THE PRICE of ASHES

THE PRICE of ASHES

THE FIRST VOLUME OF THE JAKOB'S STAR TRILOGY

BY
RICHARD BARNARD
AND SAM HERTOGS

LOUIS HUBBARD
PUBLISHING

Published by Louis Hubbard Publishing
1350 South Frontage Road
Hastings, Minnesota 55033-2426

Edited by Barbara Field

ISBN: 0-9644751-3-8

First Printing March 2000

10 9 8 7 6 5 4 3 2 1

Cover artwork by John Keely

Cover design by Richard Barnard

Printed in U.S.A.

PREFACE

HE WHO FIGHTS WITH MONSTERS MIGHT TAKE CARE LEST HE THEREBY BECOME A MONSTER. AND IF YOU GAZE FOR LONG INTO AN ABYSS, THE ABYSS GAZES ALSO INTO YOU

—*Friedrich Nietzsche*
"Jenseits Gut und Böse"
(Beyond Good and Evil)

The Jakob's Star Trilogy is a work of historical fiction. Fictional events and characters have been interwoven with the factual historical period from the end of the First World War through the end of the 1980s. Names, characters, places, and incidents in the fictional scenarios are either products of the authors' imaginations or are used fictitiously. Any resemblance of those fictional persons and situations to actual events or persons, living or dead, is entirely coincidental. Due to the extensive number of characters, we have included a list at the back of the book indicating which characters are fictional and which are based on actual people. Sam Hertogs and I have made efforts, through extensive research, to produce an accurate historical background, but we have also taken license with historically ambiguous episodes based on popular conjecture of that time.

While writing the *Jacob's Star Trilogy,* I spent considerable time interviewing Rolf and Ruth Jacobus. Rolf told me how he and Ruth met as they escaped Germany in 1940, only to be loaded aboard a ship named the *Patria* when they had finally arrived in Haifa as the British planned to deport them to a refugee camp on Cyprus. The *Patria* was accidentally sunk by Haganah men with the refugees aboard when the Haganah had tried to forestall the British by disabling the ship.

One of Rolf's great contributions to this work was his repeated question: "Why are you writing this book?" I suppose you can't write fiction without having a message in mind. Our message is embodied in the preceding quote by Friedrich Nietzsche. People are too ready to find simple answers in their lives, and that desire often leads to bigotry, dogma, and fanaticism. It is said in the Jewish tradition that it is better to have a good question than a good answer. Fanaticism is the enemy.

When the Nazis were on the rise, their principles of racial hatred were based on what they considered the "science" of eugenics. At the same time, they were looking for someone to blame for Germany's defeat in the First World War. Their belief that they had an absolute answer to those questions led directly to the deaths of tens of millions of people. The Holocaust, or "Shoah", was a unique event in history as a major, modern twentieth-century nation brought its technology to bear in a systematic policy of genocide. The lesson of the Shoah is about institutionalized racism. Why did the Shoah occur in Germany against the Jews and not in America against African-Americans, for example? It would not be inconceivable given the long history of lynchings and other violent acts in America. We in America would like to think such a concept is impossible, but how many Germans in the decades before World War II would have believed it could happen in Germany? Why were Japanese Americans imprisoned in American detention camps during World War II and not Germans and Italians? The lesson of the Shoah is to learn the lesson of institutionalized racism. Millions of voices silenced before their time should now be shouting that lesson in our ears.

RICHARD BARNARD
MINNEAPOLIS, MINNESOTA
NOVEMBER 1999

ACKNOWLEDGMENTS

We gratefully acknowledge the assistance of the following institutions and individuals:

The staff of the archives of the City of Munich, Germany
The staff of the archives of the City of Berlin, Germany
The staff of the National Archives of the
United States of America
The staff of the United States National Holocaust Memorial

Mr. and Mrs. Ralph and Ruth Jacobus
Frau Brigitte Schmidt
Mr. and Mrs. Wilhelm Schwartz
Mr. and Mrs. Gottfried Loescher
Mr. Ludwig Hirsekorn
Mrs. Kathy Murphy
Ms. Jean Weissenberger
Ms. Myra Dinnerstein
Mrs. Zemta Fields
Professor Herbert Jonas
Rabbi David Nussbaum of Salzburg, Austria
Mrs. Bobbie Jean Tervo
Ms. Dorothy Fritze
Ms. Jaci McNamara
Ms. Jeri Parkin
Mr. Brett Zabel
Mrs. Tamara Winn
Mr. Noah Anderson
Ms. Misha Dille
Ms. Michelle Russell
Mr. Nathaniel Edward Olson

This map approximates points of interest from the story. Please note that the liberation of France began with the Allied invasion of 6/4/44, so by 1945 the entire country was liberated.
East Prussia
Route of journey across France
Rail transport rout
England
Ipswich
London
Netherlands
Westerbork
Berlin
Essen
Germany
Cologne
Belgium
Wroclaw (Breslau)
Coburg
Lidice
Teresin
Prague
Polan
Auschwitz
Paris
Occupied France (1940 - 1945)
Dachau
Munich
Spital
Bratislava
Vienna
Budapest
Zurich
Bern
Switzerland
Lyon
Moreno
Vichy France (1940 - 1945)
Italy
Marseilles
Toulon
Corsica
Rome
Sardinia
Mediterranean
Sicily
Algeria
Tunisia

The Jakob's Star Trilogy
is dedicated to the innocent victims
of racial hatred. Just as there seems to
be no reason, so there seems to be no end.

CONTENTS

CHAPTER 1

In an society of such short memory, we might as well be talking about Atlantis or Camelot when considering the world that became engulfed in war in 1914. It seems we are doomed to be so blinded by the present that we quickly forget the hard-learned lessons of the past. As an obvious example, the same petty nationalism and mindless ethnocentric hatreds that focused attention on Sarajevo eighty years ago now thirst for the blood of new generations in these late days of the twentieth century.

The First World War is an historical boundary of such magnitude that it might be seen almost as a wall separating the nineteenth and twentieth centuries in the European community, a wall that had been carefully pieced together brick by brick, conflicting treaty laid atop conflicting treaty—all held in place by a mortar of rabid nationalism and oppressive colonialism. There had never been an armed conflict such as the Great War in the history of mankind up to that time, played out with the cooperation of so many people from so many different cultures and fought with modern weapons that, compared to those of the previous century, leapt beyond all superlatives of horror.

German armies stood within a hundred kilometers of Paris as the autumn of 1918 came to an end. The Great War had dragged on for four long years, and the front lines cut deep into French territory.

Erich von Ludendorff, the quartermaster general of the German High Command, gambled on one final offensive to break the stalemate of trench warfare and bring victory to Germany. When that final offensive failed, it became apparent to Ludendorff that his troops could not hold out much longer. He knew that the German armies simply didn't have the men or materiel to stand against the French, Britons, and most of all, the fresh manpower resources and great industrial strength of the Americans. He therefore advised that emissaries be sent to discuss the terms for a peace settlement.

The armistice of November 11, 1918, brought great disorder to the German front lines as many soldiers began to leave their posts. A rising revolutionary sentiment was sweeping across Germany, and once word of the armistice came through, many of the German soldiers at the front who would have fought to the end felt there was no more reason to stay. German officers began sending reports stating that the troops were disappearing so fast there might not be an army left to march back to Germany by the time the High Command issued such orders. When those orders finally came, senior German military officers had the unpleasant duty of informing Kaiser Wilhelm that, while the troops would "be honored" to have him return among their ranks, they would no longer obey him.

Once German troops put up their rifles, hundreds of thousands of families began their wait for a moment that would become a dramatic part of personal histories—the day when father, son, husband, brother . . . when "he" came home.

One might also note as an aside that in that time of humanity's lost hope and virtue, a prayer so childlike in its innocence and so seemingly hope-

less in the face of man's apparent nature had spread across the world. It was a prayer from the victims on all sides asking humanity and God that this war might be the war to end all wars. The war to end all wars . . .

Hardly anyone took notice of the screams that echoed down the frigid, barren white hallways of the Salzburg hospital on that cold November morning. Amalie could actually see her breath as the sweat poured off her face while she fought for air and then screamed again. The war had been on for just over two years, and coal shortages on the home front dictated that the hospital be kept uncomfortably cold.

"Again!" the doctor commanded. "You must push."

"Shut up!" she shrieked. "Shut up, you bastard!"

Profanity was completely out of character for Amalie, but she could no longer stand the doctor's calm directions as she was being torn to pieces!

"You *must* push," the doctor repeated calmly.

"I can't" she sobbed hysterically. "I can't do it! What the hell do you want . . . ? I can't!"

"Frau Metzdorf, you must push. We can barely see the head. It's all up to you. Take a deep breath and give us one more big push."

Amalie was at the end of her rope. She had been in labor for so many hours that she couldn't even remember what day it was. She was sweating so profusely that steam was rising from her body in the icy hospital delivery room.

The nurse patted the sweat from Amalie's forehead and tried to calm her as the doctor glared at both of them.

"You're breathing too fast," the nurse said gently and quietly next to Amalie's ear in dramatic contrast to the doctor's cajoling presence. "I know it's not easy, but try to calm down and then give one more big push."

From somewhere deep inside, just as always seems to happen in cases like hers, Amalie somehow found the strength—the final push needed—and suddenly it was done as she fell back again into the bed. She felt as if she was floating when she laid back and heard that little cry off to her side where the doctor and nurses were tending to her newborn son, and she started to laugh weakly as tears streamed down her face. It was over!

She was completely exhausted, but when the nurse said they would take her son away so she could get some rest and bring him around later, she insisted she had to see him right then. They brought the boy to her and laid him in her arms. Enraptured, she studied his face and hands and gently stroked his head. It was just the beginning.

That night was little more than a week and nine months since her husband Gunther had managed to get a rare pass from the Russian front in Galicia. She had known she was going to have a son. She named him Jakob after her mother's favorite Emily Dickinson poem, just as Amalie herself was named after the American poet.

Ethan, Amalie's father, refused to acknowledge that his daughter was turning away from her Jewish heritage and took it for granted that Jakob would have a bris, the Jewish ceremony of ritual circumcision, even though Jakob's father wasn't Jewish. Ethan arranged for it while Amalie was still recovering from the difficult delivery, and so she didn't even know about it until it was over. Ethan's presumption put an even greater strain on his relationship with his daughter, but Amalie didn't say anything outright. She decided she would just bide her time until Gunther returned for good so that they could start their own life together.

HUNDREDS OF MILES to the north while Amalie was daydreaming about their reunion, Gunther sat waiting for the sound of a whistle. He looked up at a pale cloud floating by and noticed how much it resembled the head of the Medusa as it drifted lazily over the upturned mounds of black dirt. The air had a salty taste to it, the piquant residue of cannon fire over the battlefield.

The haunting silence was prelude to an impending charge across the field by the Austrians . . . or was it the Russians . . . ? It was easy to lose track as one army would charge and the other retreat—then the reverse as the loser tried to regain and the winner tried to hold.

He had perched on the earthen wall of the trench by digging his feet into the dirt. As he stared down into the wash of mud below him, the water looked gray, but he decided that the grayness was only the reflection of the sky. Its real color was a sickly reddish black made so by the blood of his comrades. The dirt was black and brown. *It must be good for farm-*

ing, he thought for an instant, but then it seemed ridiculous to be thinking about life springing from that earth. This was the same earth that had consumed so many of his friends. The images replayed in his mind of his friend Luther Scheutzman being blown to pieces with all the bits of arms, legs, and the rest raining down into a neat pile as great mounds of dirt fell in after him into the man-made crater that became his grave.

It then occurred to Gunther that something wasn't quite right. Why was he, a captain, huddled against the dirt wall waiting for the call of a brass whistle? He should have been the one calling the men up—sending them over the top to rush out with bayonets fixed, hoping to cut deep into the belly of some poorly trained Russian peasant before the same was done to them.

There wasn't much time to wonder about such things, however, as the eternity between the silencing of the artillery and the charge was suddenly ended by the shrill whistle, and he and the others began scratching and clawing their way to the top of the trenches. They quickly broke out onto an open field, the "no-mans-land" that had been crudely plowed again and again by the recurrent artillery fire.

No sooner had they cleared the trenches when the deep, guttural barking of enemy artillery warned of another volley hurtling toward their lines, and they all threw themselves to the ground as though the cannon were some pagan god demanding their devotional submission.

The artillery paused for a moment, and Gunther

rose up from the mud and looked out across the field as his comrades continued their labored, hunched-over charge toward the Russian guns. A strange feeling came over him, and he stood tall, almost at attention, as he watched.

From somewhere across the field, a machine gun began to sputter out its lead issue in a staccato melody, and the bass of the cannon sounded a mighty counterpoint. This strident symphony was fitting accompaniment to the awful ballet playing out before him. Here and there he saw the dancers fly off one foot and land gracefully in the dirt. A rifle was flying over a man's shoulder as he convulsed in pain, and yet further down the line a boy tumbled with the perfect form of a well-trained acrobat.

All at once Gunther wanted a better view. He wanted to understand it all and thought that maybe if he could just see it all at once he might grasp the meaning of it. But how? It occurred to him that if he could fly . . . and with that he jumped. He jumped up as high as he could, feeling his feet leaving the ground and not allowing himself to consider the possibility that he might fall, thinking that if he believed he wouldn't fall back to earth, then maybe he wouldn't, and it worked. He just kept rising higher and higher. He saw the whole battlefield, the place that was the whole black world to him, made up of burnt trees and battered little buildings and rotting human flesh. He flew higher and saw that the whole great, black, bloody battlefield was only a spot on the countryside, getting smaller and smaller as he flew.

And he felt so free.

"Time to go," the corporal said as he shook Gunther awake. Gunther desperately grabbed the corporal by the coat, holding on for dear life so he wouldn't fall.

"It's all right, Captain. You were just dreaming," the corporal continued without a laugh or a sideways look, because it was so common. They all had nightmares there.

MONTHS LATER, far from what had been the Russian front, Gunther sat at a table with a blank expression. He had thought that all of those terrible visions would disappear when the guns fell silent, but he still found himself lost in the memory of it. Why couldn't he get the face of Lorenz Weber out of his mind? There he was again in that wooded hollow, Lorenz looking back at Gunther and waving him ahead, and then suddenly there was a bayonet in Lorenz's chest. Gunther didn't know why he was so constantly haunted by that particular incident out of all the others. Maybe it was the look of complete surprise on Lorenz's face. A lone Russian who seemed to come out of nowhere, giving all his strength to the thrust of that rifle, as though he might lift his impaled victim off the ground and just toss him aside. Although it seemed like a long time, it was only an instant before the forest erupted in gunfire as they stumbled into an ambush.

Some men had made it through without these scars. Gunther had believed in the war. His belief in some holy cause of courage and glory was the drug that kept him going.

When he'd joined the infantry, it was as a common soldier, but he was soon promoted in the face of horrific battles that decimated his brigade. He'd managed not only to stay alive, but also to rally and lead the others in his squad as the Austrians and Germans drove into eastern Galicia. Through the next years of seemingly endless attacks and counter-attacks he received more field promotions, achieving the rank of captain by the time of the armistice.

When it was finally over he'd had to take a roundabout way home because of problems with trains and transportation in general throughout Europe. He'd had to go to Berlin and then travel south from there.

That was how he came to be sitting at a table in a restaurant on the Alexanderplatz in Berlin. He had never been to Berlin before and found it vastly different from his home near Salzburg. Even the Munich of his youth couldn't compare. Munich had a personality, while Berlin just seemed to happen somehow in its vast, sprawling randomness. Berlin simply was.

Gunther was musing over these differences when he suddenly looked up. It was one of those times when a person senses there's something he ought to look at without knowing why. There across the dining room of the restaurant stood Klaus Grunewald. It was an incredible chance of fate that Klaus and Gunther should meet again.

At the onset of the war, Germany's Austrian allies had agreed to defend Germany's eastern border while German armies marched off to France, but additional troops were soon required to hold off the Russians, so German soldiers were brought from

France to fight alongside the Austrians. That was how Gunther and Klaus had met, but Klaus had returned to France with the rest of the German troops after the Treaty of Brest-Litovsk. The Russians had made a separate peace with the Germans when they signed Brest-Litovsk, quitting the war to concentrate on their revolution. The Austrians were then left to garrison the border for the last few months of the war.

"Klaus!" Gunther shouted, almost knocking over his table as he jumped to his feet and began working his way across the crowded room. He threw an arm around his friend as they came face to face. "You made it home!"

"Metzdorf? What are you doing in Berlin?"

"Waiting for a train . . . or maybe a horse cart . . . something going to Salzburg. I'm trying to get home."

"Home? Are you out?"

"I'm just waiting for paperwork. It should be done tomorrow."

"Why? Do you have something else lined up?"

"No," Gunther said solemnly, "I'm just going home."

"No, I mean work," Klaus countered with a lighter attitude. "What are you going to do for work?"

"I don't know. I haven't planned that far ahead yet."

"You should have stayed in. Believe me, with all these others coming home, it's going to be hard to find work."

"I've had enough. I've got a wife and son that I hardly know."

"What good is it if you get to know them while you're all starving?"

"Haven't you had enough?" Gunther asked incredulously as the two of them went back to his table and sat down. "You had it harder than me. I haven't had much of a war since the Russians quit, but I hear it was far worse in the west than it ever was in Galicia."

"Harder?" Klaus asked with a sardonic smile that quickly faded. "I don't know if you can say it like that. It's like the weather. If it's zero degrees out, how cold would it have to be to be twice as cold?"

"But you're staying in?"

"Yes," Klaus answered adamantly. "I decided before leaving the front. I'm just waiting to see where they send me . . . that is, if they keep me. The army will be cut down to nothing. And just when they need us more than ever at home. You've heard about the mutiny in Kiel?"

"Yes. They say it's like that all over."

"Damned Communists . . ."

"I thought it was Social Democrats."

"It's all the same," Klaus answered. "Different brands of anarchy."

They lapsed into silence for a moment, but the silence was soon broken as they abruptly changed to making plans for the evening. They decided to go out drinking, or at least looking for something suitable to drink in a city whose only bounty was its abundance of shortages after years of war.

Within a day Klaus found himself assigned to the Munich Garrison. Gunther conceded that if he insisted on staying in, then Munich was the place to be. Since Munich was so close to Salzburg, Klaus managed to secure passage for Gunther on the same train, and they traveled together for the first leg of Gunther's journey home.

It was on the train that Gunther confessed to his friend that he was not looking forward to returning to Salzburg. His father had all but disowned him for marrying a Jewish girl, and besides that, Salzburg, while not being a little town, was not large enough to supply returning soldiers with jobs.

Klaus had the good fortune to inherit an apartment from the officer he was replacing in Munich, and so he insisted Gunther stay the night before taking the train to Salzburg the next morning. That night Gunther gave Klaus a grand tour of Munich, at least as much as he remembered from his childhood, and then they spent the night talking. It was Klaus who brought up the idea of Gunther and his wife and son staying with him while Gunther looked for work and a place to live in Munich. Klaus even argued for it, bent on winning his friend over so that the four of them might share the one-bedroom apartment. The next day Gunther sent word to Amalie that they were going to live in the city where Gunther had lived as a boy, and they all waited with excitement—and apprehension—for the day when it would happen.

THREE WEEKS LATER Amalie's train slowly moved into a dark, overcast night with its passenger cars groaning in tempo with the clanking of cold metal couplings as the line of cars drew taut. Amalie was so anxious that she stayed awake for some time after the kerosene lamps in the battered old coach car were turned down, finally being lulled to sleep by the roll and sway of the train.

She awoke with a start as another train passed by going the opposite direction, causing a sudden explosion of wind through the narrow slit of a partially opened window. She then realized that she had fallen asleep on the shoulder of the old woman sitting next to her. The woman appeared to be asleep and didn't stir as Amalie pulled away, but Amalie watched her for a moment just to make sure. The old woman's head was slouched forward and her many chins, which cascaded down to ample breasts and a huge stomach, moved in rhythm with a pronounced wheeze of a snore.

The only light in the compartment came from the faint glow of a kerosene lamp in the passageway and a hint of moonlight that occasionally filtered into the windows through the cloudy December sky. Amalie looked around at the other people in the crowded, stuffy compartment. It was cold and smelled of musty clothes and unbathed bodies. Many people were on the move since the Armistice—soldiers returning home and families, like Amalie and her son Jakob, going to be with their soldier-husbands and -fathers.

Her thoughts drifted to all that she was leaving behind in the city of Salzburg where she had been born and raised. Her mother, Ruth, had died there in 1908 after a brief battle with influenza, leaving twelve-year-old Amalie and her ten-year-old sister Eleonore alone with their father, Ethan. Amalie, as the eldest daughter, became the woman of the house and remained in her father's home even after Eleonore married on the eve of her seventeenth birthday and moved with her husband, Louis, to Vienna. Amalie even remained after she herself married a few months later in 1914 and Gunther volunteered for duty in the Austrian infantry just as the war began. She attended a university as she waited for the war to end, partly out of an interest in getting an education and partly just to pass the time so that she would have somewhere to go rather than sitting about the house all day.

When she finally received word from Gunther that they were going to live in Munich, she was put off because the instructions sounded more like an order issued to troops than a decision made between husband and wife, but she was tired of waiting. She was tired of living in her father's world as though it were her own, and so she accepted Gunther's plan without question and began preparing for the day when her journey would begin.

It had been a long day, but she'd managed to get everything together just in time to board the late train. Jakob, who was usually such a good and quiet little boy, had fussed and cried incessantly. He was upset about leaving his home in Salzburg and his grandfather, as though he somehow knew he wouldn't be seeing either again for a long time.

One of the many thoughts that ran through Amalie's mind as she sat in the shadowy train compartment was that it wasn't easy to picture how Gunther might look now. They had been apart for so long. What would it be like living together for the rest of their lives in Munich?

She could only remember him as he looked when he held her face in his hands at the train station when they last said good-bye. The end of a furlough more than two years before. A last kiss. The way she had pressed her face so tightly against his so that he would not forget her, forget her touch, so that she could still feel him when he had gone.

"Mutti[1] . . . ?" came a little voice from beside her.

"Sleep, darling. It's late . . . very late," she replied as she gently brushed Jakob's hair from his eyes, gently pulling his head against her side and putting her arm around him. Jakob had his father's light blue eyes. Amalie thought how strange it was that Jakob wouldn't know his father, and then she realized that she might not recognize Gunther, either.

What a frightening thought! Here she was, traveling from her home in Austria, leaving all her friends and family behind and heading to Munich, which she had heard was bordering on anarchy since the war ended, to be with a husband whom she hadn't been with for more than four months in the four years they had been married.

Jakob looked up at Amalie from his nesting place in her dark wool coat and laughed as he pointed at her head. She reached up and found that her hat had been pushed to one side when she had fallen asleep on the old woman next to her. She thought of taking it off and putting it up with her luggage, but she was afraid she would wake the old woman and possibly everyone else in the compartment, so she just pulled out the hat pin and straightened the hat before settling back into place on the wooden bench.

Jakob looked up at his mother again and, almost as though he had read her thoughts from a moment before, asked, "Mutti, Vati?[2] Vati?"

Amalie looked down with a tender smile. "Yes," she said, interpreting and answering the question of her two-year-old son in a quiet voice, almost a whisper. "We'll see your father soon." She knew that Jakob's question was only a reflex at this point. Amalie had tried to explain to Jakob over and over again where they were going and why they were leaving his grandfather. By the time they left Salzburg, Jakob was filled with excitement that he was going to meet this wonderful new person in his life—someone named "Vati."

"Would you like to hear a story about your father? Did I ever tell you how I met him?"

"Ja," Jakob quickly replied, eager to hear a comforting bedtime story in this strange place. "Story."

"Let me see if I can remember . . . it was a long time ago in a much different world." Jakob settled back against his mother's coat as she continued. "My father, your Grandfather Ethan, is a publisher. That means he prints and sells books that other people write." Amalie stopped and looked at Jakob to see if he was asleep before she continued. "Well, a long time ago, almost ten years, Father took me to Paris with him when he had to go there to buy a book."

"Book," Jakob said sleepily.

"Book?" she asked, surprised that Jakob would repeat that word as though it had great significance,

---

[1]The familiar German form of "mother."

but then she realized he only spoke to show that he was still awake.

"I don't remember what book it was, but the important part is that we were in Paris. It was so wonderful! I was only fourteen, and I could do as I pleased while Grandfather Ethan was busy with his book, even though he had told me to stay at the hotel while he was working. One day I went to a great museum in Paris called the Louvre."

"Loove," Jakob repeated without stirring, having found a word he had never heard before.

"No," Amalie chided gently. "It's a French word and you say 'La Looov vreh.'" Amalie made a funny face as she exaggerated the pronunciation and put her face close to her son's, touching her nose to his, as Jakob giggled.

Jakob dutifully tried to repeat the correct pronunciation, making the same funny face as he said, "La Looovvv."

"Very good!" Amalie complimented, then went on with the story as Jakob again rested his head against her coat. "I entered one room in particular and saw a painting by a man named Raphael, a great Italian painter who lived long ago, and there was a young man standing in front of it. He was tall and awkward, a couple of years older than I was. I noticed something special about him, but I pretended as though he wasn't there . . . I guess it's a kind of game that boys and girls play." Amalie paused for a moment as she gathered her thoughts to continue the story. "But it was strange . . . even though I was pretending not to notice him . . ." As she spoke, it was only then that she realized she was telling this story for herself rather than for her son. "I had a picture in my mind, as though I had taken a photograph of him in the best possible light at the perfect moment of his revealing his true nature. He was such a beautiful boy, like a colt that has only recently learned to stand. A mix of boy and man. He was a bit clumsy . . . and shy. I remember him fumbling with some pamphlet and almost dropping it, and then clenching it tightly as we talked. I felt so wicked, a young girl day-dreaming of him taking me in his arms. As I recall, I lost the power of speech when he looked at me. And when he tried to be friendly and say hello in that horrible French he spoke, I couldn't respond."

Amalie looked down at Jakob, wondering what her little boy would make of her ramblings. He was fast asleep.

The train was slowing down as they approached the German border. Salzburg had been her home for all of her twenty-three years, and even though she had often gone with her father when he traveled for business, it felt as if she was leaving for the first time because she feared she might never return. At the same time, though, leaving Austria behind filled her with excitement and anticipation. It was going to be a new life! Life in Salzburg had been comfortable before the war, but the war had changed the whole world and now it was time for her to change, too.

She had certainly done her share of changing already. She had married a gentile, kept her last name, and even ignored Kashrut, the Jewish dietary laws. Amalie Stein-Metzdorf was not going to be the typical Deutsche Hausfrau[3] . . . and what a scandal for the Stein household! Amalie's mother and father knew she was headstrong as a child, and she became even more so after her mother died, but this was too much. To marry out of the faith . . . Amalie could still hear her uncle reminding her of the words of the rabbi: "The lost tribe of Israel is not lost as one would be lost in the wilderness; they are lost as a drop of wine is lost when spilled into the ocean."

Amalie looked up as the conductor stopped a moment to check on the crowded compartment. "How much longer before we get to Munich?" she asked softly.

"About three hours," the conductor replied.

"Three hours?" Amalie repeated with surprise in her voice. The trip to Munich from Salzburg would only have taken an hour and a half total from station to station before the war, but with fuel scarce and so few trains running, it took three hours just to go from the German border to Munich.

"Thank you," she said quickly, so that the conductor wouldn't think she was blaming him for something that was obviously not his fault. She then curled herself around Jakob on the hard wooden bench to keep him safe and warm.

"Three more hours," she signed to herself as she drifted off to sleep while the weary old train pushed its way through the darkness toward morning.

IN MUNICH, Klaus and Gunther decided to pass the time in one of Munich's famous beer halls until the hour arrived for them to go to the train station.

---

[3]"Typical German housewife," a phrase meant to describe a stereotypical wife at the time of the First World War who was quiet and subservient to her husband.

"I have to thank you again, Klaus. It'll be crowded, but I'm sure we can all get along until I find work."

"I told you not to worry about it," Klaus said sternly. "We old soldiers have to stick together. Besides, after all those years of living in trenches with hundreds of other men, I'm afraid I might get lonely all by myself." Klaus laughed and waved to the barmaid across the crowded room of the Hofbräuhaus, and as she came close enough to hear over the dull roar of the crowd, he pointed to Gunther and himself. "Beer! he shouted. "And keep them full! We're celebrating."

Gunther put a hand on his friend's shoulder. "Not too much, Klaus, or we might not make it to the train station on time."

"That would never do," Klaus retorted in mocking fashion. "Not seeing your wife for almost two years and then missing her train . . ."

"Miss the train?" Gunther repeated ominously. "God in heaven . . . The war would seem like a schoolboy row compared to the fight Amalie would put up."

"She's a fighter?"

"No, no . . . well, not often, but when she does fight, she comes from out of nowhere with everything she has." Gunther paused a moment before continuing the banter. "And I, of course, being a gentleman, raise a white flag."

"You? The regal Captain Metzdorf, sprung from generations of proud officers, a tiger on the battlefield, surrendering to the wrath of a little woman?"

"She was a little woman when I last saw her,"

Gunther answered, smiling. "I haven't seen her for a while. She might have put on weight."

"So you think that by now she may be able to wrestle you to the ground in a fair match?" asked Klaus, once again baiting his friend.

"One never knows!"

Klaus looked down at his beer for a moment as the boisterous sounds from the other tables rose and filled the room. "How did you ever meet this terror of a woman?" he finally asked.

Gunther smiled and his eyes took on a faraway look as he recalled a cherished memory. "It was on holiday. My parents had taken my younger brother and sister and me to Paris to visit my father's uncle."

Gunther snapped out of his musings and leaned forward to inform Klaus of the details. "My Great-aunt Greta had sent word that Great-uncle Berchtwald was on his deathbed and that the family should come to pay final respects. By the time we got to Paris, Berchtwald was up and around, and as a matter of fact, the last I heard he's still a strong old bull, ready to take on the world. Aunt Greta, however, died the next year of pneumonia after insisting for weeks that she only had a cold. But, anyway, there we were in Paris without a funeral, so father proclaimed it our holiday for that year."

"What else could he do?" Klaus asked facetiously.

"As I was saying," Gunther continued, leaning back in his chair and gazing upward before closing his eyes, as though trying to see everything just as it had happened. "I had just turned fifteen that year, and to my embarrassment, I found I was often the unwilling victim of spontaneous sexual arousal."

"Ah! A sexual deviant even at that tender age," Klaus piped in accusingly.

Gunther opened one eye to glance crossly at Klaus, clearly annoyed at the unsolicited interruption. Klaus reacted like an unruly child scolded by a disapproving teacher.

"It was extremely unnerving," Gunther continued, as his gaze returned to the ceiling, "especially since I considered myself at the time to be so well endowed that no one in the vicinity could help but notice."

Gunther stopped again and stared at Klaus, almost daring him to comment, but Klaus just sat quietly waiting for Gunther to continue.

"One day Father took us all to the Louvre, and being 15 years old, I certainly didn't want to tag along with my family. So with guidebook in hand, I pestered my father until he finally agreed that I might go my own way, providing I agreed to meet them all later at the Place de Pyramid by the river. So there I was, standing in front of a fantastic Raphael nude, a buxom pink-skinned beauty with dark hair and just the slightest hint of a mustache, sporting the ever-present erection... mine, not hers," Gunther interrupted himself with a sidelong glance at Klaus.

"Thank God," Klaus whispered.

". . . when there appeared beside me a vision. I would have sworn before God that the girl beside me was the younger sister of the immodest lady rising above me in that incredible portrait. I quickly adjusted the guide program to disguise my interest in this great work of art . . ." (Gunther gestured discretely, demonstrating for Klaus's benefit as he covered his groin with his hand) ". . . and turned ever so slightly toward the girl. I wanted to sound clever, but she saw through me. I was fluent in French, and I said something about the unequaled artistry of the Renais-sance, but she just stared at me as though I had told her that my parents were pigeons and I could spread my arms and fly if I really wanted to."

"Does she still look at you like that?"

"Only sometimes, but, of course, now she knows my parents . . . As I was saying, there was an awkward pause when I could have just walked away and not risked further embarrassment, but we stared at each other as I noticed her deep brown eyes."

"Ah, yes, the eyes . . . a typical woman's trap," Klaus interjected.

Gunther sat up and turned to Klaus, trying to explain. "I still stare into her eyes. We talked. I told her where I was from, and we found to our amazement that we lived within a few kilometers of each other. She was with her father, who had come to Paris for business, and she was staying at a hotel not far from my family. It seems our lives were almost parallel up to the time of our meeting. We spent that week together as much as we could, and talked about school studies and friends and other such nonsense. She returned home the day after my family, and we began to see each other as often as we could. Three years later we married."

"How old were you?" Klaus asked.

"The men in my family have always married young, and I've never been one to break with family tradition. Nineteen. I've always followed in the footsteps of my father and my father's father. That's why

I joined the army so quickly. They certainly would have joined if they could have."

"Yes," Klaus agreed. "My father said the same thing."

"But Klaus, look where it's brought us. What have we become? The world has changed, and men like you and me just sit and wonder at it."

"My God, you take a quick turn," Klaus said with annoyance. "From the sublime to the morbid with hardly a pause."

The conversation soon took on a lighter tone as the two old friends began to talk about the early times of the war, when they were the victors and still boys. It seems that youth is not always a matter of age, but of the roads one takes. They were still young, but now they were on a rough, darkened road as they trudged through the defeat that Ludendorff had orchestrated, the defeat of the Kaiser and all that the monarchy had meant to the imperial German Reich, which Bismarck himself had fused together through sheer force of will some fifty years before.

The animated discourse was about the antics of two boys. They spoke of romantic adventures, real and imagined, and their experiences before they met. They competed in telling stories of times when they had bent the rules, such as when Klaus had "found" a stray goat that became a feast for his squad, and the time when Gunther disappeared in the smoke of an artillery burst and Klaus rushed in to save him, only to find that Gunther had fallen into a wine cellar and the blood that covered him turned out to be wine hoarded and hidden by a farsighted merchant. They laughed away the hours until they were due to leave for the station to escort Amalie and Jakob to their new home.

At three o'clock in the morning, it had already been snowing for hours as Klaus and Gunther stumbled out of the beer hall on their way to the train station. It was a heavy snow that was quickly filling the dark streets of Munich. A strong wind rose, sending flocks of snowflakes stinging against their faces, blinding them from time to time.

They were weaving from side to side as they walked, each with his arm around the other in a fruitless attempt to steady one another. They both knew, though they never spoke of it, that they only allowed themselves to feel drunk. They welcomed the numbing effects of the alcohol, and they made the feeling last as long as they could. Gunther knew how to drink. He knew how to feel full of laughter in the most damnable places that a man could find himself, but he knew also to be ready to fight. He learned young to always be a soldier, and it would stay with him for the rest of his life. The two young-old comrades leaned against the dirty, gray cornerstone of an old bank building, laughing at their apparent inability to negotiate the corner, when they noticed a delivery man getting down from his horse-drawn wagon to push it through a snowdrift in the middle of the street.

"Wait!" Klaus shouted exuberantly to the old delivery man. "We'll be right there to help."

The delivery man was startled, as he hadn't noticed the two of them in the shadows, and he peered through the swirling snow to see who was there as they moved into the glow of a guttering street lamp. It became apparent as they struggled through the snow in their military greatcoats that they were drunken soldiers, and the delivery man waved them away. "Gott in Himmel," he said under his breath, "just what I need."

"Ja, we are experts at pushing wagons," Gunther shouted, even though they were now close enough to be easily heard. "The army only let us in because of our strong shoulders!"

Again the delivery man waved them away. "Go back. You'll only get hurt, you drunks!"

"Drunks?" Klaus said indignantly, looking at Gunther.

"Nahnshennsshh," Gunther replied.

"What?" Klaus asked, laughing at his friend.

"I said *nahn . . . shhennsshh,*" Gunther drawled, slowly and deliberately, so as to be understood this time, which made Klaus laugh even more.

"We've pushed wagons through mud . . . snow . . . even fire. Why, we pushed wagons all the way to France," Klaus said through his laughter.

"Ja, ja," said the exasperated old man. "Do what you want, but it's none of my fault if you fall under a wagon wheel." He started to move ahead of the wagon, but then stopped and turned back, shaking a stubby crooked finger at them for emphasis as he spoke, "And if you do fall, don't think I'll stop for you when I get moving!"

Gunther smiled at Klaus as they got ready to push. "I'm beginning to like the old bastard."

The delivery man trudged up behind his horse and pulled the reins from the driver's seat, then gave the horse a pat on the rump. "Come, Gertie, show them how it's done," he said wearily, positioning himself in front of the animal to urge her through the snowdrift.

"When shall we push?" Klaus shouted impatiently.

"Whenever the spirit moves you," came the curt, sarcastic reply from in front.

"I'm not so sure he appreciates us," Gunther said to Klaus as they put their shoulders to the back of the wagon.

"Come, Gert! Come on!" urged the driver, and Klaus and Gunther threw their weight against the creaking back gate of the old wagon with little result.

"Verdammt!" muttered the old man. He now realized that he would really need the help of the two soldiers and addressed them seriously for the first time.

"Once again, when I count to three," shouted the delivery man as he patted the horse on the shoulder. He then wrapped the reins around his hands several times and drew them up tight in front of Gert.

"Eins!" the old man shouted.

Gunther repositioned himself for a better stance and in so doing turned his back to Klaus.

"Zwei! " came the call from in front.

As Gunther put his left shoulder to the wagon, he looked up the street, as suddenly a sparking blue light appeared around the corner.

"Jump, Klaus!" Gunther shouted.

"What?" Klaus asked, as he turned toward Gunther in time to see the electric street trolley moving toward them. Klaus and Gunther leapt through the snow, away from the wagon, and the delivery man's eyes filled with horror as he tried to pull his horse out of the way just as the trolley plowed through the snowdrift and rammed into horse and wagon, driving them into the snowbank and dragging the old man along with his hands tangled in the reins.

The impact of the crash was muted by the snow, creating a strange "whuummppff" sound that filled the empty street. The old man was cursing at the top of his voice: "Damn! Damn! My Gertie! What have you done to my Gertie?"

The trolley operator had been thrown over the horse and wagon into the snowbank, while the only two passengers on the early-morning trolley had merely been forced against the wall at the end of the bench without being hurt.

The windows of surrounding apartments quickly filled with faces as Gunther and Klaus worked their way over to the wagon. The delivery man's horse had been pinned between the snowdrift and the trolley, and the old man, who continued to rant and swear at the trolley and its snow-covered driver, had broken his right hand and dislocated the wrist of his other hand.

They were all surprised to see a policeman come around the corner within a few short moments. He checked on the trolley passengers and the old man, then stood looking down at the horse. Gert was struggling and panting heavily as she lay pressed against the snowbank with her front legs bleeding and twisted beneath her. Without saying a word, the policeman drew his revolver and pointed it at the horse's head.

The old man's shout of protest was overwhelmed by the explosion of the bullet as the horse instantly stopped struggling in the snowbank.

The first to come out of the apartment buildings was a short, middle-aged woman wearing nothing but a nightgown. She slipped and slid in the deep snow as she hurried toward the wagon, while the policeman, Klaus, and Gunther untangled the delivery man's hands from the reins.

"I'll get help. You just wait here," the policeman said to the old man, and as he rushed off down the street, the woman was soon followed by others coming out of the apartments in various states of dress, some in pajamas with overcoats, some wearing only pants and shoes.

Klaus caught only a glimpse of the knife in the woman's hand as it flashed a reflection of the dim streetlight when she drew it above her head and fell upon the horse, driving the blade deep into its shoulder.

"N-o-o-o," moaned the delivery man in disbelief as tears filled his eyes. The old man tried to get up, but Klaus and Gunther held onto him and pulled him back a few yards, away from where Gertie was being set upon.

"There's nothing to be done," Gunther said in a low voice next to the old man's ear as he held him down.

The people from the apartments, not having seen meat for months, butchered the horse in less than a quarter of an hour. Greedily they carried away the heart and liver and chunks of meat, still dripping with warm, deep-red blood, back to their apartments, struggling through the deep drifts, trying to get in from the cold as quickly as they could.

Klaus, Gunther, and the old man witnessed it all as they waited for the policeman to return with help to get the old man to a doctor.

"Just like the war," Klaus finally said in a low, overly dramatic tone. "Some would feed upon the still-living body of our Germany. They cut it up and take it for themselves, so they can grow fat and strong off our demise." It was a statement born of Klaus's bent for theatricality, but nonetheless, Gunther nodded in agreement without comment as they watched the last man in pajamas and overcoat slip in the snow and fall flat on his back, spattering himself with Gertie's blood all down his front and on his face. He got up without saying a word, not even a curse at having fallen, and made his way through the snow back to his apartment.

In a few moments, the policeman returned with a wagon to take the old man to a hospital, and Klaus and Gunther continued on their way to the train station. When they arrived, they learned that Amalie and Jakob's train was more than an hour behind schedule. They didn't talk as they sat in the dark cold station.

The snow delayed the train even more, so it wasn't until four-thirty in the morning that it finally dragged into the nearly deserted Hauptbahnhof.

Gunther and Klaus stood up from the cast-iron bench in the open waiting area and walked toward the train as it came to a stop. Gunther waited for several minutes, but when no wife or child appeared, he threw an anxious glance at Klaus. Klaus snapped to attention and clicked his heels together: "You've waited long enough, Mein Kapitän. It is time you took the train."

Waving off Klaus's sarcasm, Gunther rushed up the steps of the passenger car, working his way down the narrow passageway as he checked the compartments one by one. Everyone had already left the first compartment, and the next was crowded with people getting their baggage down off the racks over the seats. Once he could be sure Amalie was not in that compartment, he turned quickly and almost knocked over a large old woman who was trying to pass by him in the narrow aisle. "Entschuldigung Sie bitte," he said, apologizing as he slid past and twisted around to look into the compartment from which the woman had just come.

He had found her. She was still asleep with Jakob curled up beside her. Gunther couldn't move. She was more beautiful than he remembered, her face more gentle, her son—his son—so handsome and frail and safe beside her. All the war was done in that instant. He knew it was right that they had come here to be together. This would now be their home, the home he would build for his own family.

Gunther slowly and quietly knelt in front of his Amalie. Gently he took her hand in his and kissed it. She still didn't stir. He kissed her again and this time nuzzled her hand with his mustache. At that, she awoke with a start and pulled her hand away. She hadn't seen Gunther with a mustache before, and she started to protest, "Oh, my God! What are you . . . ?" Then, realizing it was him but still confused at having been awakened from her sound sleep, she cried, "Oh, Gunther! Are we home?"

"Well, we're at the Munich station . . ."

"Mutti?" Jakob said sleepily, rubbing his eyes. When he saw the man kneeling in front of his mother, he drew back into the folds of her coat.

"Good morning, my fine little soldier. Do you know who I am?"

Jakob slowly shook his head from side to side, but then a bright expression filled his face as he was struck with a revelation: "Vati?"

Gunther smiled a great smile and could feel a tear sting at his eye, even though he would not show it, but his strained voice betrayed emotion as he replied, "Yes, yes. It seems about time that we should meet."

CHAPTER 2

The role of General Erich von Ludendorff in the events of 1918 far exceeded the authority of his position as quartermaster general of the German High Command. Ludendorff's victories at the beginning of the war earned him a reputation that carried him far beyond the time of German victories and likewise earned the confidence of Kaiser Wilhelm to a point that even eclipsed the Kaiser's respect for Paul von Hindenburg, the chief of the German High Command.

Ludendorff determined in September of 1918, after a final failed German offensive, that Germany could not continue the war. In that desperate moment, he decided he must somehow salvage the honor of the German military by finding a way to end the war without admitting military defeat. The answer was handed to him by Woodrow Wilson, the President of the United States. Wilson, acting as spokesman for the Allies, stated in no uncertain terms that the first condition of any peace talks was that the Kaiser must step down as emperor. Based on this demand, Ludendorff decided that if the government were turned over to a group that was in opposition to the Kaiser, then they would be the ones to actually sue for peace and bear the onus of surrender.

The Social Democrat party was just such a group. At one time, some fifty years before the Great War, they had been considered a radical revolutionary force in German politics. Over time, however, their leadership had moved toward a more conservative position, and so, although they spoke of republicanism and democracy in contrast to Germany's autocratic monarchy, they were no longer considered to be radical revolutionaries. For Ludendorff's purpose, they were certainly the lesser of evils in a choice between them and the Communists. The Social Democrats represented the scent of rebellion without the fires of revolution.

It was Ludendorff who told the Kaiser that Germany must surrender before the war was pushed onto German soil, and in order to achieve that end the government must be turned over to the Social Democrats, with Friedrich Ebert installed as president of a new German Republic.

Months later, completing his plan to produce a scapegoat without ever acknowledging his role in the transfer of power, Ludendorff would say that the Social Democrats had betrayed Germany; that they had stabbed the army in the back by surrendering while the army still held the field. "Dolchstoss," or "the stab in the back," became a catchphrase among those opposed to the Weimar Republic for years to come.

The abdication of Wilhelm Hohenzollern was in itself a strange example of the turmoil of the times. The Hohenzollerns had been Germany's ruling family from the time of German unification in 1871 until 1918, when Kaiser Wilhelm was informed that he no longer had the support of the military. On November 9 of that year, Prince Max von Baden, an intermediate Reichschancellor, announced the abdication of the Kaiser and the formation of the new German Republic led by Friedrich Ebert.

The Kaiser, however, had not intended to abdicate! He had been willing to step down as emperor, but he had expected to continue influencing his country by retaining the title of King of Prussia.

Original intentions aside, once the Kaiser heard of the premature and incorrect announcement of his abdication, he shouted angrily that he had been betrayed and then fled to Holland, fearing for his life in the face of a revolutionary uprising. That fear was certainly well founded, considering the fate of his cousin, Czar Nicholas II of Russia, less than a year before, when revolution had swept the Romanoff dynasty out of power. Nicholas and his family had disappeared without a trace.

It was not until some three weeks after Prince Baden's announcement that the Kaiser officially abdicated while in exile in Holland.

One of the oft-cited examples of the revolution that the Kaiser feared was the mutiny by German sailors in Kiel. The irony, however, is that it wasn't a Communist revolution, even though it certainly had all the earmarks of such. The mutiny was not a spontaneous act of revolution, but a response to an attempt by a group of naval officers who sought to defy orders from the new Weimar Republic to stand down and wait for developments in the peace talks. The officers decided that they could not allow Germany to go down to defeat while there was still a functioning military. Their reasoning was not unlike the course of action being attempted by Ludendorff, but while Ludendorff sought to set up scapegoats to take the blame for the surrender, the naval officers were determined to renew hostilities.

It was at this point that the sailors mutinied. If you look at the events from this perspective, the truth would seem to be that it was the naval officers who were engaging in mutiny against the government. The sailors were putting down that mutiny and standing up for the new republic by refusing to fight on.

Gunther was dressed in civilian clothes for the first time in years, and he felt out of place. He was a soldier, and now he was pretending not to be. He still wore his military coat and highly polished boots, but only because he had no others.

The brilliant sunlight cutting through the frigid blue sky and reflecting off the fresh white snow was enough to blind a man. The snow crunched loudly with each step as he walked down Arcisstrasse.

He had been looking for work for more than two weeks, ever since Amalie and Jakob had joined him in Munich, and was once again off to beg for a job. He stopped for a moment and felt through the deep pockets of his greatcoat until he managed to fish out a small book. BAEDEKER'S MÜNCHEN UND SÜDBAYERN was spelled out in gold type against the red cover. He opened the book to one of the delicate foldout maps, which he had marked off the night before.

When he left the army, Gunther had thought he would be able to put his leadership experience to good use in civilian life. Unfortunately there were hundreds of thousands of other men across Germany with the same delusions. Amalie, Klaus, and he had sat around the small kitchen table in Klaus's apartment the night before, suggesting possible jobs, and had all concluded that Gunther should try at the Hauptbahnhof.

When he decided to return to Munich, he had been sure that he still knew the city like the back of his hand, but when he had attempted to give Klaus a tour on that first night, he found that his memory was not as clear as he thought. Thus he resigned himself to the embarrassing experience of being a native who was forced to buy a tourist's guidebook. As he traced the route toward the main train station with his finger, the street was suddenly filled with the explosive sound of an old truck coming around the corner, its four cylinders banging irregularly, indicating a desperate need for repairs.

Gunther looked up as the Lastkraftwagen came into sight. The lorry was filled with soldiers of the revolution. Almost a dozen men rode on the running boards and front fenders of the beaten and abused old truck, all with rifles slung over their shoulders, one of them holding a crimson flag of the revolution that barely fluttered due to the slow pace of the truck.

One of the soldiers waved at Gunther as they passed, and Gunther found himself reflexively raising a hand to return the greeting to fellow soldiers before catching himself. *What am I doing?* he thought to himself.

"Dolchstoss," he whispered bitterly under his breath.

It was what many Germans were saying to themselves. These were the back-stabbers who had betrayed Germany in its hour of need. They were part of the revolution begun by the sailors who had mutinied in Kiel. They had forced a disgraceful surrender by their revolution, and suddenly Germany was caught up in a political, economic, and social nightmare.

Even though the streets of Munich were quiet,

there had been great political upheaval across the country. Kaiser Wilhelm had fled to Holland and left the ruins to Friedrich Ebert, head of the Social Democrats, and "his friend," Kurt Eisner in Bavaria.

Eisner was the head of the Independent Social Democrat party in Bavaria, and it certainly didn't help matters that he was Jewish, since it added a distinctly anti-Semitic quality to the "Dolchstoss" sentiment in Germany. It was Eisner who had marched to the royal residence on November 7 and, with the support of the royal guard, declared the Freistaat Bayern, the Bavarian Free State, in place of the Wittelsbach's provincial monarchy, which had ruled the regency of Bavaria since 1180.

Members of the Wittelsbach family, including Ludwig III, quickly left the royal residence as Eisner began to set up office. The royals raced out of Munich in their great black automobile, eventually ending up in a ditch outside of town, the result of a minor accident caused by their excessive speed.

The end of over two hundred years of Hohenzollern rule, the defeat of Germany in war, the imposing threat of Communist rule, it was all too much. It was unbelievable. But Gunther had his wife and son to care for, and so his was not a political world. He needed to put bread on the table and find a place to live so that he would not have to continue imposing on Klaus's hospitality. They couldn't go on forever with Gunther and Amalie sleeping on the floor in the living room and their son sleeping on a sofa.

He returned to the map and once again located the Hauptbahnhof before carefully folding it and continuing on his way.

He soon arrived at the station, stamping his boots and shaking off the cold as he stepped inside, but when he turned to find the stationmaster's office he almost walked out again. More than two dozen men were lined up outside the office, and Gunther could tell by looking at them that they were in the same situation as he, looking for the same job that he had hoped for. Even the rumor of work would bring men from miles around to apply—well-qualified men, young and strong. It was all power to the man with a job to offer, and many employers knew it and took advantage. New men would be paid less, expected to work longer and not complain. Gunther became angry at the thought of going from an officer in the army to a nobody on the streets of Munich.

He stood for a moment, indecisive, until he remembered Amalie and Jakob, and then walked over to the group of men and leaned against the cold whitewashed wall. The young man sitting on the floor beside him looked up, sizing up this new competitor for the job, then turned back toward the opposite wall, choosing a blank space to stare at.

Gunther reached into his pocket for a cigarette, a rare commodity in these times, and as he did so he heard a crunching sound. The man sitting on the floor was surreptitiously eating an apple, another scarce commodity. Pulling his last two cigarettes out of his pocket, Gunther put one in his mouth, then offered the other to the young man on the floor. The man continued to stare at the wall until Gunther tapped him on the shoulder and extended the cigarette to him again. This time the man smiled and took the cigarette. He then took out a pocketknife and cut the apple in two, offering half to Gunther. Gunther thanked him with a nod and slipped the piece of apple into his pocket, then ran a wooden match against the wall to light his cigarette.

"Which division?" Gunther asked as he offered the young man a light.

"Medical corps," the man replied as he drew on the cigarette. "I drove ambulance. And you?"

"Austrian infantry. Galicia."

"I was in Rheims at the beginning," the young man explained, "and then I was transferred to drive at the Russian front, but I was far south of Galicia."

"I heard Rheims was bad."

"It was hell. After I was sent to Russia, my brother ended up at Paschendale. He died there just before the end."

"Those are the hardest," Gunther said, trying to offer sympathy, "when they die just before it's over."

There was an awkward pause as each thought of what they might say next.

"Now if there was just some way to find work," the young man finally said with a forced smile.

Gunther just shook his head from side to side and took a long drag on his cigarette. "It's the revolution. First they defeat us on the battlefield, and now they terrorize the businessmen, trying to get them to either close down their factories or turn them over to the workers."

"When I first heard about the revolution," the young man recounted, "I was on the Russian front, and I had come to town to get the rations for my squad, and the quartermaster laughed at me. He tells me I'm an idiot for not knowing. 'They've quit the war,' he says, 'and now we should just leave and find our way home.'"

"Chaos," Gunther interjected. "At least when I came home, it was on a troop train."

"I had to get rides where I could . . . horse cart, even a motorcycle once," the young man said. "My suit had been stolen, the one the army gave me, and then one day there I was at the door of my family's apartment."

The young man paused for a moment, recalling the scene. "My mother . . . ," he began, as a rush of emotion suddenly broke across his face, but he quickly composed himself. "My mother cried out, 'Friedrich! Friedrich is home at last!' I stood there in that damned flea-ridden uniform thinking how strange it was, because my father died earlier this year of a heart attack and my brother died in the war. We were the only two left. There was no one else to hear her when she called out."

There was another awkward pause until Gunther reached out his hand, introducing himself.

"Gunther . . . Gunther Metzdorf."

"Friedrich Haas," the young man countered as he reached up from his spot on the floor.

"How long have you been waiting here?" Gunther asked.

"Almost two hours."

"What's the job?"

"I don't know. I heard they might be looking for baggage men, but I don't know for sure."

A short, balding man with graying hair and thick round glasses came out of the stationmaster's office and stopped dead in his tracks when he saw the line of men. His face instantly turned red, and he began to shout, "What is this? What do you want here? I have no work, do you hear? No work! When there is a job, it is posted. When there is no work, nothing is posted. Nothing is posted, so stop blocking the hallways. Get out! Get out, all of you, or I'll call the police!"

One of the men, a gaunt and drawn young veteran who had been waiting longer than most, was clearly angry and started to walk toward the stationmaster. The stationmaster took a small step backward, but then, determined not to appear afraid, he stood up to the young man.

"No trouble!" the short man said in a loud, threatening voice as he raised a finger in warning. The other men in the hallway froze as they waited to see what would happen. The angry young man stopped and glared at the stationmaster for a moment without saying a word. He then spat in the little man's face and stormed out the door.

The stationmaster pulled a balled-up handkerchief from his back pocket as he removed his glasses. "Little bastard," he cursed under his breath as he cleaned the glasses and angrily wiped his face.

The rest of the men started moving toward the door one by one. They moved slowly, not wanting to let the stationmaster win so easily, but he had won. The little gray-haired man with the thick glasses had the power; he decided who would be able to eat and pay rent and who would not.

Gunther closed his coat and moved for the door, but stopped when he heard something fall behind him. He turned and saw a wooden cane on the floor.

"That's mine," Friedrich said as he struggled to his feet, reaching for the cane. Gunther quickly scooped it up and held it out for Friedrich to take. "Thanks," Friedrich said, quickly buttoning his coat and buckling the belt around his waist before taking the cane.

Friedrich didn't wait for Gunther to ask about his limp. "This was a last-minute bit of bad luck. My squad drove ambulance, and about two months before the war ended I took a corner too fast and the damned thing rolled over. I wasn't carrying any wounded, but when I came to, the cab was crushed in around me and I turned my head to find my boot next to my face."

"It came off?" Gunther asked.

"No, no," Friedrich continued, "my foot was still in the boot. My leg had snapped like a twig and twisted back up toward my head."

"Weren't there any doctors?" Gunther asked with a mixture of empathy and astonishment in his voice.

"You might better ask if there weren't any good doctors. They set the leg wrong, and every time I told them it felt like something was wrong, they told me that I was bound to be uncomfortable and I should just take their word that everything would be all right. Now it's too late. Nothing can be done to correct it."

"That's a horrible shame," Gunther said.

"Well, it should get better to the point where I won't need the cane in a few months, but it'll never be the way it was."

Gunther didn't know what to say, and Friedrich

sensed the awkwardness. "Well, I guess I'll be off. We'll see if there isn't better luck tomorrow." With that, Friedrich extended his hand to Gunther. "Wiedersehen."

"Where are you going now?" Gunther asked, stepping up beside him.

"I might as well head for home," Friedrich answered. "I'm living with my mother until I can get a job and find a place of my own."

"I was just about to meet a friend of mine at the Sterneckerbräu. Would you care to come?" Friedrich looked at Gunther for a moment, considering the offer. "Ja," he finally said. "I can afford one beer." And with that they left the train station to meet Klaus.

When they arrived at the small beer hall, Klaus was waiting. He had been leaning back in his chair, watching the world go by the window, and he brought the front legs of the chair down with a bang as Gunther spotted him.

"What a day!" Gunther grumbled.

"I take it you have not yet joined the proletariat?" Klaus asked with a grin.

"To hell with you," Gunther tossed back. "Klaus, this is Friedrich. We've come for beer after a long day of chasing down nonexistent work."

"Yes," Friedrich added, "but next time maybe that stationmaster will think twice before shouting out a group of soldiers."

"Why?" Klaus asked. "Did they kill him?"

"No," Gunther replied, "but one of the men spit right in his eye."

"Did he get the job?" Klaus asked with a straight

face. Friedrich started to laugh.

"I don't know," Gunther replied pensively. "I don't think they had a job opening for men to spit on people. I think that's a government job."

Gunther then glanced casually around the room and was surprised to see Amalie working her way across the room with Jakob in tow.

"Amalie!" Gunther called, waving to her. She had obviously already seen them, as she made straight for their table.

"Gunther, at last some good news," Amalie said eagerly as Gunther held open his arms for Jakob, who gladly jumped up on his father's lap.

"What news?"

"A letter from Father," Amalie said excitedly. "He has contacts with a couple of publishers here in Munich and has sent a letter of recommendation for you."

"Publishers? What do I know about publishing books?"

"Well, there are many things you might start with," Amalie began to explain.

"I'm not a writer! I don't really have much interest in books," Gunther interrupted.

Amalie looked hurt. She had been so excited about her news, and Gunther had closed the door on her.

"I'm sorry, Liebling," he said after a moment. "I just don't think I would be much good at that sort of thing."

"I just thought . . . ," Amalie began hesitantly. "Jobs are so scarce . . . I thought maybe just for a little while you might try."

"This sounds more like something you might like to do," Gunther said. "I was raised with soldiers, architects, and builders. I know absolutely nothing about books."

"You're right," Amalie said quietly, looking down at the floor. "I just know how badly you want work."

"Don't worry, Liebling," Gunther said, reaching for her hand. "I'll find something soon."

Gunther then realized that Klaus and Friedrich had been paying close attention to their conversation. "We certainly can't continue to stay in the asylum," he continued as he shot a look at Klaus and Friedrich, acknowledging their presence with a nod and wink.

"The asylum?" Friedrich asked incredulously. "Where do you live?"

"With me," Klaus said dryly.

"Well," Amalie said as she lifted Jakob from Gunther's lap, groaning softly as she strained at the little boy's weight. "I will take our chubby little boy home and get dinner ready. Will we have another for dinner?"

Embarrassed, Gunther realized that he hadn't introduced Amalie to Friedrich. "I'm sorry . . . Amalie, this is Friedrich Haas. Friedrich, this is my wife Amalie."

Struggling to get up, Friedrich extended his hand. "A pleasure to meet you, Mrs. Metzdorf."

"Are you able to join us for dinner, Mr. Haas?"

"Oh no, I couldn't impose."

"But you must!" Klaus piped in. "I've just come back from the country with a suitcase full of food."

Friedrich's eyes grew large for a moment at the

thought of a decent meal, but then he thought better of it, remembering his living arrangements. "No, my mother would be all alone."

"Bring your mother along. For a couple of days we eat well . . . you shouldn't refuse hospitality in times like these," Klaus continued.

"Yes, you really should come," Gunther added.

"Are you certain?" Friedrich asked, giving them a chance to change their minds.

"Absolutely," Klaus insisted.

"Then I would be honored."

A FEW HOURS later, in the Schwabing district of Munich, Gertrude Haas looked up from her book with a start when she heard footsteps stopping at the door to her apartment. Her body tensed and she sat very still and quiet, waiting to see what would happen next. Her instincts told her to rush to the bedroom, lock the door, and grab the long kitchen knife she kept under her bed for protection.

Ever since her husband had died, and especially now with revolution in the streets, she was constantly afraid. Suddenly it came to her as she sat there holding her breath . . . *Friedrich!* She had almost forgotten that he had come home from the war. She was sure it was just Friedrich coming home, but she still held her breath as she heard someone try the door.

"Mother," Friedrich called as he came in, "I'm home."

Gertrude didn't even realize she had been holding her breath until she let it out in a loud sigh, startling her son. "Oh, there you are," he said as he turned. "Have you started dinner yet?"

"Started what?" Gertrude asked with a cutting edge to her voice. "All we have is a potato and a moldy turnip. Have you found any work?"

"No, but today I found something better."

"Better than a job?"

"Yes. I found a couple of friends who have connections in the farmlands. They've invited us for dinner."

Gertrude looked at her son's smiling face but didn't share his sense of triumph. Friedrich was confused at her lack of enthusiasm. "What's wrong? We'll have a good meal tonight."

"Tonight," Gertrude repeated as her face suddenly contorted with grief and she began to cry. "Tonight we can eat, but what about tomorrow?"

"Mother . . . ," Friedrich began, about to explain to her the way that things were now that they were the defeated and the world was turned upside down.

"Damn!" Frau Haas shrieked.

"Mother!" Friedrich exclaimed in shock. He couldn't remember ever hearing his mother swear. Not that it was such a horrible thing, but this was his mother, a soft-spoken, gentle woman of impeccable manners.

"I hate being poor!" she cried. "I hate being alone! I hate being afraid all the time and not knowing whether or not there will be food to eat." Gertrude began to sob uncontrollably as her son knelt beside her.

Friedrich's father had always been there to take care of his mother, and Friedrich had never given it a second thought. He knew his parents would always be together to take care of each other.

Friedrich's father had been a great, barrel-chested bull of a man. Manfred Haas was a man who could carry the whole world on his shoulders if need be, and Friedrich had been sure he would outlive his own children. Thus he couldn't believe it when he had received a tear-stained letter six months before, while he was still on the Russian front.

The letter was a departure from the perfect examples of calligraphy his mother had always sent him before. She had written the wrong date at the top of the letter and then scratched it out. Scratched it out! His mother would *never* do such a thing. Each letter she wrote was a work of art in grammar and style and penmanship, yet here was this smudged note with scratched-out mistakes—he knew that something was terribly wrong as soon as he saw it.

"HEART." The word was written larger than the other words on the page, perhaps because it spoke of two broken hearts, or perhaps because Frau Haas had to remind herself that it was true. Manfred Haas had gone to work on a Monday morning in March in the small machine shop where he operated a metal lathe. The shop made parts to supplement the enormous industrial war production of the Krupp Works in Essen, far to the north. Manfred had lifted a half-empty box of parts to be finished and begun carrying them to his lathe when he suddenly stopped in the middle of the shop floor. One of the other workers, Karl Werthers, an old friend of Manfred's, had noticed him standing there, staring straight ahead, and had asked if something was wrong. Manfred had looked at his friend, smiled a half smile as his chin began to quiver uncontrollably, and then staggered a half step before dropping the wooden crate. His arms fell to his sides, and he watched as the shiny metal cylinders bounced out of the fallen crate, seemingly in slow motion, each piece ringing like a bell as it hit the cement floor, the parts tinkling softly as they continued to roll in a broadening pattern, like ripples rolling away from a stone dropped in a pond. A couple of the other machinists rushed over to help him, and Karl heard him whisper "Oh, Gertie . . ." in a sad, low voice, as his knees buckled and he collapsed on top of the wooden crate, crushing it as he fell. It was a massive coronary, striking just a week short of his fifty-first birthday.

"You're not alone," Friedrich said. "I'm here."

"But not for long," Gertrude said amid her sobs. "I know you'll leave too. You'll find a girl and make your own life, and I'll be all alone."

"Mother, don't think of that. I'm here now, and I won't be leaving for quite a while. We've got to just get through today. The whole world is changing, and you just have to try to be strong."

"I can't," she sobbed even louder than before. "I can't be strong anymore. I don't want to be strong."

Friedrich stood up beside her and said matter-of-factly, "I'm afraid you have no choice, Mother. I'm sorry, but the world has not stopped, and I'm not going to let you stop. Now get dressed. We're going to have dinner with my new friends, and we'll both feel better for it."

"I'd rather not go out," Gertrude said as she wiped her eyes.

"Of course you'd rather not go out," Friedrich scolded. "You'd rather sit here and feel sorry for yourself."

"Friedrich!" Gertrude cried indignantly. "How dare you speak to me like that. If your father were here . . ."

"He would say the same thing," Friedrich said, finishing her sentence with more than a hint of smugness.

Gertrude eyed him coldly and continued drying her tears, getting up without saying a word and going into her bedroom, not slamming the door, but certainly closing it with force.

Friedrich went into the kitchen and put water in the teapot. "Would you like tea?" he called out to the bedroom, hoping to resume the conversation on a more casual note.

Normally, after such a confrontation, his mother would stay in her bedroom for the rest of the night and remain cool to him for days. It had been like this for the past month, ever since he had returned home. It certainly portended a depressing Christmastime, with just the two of them left of the family, no money coming into the house, and his mother's meager savings running low.

The bedroom door opened. "What time will we meet your friends?"

Friedrich stopped for an instant, surprised that she had changed her mind. "Half past seven," he replied.

"How far away do they live?"

"By the Schwabing barracks on Turkenstrasse."

"Schwabing barracks? Are they soldiers?"

"Yes."

"Not part of that revolutionary mob?" Gertrude

asked with a note of apprehension.

"I'm sure not," Friedrich said reassuringly. "They were infantry officers in the trenches, not sailors."

"Are we to have dinner in the barracks?" Gertrude asked in a disapproving tone.

"No, mother," Friedrich said, clearly annoyed at her insinuations. "They're two officers, one married with a little boy. One of the officers just came back from the countryside with food. I met the other man at the train station while looking for work. We got to talking and hit it off, and the next thing I knew, his wife invited us to dinner."

"Just the same," Gertrude cautioned, "you can't be too careful these days."

"They didn't seem to care much for Ebert or Eisner, or the rest of that Social Democrat bunch, much less for Communists."

"Well," Gertrude continued, "if the conversation turns to politics, just agree politely with whatever they say. It's worth it for a good meal, even if they are Communists."

The teapot began to whistle, and Gertrude brushed past her son on her way to the kitchen, taking over the preparation of the tea. "You should take a bath," she said. "We might at least pretend we are still civilized."

Friedrich's face took on a smirk as he headed for the bathroom. "Please, Mutti dear, have the maid bring my tea to the drawing room while I draw my bath."

"Friedrich, Friedrich, " Frau Haas lamented, "when did my little boy become so insolent?"

"Mother, dear Mother," Friedrich retorted, "the

world became insolent . . . I have only joined in." And with that, he moved toward the bathroom, his mother watching with sudden sadness the measured movement of his cane and the accompanying limp that had been returned to her in place of her little boy.

FRAU HAAS and her husband had lived in the southern part of Schwabing district for almost twenty years, in an apartment at 23 Franz Joseph Strasse. South of them there were army barracks still full of soldiers, many of them caught up in the revolutionary fervor of the time, disillusioned by the drawn-out war and the abdication of the Kaiser.

These troops had played a significant role in the revolutionary uprising in the area during the past months by refusing to act against the revolutionaries. While the streets were alive with voices calling for a new government—a leftist government—the soldiers stayed in their barracks playing cards.

It was about eight blocks to Klaus's apartment, but Gertrude and Friedrich couldn't spare the few pfennigs for the trolley car, so they started their journey early to make sure they would get there in time. Friedrich knew his mother was worried about walking through the area at night, but he had done so in his uniform many times and had never had any trouble. There was still a bond between soldiers, and when the army had refused to fire on their fellow soldiers who had taken up flags of revolution, that bond seemed to grow even stronger.

Gertrude was only fifty-two years old, but the constant noises she made as she moved over the snow-encrusted sidewalks irritated Friedrich. It made her sound like an old lady, a role it seemed to him she had adopted as a consequence of his father's death. She was now content to be the little old widow lady who needed help with everything. He found it pathetic, and worse, he found himself growing constantly more annoyed and angry with her. She was giving up. She was gladly leaping into the role of the neglected old grandmother whom no one cared about. Although she constantly acknowledged that Friedrich would be leaving her soon for his own life, her implication was that he must stay. He had to stay because she was old and feeble and could not care for herself, and now that Manfred and Kurt had left her, there was no one left but Friedrich to care whether she lived or died. When Friedrich dwelled on it, he could feel himself become infuriated. How dare she place that on his shoulders! Just because she had given up all hope of living and being happy didn't mean that she could expect him to leap with her into the grave she was digging for herself.

Friedrich slowed down a bit and let his mother walk ahead of him as she carefully navigated through the snow and ice. Afraid of falling, she kept looking down, paying no attention to the street ahead of her.

Friedrich had fallen behind so that she would not see his face—so that she would not notice the anger there and ask him what was bothering him. He truly was just living for the day, as he had told her at the apartment. If he could only get through the day without another argument. If he could just get through until he could get work and move to his own place. A little distance—that was all he wanted. Not that he would never see her again—he would certainly help her as much as he could. He knew that he still loved her and that she loved him, but he was not going to let himself be a replacement for Manfred.

Friedrich regained his composure and caught up with his mother as they came to a cross street. He grabbed her arm and stopped her as she was about to step off the curb in front of an oncoming truck, and she looked up with a start.

"Careful!" he said. "You've got to watch where you're going."

"It's a good thing you're with me," Gertrude said as she smiled up at her son, catching the glint of annoyance but not quite understanding the reason for it and not wanting to ask him what was wrong.

"Yes . . . well, it's only a few more blocks," he said, looking ahead at the dimly lit street signs. They continued on in silence until they reached the apartment house.

"Here we are," Friedrich said as he opened the door for his mother, then walked over to the mailboxes. "Grunewald . . . Klaus Grunewald," he said, looking through the names. "Here it is. Apartment Two-B." With that, Friedrich made his way up the stairs, using his cane expertly to vault his bad leg up each step, leaving his mother to follow behind at her own measured pace. Friedrich leaned against the doorjamb, waiting for Gertrude to catch up before he knocked on the door.

The door opened only a crack, and Friedrich smiled as a little boy peered out at him, looking him up and down, then turning his gaze on Gertrude as she stood stiffly, looking straight ahead, pretending to be oblivious to the child's impolite stare.

"Jakob, you have to move so they can come in," Amalie said, opening the door wider. "Grüss Gott," she said warmly to her visitors in the traditional Bavarian greeting, which translates to "greetings from God."

"Grüss Gott," Friedrich replied. "Mother . . . ," Friedrich said hesitantly, as he realized that his mother was still staring straight ahead, not even making eye contact with Amalie. "This is Frau Metzdorf." Gertrude finally looked at her hostess once she had been introduced, as though a curtain had been opened and she could now acknowledge the young woman's presence. "And Amalie," Friedrich continued, "this is my mother, Frau Gertrude Haas." Gertrude extended her hand to Amalie, who took it gently.

"Welcome to our home, Frau Haas. Won't you please come in?"

Amalie nearly knocked Jakob over as she turned into the apartment. "Oh! Frau Haas, you haven't met my little Jakob." Amalie positioned Jakob in front of her and bent down, presenting him to Gertrude. Gertrude's manner instantly softened as she looked into the big blue eyes taking her in warily. "Good evening, Jakob," Gertrude said. Jakob did not reply; he just continued staring at her. Friedrich was then astonished to see his mother take the little boy's hand. "How old are you then, little one?"

"He just turned two last month," Amalie answered for her son. "Klaus and Gunther should be here any minute now," she continued, taking her visitors' coats. "Dinner will be ready in about half an hour."

"It smells terrific," Friedrich said enthusiastically, as he caught the smell of food cooking in the kitchen.

"It's only Kartofflesuppe mit Wollewurst," Amalie said apologetically. Potato soup was standard Munich fare, and it was common to slice a couple of sausages into the mix when one had such. Wollewurst, or "wool sausage," is one of the many different kinds of sausages made in Bavaria, whose names rarely reflect the ingredients. For example, there isn't any wool at all in wool sausage.

"It sounds wonderful," Gertrude assured Amalie. "It is so kind of you to have us, especially with food being so hard to come by these days."

"Yes, well, our friend Klaus travels to the countryside regularly for the army, and he has friends . . ."

"You are very lucky, Frau Metzdorf," said Gertrude.

"Yes, I thank God for Klaus. Not so much for Gunther and myself, but for Jakob. Children shouldn't have to pay the price for the war . . . they shouldn't have to starve when they had nothing to do with it."

Jakob had warmed up to Frau Haas a bit and now stood close beside her. It seemed so natural to see her reach over and lightly stroke his hair. "I'm afraid we will all have to pay the price," Gertrude said in a soft voice.

"Now, Mother . . . ," Friedrich reproached, trying to forestall her prophesy of gloom. "These hard times are only temporary. Things will settle down."

"Friedrich, I was only five years old when Bismarck's war with France ended, but I knew even then how much the French hated us. All my life I've known how the French hate us, and now we're at their mercy. Our soldiers aren't in France ready to fight. They're in the streets of German cities carrying red flags! Even the emperor has left. We have no Bismarck now . . . nothing will be the same."

"Maybe we could just leave that behind tonight?" Friedrich asked plaintively.

Gertrude's first reaction was to shoot Friedrich an angry look, but at the same instant, she thought how nice it might be to leave the war behind. "You're right."

"Shall we sit?" Amalie asked, motioning her guests to the living room. "I'll be right in. I have to check the soup."

The two old chairs and settee in the living room were similar in style, although they didn't quite match. The two chairs were covered in a coarse, dark red fabric that showed signs of being neglected at one time, but still, the entire apartment and its contents were very clean. The settee looked brightest, upholstered in a dark blue. It must have been a more recent acquisition. The furniture was obviously secondhand, but it was comfortable. Friedrich sat on the settee, where Jakob joined him, while Gertrude settled in one of the chairs. Jakob looked down at Friedrich's cane, which leaned against the settee between them.

"What's that?" Jakob asked.

"I need it to help me walk," Friedrich replied.

"Why?" Jakob asked.

"Because I hurt my leg in the war."

"Vati and I saw a man . . . a man hurt his leg,"

Jakob said in the measured cadence of a child. "In the war . . . they cut it off." Both Gertrude and Friedrich were surprised to hear such a comment coming from a little boy, but then it wasn't unusual to see wounded men these days. Lost arms, amputated legs, blind men trying to survive in the streets of Munich. What should a father tell his son of such things? They exchanged a quick glance, but Jakob, oblivious to the looks, and certainly oblivious to the macabre nature of what he was saying, continued: "Will they cut off your leg?"

"Child!" Frau Haas exclaimed in shock at the question.

"I don't mind, Mother," Friedrich said calmly. "He shouldn't be afraid to ask questions." Friedrich then turned back to Jakob. "No, they won't cut my leg off because it wasn't hurt as badly as that other man's leg must have been . . . I suppose I was lucky."

There was a crackle from the fireplace as the coals settled, and as always happens with young boys, Jakob's attention shifted quickly.

"Mutti . . . the fire?" Jakob called out to his mother in the kitchen, using the shorthand communication families with small children typically use, in this case asking if he could put more coals on the fire.

"No," Amalie said as she reentered the living room. "You're not old enough to tend the fire yet."

"You can help me do it," Friedrich offered as he moved to the fireplace.

Everyone watched as Friedrich used his hands to bend his leg and knelt in front of the fireplace. Jakob knelt beside him and offered him the small coal shovel. Friedrich scooped up a couple of the briquettes, stopping for a moment to read the words that had been stamped into each piece: GOTT VERNICHTE ENGLÅND.

"I always thought this was ridiculous," Friedrich said to the piece of coal.

"What's that?" Amalie asked, thinking he was talking to her.

"'God destroy England,'" Friedrich replied. "'God destroy England' stamped into each piece of coal. What possible reason could there be?"

"Perhaps they thought the soot would be carried up to God and he would get the message?" Amalie offered.

Friedrich and his mother began laughing loudly and Jakob smiled, although he didn't understand the joke. Klaus and Gunther arrived amidst the laughter, making a noisy entrance as they put up their coats and hats.

"Vati!" Jakob shouted as he ran to his father's side. Gunther picked up Jakob and gave him a hug and a peck on the cheek as he spun around in a circle. "Grüss Gott, Friedrich!" Gunther said as he put Jakob down and entered the living room. Jakob followed closely, clinging to his father's leg. "And this must be your lovely mother."

The two young officers snapped smartly to attention and brought their heels together as though they were meeting a general. "We are glad you could join us this evening, Frau Haas," Klaus said, bowing slightly.

"Thank you so much for inviting us, Herr Grunewald. As I was saying to Frau Metzdorf, it is especially kind of you in times like this."

"Please, Frau Haas, we are all friends here. Call me Klaus."

"My friends call me Gertie."

"Well, I'll be ready to serve in a moment, so everyone should come to the table," said Amalie as she got up and put her hand on Jakob's shoulder. "Come, Jakob, you can help me."

Klaus, Gunther, Friedrich, and Gertie began to move toward the small table in the dining area of the apartment, engaged in small talk, as Amalie handed Jakob a plate with slices of heavy, dark "war bread." Made from old potatoes, old bran, and more often than not, sawdust, it had been a staple of the German diet for both civilians and soldiers throughout the war. The thing that caught Friedrich's eye, though, were the slices of fresh, yellow-orange cheese that accompanied the tired, old black bread.

Jakob walked slowly and steadily toward his father, keeping close watch on the plate, as though it might unexpectedly fly off into space at any moment. Gunther loved watching his son's face. He loved seeing that intensity and seriousness. He was sure it was a sign of intelligence and character.

"Thank you, son," Gunther said as he relieved Jakob of his burden and found a place for the plate on the small table.

"He is a charming little boy," Gertrude commented after watching the exchange, as Amalie began to serve the soup in mismatched bowls.

"Excellent!" Friedrich proclaimed, taking a drink of water after tasting the soup.

"I'm sorry it could only be soup and cheese," Amalie said.

"One forgets," Gertie responded, "just how good simple meals can be—until one has to do without."

"Yes," Amalie said, feeling a bit guilty at their good fortune. "We eat well a couple of days a week, thanks to Klaus, but the rest of the time we just barely manage to get by."

"But let's not forget the cook!" Klaus interjected good-naturedly, countering Amalie's apologetic tone. After all, there was certainly nothing wrong with their good fortune.

"Yes," Gunther concurred, "one of the best in Munich."

There was an awkward pause as they ate in silence, until Jakob finally popped up his head. "Mutti . . . marmalade?" he asked, his eyes aglow in anticipation.

"No," Amalie replied.

"Why?" Jakob whined.

"Because I said no," Amalie said firmly. She was embarrassed in front of her guests and peeked to see Frau Haas's reaction, but Gertie continued eating slowly, looking down at her soup.

"Why, Mutti?" Jakob whined again.

"He knows what he wants," Gunther said, trying to keep Amalie in good humor, but she was clearly exasperated.

"Dear," Amalie began, almost snapping at Gunther, "how will Jakob learn manners if we always give in to him?"

Amalie addressed Frau Haas: "I'm sorry for Jakob's behavior." Then, turning to Jakob, she scolded mildly, "Jakob, we haven't enough marmalade for everyone, and it is very bad manners to have something that you cannot offer to your guests."

Jakob had never felt a disciplinary swat on his bottom because one had never been needed. Just his mother's or father's disapproval was always enough to get him to change his behavior. Amalie's scolding affected him deeply, and he felt like crying, but he did not. He just sat there looking sad, so sad it prompted Gertie to speak.

"Actually," she began, "we've never cared much for marmalade."

"No," Friedrich concurred. "We rarely had marmalade in the house . . . I think Kurt was the only one who cared for it."

Friedrich almost caught himself as he said it. He had invoked the name of his dead brother, which he usually tried desperately to avoid doing. Not that he didn't think of Kurt; in fact, he thought of him often. He had admired his brother and loved him deeply. Gertrude, however, wore her grief like a crown, and now he had given her license to pull out Kurt's death shroud and wrap it about herself.

But Gertie only made passing mention of it. "Kurt was my other son . . . He died at Paschendale. Yes, he loved his marmalade." She lost only a moment in wistful memory of her dead son and his love of marmalade, and then came back to the matter at hand. "So you needn't deny little Jakob because of us."

Amalie had no choice but to recant: "Jakob, do you want some marmalade then?"

"No, thank you," Jakob said quietly and politely.

"Very well," Amalie replied, with no thought of trying to make him feel better and reconsider his about face. Friedrich couldn't help but smile at

Jakob's contradiction. The dining room fell silent again as the dark little cloud floated over Jakob's head.

Finally, Gunther addressed Friedrich across the table. "Have you heard any good rumors about jobs?"

Again Friedrich smiled as he kept eating. "It seems, my friend, that the rumors far outnumber the jobs."

Klaus laughed. "It's the damned revolutionaries!"

"Please, Klaus . . . ," Amalie begged softly under her breath. "Children repeat what they hear."

"But it's true!" Klaus insisted "They want everyone to share equally in the poverty."

"Yes, you're right," Frau Haas agreed. "If only the Kaiser were still with us."

Friedrich was surprised at his mother speaking out like this. It was the first time he had ever heard her say anything political. It was certainly not unusual in European households for children to be unaware of their parent's financial situation or political beliefs. Parents rarely discussed matters of money or politics with their children in those years. But apparently that had all changed with Frau Haas. With the death of her son and husband, and the uncertainty of the future, politics was now a very personal thing to her.

Friedrich found himself responding automatically as he always had to discussions regarding the Kaiser's abdication. "He ran away!"

Everyone looked at Friedrich. Perhaps he had spoken a bit loudly.

Gertrude responded in the tone of a schoolteacher

correcting a below-average student. "No, Friedrich . . . he was forced to leave by the revolutionaries."

"Mother," Friedrich began, speaking slowly, as though addressing an elderly woman who had lost her faculties. "The revolutionaries were his people. If the Kaiser had been a good leader, they would not have rebelled against him."

Klaus, Gunther, and Amalie had listened quietly to the exchange. Recognizing that it was just family bickering, Gunther and Amalie held their peace, but Klaus couldn't help expressing his opinion.

"The revolutionaries," Klaus began, "want something for nothing."

"So, you think we would be better off if the Kaiser were at the head of the government?" Friedrich cautiously asked his host, clearly not wanting to offend him.

"No, certainly not," Klaus replied. "Wilhelm was not the man for the job, but we do not live in a country whose people are inclined to be ruled by committee."

"'Not by speeches and majority votes are the great questions of the day decided,'" Gunther quoted, "'but by blood and iron.'"

"Bismarck," Friedrich responded reflexively, accrediting the quotation.

"You're all so young," Frau Haas interrupted the exchange, "but your politics must acknowledge a frightening reality. We have lost the war . . ."

"Lost the war from within," Gunther stated unequivocally.

"We lost because of the Jewish revolutionaries," Klaus said almost simultaneously in a knee-jerk response.

Amalie felt a strange twinge at Klaus's statement. Certainly there were Jews among the revolutionaries, and some of the leaders were Jewish, but the two were not synonymous. She didn't say anything, though. She didn't consider herself a Jew, and she wouldn't defend someone just by virtue of their being Jewish. Her family had lived in Austria for hundreds of years, and she considered them Austrians who practiced the Jewish religion, not Jews who lived in Austria. Now she was a German who had left her Jewish past behind her, not in the sense of denouncing her past religion, but in the sense that she no longer practiced any religion. She merely left it behind along with other things she had decided not to take with her when she left her father's house to be with her husband. She would not stand up and defend the revolutionary radicals, yet she felt her husband and Klaus were wrong to link the Jews, the revolutionaries, and the Bolsheviks all together with the defeat of Germany. In her opinion, they were only parroting what they had heard from others.

"I was saying," Gertrude continued persistently, "that we lost, for whatever reason, to the French."

"An excellent point," Klaus conceded, "and all the more reason we need a single strong leader, someone representing the interests of our nation as though we were his sons and daughters. Someone to keep faith with his people in their most desperate time of need."

"Perhaps you?" Gunther mused, arching his right eyebrow comically.

Klaus looked as though someone had just poured a huge bucket of water on him from the top of a building. He glared at his friend.

"Well, Klaus, you're constantly telling me that I should let you know when you're getting carried away," Gunther said, defending himself against his friend's venomous stare.

"Yes," Klaus responded, "but this is something I know about."

"We would all like to be able to draw simple lines. It would make life so much easier if we could tie all the different parts of our world together into one great, comprehensible truth. But I don't think that's possible," Amalie said, responding to Klaus's great declaration.

"Well, this is a fine state of affairs!" Klaus said theatrically. "The whole family turns against me." Klaus then turned to Jakob. "How about you Jakob? Do you have anything to say?"

Jakob looked up at Klaus innocently. "Dessert?"

Everyone at the table laughed as Klaus declared, "Now there's a true proletarian!"

"But what about God?" Gertrude asked Amalie. "Don't you think he links everything together into one great truth?"

Friedrich began to feel a little nervous as his mother broached the subject of religion. Wasn't it she who had said less than two hours ago that they shouldn't risk offending their guests by discussing politics or religion? And now she had brought up both topics.

"God certainly was not on the battlefield," Gunther answered for his wife. "How could he then possibly have a hand in politics? No, that has to be the devil's field."

"It's not unusual," Frau Haas countered, "for young men to lose faith after seeing the ugliness of war."

Suddenly Klaus was serious, without making his usual retreat into sarcasm and facetiousness. "With all due respect, Frau Haas, you cannot possibly know what it was like for any of us, even your own son—perhaps especially your own son—and we could never completely explain what it was like."

"I know that," Gertrude said, looking down at the table in a defensive posture, as though Klaus had physically attacked her. "I only mean that we cannot know what God knows, and so we cannot understand what God does."

"Then how do we even know that there is a God?" Klaus asked.

"You can see it in the good in the world, in the beauty of nature, in the best of men and the greatest things that men have done for the world," Gertrude answered.

"If I were to tell you the truth of life, Frau Haas," Klaus began thoughtfully, sadly, "it would be that there is something missing in the reality of life, an absence if you will, an absence of honor, love, justice . . . an absence of superlatives in our little world. Who is the best, who is the worst, who is right and who is wrong. We are constantly surprised in our lives, such as when a good man commits an evil deed or, even more surprising, when an evil man commits a good deed. Yes, there is a distinct absence of superlatives in our little world."

"My father would say," Amalie offered after a brief pause to contemplate Klaus's pronouncement on the nature of modern man, "that all men are capable of good, if only they make a personal commitment to honor, justice, and love."

"But my point is that you will not find many men willing to make that commitment," Klaus countered.

"I agree with Frau Metzdorf," said Gertrude. "It is like a living testament to Christ."

Klaus laughed a little at this. "But, Frau Haas, Amalie's father is an old Jew."

"A Jew?" Gertrude exclaimed.

Amalie was embarrassed at Gertrude's dismay and for an instant was conflicted by feelings of shame, mostly because of the way that Klaus could make the word *Jew* sound like such an insult, and of anger that Frau Haas would be upset to learn Amalie's father was Jewish.

"Of course, there's nothing wrong with being Jewish," Gertrude bubbled, trying to cover her faux pas. "I just didn't know . . . still, your father's words show a Christian hope, that we must work against evil."

"Well, actually," Amalie ventured in again, "to me the point has always been to work *for* good, not to work *against* evil."

"Isn't that the same thing?" asked Frau Haas.

"I don't think so," said Amalie. "When we concentrate on fighting something we consider evil, we fail to see those things that we consider 'good' as well as we might. And once you center your life around looking for evil, then you come to change your whole perspective of the world, from what it might be to what a terrible place it is."

"You must often be disappointed," Klaus said.

"Well," Gunther said with a heavy sigh, "*is* there any dessert?"

Friedrich laughed at Gunther's attempt to lighten the conversation.

"Yes, as a matter of fact, I made some Apfeltaschen for our guests," Amalie replied.

"Apple pockets?" Gertrude exclaimed in disbelief. "With flour? I haven't seen real flour for so long."

"We so rarely have guests, I wanted to do something special," Amalie confided.

"Just for the guests?" Gunther asked "What about Klaus and me? . . . And little Jakob?" Gunther picked up his son and set him on his lap, bringing their faces close together, both expressing sadness at this terrible news.

"Why don't you all go to the living room while I dish up dessert?" Amalie said as she began taking the supper dishes to the sink.

"This is so kind of you," Gertrude said, rising to move with the others to the living room. "It reminds me of times before the war. I had almost forgotten what it was like." She wiped a tear from her eye. "My God!" she cried, gesturing broadly with the hand she had just used to wipe away the tear. "I really am a foolish old woman! Crying over Apfeltaschen!"

"It's all right, Frau Haas," Gunther said in a comforting tone. "We take things for granted in easier times, and then suddenly hard times befall us and we associate these little things with times gone by."

"Ah, yes," Friedrich mused, "the things we take for granted. I was only seventeen when the war started. That was such a long time ago."

"Let me see ," Gunther began, "Amalie and I had just gotten married a few months before the war broke out—"

"And I," Klaus interjected, "was a fresh young lieutenant in the greatest army the world had ever known."

"The greatest army the world had ever known . . . ," Friedrich repeated wistfully, his eyes drawn by the orange glow of the coal burning in the cast-iron fireplace. "I just heard from a friend of mine about another friend who was a lieutenant in the cavalry. He and another officer had found a bottle of cognac in a bombed-out restaurant in a small Belgian town, and they were drinking it when they heard about the surrender. They finished off the bottle, then each put his pistol in the other's mouth, and on the count of three they fired . . . "

"The thing I miss most are the Christmases," Gertrude said, appearing to ignore her son's story, and Friedrich was content to let it go by.

"A big goose roasting all day," Gunther offered, shuddering a bit, recovering from Friedrich's story.

"As a child, I always loved the candles on the tree," Klaus added.

"When Gunther and I got married," Amalie began tentatively as she entered the room, passing out the apple pastries to her guests and family, "I saw my first Christmas celebration, and I shall never forget the great crowd of family on the evening before, and the closeness and warmth."

Gunther smiled at his wife at the thought of this shared memory.

"I wonder what we'll do this year, with only a couple of weeks to go," Gertrude said to no one in particular.

"What is it now? Two weeks?" Klaus rejoined.

"Ten days," Amalie answered.

"Well, at least we'll be together," Gunther said, knowing that there would be no Christmas feast this year and no wonderful gifts for his son. He couldn't even find candles for a Christmas tree.

"I do have some 'coffee,'" Amalie offered meekly.

"From roasted corn?" Gertrude asked with a smile.

"Ja," Amalie said, now at ease with her ersatz coffee.

"You have given us such a lovely evening," Gertrude said, "there is no need to be embarrassed."

"Oh no!" Friedrich agreed emphatically with his mother. "You've been so kind."

"We were happy you could come," said Klaus. "In these days, we soldiers who fought at the front must stick together."

"Well, I didn't actually fight at the front," Friedrich corrected his host.

Klaus shot a look of surprise at Gunther.

"I didn't say he *fought* at the front, I said he was *at* the front," Gunther stated defensively.

"I was in the medical corps," Friedrich explained. "I drove ambulances."

"Ah," Klaus replied, "then you were still in the thick of it."

"Yes," said Friedrich. "I often went right to the trenches to take men out."

"Is that how you hurt your leg?" Klaus asked.

"No . . . ," Friedrich said as he began to describe the circumstances of his injury to a third member of the household. "My ambulance tipped over on a bad stretch of road near the Russian front. The ironic thing is that it happened after all the fighting was over." Friedrich paused a moment, then added, "That's how I earned this lovely cane."

"Well," Klaus explained, "when I speak of soldiers at the front, I mean to say those who really knew what the war was like. You would certainly qualify."

"You make it sound like a club . . . some kind of fraternal organization," Friedrich said in an analytical tone.

"Exactly," Gunther exclaimed, jumping back into the conversation. "A brotherhood of front-line soldiers. We have experienced things firsthand that others could not imagine, much less endure."

"I see what you mean," Friedrich said thoughtfully as a thousand images raced through his mind, experiences that he could only tell to other soldiers. Who else could understand? Who else but another soldier could appreciate the things a man feels when he is forced to hide from a relentless artillery barrage in a tiny hole in the ground with the entire world threatening to collapse in on him. Who but another soldier could imagine the things a human body can endure? One moment you and a friend are diving into a trench to escape an incoming artillery round, and in the next instant your friend is nothing but a mass of splintered bone, blood, mud, and gore—giving out a pitiful whimper and calling for his mother—before falling dead into the water at your feet.

Friedrich quickly looked back at the glowing

embers in the fireplace so that he would not have to look into anyone's eyes. What if they looked into his eyes and saw within him the terrible things that he had seen? Surely they could never look at him again.

Jakob had been sitting quietly next to Friedrich through all this, slowly eating his Apfeltaschen, knowing without even being told that it would be a long time before he ever got such a treat again.

Jakob sensed that Friedrich was feeling sad, as did all the others in the room, and he climbed up on Friedrich's leg and rested his head against the young man's chest. Friedrich was surprised at first, but then he put his arm around the tired little boy. Everyone else watched in silence, knowing that Jakob was the only one who could have gotten close to Friedrich at that moment. This sad young man, only just turned twenty-one years old, marked by this hellish war for the rest of his life.

Gradually the conversation returned to lighter topics than those of war, defeat, and religion, and the remainder of the evening became a pleasant diversion. Friedrich and his mother got up promptly at ten o'clock and insisted that they must be getting home. They were both keenly aware that they did not want to overstay their welcome. On the cynical side, they hoped to be invited back to share in the good fortune of their hosts, but they really had enjoyed their evening and genuinely liked their new friends. Frau Haas even picked up Jakob and rested him on her hip as she gave him a little peck on the cheek. "You must promise to be a good boy until we meet again," she said with a kindly smile.

"Christmas?" Jakob asked innocently.

Amalie shot an embarrassed glance at Klaus, then looked down at the floor. None of them had any idea if their fortune, such as it was, would continue, and to plan ahead even two weeks seemed highly presumptuous.

Klaus looked at Gunther and then at their guests. "Of course," Klaus said, "you must come for whatever kind of Christmas dinner we have."

"But we can't promise a goose!" Gunther added.

Frau Haas smiled appreciatively, realizing that they had made such a generous offer based on a child's slip of the tongue.

"Thank you so much, but I think we have plans," she said, turning to Friedrich for his concurrence.

"Yes," he said, "I think we promised to visit family and would be gone for most of the week."

Amalie stepped over to Frau Haas to relieve her of Jakob. "If your plans with your family fall through . . . ," Amalie began hesitantly," looking at Klaus and Gunther for a glimmer of acquiescence and, seeing it in their eyes, continued, "we would very much enjoy your company."

Frau Haas then knew Amalie was being sincere. "Well, if things don't work out, and if you allow us to bring something with us next time," Gertrude insisted sternly, "then I think we would be happy to come." Friedrich agreed with a nod and offered his hand to his new friends, and with that, he and his mother left.

Klaus returned to the living room while Gunther took Jakob from Amalie so that she could go into the kitchen to finish cleaning up. A dirty supper dish never saw the light of day in Amalie's kitchen, even if it was really Klaus's kitchen. Klaus went in search of the daily newspaper while Gunther hoisted Jakob to his shoulders for a piggy-back ride into the living room. "Now, young man, it's long past your bed-time."

Klaus went to bed soon after, and Amalie and Gunther were left alone to lay their bedding on the floor in the middle of the living room. Once they had settled in, Amalie nestled beside her husband with her head on his chest, Gunther spoke quietly so as not to wake Jakob.

"I don't know how we're going to get an apart-ment. I didn't think it would be so hard to find work."

"It's not your fault," Amalie said. "No work, no food. . . I'm afraid to say anything that might offend Klaus because I don't know what we would do with-out him."

"You shouldn't worry about Klaus," Gunther reas-sured her. "He's been a good friend, and he knows how hard things are."

"He worries me, though."

"Worries you? Why?"

"Well . . ."

"Go ahead and say it."

"He hates Jews."

"So what?"

"How can you say that?" Amalie asked incredu-lously, sitting up.

"What do you mean?"

"How can you say 'so what' when you know I'm Jewish?"

"But you're not that kind of Jew," Gunther said in

a comforting tone, trying to placate his indignant wife. "Klaus doesn't mean you."

"Then who does he mean?"

"Well, he means the Bolsheviks, of course!"

"But they're not all Jews. If he means Bolsheviks, then why doesn't he say that?" Amalie continued to press.

"You're being too sensitive. He doesn't mean all Jews," Gunther replied, putting his arm around Amalie and gently pulling her head to his chest. "In any group of people you have good and bad. There are good Germans and bad Germans, good Frenchmen and bad Frenchman, the same as there are good Jews and bad Jews. Klaus hates the bad Jews."

"You make it sound so reasonable, but it frightens me when I see that look in his eyes. And there's such a strange edge to his voice sometimes."

"You're just anxious because you feel we're imposing. Just hold on. Things will be better after Christmas."

"Christmas . . . ," Amalie said with a hint of foreboding as the subject changed, finding that she was happy to let it go. She was afraid that if she dwelled too long on Gunther's anti-Semitism, well, she just didn't know how they could ever resolve it. It was like a monster hiding in a closet, waiting to rush out some day and devour them both.

"That reminds me," Gunther said, planting a little kiss on Amalie's forehead, "it's been a long time since you've given me a gift."

"A gift?"

"Like this . . . ," he said, moving his lips down to

kiss her on the shoulder.

"Gunther! Our son is right there!"

Gunther looked over at Jakob curled up against the back of the sofa.

"He's fast asleep. We can be quiet. I've heard that if you hold your breath at the last minute, it can make it even better."

Sliding his hand gently under her nightgown and across her stomach, he kissed her on the lips and then on her throat, his hand moving slowly up her side as his passion rose.

CHAPTER 3

Kurt Eisner. Rosa Luxemburg. Karl Liebknecht.

These were the names and faces of revolution in Germany in 1919. There were certainly more, tens of thousands more, but these were the names known all across the country. Karl Liebknecht's had been one of the few voices in 1914 that called for peace instead of war, and in that time of war fever he was sent to prison for his beliefs. Rosa Luxemburg had been a Communist for most of her life, fighting for the rights of the poor and disenfranchised and believing that the only way their lot could be improved was through Communist rule. She, too, was put in prison for her willingness and commitment to speak out about those beliefs. Both Liebknecht and Luxemburg were released from prison just days before the end of the war. Although their political philosophies differed on many points, together they led a group known as the Spartacists, named after Spartacus, the slave who led a revolt in ancient Rome. The Spartacists were a Communist organization in Berlin, and many believed they were the leaders of the revolution in Germany. The truth, however, was that the actual revolution that spread across Germany was a more popular rising of ordinary citizens. Those citizens just wanted the war to end, and they believed that they were merely supporting the new Social Democratic Republic.

It was that idea of a new German Republic putting an end to the Kaiser's war which emboldened Kurt Eisner to stroll into the Bavarian provincial palace and declare the new republic in

Munich and Bavaria.

Trouble lay ahead in Munich, however, as it always does when a change of such magnitude is begun. As an anonymous revolutionary once so appropriately put it: "The problem with revolutions is that they always degenerate into governments."

Christmas came and went quickly in 1918. Frau Haas and Amalie had become fast friends. It was to their mutual benefit, since Frau Haas enjoyed sitting with Jakob and Amalie was willing to share whatever she could with Frau Haas and Friedrich as repayment for services rendered.

Gunther and Klaus quickly adopted Friedrich, and they would often go to one beer hall or another whenever they could afford it. Friedrich and Gunther would find odd jobs about the city, filling in the time until they could find steady employment.

They all felt that Christmas was mostly a time for children, and so when they met for Christmas Eve, the presents for the adults were modest and utilitarian while Jakob was showered with gifts. They were mostly home-made toys from the men and clothing Amalie and Frau Haas had made by cutting down adult clothes.

Friedrich was especially proud because, while everyone expected that Klaus, with his connections in the countryside, would be the one to provide their Christmas Eve dinner, it was Friedrich who had "gone weaseling," as they called it in Munich, into the countryside near Rosenheim and traded some of his father's old metalworking tools to a farmer in exchange for two large chickens.

Gunther had liberated a small Christmas tree for the apartment. He never told anyone where the tree came from, but his silence caused his wife and friends to speculate that it must have come from somewhere in the English Garden by the river, a practice all too familiar to the park managers in the time after the war.

Gunther's mother, Marie, had sent a few treasured tree ornaments with Amalie when she left Austria. Marie had been upset all along at the way her husband, Oskar, had treated Amalie and the way he ignored his own son, but Marie was not strong enough to stand up to him. When she heard through friends that Amalie was leaving for Munich, she packed a small crate with some personal things for Gunther, the son she hadn't seen in four years and didn't know if she would ever see again, and managed to sneak out of the house without her husband's knowledge. The meeting with Amalie was very emotional for her, as she tried to excuse her husband's actions and then embraced Amalie with tears in her eyes. "Take care of him" was all she could say as she left Amalie at the train.

There were no candles to be found that year because of continuing wartime shortages. Klaus, however, managed to improvise some ersatz candles for the tree. He polished empty rifle cartridges so that they shone like little brass mirrors and filled them with carbon sticks such as the miners used in the lamps they wore on their hats. The candles were traditionally lit for only a short while, which was a good thing, because the burning carbon gave off a nasty smell along with a dirty, sooty flame, but at least they had candles. Everyone commented on how nice they were. They were just tiny smoldering candles on a Christmas tree, but as revolution shook their world and they waited to see what the price of peace would be, those candles were a tiny light against the darkness of what tomorrow might bring.

There was a sizable snowfall in Munich a few weeks after Christmas, which meant a lot of shoveling work for Friedrich and Gunther, so with a few coins in their pockets, they decided to meet at the Hofbräuhaus. Friedrich was passing through the Altstadt, or "old city district," on his way to meet Klaus and Gunther when he heard someone call his name from across the open-air market.

Friedrich turned to see who it was and immediately recognized the mop of red hair settled atop the head of the young man crossing the viktualienmarkt. At first he couldn't put a name with the large, oafish-looking face coming toward him, but then he remembered. Werthers . . . that was it. Richard Werthers, the son of one of the men who had worked with his father in the machine shop.

"Friedrich!" Richard repeated, slapping a meaty hand on Friedrich's shoulder. "I haven't seen you for years! How are things?"

Friedrich looked at the young man as though he were a child, even though Richard was only two years his junior. The difference wasn't so much their ages as the fact that Richard, in his clean, new uniform, had never left Munich during the war. He had only been conscripted some two months before and had barely finished training when the armistice was announced.

"Fine. Just fine," Friedrich replied reservedly.

Just then Richard's gregarious mood changed as he remembered the death of Friedrich's father. "We were all so sorry about your father," he said earnestly. "My father was with him at the last, you know."

"Yes," Friedrich said, grasping for some sort of appropriate acknowledgment. "We were glad that his friends were there."

"So . . . what are you doing now?" Richard asked.

"Anything I can until I find steady work. And you?"

"Me? Well, I've just started as an apprentice machinist with Father."

It was strange how those words hit Friedrich. Even though he had never wanted to follow in his father's footsteps and become a machinist, he was still somehow offended that Richard should not only be spared the horror of war, but was even spared the economic hardships visited against veterans afterward.

"You're very lucky," Friedrich commented coolly.

"Yes, I know," Richard agreed in an embarrassed tone, averting his eyes. He could tell what Friedrich was thinking. "Where are you off to?" he asked, trying to change the subject.

"Hofbraühaus . . . to meet friends," Friedrich replied.

"That sounds like a fine idea. Would you mind if I tag along?"

Friedrich was not thrilled with the idea, but he had grown a bit cynical. Perhaps his fortunate young friend would feel guilty enough to buy.

"Sure, why not?" Friedrich acquiesced, then smiled to himself as he realized that Klaus and Gunther would have this young upstart for dinner, and yet he would knowingly lead Richard into the lion's den of his friends' company.

It was just after three o'clock as they walked through the cobblestone streets, passing the Heilige Geist Kirche[4] and the city hall with its gothic spires. The streets were dark and ominous under a shroud of gray winter clouds. People seemed to move slower than they had before the war. The smiles seemed more forced and infrequent, the buildings more faded and inhospitable.

So much of the city seemed homogenous, with its gray five-story buildings, all with the same basic structure, the same windows, the same doorways, interrupted here and there by a gothic church or a square. It was the embodiment of the Germanic sense of order and utilization of space.

The Hofbraühaus, however, was its usual loud and boisterous self. The patrons always made a good show of being noisy and raucous. This had been the tradition of the beer hall for generations, as patrons banged their two-liter, earthenware steins on the tables and sang along with the carnival-like music. The hall was garishly decorated, with canary yellow walls ascending to renderings of bright green vines and red foliage with berries, all climbing to the pinnacles of the cathedral vaults. The ceiling did much to augment the noise from the crowd below, amplifying the revelry of even a small crowd. It was an embellishment that made the participants seem

[4]Church of the Holy Spirit.

much larger than normal, stronger and more alive.

Richard followed Friedrich as he made his way to a table against the far wall, where Gunther and Klaus waited. Klaus was smoking a cigarette, and he and Gunther sized up Friedrich's well-turned-out companion in his flawless uniform.

"Parade inspection today?" Klaus asked.

Klaus's sarcastic tone and the fact that he was an officer put Richard immediately on edge.

"No," he replied, "I just wanted to look good for the meeting of the soldier's council."

Friedrich nearly burst out laughing. Of all the things Richard could have said to antagonize these two men, that was the most damning, delivered with the utmost innocence. Friedrich waited for the explosion.

"The soldier's council?" Gunther repeated. "Are you a member?"

"Oh no!" Richard responded emphatically. "I have no qualifications for such work."

"Then why are you going?" Klaus asked.

Friedrich was astonished at the tone of his friend's questions, the lack of condemnation, the seeming acceptance. He didn't say a word, though, but simply pulled up a chair and offered one to Richard.

"I was curious," Richard offered as he sat down.

Gunther and Klaus had seen many boys like Richard, and just as Richard was curious about the soldier's council, they were curious how such young men got swept up in the revolution.

"About what?" Klaus asked.

"Well, I guess I thought there was more to a revolution than this," Richard replied.

"More?" Klaus asked.

"More blood," Gunther interjected, answering the question for Richard.

Richard, a bit embarrassed at Gunther's astute observation, broke eye contact as he meekly replied: "I suppose."

Klaus stared at Richard relentlessly as he ominously prophesied, "It may not yet be over . . . There may be a few cards left to play."

"Cards to play?" Richard asked, returning Klaus's stare.

"Look to Berlin," Klaus said, nodding his head, referring to the formation of counterrevolutionary forces called Freikorps, or "freebooters," which had been organized under Friedrich Ebert's defense minister, Gustav Noske. Noske sought to abolish the worker's, soldier's, and sailor's councils in Berlin and had begun to do so with machine guns and artillery in the heart of that city only the day before.

"But almost everyone agrees that they've done some good," Richard offered in defense of the councils.

"What good?" Gunther challenged.

"They . . . ," Richard began hesitantly, trying to gather his thoughts, "raised old-age benefits . . . helped men without jobs . . ."

"They destroyed jobs, betrayed the nation, and dishonored us all," Klaus declared.

"Gentlemen," Richard said curtly as he stood up, realizing he had been led into a trap, "it was interesting meeting you, but I'm afraid I must be going." He then looked pointedly at Friedrich, who had not said a word throughout the entire exchange. "My best to your mother," he said, and with that turned and wound his way through the crowd toward the door.

"Coward," Gunther said under his breath as he hoisted his stein for a drink.

"Why on earth did you bring him?" Klaus asked Friedrich.

"He has a job," Friedrich said morosely. "I thought he might buy."

Gunther nearly choked on his beer as he snorted with laughter, and Klaus gave Friedrich a good-natured slap on the back.

Richard walked briskly as he left the Hofbräuhaus and quickly covered the five blocks to Marienplatz. He should have seen it coming, he thought to himself, that an officer would try to pick a fight when he mentioned the council, but he couldn't understand why Friedrich had let it happen without saying a word.

Richard reached the trolley stop just as a trolley pulled up to the siding and people began to disembark. "Excuse me!" he said, almost stepping on a tiny woman who was getting off just as he leaped onto the running board. "No harm done," Rosa said as she stepped off the trolley, making her way through the Marienplatz square and down the street to one of the nameless gray buildings.

Rosa had traveled for six hours to get to Munich from Berlin so she could approve the galleys for a book of her speeches. The publishing firm tended to the left politically, to the far left at that time, and was located far enough from Berlin that they dared to take the chance of publishing her works.

She had spent most of the war in prison and had only been released within weeks of the armistice, just as many political prisoners were being released by the Social Democrats. It was one of the great paradoxes of the revolution in Germany that she was considered a leader of the revolution when, in fact, she'd had no hand whatsoever in the overthrow of the Kaiser.

Rosa Luxemburg was a Communist and an important figure in the cause of revolution in Germany. She had opposed the war from early on, and it was this opposition that landed her in prison, but the revolution at the end of the war was a spontaneous movement of the people. This fact is most clearly demonstrated by the revolution's tragic, and eventually self-defeating, lack of leadership and direction. Rosa was associated with the revolution by virtue of her revolutionary career prior to the war, not by her actions during the revolution. It was the speeches she had made before the war that were about to be published.

Amalie sat patiently with her hands folded in her lap, the letter of recommendation her father had sent for Gunther and her résumé pressed tightly beneath them. She had left Jakob with Frau Haas in plenty of time to arrive early for her appointment. Mr. Frieder had kept her waiting for over half an hour, but she wasn't about to raise a fuss because she was so nervous she had seriously considered just walking out. Gunther had made it obvious he was not interested in using her father's connections to get a job, but Amalie was afraid Gunther wouldn't be able to find anything else. On the other hand,

Amalie was fairly sure that Gunther would not be happy with her getting a job, but they had to find a way to get their own apartment and stop taking advantage of Klaus's good nature. Or was it just that she wanted to get her husband away from Klaus because of his anti-Semitic sentiments and right-wing politics? Whatever the reason, here she was, afraid to get a job and just as afraid of not getting a job.

Tired after rushing up the three flights to Mr. Frieder's offices, Rosa let out a loud sigh as she entered the lobby area. Amalie, who had been caught up in her reverie, reacted with a startled jump so exaggerated that Rosa couldn't help laughing.

"I'm so sorry!" Rosa offered apologetically, stifling her mirth. "I didn't see you. I didn't mean to frighten you."

"No, no, it's not your fault," Amalie assured her. "I didn't realize how nervous I was."

"Oh, are you waiting for a verdict on a book?"

"What?" Amalie asked, not at all understanding the question.

Rosa restated her question: "Are you an author waiting to hear about a book?"

"Me? Oh no. I'm just looking for a job, something in administration."

"I see," Rosa said measuredly, not sure what to make of Amalie's reaction, as though she looked on Rosa's suggestion that she might be an author as a criminal accusation.

"Well, good luck," Rosa said as she went up to the receptionist's desk and asked for Mr. Frieder.

"Do you have an appointment?" the receptionist asked.

"Yes. I'm a little late, though. Luxemburg. Rosa Luxemburg."

"Of course, Miss Luxemburg. He's been expecting you. Go right in."

Amalie was impressed. She may have been kept waiting, but she at least felt better to learn that someone like Rosa Luxemburg was the cause of it. And she had even spoken to her! This was certainly not something she would talk to Gunther about, but someday she would tell her father, and she knew he would be impressed.

Amalie waited for another half hour, and finally Rosa came out of the office with Mr. Frieder. Once they had finished saying good-bye, Amalie got up and extended her hand.

"I didn't realize who you were, Miss Luxemburg. My name is Amalie Stein. My father . . . my father and I have admired your work, your courage."

"Thank you," Rosa replied politely. "Are you a member of the party?"

"No," Amalie responded meekly, "but I agree with many things you've said and I have a great deal of respect for you, for the way you stand up for what you believe in."

"Well," Rosa said with a bit of a laugh, "that's a start." Then, becoming more serious and looking Amalie straight in the eye, she added, "But remember, now is the time to stand up for what you believe in." Rosa shook Amalie's hand one last time and left, returning to Berlin that same day.

At last Amalie was invited into Mr. Frieder's office,

and they went over the hand-written résumé listing her educational background and experience working with her father, some of it actual and some of it contrived. She then showed him the letter of reference from her father, and eventually, she talked her way into a job.

The problem now was that she had no idea what she was going to say to Gunther. How could she tell her husband that she had gotten a job when he could find nothing? Would he let her keep it?

The impending confrontation with Gunther loomed large in Amalie's mind. It was the only thing she could think about as she walked home, as she made dinner, and while they ate.

The dinner was certainly nothing to talk about—boiled turnips and war bread with only water to drink. Klaus and Gunther were content to talk between themselves as Amalie ate in silence. She didn't seem upset. Nor did she snap as she sometimes did when she was angry. She merely ate in silence and then cleared away the dishes and washed them. Afterward she put Jakob to bed and finally laid out the bedding on the floor for Gunther and herself.

"Could you make us some coffee before you go to bed?" Gunther asked, still not questioning her silence.

Amalie made the coffee while Gunther and Klaus continued talking at the table and then went to change into her nightgown. Her mood was not lost on Klaus, however, who rolled his eyes at Gunther as Amalie went into the bathroom. "I don't know what you did," he said sympathetically, "but you must have really upset her."

"I can't imagine how," Gunther countered emphatically, shrugging his shoulders and tossing a glance at the closed door of the bathroom.

"A women's thing?" Klaus offered feebly.

"No, that was just over a week ago . . . ," Gunther replied, just as Amalie came out of the bathroom.

". . . and then they threw them out." Klaus said quickly, completing an imaginary sentence so that Amalie wouldn't know that they were talking about her.

Amalie paid no attention to them as she put a last scoop of coal on the fire and banked the ashes before laying out the makeshift bedding on the floor.

The two men continued talking for another hour or more as Amalie lay still, eyes open, watching Jakob as he slept on the sofa, wondering if she would be able to sleep at all. When Gunther finally came to bed, he leaned over to kiss her on the cheek as she lay on her side, facing away from him. As he did so, he noticed she wasn't asleep.

"I'm sorry, did I wake you?" he whispered.

"No," Amalie whispered back.

"Can't you get to sleep?"

"No," she answered again.

Gunther reached an arm around to embrace her, rolling her on her back at the same time. He kissed her lightly on the lips, but Amalie didn't respond.

"All right," he said quietly, "what's wrong?"

"It's nothing."

"Nothing? You've been moody all week and you haven't said two words all night. You didn't even read to Jakob tonight."

"I'm just tired," she offered unconvincingly.

Gunther rolled onto his back beside her. "I'm not always sure how to love you," he said with a sigh, gazing up at the ceiling.

Amalie felt a twinge of sadness when he said it. "I know," she replied. "I know it isn't easy. We were apart for so long . . . we were so young."

Gunther was confused by the strange turn the conversation had taken. He had hoped it would be some sort of little problem, and now they were talking about the quality of their love.

He couldn't have known that the past week had been a time of decision for Amalie—starting with her first thoughts of getting a job, then deciding where to get a job, and finally, working up the courage to actually do it. Gunther only noticed the sudden change in her. She had become quiet and withdrawn, and now he had to face the possibility that he was the cause—that he was not being a good husband, that she was losing faith in him because he couldn't find work to support his family, that she was giving up on him because he continued to accept the charity of his friend.

"Do you love me?" Gunther asked.

Amalie couldn't believe her ears. This was something he might have said when they were first married, but not since he went to war, not since the war ended. It seemed to be a given. She could imagine herself asking him that, but not Gunther asking her. When she asked, it was because she wanted to be reassured, to hear the words and know for certain, but he seemed to be asking because he feared the answer might be no.

"Of course I do," she whispered as she drew close and lay her head on his chest.

"I don't know what I'd do without you and Jakob. You're all I live for," he said quietly.

"Oh no, it's nothing like that," Amalie said warmly as she kissed him on the cheek and wrapped her arms around him tightly.

"Then what?" Gunther asked, taking her chin in his hand and raising her face to his so he could see her eyes in the pale moonlight.

"I guess . . . ," Amalie started hesitantly, averting her eyes as she ran a finger across Gunther's chest, "I guess I just want us to move to our own apartment."

"We've talked about this before," Gunther said calmly. "We'll find a place as soon as I get work."

"I know," Amalie said, "but . . . Gunther, I have something to tell you but I don't know how to say it."

"Just come out with it," Gunther said firmly.

"Do you remember the letter Father sent?"

"Letter? What letter?"

"The letter of introduction. The recommendation to the publisher here in Munich."

"Yes, yes," Gunther said. "Now Amalie, I told you I wasn't—"

"I used it," Amalie interrupted.

"You *used* it? What do you mean?"

"Gunther, I got a job with a publisher."

"You what?" Gunther exclaimed in a loud whisper, rousing Jakob, who began to toss and turn.

"Shhh," Amalie said, touching a finger to Gunther's lips and turning to watch Jakob as though her watchful eye would keep him from waking. Her real goal, however, was to distract Gunther and keep his temper from flaring. Jakob made a little sighing noise, then turned toward the back of the sofa and settled in again.

Gunther turned on his side, moving Amalie from on top of him onto her side, so that they faced each other.

"What have you done?" Gunther asked in a tone that was once again calm.

"I told you. I got a job with a small publisher. As an assistant editor."

"What about Jakob?"

"Gertrude said she would be glad to watch him. Her apartment is on my way." Amalie said, ready to meet any obstacle that Gunther might throw in her path.

Gunther sighed. "My wife working while I shovel sidewalks," he said glumly, then sighed again. "I don't know, Amalie, I just don't know. It doesn't seem right. What will people say? What will my friends say?"

"What can they say? Most of your friends are out of work too."

"Oh, Amalie!" Gunther said, clearly exasperated by his wife's persistence. "This is just too much."

"Please, darling," Amalie said as she lay a hand on his cheek. "Please let me try. Let's just try it and see how it goes."

Gunther sighed again and rolled onto his back. "Don't you know how this makes me feel?"

"I know, dear," Amalie said sympathetically.

"Women only work until they get married,"

Gunther asserted. "I have never met a man whose wife works, except for farm women. Peasants working in the fields." The way he said the word *peasants* made it sound as though they were animals of some kind and now his family had sunken to that level.

"Gunther," Amalie began delicately, "these are unusual times. We need to do whatever we can to get by." They lay in silence for a moment until Amalie added: "I'm not doing this to hurt you."

"As soon as I find work, you must quit," Gunther said with finality, acknowledging that they would try it, but still making it clear that he was the master.

"Yes, Captain," Amalie said contentedly and smiled as she kissed him gently on the cheek, then turned on her side to go to sleep.

"You're so easy to get along with when you get your own way," Gunther commented icily as he too rolled onto his side, turning his back to Amalie.

Amalie turned onto her other side and moved close to Gunther, putting her arm around his waist and pulling her body close to his as they drifted off to sleep.

KLAUS WAS the first one up the next day, off to his administrative duties at the Schwabing barracks after a quick breakfast of bread and coffee. Gunther didn't say anything about Amalie's job as she got herself and Jakob ready for the first day of her new routine. It wasn't that he was cold, just apprehensive. For that matter, so was Amalie. Gunther picked up Jakob and tossed him in the air, then gave him a kiss on the cheek. Amalie smiled as she watched them, then took Jakob from Gunther as he leaned over to give her a quick peck on the cheek too. They all went out the door at the same time, but Gunther stopped to lock the door, then stood watching his wife and son until they were out of sight, wondering if he had made the right decision.

The day went by quickly, and before she knew it, Amalie was on her way to pick up Jakob. Neither Gunther nor Amalie told Klaus about her job at dinner that night, but they did so the next day, and although Klaus didn't betray the sentiment to his friends, he was glad that Amalie was taking the first step toward moving to their own apartment. It was this sentiment on Klaus's part that saved Gunther from the endless stream of jokes and barbs he had feared.

Amalie quickly learned the ins and outs of her job at Frieder and Son Publishing and was glad that she had chosen that particular firm. In her free moments at the office, she read the galleys of the speeches by Rosa Luxemburg, more because she had met Rosa rather than for any political reasons, but she wouldn't have dared to take them home for fear that Gunther or Klaus might find them. She finished reading the last of the galleys just before going to pick up Jakob on the tenth of January.

IN BERLIN on that day, Rosa was staying in a house in Wilmersdorf. She was actually in hiding, since the Freikorps, the soldiers of counterrevolution, had named her as a leader of the revolution and put a price on her head.

Karl Liebknecht, another revolutionary figurehead, was staying at the same house. He was much like Rosa in that he was associated with the revolution because of his prewar activities and his open opposition to the war, even though he actually had nothing to do with leading the revolution. Liebknecht likewise had the dubious honor of having a Freikorps price on his head.

Someone betrayed them both to the freebooters, and it was on this night that the Freikorps had come to "arrest" the two of them. The troops, led by a Lieutenant Linder, invaded the house and caught both Rosa and Karl at home.

Rosa sat writing a letter as three men exploded into her room.

"What is the meaning of this?" she shouted as she stood up, knocking over the chair and surprising the soldiers for an instant.

"Rosa Luxemburg?" one of the soldiers demanded.

"Yes," Rosa answered, not backing down. "What do you want?"

"You're under arrest," the soldier said as he took a step toward her.

"Under arrest for what? By what authority . . . ," she began, but before she could go on, the soldier struck her with the back of his hand, knocking her to the floor. Spotting her coat on a hook on the wall beside him, he grabbed it and threw it at her.

"Put it on," he ordered.

Rosa slowly and deliberately put on the coat, all the while trying to plan what she would do next. This was certainly not the first time she had been arrested. In a way, it was a good sign. It meant she was being taken seriously and still had an effect on the politicians, but now she was thinking of who she would call and how she would get the money to bribe her way out.

"Take her," the lieutenant said to the other two men. It was a comical sight—the two burly soldiers dragging the small woman between them—but the men's faces showed no humor. It was clear they hated what she represented and enjoyed the thought of torturing her. Rosa missed a step as the men pulled her along, and as she tripped, they let her go, joking and laughing as she tumbled down the rest of the stairway. She was pretty banged up, but the soldiers took no notice of her injuries as they met at the front door of the house with another group of soldiers, who had rousted Karl Liebknecht from his room. It was obvious he had been beaten.

From there the group drove to the Eden Hotel, with Rosa and Karl in separate cars. The two managed to exchange glances as they arrived at the hotel, where they would soon be questioned by a Captain Pabst. Both of them had been through this type of thing before, but they found it strange that they were both there together. Their paths had only crossed by coincidence in the past, but now they were both working on a Communist newspaper called *The Red Flag.*

Rosa's politics were farther to the left than Karl's. If one were to define the difference between them, it would be that Rosa would want to scrap the entire government and start anew, while Karl would want to rebuild the existing government, saving what he felt was useful.

In the final analysis, of course, these differences

meant nothing, because they would both share the same fate, and ironically, they would share that fate because of what they appeared to be rather than what they were, although there was another, more immediate reason for their adversaries wanting them out of the way.

The Red Flag had been printing constant and accurate statements about the connections between the Social Democrats and the Freikorps. The Freikorps was made up of right-wing German military units not associated with the regular army. Neither the Freikorps nor the Social Democrats wanted to be associated with each other, and they especially didn't want such associations to be made public. Members of these groups at opposite ends of the political spectrum had only allied out of what they all believed to be the absolute necessity of crushing the revolution. The task at hand demanded that Luxemburg and Liebknecht be stopped, not only because they appeared to be leaders of the revolution, but because they were exposing the alliance between the Social Democrats and the Freikorps.

Rosa and Karl were taken in turn to a room on the first floor of the hotel, where Captain Pabst was to question them. Rosa began to get nervous, although she didn't show it, when it became apparent that the purpose of the questioning was only to verify her identity. There were no charges or outrageous accusations, as there had been whenever she had been arrested before. This time, it seemed, they only wanted to make sure they had the right person.

After Pabst finished with them, Karl and Rosa were taken to a side door of the hotel, where cars were waiting in a side street that had been closed off to traffic. Just as they got to the door, a guard who was stationed there suddenly brushed past his fellow storm troopers and brought up his rifle, gathering his whole body into a powerful thrust as he drove the rifle butt against Karl's cheekbone. There was a sickening cracking noise as the impact fractured bone and Karl fell to the floor, blood flowing freely from the wound.

Rosa was knocked aside in the mêlée and ended up being slammed against the wall near the stairway, where she fell to the floor. That was where the assailant found her as he thrashed around with his rifle, the butt finding its mark and fracturing her skull, rendering her unconscious. Karl was still conscious, but bleeding badly from the head and speaking incoherently.

The guard had been hired by an unknown party and ordered to kill the two Spartacists, but since he had only wounded them, the officers moved on to the next step of their plan and had the soldiers load their victims into cars. A young lieutenant named Vogel was in charge of Rosa's fate.

Vogel took out his pistol as soon as he got into the car. Once the car pulled away from the curb, he pulled her coat up over her head and doubled the heavy fabric, using it to muffle the sound of the explosion as he shot Rosa in the temple as she lay unconscious on the seat beside him. Vogel then commanded the driver to proceed to the Liechtenstein Bridge and stop in the middle, where he ordered the other two soldiers to carry Rosa's body to the side of the bridge and throw her into the canal. The two stood and watched for a moment as the body was quickly swept away.

In the end, when doctors examined Rosa's body after it washed up on the banks of the canal months later, they could not determine the cause of death. It seems that they found water in her lungs, indicating that even after the vicious bludgeoning and the gunshot, Rosa had actually survived and may have finally drowned as she was carried away by the frigid water of the canal.

Karl Liebknecht had also been killed that night. The soldiers who drove him away from the Eden Hotel took him out to the lake called Neue See and politely asked him to step out of the car. When he did, they shot him once in the back of the head and threw his body back into the car. They then drove the body to the local morgue and left it there, claiming it was the body of an unknown murder victim.

All of this was only overture to the fate of revolution in the south, in Munich.

LESS THAN two weeks after the deaths of Luxemburg and Liebknecht, Kurt Eisner was walking through the "old city" of Munich on his way to a ten o'clock meeting of the provincial assembly, a letter of resignation in his pocket. His organization, his bloodless revolution, which had come about so unexpectedly, was now falling apart under the weight of petty demands by Parliament members, each wanting more than the others. Perhaps the resignation was his final answer to Parliament, or maybe it was just a threat. No one will ever know exactly what Eisner might have done.

It had been typical weather for Munich at that time of year. The sun hadn't shown itself for almost a week, as light rains periodically swept through the city, keeping the streets dreary and wet. The dark clouds were mirrored on the wet cobblestones and in the puddles on the sidewalk, so that one could almost become confused as to which was earth and which was sky.

A young man stood hidden in the shadow of a nondescript doorway. Dropping the butt of his last cigarette on the damp threshold, he glanced down at the fading orange glow before crushing it out with his heel. He knew that Eisner would be there. He knew it would be soon. He knew in his heart that the German people did not want revolution. They had been seduced. They were tired of the war and thought this was the only way to end it. He could forgive them for this; it was understandable that they wanted the war to end. But he could not forgive Eisner for taking advantage of their war-weariness.

Count Anton Arco-Valley had something to prove. As one of the rightful rulers of Germany, a member of the nobility, he believed it was his duty to stop Eisner. A half-Jew, the young count was also eager to prove to his friends at a right-wing club—"friends" who had rejected him for membership because of his Jewish background—that a half-Jew could do something great. That was Anton's last thought as he stepped out of the doorway—that he was about to do something great. As Kurt Eisner came around a corner onto Promenadestrasse, Anton slipped his hand into the pocket of his black raincoat, drawing out a revolver and firing point blank at Eisner's head.

Richard Werthers, the young apprentice machinist whose father had worked with Friedrich Haas's father, was stunned when his two friends told him what had happened.

"Where?" Richard asked, staring down at the table around which the three young men were seated in his friend Alfred's apartment.

"Promenadestrasse," Alfred reported.

"Do they know why he did it?" asked Otto, the third young man.

"Right wing," Alfred answered. "I don't know . . . maybe he wants the Kaiser back."

"I want to see where it happened," Richard said after a short pause.

The other two looked at him and agreed.

"But I'm going to bring my rifle," Otto said.

"What on earth for . . . ?" Alfred began, but then answered himself. "I suppose they might try something."

"We might as well," Richard said, and with that Alfred went and got his rifle, sliding the bayonet into his belt, and the three of them left his apartment, stopping at the apartments of the other two as they armed themselves on their way to the site of Eisner's assassination. When Richard stopped at his apartment for his rifle and bayonet, he picked up a photograph of Eisner that he kept on a small table by the door and slipped it into his coat pocket.

It was almost dark by the time they got to Promenadestrasse. A block from the square, the Glockenspiel[5] in the Neuen Rathaus[6] chimed off four o'clock. A mist spread over the crowd of hundreds who had come to view the blood-stained sidewalk.

Once the three young soldiers were sure that no battle was brewing on the street, they worked their way through the somber crowd and, after about twenty minutes, found themselves confronted by an elliptical red stain on the sidewalk representing the last moments of Kurt Eisner. His blood had pooled about his fallen body and then run down to the curb.

The three stood there in silence, not moving, their eyes roving back and forth, taking in the color and size and shape, the gray of the street contrasting with the red bloodstain, not knowing what to do next. At last, Richard slid his rifle off his shoulder and fixed the bayonet; Otto and Alfred watching intently, wondering what he was up to.

"Fix your bayonets," Richard told his friends. Otto and Alfred exchanged confused glances but then followed the order. Richard rested his rifle on the sidewalk as he waited for his friends, taking Alfred's rifle and hooking it to his bayonet catch, completing a tripod with Otto's rifle. He then took off his coat and cloaked it around the tripod, forming a small tent. Finally, he took the picture of Eisner out of his coat pocket and placed it on the ground under the tent to protect it from the rain.

"A shrine," Alfred said.

"What about your coat?" Otto asked pragmatically.

"I've got another," Richard said.

---

[5]An intricate mechanical display of figurines in motion that is activated by the hourly chimes in a city clock tower.

[6]New city hall.

"What if they steal it?" Otto persisted, but just then a young woman walked past them and knelt in front of the picture. They stood watching as she produced a red votive candle from her pocket and lit it, placing it beside the picture.

"Never mind," Otto said.

The three men stepped back, not knowing that the doorway in which they sought shelter was the very same doorway that had sheltered the noble assassin. They watched for a while as the crowd passed by quietly and reverently, as though viewing the blood of the revolution itself, and one might say that they were.

By sheer force of will, Kurt Eisner had focused the desires of the people and formed a government that matched the mood of a bloodless revolution, riding a wave of sentiment that could best be described as populist. By sheer force of will, a single man had seized the spirit of this part of the German nation and molded it into the image of a government. It was not unlike the way Otto von Bismarck had brought together hundreds of small German kingdoms and principalities in 1871 to form the modern German nation following the Franco-German war.

Who would be the next man to harness the power of this fickle crowd? Eisner tried to focus the democratic will of the people, but the demagogues who would come after him would capitalize on the fears of these same people. Subsequent leaders of Bavaria would seek control and order above all else, certainly above the freedom of the individual and the right of the individual to have a voice in his government. The phrase "a republic without republicans" seemed to strike a chord deep within the essence of German existence, as though it were not only their history, but their destiny as well.

CHAPTER 4

The assassination of Kurt Eisner created a sense of urgency throughout Munich as local politics took a turn even farther to the left. The revolutionaries knew they would have to fight to keep control from other factions, and the counterrevolutionaries saw it as a collapse of the government. Another member of Eisner's cabinet was attacked within an hour of Eisner's assassination, while still other cabinet members fled, leaving only two of the original eight members to try to keep the provincial government running.

After several days of confusion, a council was formed to run the government, made up of members of the worker's and soldier's councils that had been created when the revolution began.

The next change came a few months later. Inspired by the success of a man named Bela Kun, who took over the Hungarian government to form a Communist state, a poet named Ernst Toller formed a new government in Munich in yet another bloodless revolution.

It was only a few days after the formation of this new government that a former schoolteacher named Hoffman, a member of a right-wing political faction, led an attempted overthrow of Toller's government. The soldiers of the Munich garrison chose not to fight for Toller's government, which gave Hoffman an advantage, although it wasn't enough to help him win. The Hoffman Putsch came close enough to succeeding to motivate Eugen Levin, a Russian Bolshevik who had been sent to Munich to lead the faltering revolution, to force

Toller out and take over the government of Munich. This move, of course, lent credence to the Freikorps' assertions that the revolution had been instigated by Russian Bolsheviks all along.

All the while, the counterrevolutionaries were gaining strength.

The Freikorps were engaged in a dance of propaganda in 1919. On the one hand, they wished to maintain the illusion that the military was no longer a force in Germany in hopes that they might thereby elicit less severe terms of peace from the Allies. On the other hand, they were driven to organize an effective military force that would crush the revolution. A paradox of the times was that the Allies were already inclined to close an eye to the military force of the Freikorps, hoping for the defeat of a Communist revolution just as much as the German counterrevolutionaries. Proof of this is the fact that little more than a year earlier, the Allies had each sent military contingents to Russia to try to crush the embryonic Union of Soviet Socialist Republics.

The Freikorps, however, still went to great lengths under the watchful eye of the occupation armies of the Allied governments to appear as civilians who were moved to protect their country against Russian Bolshevism.

In Munich and throughout Bavaria there is something called "Gemütlichkeit," which translates into English as an easy-going attitude toward life and is most often characterized by Bavarian folk in traditional costume drinking beer. The Freikorps propaganda in the Munich area often featured photographs of its soldiers dressed in Bavarian costume: Lederhosen[7] and mountainclimber's cap with a feather tuft, complemented with a rifle, bayonet, and forty rounds of ammunition. The idea was to suggest the existence of a "Gemütlichkeit counter-revolution." It was an interesting political strategy, but Gunther and Friedrich, along with hundreds of other Freikorps recruits, had no such costumes. They only had their old army uniforms, which had been changed to make them look more like civilian clothes.

When they first heard the news of Eisner's assassination, Klaus advised his friends that it was time to offer their services to one of the Freikorps units. Noske's counterrevolutionary forces had been moving south for several months by that time and recruiting posters for Freikorps units had been seen in Munich for quite a while. Gunther and Friedrich waited for weeks, through all of the changes of governments and political leaders in Munich, for when the local fighting was about to begin.

Meanwhile, in the midst of this political chaos, Klaus, who was still a member of the small forces left to the regular German army, decided to move into the barracks for a few weeks as he waited to see how events would unfold. For the first time, Gunther, Amalie, and Jakob were alone together as a family.

The next day Gunther finally got word that he would be needed in his Freikorps unit. Since he had no idea when he would return, his first thought was to put Jakob to bed early and then spend the

---

[7]Part of the traditional Bavarian costume, they are short pants with suspenders, usually made of leather or suede.

evening making love. But in planning this night of passion before going off to join up with the Freikorps, he hadn't considered Amalie's feelings.

Gunther had a hard time explaining to his son why he was going off to join the Freikorps. He finally just put him to bed on the sofa, telling him that his Vati would be gone for a little while and admonishing Jakob to be especially good while he was away.

He had an even harder time explaining it to his wife.

"But why does it have to be you?" Amalie asked as she closed the bedroom door, clearly annoyed at his decision.

Gunther felt Amalie was being too assertive. Why couldn't she just accept his decision like a wife was supposed to? His mother would never have questioned his father in such a situation. They turned away from each other as they began to undress for bed.

"What would you expect me to do?" Gunther asked, an angry edge to his voice as he stopped in the middle of taking off his shirt. "Do you think I could stay here, safe and quiet, hiding with my wife and son while men are fighting in the streets?"

"You wouldn't be hiding," Amalie corrected, a pleading tone to her voice. "You've done enough fighting."

"Enough fighting? It is not enough until it is done."

"But the war is over!" Amalie shot back, raising her voice. "It's over!"

"No!" Gunther declared adamantly as he spun around to face her. "The war didn't end. It just moved to within Germany itself."

Amalie was stunned by this assertion. Not only was the war not over, but it would never be over until her husband said it was. She quietly sat down on the bed, her back to Gunther, making every effort to keep from crying. Gunther had no respect for tears. She was determined not to lose this argument by default, by crying and giving Gunther what he would consider justification to storm out. Her head felt as though it were spinning.

"It seems," Amalie began slowly, fighting to maintain her composure, "that you've just come home. We have really only started to get to know each other again, and now you want to go back to war."

"It is not what I want," Gunther said firmly. "It is my duty."

"Duty?" Amalie exclaimed as she turned to face him. "What about the duty to your family? What about your son? Don't you think he should know who you are?"

"He will know who I am through the things that I do," Gunther declared dramatically, waving his hand through the air as though cutting through words to command action.

Just then they heard Jacob cry out from the other room, probably having a nightmare.

"I'll take care of him," Amalie said, rushing out to the living room and closing the bedroom door behind her before Gunther had a chance to respond.

By the time she got to the sofa, Jakob had rolled over and was fast asleep again, but Amalie knelt beside her son for a moment in the darkened room, watching him sleep and thinking about her argument with Gunther. She knew he had made up his mind and there was nothing she could do to change it.

Suddenly the bedroom door opened, Gunther's form casting a long shadow that ran up alongside Amalie in the muted light from the bedroom. Gunther's eyes fell to where his wife knelt before their sleeping son, dressed in her white nightgown, looking up at him with a single tear on her cheek. She quickly brushed it away—no victory through the default of a single tear.

"Is he asleep?" Gunther asked.

"Yes."

"Are you coming to bed?"

"In a moment."

Gunther made no move to go back into the bedroom, but stood watching as Amalie gently combed the hair back from her sleeping son's face.

"I have to go," Gunther said matter-of-factly, ending the argument with this final declaration.

Amalie stood up and moved toward the bedroom. Purposely averting her eyes to avoid looking Gunther in the face, she said coolly, "The truth is that you want to go." With that she passed him in the doorway and got into bed.

Her words were like a slap in the face to Gunther. He stood in the doorway for a moment, considering his next move, then followed her into the bedroom and got dressed without saying a word. When he said he had to go, he had meant that he would be leaving in the morning, but now he couldn't stand it. He packed a small bag and finally stood at the door once again. Amalie had not once turned to look at him all the while he had been dressing and packing.

"Someday you'll understand," Gunther said, like a father talking to a child. He might even have used those same words earlier when he had tried to explain to Jakob. "I'll spend the night with Friedrich and leave in the morning."

"Will you come back?" Amalie asked without emotion, still clutching a pillow and refusing to look at her husband.

"Of course!" said Gunther with an exasperated sigh. He then turned and, making no effort to be quiet as his boots thudded loudly against the floor, strode purposefully out of the apartment.

Jakob cried out again and Amalie rushed to the living room once more, this time to find her small son awake and crying.

"Oh Jakob, Jakob," she said soothingly. "What is it?"

"I had a dream," Jakob said in a quiet, little-boy voice as he rubbed his face with the back of his hands. "I dreamed that Vati went away again."

IT WAS only ten-thirty at night when Gunther reached the Haas apartment, but Frau Haas had a habit of going to bed early, so Friedrich was sitting alone, reading, when Gunther knocked at the door.

"What are you doing here?" Friedrich asked with surprise.

"It seems Amalie doesn't support us."

"Oh," Friedrich said sympathetically. "Well, she certainly has spirit."

"Perhaps too much."

ONLY A few blocks from the Haas apartment, as Gunther and Friedrich were settling in to sleep, a man sat watching a shadow dance around the base of an old brass candlestick. His mind wandered as he wondered absent-mindedly where the shadow came from, and then he realized that it was the shadow of the candlestick itself as the flame shifted in some breezy draft of unknown origin. It occurred to him that it was symbolic of the recent turn of events: the light of the candle casting a shadow on itself because they went hand in hand—the light and the shadow. One could not exist without the other, and so it was with the revolution—the light of its hope creating the shadow of political undercurrents.

Now that Eisner's government was collapsing, the Communist party had sent Eugen Levin to Munich to try to save the revolution, or rather, to turn it into a Communist revolution.

Suddenly the man looked up as he sensed that the other men around the table were looking at him. They must have asked him a question, he realized, but he didn't have the slightest idea what that question might have been as he snapped out of his communion with the guttering flame.

"Will you support him, Ernst?" one of the men finally repeated.

Ernst still hesitated. Now that he knew the question, it was no easier to answer. Would Ernst Toller support Eugen Levin as he attempted to reform the faltering revolution into some organized form of government? Ernst was not a Communist . . . well, certainly not a Russian Bolshevik. These were difficult times for Ernst and his friends. It had been easy in the past to join in the debates and political banter at Alten Simpl, the Schwabing district café that catered to radicals who did much talking and writing about their political convictions without committing those thoughts to action. He now had to face the realities of this faltering revolution, putting his words and great ideals into action. Would he ally with Levin when his own political beliefs were actually quite different from the Russian's, just because Levin might stand the best chance of organizing the forces of revolution and keeping that revolution from total collapse?

"I don't know," Ernst finally said, giving the answer to himself as much as to his three comrades gathered around the table in the dark apartment.

They all knew this was a critical time. That was why they were being so cautious, sitting in the dark apartment, away from the window facing the street, with just a single candle to light this dangerous meeting.

"We must decide!" said Hans, a middle-aged man with bushy, unkempt sideburns. "In a few days there will be no time for discussion. We have to decide where we stand and who we stand with," he declared, clearly frustrated at the impasse in the discussion.

"I will not oppose nor endorse Levin," Ernst interrupted his friend. "I will stand for the councils, not for politicians."

"That is not a decision, Ernst!" said Peter, the reflection of the candle flickering across the lenses of his wire-rimmed glasses. A young man, Peter was surprisingly controlled for his age, considering his passion for politics. "Hans is right. This is an important decision if we are to represent a unified force on a field of battle."

"Peter, I think you two are missing a point here. The men we are talking about leading into battle are defending their homes. We are not leading them. We are merely trying to help them do what they would naturally do."

Finally, Stefan, the fourth member of the group spoke: "Ernst, you are naive." Stefan was about the same age as Hans and Ernst, but he was the only one in the group who had seen action in the war. He was very clean-cut and quite reserved, but when he eventually joined a conversation, it was usually with a keen grasp of the various positions being offered.

"Any fighting army needs clear leadership and direction," Stefan continued. "Their cause and leaders must be kept constantly in front of their eyes—"

"Their cause above any leaders," Ernst interrupted.

"No!" Peter disagreed.

"Their leaders," Stefan began again, "are the focus of the cause. They are a visible representation of what we all hope to bring about."

"But Levin does not represent our revolution!" Ernst countered. "He has his own revolution in mind."

"That is not important," Hans said patronizingly, speaking in measured cadence and carefully enunciating each word, as though doing so might slow Ernst's thinking and make him understand.

"Of course it's important," said Ernst, brushing Hans's comment aside.

"I'm sorry to be the one to tell you," Stefan began, lacing his fingers together and resting his elbows on the table. Leaning closer to Ernst, he bowed his head for an instant before looking him directly in the eyes, then continued: "Soldiers need simple truths. One leader, one direction, one cause."

"With all my being," Ernst began, "I believe that the men, the soldiers you speak of, have found the greatest truth, the greatest justice they could hope for, held within the spirit of this cause, of their own popular revolution. Not Eugen Levin's vision of revolution, but the revolution that these people brought about on their own, a revolution that deserves to live by its own virtue. I will not sell this revolution for political expediency."

"I hope your idealism will stand up to the point of a Freikorps bayonet," Peter said as he stood up from the table.

"I suppose this means we just go on as we have been," said Hans, also rising to leave.

Stefan and Ernst remained seated as Stefan took Ernst's hand in a firm grip, a tactic Stefan had developed throughout a career of presenting arguments that he knew would get his adversary's complete attention. "Think about it Ernst . . . consider what is the best hope against counterrevolution."

Ernst looked Stefan in the eye, and Stefan knew that Ernst would consider it. Ernst then pushed back his chair as Stefan released his hand, and the two men walked to the door, bidding each other good night. Finally alone in his apartment, Stefan crossed the room to the candle and drew close to the flame, blowing it out with a single short breath.

THE NEXT day, Gunther asked Frau Haas if she would do him the favor of watching out for Amalie and Jakob while he was gone. He also mentioned that they had managed to stockpile some black market food, since there was sure to be trouble in the next few weeks. Gunther and Friedrich then shouldered their rifles and homemade packs and left for the northern outskirts of the city, where the Freikorps unit was waiting for their time.

In the weeks that followed, there were a number of battles for Munich. In the beginning, the revolutionaries, led by Ernst Toller, were able to push back the Freikorps soldiers. Toller's great shortcoming in the battle, however, was that he was too fair in his treatment of the enemy. Not only did he see to it that prisoners were not mistreated, he even released them at the end of the battle, long before the war was done.

Levin, now head of the revolutionary government, issued orders for Toller to be arrested for his lenient attitude toward the freebooters, only to release him later to once again lead the troops when the Freikorps counterattacked the next day.

This time the prisoners of the revolution were not so lucky. At some point during the battle, when a group of Freikorps officers was to be moved from one building to another located farther from the fighting, a group of overzealous soldiers of the revolution rushed in and shot the officers. This was all the Freikorps leaders needed to whip their troops into a murderous frenzy.

The freebooters had been known for their cruelty toward the men they took prisoner, and they had certainly murdered many revolutionaries who tried to surrender, but somehow the thought of the revolutionaries fighting back in such a way was different. It seemed the life of a Freikorps officer or soldier had meaning, whereas the life of a revolutionary soldier had none, and this triggered the psychotic rage that gave many of the soldiers license to commit any atrocity. The goal of the Freikorps leaders and many of the soldiers was not just the defeat of the Communists in battle; they wanted to break and purge the spirit of Germany, carving the German soul into an image of their liking with the blade of a bayonet. That is how the cobblestone streets of Munich, which had channeled a thousand years of growth in the heart of Bavaria, came to run red with the blood of its own citizens.

Friedrich had never actually fought in a battle before. As an ambulance driver, there had been a few times when he had been in the wrong place at the wrong time—when some officer had thrown the rifle of a dead soldier into his hands and ordered him to man the trench—but it had never come to much. He was usually back in the ambulance driving casualties to an army hospital before there was any assault by enemy troops. He had seen many artillery barrages, but he had never faced a charge or been part of one . . . until now.

His leg held him back as he limped forward into the city with the other troops, once they had finally broken through the revolutionaries' defenses. Reaching the corner of a small house, he stopped for a moment before entering the street so that he could check before going out into the open.

As he cautiously looked around the corner, he saw two other Freikorps soldiers who had captured one of the revolutionaries. Deciding it was safe to enter the street, he started to cross as one of the two free-booters took a rifle from the revolutionary's out-stretched hand. Friedrich looked away to see if anything that posed a threat was going on at the houses in front of him, but as he turned away, an image of the three men flashed through his mind, giving him the feeling that he had overlooked something significant. Then it dawned on him—a tousled heap of red hair.

Werthers. It was Richard Werthers they had captured! Turning back, Friedrich took a step toward them and was just about to say something when the freebooter who had been standing in front of Werthers while the other disarmed him raised the muzzle of his rifle to Werthers' jaw and pulled the trigger.

Richard Anton Werthers' head exploded and his lifeless, nearly decapitated corpse dropped to the street. Friedrich stumbled, his legs crumpling beneath him as the scene spun down to slow motion—Werthers' falling body, the freebooter who had been standing beside Richard moving out of the way so as not to be splattered by the bits of brain and flesh and pieces of skull. He was laughing. It was a joke!

Friedrich felt the bile rising in his throat and he began to throw up, retching uncontrollably, doubled over in the middle of the street, but he'd had so little to eat, there was nothing in his stomach to come up. The two freebooters who had murdered Richard stood watching, and then, to his utter disbelief, began to laugh as they hurried away, presumably to seek out more victims.

Now the battle was even worse for Friedrich. No longer was it just a matter of killing a nameless, faceless political enemy. Now that enemy had a face—a face he had known nearly all his life. He suddenly found himself fighting beside men who were capable of committing the most inhumane atrocity, then laughing at the carnage they had wrought. His mind suddenly flashed back to paintings he had seen in his youth that were meant to depict hell, calling forth images of demons standing at the edge of a fiery pit, flaying and torturing the damned before forcing them into the inferno, laughing at the pain and suffering of their victims. But Richard was not among the damned, nor were these men engaged in some divine judgment between heaven and hell. They were less than men—men who perversely felt more alive by proving they had the power to take life.

Just then, Gunther came up beside Friedrich, almost passing him before realizing it was him.

"Friedrich!" he called out. "Are you hit?" When Friedrich didn't answer, Gunther knelt beside him, grasping his shoulder, and repeated his question.

"No," Friedrich finally gasped.

"What happened?" Gunther asked.

"They shot him," groaned Friedrich.

"Who?"

"Two of ours . . . they shot him," Friedrich said, swinging one arm out away from his stomach and pointing at the mutilated corpse in the middle of the street.

"It was Werthers," Friedrich continued.

"Who?" Gunther asked again.

"Werthers!" Friedrich gasped, retching again, then finally straightening up so that he was now kneeling in the street. "Werthers was the man I brought to the Hofbräuhaus to meet you and Klaus a couple of months ago. We've known each other since we were kids. Our fathers worked together." Friedrich paused for a moment, fighting back tears. "He had given up his gun and had his hands up, and those two bastards shot him."

Gunther stared hard at the corpse, sickened and angered at the realization of how badly it had been mutilated. "Christ!" he said, then put his arm around Friedrich and helped him to his feet. "There's nothing we can do about it," Gunther said. "Let's get out of here . . . it's almost over."

Gunther was only partially right. The final battle ended in victory for the Freikorps units, but there were still weeks of bloody retribution to be visited against the people of Munich by their freebooter conquerors.

After the battle, Defense Minister Noske ordered the Freikorps to go from door to door in the city, searching for revolutionaries. The order stated that each house was to be searched, and if even a single weapon were found, all the inhabitants were to be taken for questioning—harsh questioning that could easily lead to summary execution under the weight of martial law, which gave the Freikorps ultimate power in the city.

As Amalie stood in the living room watching the

two men searching the apartment, Jakob's arms wrapped tightly around her legs, his face buried in her skirt, she thought it strange how the fate of everyone in the building depended on what was found in this apartment—and that her fate depended on what was found in the apartments of the others in the building, people she didn't even know.

"Have you any guns?" barked one of the soldiers.

"No," she replied, but then realizing she couldn't be certain, she modified her answer, and in doing so betrayed her anxiety. "I don't think so . . . you see, this is the apartment of a friend, an army captain who is letting us stay here."

The interrogator smiled, assuming that the captain had taken advantage of the housing shortage and the difficult situation in which a war widow might find herself in these times. Perhaps he had taken in this handsome woman and her child in exchange for sexual favors. He looked at the other soldier and winked.

This further unnerved Amalie as she tried to explain. "He and my husband were friends from the war, and he was kind enough to take us in."

"Where is your husband now?" the soldier asked, thinking he was now onto something.

"With you!" Amalie answered. "He joined the Freikorps."

The soldier was a little disappointed that he had not stumbled upon the wife of a revolutionary, as that might have put him in good standing with his superiors. He didn't altogether believe her, since she certainly wouldn't tell him if her husband was a Communist. "And the captain? Where is he?"

"I don't know. He went to stay in the barracks just before the fighting began."

"In the barracks? You mean he's still on active duty?"

"Yes."

"What does he do?"

"I'm not sure."

"What is his name?"

"Grunewald. Klaus Grunewald."

The soldier who had been searching the apartment came up to the interrogator during this exchange and stood silently as the other man wrote down Amalie's answers. "Nothing," he finally said when the interrogator looked up from his notes, indicating that he hadn't found any guns or incriminating papers. "Let's go. We have a lot more buildings to search."

"Very well, Frau . . . ," the interrogator began, searching the report he had just written for her name. "Frau Metzdorf. Guten Tag." He forced an insincere smile as he nodded at Amalie.

"Good day," Amalie repeated reflexively as the two soldiers finally left, not even realizing she had said it as an overwhelming sense of relief swept over her like a rush of cool air.

It wasn't until they had asked her if there were guns in the apartment that she realized she didn't know one way or the other. After all, Klaus was an army officer. It was quite possible he could have had a gun in the apartment.

They had been lucky so far. If something turned up in one of the other apartments, she and Jakob would soon be ordered down into the streets. She had seen it happen from the window as one of the other buildings had been evacuated. The people on the street in front of that building had looked so lost. They were herded onto a truck and taken away. *Who had kept a gun in that building?* she wondered. Was it a revolutionary, or just a soldier who had brought his rifle home from the war as a souvenir? Who would pay for that indiscretion? It was a frightening thing to let your mind wander like that, especially when you knew that yours was the next building to be searched. Next, you began to sweat as you wondered who your neighbors were.

Amalie soon realized that her fears were unfounded as the soldiers finally left her apartment building and moved on to the next. Just as the last of the soldiers had left, there was the sound of gunfire off in the distance, and Amalie rushed to the window to see if anything was happening in the street. The only people on the street were the soldiers, who were now moving to the next block. She wondered how Gunther was doing and where he was. Somewhere in the back of her mind, a thought she could barely acknowledge, she wondered if he was even alive.

She felt torn and confused. Suddenly she had the feeling that she needed to see the entire city, to find a place where she could view everything and sort it out. She gathered up Jakob and a couple of his toys.

A short time later, Jakob sat on the gravel-covered roof playing with a little wooden horse and wagon as Amalie walked to the side of the building. It was already the middle of May, and the English Garden to the east was alive with flowering trees and a fresh green carpet of grass, but Amalie couldn't see that from the top of the apartment building. She looked out over the sea of buildings as dark, billowing clouds gathered overhead, riding in on a damp spring breeze. It was late afternoon, and she could see flashes of lightning in the distance, so far off that she never heard the thunder, so far off the flashes were but tiny blossoming flowers of light that faded in the next instant.

She remembered the argument she and Gunther had had when he walked out of the apartment in the middle of the night. She hadn't said anything that night about the rumors she'd heard about the Freikorps, stories of their activities in the north that frightened her, as did the hysterical tone of their posters—the raging anti-Semitic slurs lashing out at "the Jewish Bolsheviks." She was horrified at the fate of Rosa Luxemburg, that graphic demonstration of the fierce brutality of which these men were capable, and these were the men that her husband now fought beside. These were the men with whom Gunther had cast his lot.

Amalie also thought of Gunther's parting words, his declaration that the war had not ended but had merely moved within Germany. He had sounded like a man bent on revenge. Amalie had heard the term "November criminals" at the publishing house, and when Mr. Frieder explained it to her, it suddenly came together in her mind. That was why Gunther had joined the Freikorps. He wanted revenge against those who had betrayed him and his comrades, to punish those who had lost the war. He could not accept the possibility that it was the army that had lost the war.

Amalie was overwhelmed. Her life wasn't supposed to be this complicated. What did all this have to do with two people falling in love and getting married and raising a family? In a sudden rush of anger and frustration, she grabbed the wall she had been leaning against and shouted "Why?" at the top of her lungs, then crossing her arms on the ledge and lowering her head, she began to cry. Jakob, startled by his mother's cry, looked up to see what was wrong. Even though he couldn't see Amalie's face, he somehow sensed her distress and, dropping his toys, got up and ran to his mother, wrapping his arms around her legs.

"Mutti?" Jakob said, not understanding why she didn't answer him, why she didn't even look at him.

"Mutti, Mutti," he cried, and finally Amalie looked down. When she saw the bewilderment in his eyes, her anger dissipated.

It's nothing, Liebling," she said, as she wiped away her tears. "Mutti is just sad."

"Why?"

I guess I just miss your father," Amalie said, trying to find a simple answer that would satisfy her son.

"Me, too," Jakob said, and with that, Amalie picked him up and rested him on her hip just as the rain finally broke. It started as a sprinkle, and Amalie took her time walking over to pick up Jakob's toys as he clung to her side, but suddenly the rain turned to a downpour, and as she let Jakob down, he let out a squeal and raced for the door with his mother close behind. Once they got inside, Amalie quickly closed the door and began to laugh as Jakob shook his head from side to side like a little puppy shaking himself dry. When Amalie tried to do the same, the two began to laugh hysterically as a veil of wet hair wrapped itself around her face.

When they had laughed themselves out, Amalie took Jakob's hand and led him down the stairs to the apartment. Just as she was unlocking the door, she heard footsteps echoing in the hallway and turned to see Gunther coming up the stairs.

"Vati!" Jakob cried out as he ran to his father, who swept him up in his right arm as he readjusted his rifle and pack onto his left, planting a little kiss on his son's cheek and nuzzling his ear.

"Vati, you smell bad!" Jakob exclaimed. Gunther let out a short laugh as he set Jakob down and looked over at Amalie, still standing motionless in front of the door.

"He's right. I haven't had a chance to bathe in days," he said sheepishly, moving closer to his wife. "It's done," he sighed, slipping off his pack and rifle and letting them fall to the floor. Taking Amalie in his arms, he actually lifted her off the floor as he held her tightly and kissed her.

CHAPTER 5

When a war ends, people often hope for a return to "normalcy," a period when things calm down, the shooting stops, and there is time to rebuild. The problem in Munich in 1919 was that their "war" was only a sideshow to Germany's other problems. The Treaty of Versailles was not officially released until the end of June 1919, more than six months after the armistice and weeks after the bloody suppression of the revolution in Munich.

There has long been a question when it comes to the fate of a transgressor as to whether that antagonist should be punished or reformed, or perhaps a medium lying somewhere between those two options. The Treaty of Versailles was clearly a bitter and vengeful punishment of Germany. The Allies politely denied any complicity in the situation that led to the war and fixed all of the blame on Germany, citing her as the responsible party for all civilian losses. It was to cost the nation dearly. Maps were quickly redrawn to acknowledge where parts of Germany had been confiscated and given to other countries such as Poland, Belgium, and France while other parts of Germany were to be occupied by foreign troops for the next fifteen years. Germany would be made to pay.

"ARE YOU all settled in then?" asked Klaus.

"For the most part," Gunther replied.

"Well, you've got a job, a new apartment, and your family with you . . . you've survived the revolution and become a regular member of the bourgeoisie,"

Klaus said with a subtle smirk. He considered this the de-evolution of a soldier, and Gunther could hear it in his voice.

Gunther had finally found a job in July, as a draftsman with an architectural firm. His father was an architect, and even though Gunther had no formal education in architecture, he had become a competent draftsman through casual observation of his father at work. He had made some drawings when he heard there was a position available, and mostly because of his experience in the army, having gone from private to captain in his four years of service, he had gotten the job.

The work was just enough to get by, and considering the shortage of building supplies and the consequent shortage of building projects, even that was surprising. There was one drawback for Gunther, however, in that Amalie had to keep working so that they could still meet expenses.

Amalie had been afraid that as soon as Gunther got work he would insist that she quit immediately, but he hadn't said a word. Going without work for so long had made him more pragmatic. He knew he would have to swallow his pride and that they would both have to work to get caught up and keep their heads above water.

"You're jealous," Gunther countered.

Klaus laughed. "Maybe a little," he finally conceded.

"You understand, Klaus," Gunther began, "when I heard the war was over, my first thought was to do just as I have done, to become ordinary. But now it feels so strange."

"There is something about war," Klaus said absent-mindedly, taking a drink of his beer.

"If someone had told me five years ago how I would be feeling at this moment, I would have laughed in their face."

"How do you mean?" Klaus asked.

"It's just not what I expected. I hated the war, the bloody murderous war, but now life is just so . . ."

"Boring?" Klaus finished the sentence.

"It's crazy!" Gunther said with a short laugh. "I know it's crazy. I love Amalie, and Jakob is a wonderful boy, but . . ."

"I know what you mean," Klaus commiserated. "It's a common complaint of soldiers in peacetime."

"It seems like heresy!" Gunther declared, shocked at his own feelings. "To somehow make it through that war alive and then to miss it when it's over."

"Did anyone ever tell you that life was a simple matter?"

"No," Gunther replied, "but I never asked."

"Well, if you had asked, only a fool would have said things would be simple . . . simple to do or simple to understand."

"Maybe life *is* simple—if you're a fool," Gunther mused.

It was still hot in Munich as the summer of 1919 drew to a close. Klaus and Gunther were spending the late afternoon of a Thursday in September at the Sterneckerbräu. When Klaus and Gunther would go out for beer, and they still did so two or three times a week, even though Gunther and his family had moved out of Klaus's apartment, they often chose the Sterneckerbräu because it was quieter than the more famous Hofbräuhaus a few blocks away.

AT THE SAME time that Klaus and Gunther were washing down their conversation with the watered-down beer typically served at German beer halls so soon after the war, Amalie was taking Jakob on an outing to the English Garden on the banks of the Isar River. It was unusual for Amalie to go out on a Thursday, but she knew Gunther would be out late, and she wanted to take advantage of the beautiful weather that would all too soon turn into a typical cold and blustery Bavarian autumn.

The Isar is an excellent example of a German river. In 1156, when Emperor Barbarossa gave the Duchy of Bavaria to Duke Heinrich der Löwe, Heinrich promptly destroyed the bridge on the Isar at Oberföhring. The bridge had been owned by the Bishop of Freising and had earned the bishop toll money because it was on the salt trade routes. Heinrich then built a new bridge at a small settlement called Ze den Munichen and began to collect the tolls for himself. Over the centuries, while the little village of Ze den Munichen was becoming the city of Munich, the river was mastered and controlled—locks installed, more bridges built, and the waters diverted through canals for factories and mills. The river was molded and fit into the fabric of Munich life. It conformed.

The Isar was broad by the English Garden, however, where the river was allowed to run shallow in a western fork as it split and found its way around the islands in its path. The banks were covered with smooth white stones that swept up to meet the grass of the English Garden, and this was where mothers would lay out their towels and watch as their children played in the gently moving water at the river's edge.

"Be careful," Amalie cautioned Jakob one last time as he moved toward the water. Jakob left his shoes with his mother, but when he tried to walk on the stony ground, he only made it a few steps before the rocks began to burn his feet. He quickly danced back to the safety of his mother's towel, wincing and whining all the way.

"Mutti, my feet are burning!"

Amalie laughed and helped him on with his shoes, ersatz oxfords made with wooden soles and cloth tops. He was growing fast, and it was bad enough that no decent clothes or shoes were available, but how could they afford to keep replacing them every few months on top of that?

"There you go," she said, giving him a little pat on the bottom to send him on his way again.

Jakob stepped gingerly into the cool water, ready to retreat if it was too cold, watching his submerged foot carefully as he decided on the condition of the water. The water distorted the sunlight as it sparkled and flashed, and Jakob was transfixed as the image of his foot moved about as though reflected in a funhouse mirror. Finally, he jumped in with both feet, making a splash and screeching with delight as he twisted around to look back at his mother to see whether she had been watching. Amalie smiled and waved. Taking that as approval to venture farther, he then headed to his right, splashing as much as he could as he moved through the water, toward a group of children who had been frolicking nearby since he first arrived.

"Hello," Jakob said to a little girl and two boys who were sitting in the shallow water splashing each other. The girl was about the same age as Jakob, who was now almost four, and the boys were about a year or so older. The other children greeted him and immediately included him in their play. They played together for over half an hour as their mothers lay on their towels and blankets, taking in the sun. The children eventually grew tired of the water and headed for a patch of trees bordering the stony beach. They began a game of hide and seek in the lush green undergrowth, running in and out of the small forest and then diving back in to catch one of the others hiding among the trees. The older boy showed Jakob a fortress of green brush that the three of them had found when they had played there before.

Finally, their energy collectively spent, they took shelter in their castle of underbrush, hidden from the rest of the world. The oldest boy peeked out to see if they had been missed by any of the mothers on the beach. There were still a number of other children making noise and playing in the water, so the mothers of the missing four hadn't even noticed their children's absence.

Once the older boy was sure of their privacy, he joined the others, who were sitting cross-legged under the small canopy formed by the dense foliage. The dirt- and leaf-covered floor of their hiding place was speckled with sunlight filtering down through the tall trees. The older boy finally spoke, trying to suppress a smile. "Why don't we play like we did yesterday?" he said, revealing a secret plan he had been working on ever since he led the others to this hiding place.

The other boy and the little girl began to giggle, but Jakob had no idea what they were talking about.

"Ja!" the other boy said with excitement, the girl nodding in agreement.

"What?" Jakob asked, wondering what their funny secret was. The little girl looked at Jakob with a big smile through which she could barely talk. "We pretend like . . . like we're babies . . . and we take off all our clothes!" she finally said, punctuating her sentence with more giggling.

The idea seemed strange to Jakob. He had never seen, or at least he couldn't remember seeing, anyone without clothes on before. He couldn't even remember ever seeing his parents without clothes. As he thought about it, his curiosity piqued, and he began to join in their laughter. It seemed fun, and yet he also had a strange feeling in the pit of his stomach, as though it might be wrong. The fact that they were hiding here seemed to indicate that it should be a secret thing, but he didn't understand why. The other boys had already started to take off their swimming suits, and once they had done so, they stood waiting for the little girl to follow their lead. Jakob only stared.

He looked at the other boys as they sat naked and semi-erect, watching as the little girl stood up and slipped off her suit, letting it fall to the dirt.

She had no penis! Jakob sat there amazed, staring between the little girl's legs as she stood in front of him, giggling and watching his face as he discovered the secret she and the other two boys had already found out about each other.

"Now you!" one of the other boys said to Jakob, smiling as he insisted that this newcomer join in. Still hypnotized by what he saw, Jakob slowly wriggled out of his swimsuit as he remained seated on the dirt floor of their hiding place. The earth felt cool on his backside, and he felt somehow free as he found himself naked with the others, all of them looking at one another. Jakob was surprised as he felt his penis beginning to grow a bit.

Just then, he little girl pointed at Jakob's circumcised penis. "What's wrong with it?" she asked the other boys. Not being Jewish, they weren't circumcised, and Jakob found himself in a terrible position for a child to be in. He was now different.

"I don't know," said the younger of the two boys.

"He's a *joo,*" said the older boy with an air of authority the others didn't question.

"What's a *joo*?" asked the younger boy, phrasing the same question Jakob was about to ask.

Jakob had been circumcised because Amalie was still living with her father at the time Jakob was born, but he had never been told that he was Jewish, at least not in a way that he could remember. It had never been mentioned, and he had never had any reason to ask questions about such things.

"I don't know," the older boy admitted after a thoughtful pause, "but my daddy . . . he said that *joos* were the ones who made the war."

Something clicked in Jakob's head, and he suddenly remembered his father and Uncle Klaus talking about Jews, but he had never known before that they were a kind of people. He just knew that they were bad.

How could I be one of these joos? Jakob thought to himself in a confused panic, feeling as though he was being accused of something bad.

The older boy continued talking. "My father said you can tell a *joo* because they cut off the end of his thing."

"Why?" the younger boy asked.

"I don't know," the older boy said "but look . . . ," and he reached down and held his own penis, sliding back the foreskin to expose the glans and then pointing to Jakob. "They cut off the part on the end." The other children watched as though in the presence of a scholar. Once he had shown the others the difference, the older boy continued his lecture.

"My father says *joos* are dirty and you can't go swimming if there is a *joo* in the water because he makes the water dirty." The boy said it without emphasis or emotion, as if it were an old poem that some adult had made him memorize by rote, words without any meaning.

Jakob was hurt and confused. The boy was talking about him, but neither of them really understood what it all meant. The older boy also felt bad because now he had put a face to this terrible thing that his father called a "joo," and it was a little boy who didn't look any different than he did.

Jakob started to cry. The little girl, who had been sitting and listening carefully to the lecture, moved over to Jakob and sat beside him, patting him gently on the back, both of them oblivious to their nakedness. She didn't know what to say either.

"Don't cry," she finally said, trying to find some way to make Jakob feel better. "Maybe you don't have to be a *joo*."

Jakob soon managed to stop crying, and without saying a word, without any of them saying a word, they all put their swimsuits back on and left the sheltered little world nature had built for them.

Jakob walked dejectedly toward his mother, who was still lying on her towel, reading a book. Amalie didn't actually see him as he came toward her from behind and off to the side, but somehow she knew he was there, and that something was wrong.

"What is it?" she asked as she laid the book on the stones beside her.

"Can we go home?" Jakob asked.

"Yes, it's getting late," she said as she glanced first at the sun lowering toward the city's skyline, then looked back questioningly at Jakob.

"What's wrong?" she asked, looking directly into Jakob's eyes and noticing that they were red, as though he had been crying.

"Nothing," Jakob said meekly, seeming on the verge of tears as he looked down at the rocky ground and kicked stones around with his feet. "I'm tired . . . I want to go home."

Amalie knew her little boy and she knew she would have to wait until he felt like talking about what was bothering him. He was a lot like his father in that respect. When something was wrong, he wanted to work it out alone and would only talk about it after he had spent time trying to fix it by himself.

Amalie gathered up their things, and they began walking back toward the English Garden, headed for their new apartment, but just as they were leaving the riverbank, Jakob looked up and saw the little girl from earlier. She was very pretty, with blond hair that seemed to glow in the sunlight. She smiled and waved good-bye, but Jakob didn't acknowledge her in any way. He just kept walking hand in hand with his mother. He didn't know the names of any of the other children, but he would always remember pieces of that afternoon, which had stirred up so much confusion within him.

The early evening hours found Klaus and Gunther still at the Sterneckerbräu. Around six o'clock Friedrich also joined them, just as the hall began to fill with people. There were about forty people, mostly Handarbeiter—laborers who work with their hands—who apparently were gathering for some kind of meeting.

It was hard to get drunk on the terrible beer they served at the Sterneckerbräu, but the trio did their best. Seated at a table along the back wall of the room, they laughed loud and long on this particular night, but managed to stay fairly subdued as the meeting began. It turned out the laborers belonged to some kind of worker's party, one of the many political factions that kept appearing in Munich at the time. There was to be a speaker, someone named Eggert or Ekert—a name that none of the three revelers in their semi-drunken state could hear or recognize—but it seemed this man had become ill, so the task of addressing the group fell to another man who spoke about getting rid of capitalism. The three comrades paid no attention, but they did make an attempt to keep their conversation quiet because they didn't feel like moving to another beer hall and didn't want to get thrown out. This was a little unusual, because Klaus and Gunther rarely felt compelled to avoid confrontation, especially on their nights out, but for some reason they just weren't in the mood for fighting.

The workers who had come for the meeting sat quietly and attentively at first, but spending a boring evening listening to an economist wasn't what they had expected. When the speaker finally concluded his lecture, some of the group began to leave as a free discussion period began. One man, a professor, stood and made the suggestion that perhaps Prussia and Bavaria should be recreated as separate states. The basis for his idea was that these regions were so politically different, Prussia's specifically militaristic history standing in stark contrast to Bavaria's Gemütlichkeit attitudes, that they seemed irreconcilable.

Another man who already had his coat over his arm and was preparing to leave stopped to challenge the professor, taking great exception to the suggestion that the German state once again be separated into unorganized states, as it had been before 1871. Laying out what many of the group considered to be a clear case for keeping Germany a strongly unified country, the man went on to completely discredit the professor's argument, so much so that the professor not only returned to his seat in silence, but soon beat a hasty retreat from the beer hall.

As the challenger finished speaking, Klaus stood and applauded him and was joined by a few others. The man flashed a quick glance at Klaus, sizing him up along with the other two men at his table. Klaus was the only army officer in the hall, and as such he stood out in the group.

The man was about to leave again when one of the meeting organizers caught up with him. Introducing himself as Anton Drexler, he handed him one of the group's pamphlets and invited him to come again. Thanking Drexler, the man started toward the door again, but then turned and walked over to Klaus's table.

"Thank you," he said, "for your kind applause."

Klaus stood and offered his hand. "You spoke well. It is good to hear such voices in times like these."

"Yes," Gunther agreed, as he too stood and extended his hand to the man. "Gunther Metzdorf," he said, "formerly Captain Metzdorf of the Austrian army."

"Austrian?" the man exclaimed. "I too am from Austria."

"I was born in Munich, but my family moved to Salzburg when I was a boy," Gunther explained.

"I was born in Braunau," the man added.

"You speak more like a German than an Austrian," Klaus interrupted.

"Even when I lived in Austria, I felt I was a German," the man replied with a good-natured laugh.

"I am Klaus Grunewald," Klaus interjected, "and this is Friedrich Haas."

Friedrich stood up with the others and shook hands.

"Adolf Hitler," the man said, introducing himself

to all of them.

BACK AT Gunther's apartment, Jakob was finally ready to speak as he and his mother were finishing their dinner of turnip soup.

"Mutti," Jakob began cautiously, as though he wasn't sure he really wanted an answer to the question he was about to ask. "What is . . . a *joo*?"

So that was it! Amalie thought to herself. This was a big question, one that would not be easy to answer, especially considering Gunther's attitudes.

"A Jew is a person," Amalie offered, wanting to keep things as simple as possible so that she could offer Jakob answers to his questions as he thought of them rather than overwhelming him with too much information at once.

"What makes a person a *joo*?" Jakob continued.

"Are you finished with your soup?" Amalie asked.

"Yes," said Jakob, always more than willing to be finished with turnip soup but wondering why his mother hadn't answered his question. Jakob watched as she got up and cleared away their bowls and glasses and put them in the sink, then reached above it to the highest cupboard. Finding that she couldn't quite get at what she wanted, she walked back to the table and got a chair and dragged it over to the sink, climbing up so she could reach into the back of the high cupboard. She looked at him and smiled as she pulled out a small white box, then climbed down and returned the chair to the table.

"Come in here," she said, motioning him to follow her into the small living room of the apartment and seating herself on the sofa Klaus had given them as a gift when they moved out. Jakob followed and hopped up on the sofa beside his mother, all the while watching the small white box she held and wondering what was inside. Amalie slowly removed the cover, revealing six dark brown pieces of chocolate, each set within a white paper cup with fluted edges. Jakob's eyes grew big with excitement.

"Chocolate!" he said with a great deal of surprise, as it had been a long time since he had had such a wonderful treat. It was so hard to get decent food, but to get something like this was truly rare.

"Please, Mother, may I have one?"

"No," Amalie said playfully, "they're all mine."

Jakob looked crestfallen, but Amalie quickly took one of the sweet morsels and pressed it to his lips, and they both laughed as he took it from her and began to eat it in tiny nibbles to make it last as long as possible. Amalie took one for herself and set the box on the arm of the sofa, then settled back and put her arm around Jakob, drawing him close.

"What makes a Jew?" Amalie said thoughtfully, surprising Jakob, who thought perhaps she had ignored his question because *joos* were such a bad thing—something that shouldn't be talked about.

"In the Bible, there was a man named Abraham," she began, gazing at nothing in particular as she tried to gather her thoughts. "They say that Abraham was a good man, and that he knew God and even talked to God, and he was the first Jew."

It sounded like just another story to Jakob as he listened to his mother's gentle voice—all this talk of Abraham and Moses and Egypt and God. Jakob had seen all the beautiful old churches in Munich, but only from the outside, and he had no concept of what went on there. Amalie and Gunther never talked about God. They were nonreligious, believing, though they didn't actually discuss it outright, that God had somehow abandoned man. When Gunther spoke of Jews, he spoke of a race of people, not a religion, and he had no desire to pursue the Lutheran faith his family had practiced. It was because of this that Amalie's words had no ring of truth for Jakob, no passion or deep meaning.

Amalie went on for some time, even reciting an old poem her parents had made her memorize as a child. She felt it was important to tell Jakob that being Jewish, contrary to what Gunther said, was a matter of religion and not race, because if she acknowledged a link to a people—the people of Israel—then it would be impossible to leave being a Jew behind, as she had so easily done.

Amalie seemed to be finished with her talk, but Jakob still wasn't satisfied. Nothing she had said was helping him understand why the boy from that afternoon had said that he was bad because of how his penis looked. But then a question began to form as his mind began putting things together in that strange way that little minds do. It was the sort of question that only a little boy could ask, one that conjures up up all the vicious lies and hatreds of prejudice and bigotry, all the nameless victims piled on top of each other from century to century.

"Am I a *joo*?" Jakob finally asked.

It was a simple question, one that could be answered with a simple yes or no, but Amalie was hesitant.

"Half," she finally answered.

"Half?" Jakob asked, not yet even understanding the meaning of a fraction, let alone the concept of somehow being partly a *joo* and partly not a *joo.*

Amalie offered him another chocolate and took one for herself. This was definitely going to be at least a two-chocolate discussion.

She got up and got a piece of paper and a short, blunt pencil, which as true thrifty Germans they had kept long beyond the point where it was easy to hold. She then drew seven little circles, four above two above one, with names below each circle and lines to connect them from one generation to the next, grandfather and grandmother to father and then father to son, and then she drew the same on the other side of the page.

"This is our family," she said. "These two circles are my mother and father and these two circles are your father's mother and father—and this little circle is you," whereupon she drew two dots for eyes and still another for a nose, which she underlined with a little smile.

"My mother and father were Jewish and so I am Jewish. Your father's mother and father were not Jewish, so he is not Jewish. You are part of me and part of your father, so you are part Jewish."

"Which part?" Jakob asked, looking up from the paper directly into his mother's eyes.

"What?" she asked.

"Which part of me is *joo* and which part is not?" Jakob repeated.

Amalie laughed, realizing she was facing another of those never-ending series of questions children always seemed to come up with for their hapless parents and trying to figure out how to explain it all.

"Is my pisha *joo*?" Jakob asked innocently, at which point Amalie burst out laughing so hard that tears came to her eyes and she leaned to the side of the sofa as though to keep from falling off.

"Where did you ever come up with that?" she exclaimed between bouts of laughter.

Jakob was somewhat bewildered at his mother's response, although he seemed not at all shaken at being the object of such ridicule. He knew what the question meant and it was a perfectly good question to him, so he pressed on, undaunted.

"A boy at the river told me that they cut off the end of my pisha because I am a *joo*."

"Oh! My, my . . . now I see what you mean," Amalie said, regaining her composure. "Remember what I said about Abraham?"

"Yes," Jakob replied, even though he hadn't really been paying much attention to the story.

"Well, first," Amalie began "before I tell you this, you must promise not to keep asking me why, because I'll tell you right now that I never knew why this was done."

"What was done?" Jakob asked.

"Well, way back when Abraham was talking with God, he told everyone that God had said he should make a mark on his body that would show he really believed in God. He called it a 'covenant,' like a promise between him and God, so that any man with this mark would be known as a Jew, and this mark was when they would cut off the piece of skin at the end of the penis."

Amalie hoped that going through it quickly and clinically would finish the conversation, as she found the subject embarrassing, even just talking to her own son.

"Why?" Jakob asked.

Amalie just stared at Jakob.

"I told you before that I don't know why," she finally answered. She wasn't really upset, but she did want to stop Jakob from going on.

"Jakob," she began, changing the subject, "can you do something very important for me?"

"What?"

"Don't talk to your father about this," she said seriously.

Jakob's first reaction was to ask why, but then he thought a moment and said sadly to his mother, "Father doesn't like *joos,* does he?"

It almost brought tears to Amalie's eyes to hear her little boy say this. It hurt to realize that somehow he understood this terrible thing and would have to live with it as a child. Especially since she knew that even she, as a grown-up, was having so much trouble dealing with it.

BACK AT the Sterneckerbräu, Gunther and his friends were just about ready to call it an evening.

"An architect?" Adolf repeated.

"Well, I do drawings," Gunther admitted with a touch of embarrassment. "I just fill in things for the real architects—rough outlines and so on."

"I used to paint," Adolph said with a hint of pride, but without giving details so as to leave the extent of his career to the imagination. "I was very good with buildings. I would have liked to have been an architect."

"What do you do now?" asked Friedrich.

"I am still in the army, but I think I shall somehow become a full-time politician," Adolf replied without hesitation.

"Excellent!" Klaus piped in. "It's about time we found some politicians who can do some good and help put Germany back on the right road."

CHAPTER 6

The reparations payments levied against Germany as a result of the Treaty of Versailles were the coup de grâce for the German economy after four years of total war. An almost immediate response to the demands on the economy was a steadily increasing inflation, which had already been a problem at the end of the war. When the terms of the treaty were announced, however, the inflation began to rise to unprecedented levels. The money that would have been considered a good annual salary one day could hardly pay for a single loaf of bread a few weeks later.

The economic problems, along with military occupation in certain areas of the country, made fertile ground for those who wished to reap power from the discontent of the German people. Many small political parties on the extremist fringe were formed during that period. One such group was the Deutsche Arbeiterpartei, which, under the new leadership of a former corporal of the Kaiser's Imperial Army named Adolf Hitler, soon changed its name to the Nationalsocialistische Deutsche Arbeiterpartei, or "Nazis," as it became known.

Time is a funny thing. When we look back over our lives, it is rarely a chronological process. Most often we remember things, perhaps an object or maybe a single event that we consider important, and then we try to rebuild the world that existed around our important memories in order to make sense of them.

Amalie's memory of 1922 was of a brown briefcase. It was made of the best leather, with shiny brass catches and shiny brass buckles on the leather tie-down straps. She had looked it over a few times in the store window as she passed by on her way to work one week. She finally decided that she deserved to buy herself a gift, an anniversary gift to commemorate the three years she had been working for Frieder and Son Publishing.

The other reason for such an extravagance was that people were then prone to spending their money as soon as they got it, because the longer they held onto it, the less it was worth. The common wisdom was that it was better to buy a luxury item now that you might be able to trade later, rather than holding onto the currency.

There were many reasons for what happened to the German economy in the first years of the Weimar Republic. Chiefly, of course, as with any inflation, the basic problem was money being printed without anything to back it up. The inflation problem began with the development of the artificial economy during the last half of the war when Germany directed all of its resources and production to the war effort. Civilian goods were made of substitute materials, ranging from shoes made of wood and cloth and coins made of pewter to bread made with sawdust. The next situation to exacerbate the economic problems was the harshly punitive nature of the Versailles Treaty. The German economy had no chance to recover from the economic strain of total war before having to pay a huge indemnity to the victors. There were a few people who benefited from the state of the economy. Imagine, for example, having a loan that was scheduled for a twenty-year repayment and suddenly being able to pay it all off with a single paycheck. On the other hand, the frugal German middle class found within just a few weeks after reparations payments began that the money they had saved to get them through their old age was now barely enough to get through a single day.

Amalie had only managed to hang on to her job by default over those years. Gunther had told her that she must quit when he found work, but when he first got the job in the architectural firm, they had wanted to get an apartment so badly that Gunther agreed Amalie should keep working until they "got over the hump" financially. Then the money went crazy.

Amalie walked into the offices of the Frieder Publishing Company with the coveted briefcase wrapped in a bag and tucked under one arm and carrying a cold lunch in a small bag in her other hand.

"Good morning, Mr. Frieder," Amalie said in a cheerful tone. She was a "morning person." Mr. Frieder was not. Amalie still called him "Mr. Frieder," even though she had worked with him for years now, but she did it out of respect rather than convention, although she noticed that "David" was creeping into her conversations more and more as they became better friends.

Their friendship was strictly platonic. In many ways, Amalie felt that her boss was more intelligent than she, but the truth was that while he had a better memory for facts, Amalie made better use of the things she knew. She was a better thinker.

"Something new?" Mr. Frieder asked, pointing at the bundle under her arm.

"A present," Amalie replied with a smile.

"A present? From who?" David asked.

"From *whom,*" Amalie corrected.

"And me a publisher," David said as though apologizing. "From whom have you received this gift?" he asked, rephrasing his question.

"From me," Amalie said with a smile.

David smiled back. "Well, at least that way you know you'll get a present you like."

They laughed companionably, as Amalie stopped at her desk and put down her packages. She unwrapped the briefcase to look at it again and also to show it off to David.

"Very nice."

"Thank you," Amalie said.

"Expensive?" David asked in a way that a friend would, a way that wasn't presumptuous.

"Very," Amalie answered.

"I hope you can trade it when you need to."

"Well, actually, I bought it as an anniversary present."

"For your husband?"

"No, not a wedding anniversary. I bought it for myself because I've worked here almost three years now."

"Three years! Already three years?"

"Yes. In four days."

"Amazing! Oh yes, I remember now. You showed

up on that day . . . the last day I saw Rosa Luxemburg. It seems like a lifetime ago."

"Rosa Luxemburg," Amalie said thoughtfully. "I haven't thought about her for quite a while. Come to think of it, I heard there is to be some sort of trial. They are trying some military officers in connection with the killing of her and Karl Liebknecht."

"They won't get far," David prophesied.

"Weimar and the Freikorps—back in bed together," Amalie said with a smirk.

David smiled and turned to walk away, but he stopped when Amalie began to ask a question. "Mr. Frieder?" she began, but then decided to change her approach. "David," she started over, "I've wanted to ask you something for a while now, but I wasn't sure how to go about it."

"What is it, Amalie?"

"It's very strange."

"Oh! It sounds interesting already."

"It's also very serious."

"Is it money? If it is, I'm afraid I can't . . ."

"No, no. I know how things are, and you've already. . . no, it has nothing to do with money."

"Then what?"

"David, I've never told you much about my husband."

"Is there trouble?"

"In a roundabout way. Gunther is involved with some men."

"What kind of men? Black market?"

"No. It's a political group."

"Which one?"

"It's a small group called the National Socialist

Workers Party."

"Oh, Amalie!" David said with shock.

"You know of them?"

"Yes, I've heard a lot about them. Far right. Vicious rhetoric. But Amalie," he continued, "aren't you Jewish? They hate the Jews. How could your husband belong to a group like that?"

"He tells me they just hate Jewish bankers and politicians."

"I've heard that fanatic, Hitler. I went to protest with some friends at one of their meetings last year, and he didn't sound like he made any distinctions as to which Jews he hated."

"That's why I'm worried. Do you know anything about this Hitler?"

"Not much. Why do you ask?"

"I want to find out where he comes from and how he got to where he is now."

"Do you want to bring him down? Discredit him?"

"To tell you the truth, I'm not sure. I just want to find out who he is. He seems dangerous."

"Well, he's obnoxious, but there are so many of these little groups around. I think this Hitler is just a sign of the times. He'll disappear as soon as things improve."

"Maybe you're right, but just the same, I'd like to find out more about him."

David stopped and thought for a moment, stroking his chin as he looked up at the ceiling. "My father," he finally said. "He might at least know where to start. Since his retirement, he keeps close tabs on the political scene. It's like a hobby with him."

"All right," Amalie said.

"Here's where you can find him," David said as he began to write down his father's address. "He lives over in Fürstenried."

"Thank you, David," Amalie said, taking the note and tucking it in her purse. She then slid the purse under her desk as she began organizing the day's work.

Throughout the day, Amalie began to develop a plan for how she might visit Sam Frieder. She knew that it would have to be on the sly. She didn't want Gunther to find out. But she was desperate to save her husband from his extremist friends, as though he had been coopted against his will by these people, and she would try anything to bring back the Gunther she had married instead of the Gunther who now frightened her so with his politics.

Just before lunch, Amalie asked if she could take off early for the day.

"Yes, I suppose," David replied, then stopped in mid-sentence as he realized why she was asking. "A trip to Fürstenried?"

"David," Amalie said, looking plaintively into his eyes, "you mustn't tell Gunther."

"Amalie, I've never even met your husband."

"I know, but just the same, promise me you'll never say anything about our conversation today."

"You have my word."

FÜRSTENRIED was, and still is, a residential area in the southern part of Munich. It took Amalie more than a half hour to get there from her office, but once she got to the Fürstenried station, she had no trouble finding the right house, since David had even drawn a little map on the note with his father's name and address.

The house was a pretty little red-brick country cottage with an orange tile roof around which other, newer houses had begun springing up before the war.

"Mr. Frieder?" Amalie asked the balding, white-haired man with thick glasses who answered her knock on the door. "Samuel Frieder?"

"Yes?" the man answered in a tone that implicitly asked what she wanted.

"My name is Amalie Stein-Metzdorf."

"That's quite a name," the man replied good-naturedly.

"Yes," Amalie said, trying to be polite but anxious to get to the point of her visit. "But the reason I'm here . . ." Amalie was having trouble gathering her thoughts. "Mr. Frieder," she started again, "I know your son . . . I work for your son David."

"Oh yes . . . Amalie," said Sam, his face breaking into a pleasant smile. "David called to say you might be coming by."

"He called?" Amalie asked with a note of surprise, but then realized that, of course, it was just like David to do that.

"Please come in," Sam said.

The living room was dark—dark wallpaper and heavy, dark oak trim at every corner of floor to wall and wall to door. The only bit of lightness was provided by the sheer white curtains over the windows, which had obviously suffered neglect since Sam's wife had died a few years before. In a way, it reminded

Amalie of her own father, this man who kept things a certain way as a memento of his wife rather than to suit his own preference. There was a bit of a musty smell to the house, but that was understandable, as it was nearing the end of January, and the windows had obviously been kept closed for almost four months now. It was nothing that the first fresh breezes of spring wouldn't cure.

There were books everywhere. Books of all sizes and colors, of all qualities and languages. It was apparent that, long ago, great care had been taken to fit proper bookshelves and organize the books, but now they were strewn about, stacked on top of the bookshelves and sitting in piles beside the sofa and chairs. It was clear that these books were not for display; they were meant to be read. They looked lived in.

Sam quickly and unpretentiously brushed some crumbs off the cushion of one of the chairs and directed Amalie to be seated while he moved around a low table in front of the sofa and sat opposite her. Amalie felt a bit uncomfortable, because she wasn't sure exactly what it was she wanted to know or how to go about investigating this friend of Gunther's, and she knew that would be Sam's first question. "Mr. Frieder—"

"Please," Sam interrupted. "Such a pretty young lady, it would make me feel much better if you would call me Sam."

"Yes, yes," Amalie said, her nervousness becoming more obvious in her voice. "And you must call me Amalie." They both smiled awkwardly for a moment, then Amalie continued. "When David called . . . to tell you I was coming . . . did he also tell you what I was looking for?"

"No," Sam said, as he settled back into the over-stuffed sofa. Watching the old man make himself more comfortable made Amalie realize that she had been sitting on the edge of her chair. She was sitting so close to the edge, it was amazing she hadn't fallen right off! Taking a cue from her host, she settled back into the chair, becoming noticeably more relaxed.

"Sam, all my life I've tried to be . . ." She paused for a moment, reaching for the right word. "To be rational."

Sam smiled as he concurred. "Me, too!"

Amalie flashed a smile but then became serious again. "My husband has become involved with a political party . . ."

"What kind of party?" Sam asked.

"One of those extremist groups."

"National Socialists?" Sam asked.

"Yes. How did you know?"

"They've grown quickly over the last few years. Even though they don't have a huge following, they make a lot of noise. Was your husband a soldier?"

"Yes," Amalie said again, pleased that he grasped the situation so quickly.

Sam nodded. "They've made a real effort to recruit soldiers who fought in the front lines." Sitting up and folding his hands together while resting his elbows on his knees, he studied her thoughtfully for a moment. "Amalie, I assume from your name that you're Jewish."

"My family was, but no, I'm not Jewish," Amalie

responded.

"What do you mean? If your family was Jewish . . . unless . . . Was your mother a gentile?" Sam asked, trying to make sense of Amalie's denial.

"No, she was Jewish. I just mean I don't follow the Jewish religion."

"Have you converted to another religion?"

"No. I don't follow any religion."

"Amalie, my dear, we don't know each other, but at the risk of offending you, I must tell you that is not a consideration. When people who hate Jews use the word *Jew,* they mean all people of Jewish ancestry."

"I don't mean to contradict you," Amalie said almost apologetically, "but my husband says they mean bankers and politicians and businessmen."

Sam paused, not because he was considering the plausibility of what Amalie had said, but because he was trying to think of a response that would open Amalie's eyes to the reality of this anti-Semitism.

"Amalie," he began, "sometimes when faced with ugly things, we turn away and close our eyes so that we don't have to see, but that doesn't mean those things are not still there, waiting for us as soon as we open our eyes again."

Amalie lowered her eyes to the floor, unable to look Sam in the face. She knew he was right, but she had tried to make life bearable by hiding behind the same excuses that allowed her husband to stay with her. Gunther's rationalization had become a thread that she held onto, one that allowed them to stay together. Even now she would not say it out loud. She felt she was on a mission to save her husband, so she continued the conversation without acknowledging the truth of Sam's statement.

"Sam, the reason I'm here is because I want to find out about the man who leads the group."

"What do you want to know?" Sam asked.

"I want to know where he comes from and how he got here," Amalie answered directly, showing that she was no longer nervous.

"Why?"

"I think he's dangerous."

"And you want to stop him?"

"I don't know. I'm not sure what I'll find. I don't even know what I'm looking for."

"Amalie, this could be a dangerous game you're thinking about."

"I know. I don't plan on telling anyone. I'll be careful, but I need to start someplace and I thought I could trust David."

"Yes, my son is a good man," said Sam, his voice trailing off as he thought about what Amalie was asking. "This man, his name is—"

"Hitler," Amalie interjected.

"Yes . . . Hitler. I know he comes from Austria. Let me see . . . ," he said, getting up and crossing the room to a desk piled high with notebooks and papers. After a bit of shuffling, he pulled out a notebook and returned to the sofa. "I make notes on people," he explained to Amalie before burying his head in the pages.

"Your hobby," Amalie said with a smile, repeating what David had told her earlier.

Sam returned the smile as he looked up again. "Some people collect butterflies. I collect politicians."

He returned his attention to the notebook, then held up a finger as he came upon the information he sought. "Braunau, about a hundred kilometers east of us." Sam stopped to think again. "I know he was in the army . . . a corporal or sergeant, I think . . . no, definitely a corporal . . . in the trenches. I'm afraid that's about all I know."

"What would you suggest, Sam?"

"Well, an investigation is a tricky thing. First of all, you don't want people to know who you are or what you're up to."

"Yes, of course," Amalie agreed.

"You might pretend to be a reporter. Use an assumed name."

"But who do I ask and what do I ask them?"

"Well . . . first you'll want to find out what his family was like. If I were you, I would go to Braunau and see if you can check the church records. Then you would not only be able to find out who his parents and grandparents were, but you might also find out where the family went from there. They might still be living in Braunau."

"Go to Braunau?" Amalie exclaimed. Even though it was a logical suggestion, it stunned her. Where would she find money to travel? How would she find the time, and how could she possibly hide the purpose of the trip from Gunther?

"Amalie, this may be presumptuous of me, but maybe you could talk to David," Sam suggested.

"Why, what could he do?"

"David travels a lot."

"Yes, I know."

"If David thinks what you are considering is

important, and I think he will, then he might send you on a business trip to Braunau and you could do research while you're there."

Silence filled the room as Amalie became lost in thought. Finally she looked up at Sam. "Do you think so? I mean, do you think David would trust me to go to Braunau on business?"

"Judging from the way he spoke of you on the telephone . . ."

"What do you mean?" Amalie asked.

"He obviously holds you in high regard, Amalie. He says you are an intelligent woman, and if my son has a flaw, it's that he doesn't compliment people easily. It's high praise when he does so."

Embarrassed by this revelation, Amalie averted her eyes. "Thank you, Herr Frieder."

"Sam," he corrected. "And thanks for what? It was David who said it."

"Then thank you for repeating it."

"You're welcome," Sam replied. "Well, I'm not sure where you can go with this or what you may find, but now it remains to talk to David and see what he has to say." Sam stood and crossed over to Amalie, extending his hand as she took his cue and rose to leave. "It was nice meeting you, and I wish you luck."

"Thank you, Herr . . . Sam," she corrected herself. "You've been very kind."

"If I can help you further, let me know. And I assure you I will tell no one."

Amalie felt a sense of relief as she left the house. She was no longer alone in this risky venture.

When she brought up the possibility of business

travel with David the following day, he was most accommodating. It so happened that he was scheduled to go to the city of Ried in Austria in a few weeks to go over galley proofs with an author. Since the author had written several books already, the proofs were little more than a formality—something Amalie could certainly handle. The town of Braunau am Inn was between Munich and Ried. The work would take about four or five days, working from ten o'clock in the morning until two o'clock, so Amalie could spend about three hours each day in Braunau for the entire time, if necessary.

Gunther was not overly excited when Amalie told him about her "promotion" and that it meant she was being sent to represent the publisher out of town. But Amalie had already arranged for Gertie Haas to come over and make dinner for the week, so it wouldn't be a such terrible inconvenience. After all, he reminded himself, it was only temporary—this three-year job of hers. She would leave at eight in the morning and be back by eight at night, Amalie told everyone, and they all sympathized with her for the long hours she would have to work.

It was the week after Valentine's Day when Amalie finally found herself on the train to Ried. After about an hour and a half, the train made its stop at Braunau station, where the border guards went from car to car asking for passports and customs declarations.

The guards were humorless and curt. There had been so much illegal traffic back and forth between Austria and Germany that they trusted no one, and since it was a Monday and there were relatively few travelers, they had time to make virtually all of der Reisender[8] feel uncomfortable and suspect.

Amalie was particularly nervous, but not because she was carrying any contraband. She felt uneasy just being in Braunau. In a few hours she would return to begin her clandestine research. Would she find anything? Would she uncover some scandal or disgrace in Hitler's family that she could somehow use to steer Gunther away from the party? And where should she begin? Now that she was finally about to begin her search, the task seemed more complicated. She decided just to take it step by step, to try to find out what she could in Braunau and see where it might lead her.

When Amalie arrived in Ried, she got lost and ended up being more than a half hour late for her meeting with Otto Maus. He had authored a series of books on the American West that were extremely popular with German and Austrian boys. Perhaps the romance of a great frontier being conquered by heroic white men struck a chord in a psyche that also revered the ageless legends of Teutonic knights.

David had been right in thinking he could send Amalie in his place to work with Herr Maus. Otto trusted David, since this was his sixth book and he knew that David was a careful professional, bordering on being a perfectionist. It also didn't hurt that Amalie was pretty. Otto was a rather shy man, and he especially enjoyed taking Amalie to lunch at the restaurant around the corner, where he always ate his midday meal during the week. The two waiters and the bartender were all smiles and made admir-

---

[8]The travelers.

ing remarks as Otto directed Amalie to his usual table in the corner.

The lunch was surprisingly good for such a small, out-of-the way café, but it soon became apparent that the waiter and cook had made a special effort for their friend Otto and his "date." The lunch was pleasant and went by quickly, as did the next several hours of checking over the proofs. Although they didn't get as much accomplished as Amalie had hoped, it was just as well, for it meant she was virtually guaranteed five days' work and thus would have more time in Braunau if she needed it.

It was a little after three o'clock when Amalie arrived at the small train station in Braunau again. She had decided to leave the galley proofs with Otto rather than dragging them with her each day, especially since she would be stopping in Braunau on the way. She did carry her new briefcase, though, in hopes of impressing those she might be "interviewing." She decided on using the name of Liesl Kraus, a new reporter for the *Munich Tageblatt.* She hoped no one would question her story, but if they did, she thought that by using the name of a new reporter, she might be able to talk her way out of any trouble if someone checked with the newspaper.

As she stepped out onto the cobblestone street in front of the station, she immediately spotted a church steeple and quickly covered the few blocks between the train station and the church. When she got to the church, she stopped for a moment, deciding whether to go inside or to first look through the headstones in the small graveyard nearby. She opted for the latter.

The short wall around the graveyard was built of mismatched stones and needed repair in several places where they had come loose. After looking for a while, she found a headstone that read: "Otto Hitler, born 1887, died 1887, beloved infant of Klara and Alois." Was that the same Hitler family, she wondered. She went on to find three more headstones with the name Hitler, all of them bearing the names of children, the oldest just six years of age. Oddly, none bore the names of adults named Hitler. She would have to ask the priest.

Amalie had never been inside a Catholic church before, and it seemed very foreign to her. The building was old, the floor and wooden pews worn smooth with time, but also very clean. The candles on the altar flickered as a draft swept by, and her eyes were immediately drawn to a garishly painted statue that hung on the wall behind the altar, depicting the crucifixion of Christ.

"The Jews killed Christ! The Jews killed Christ!" The childhood taunts echoed in her mind, frightening recollections of an incident from her school days in Salzburg. The boys had not attacked her, but she had heard them shouting at a young Jewish boy and had seen the hatred in their faces. She hadn't understood what it all meant back then, but now here it was before her—the image those children must have seen every week when they went to their churches on Sunday. They had blamed a little schoolboy for the bright, red blood running from the side of Christ, from the nails in his hands and feet.

"May I help you?" came a high-pitched voice from

behind her.

Amalie turned with a start and let out a small cry, so engrossed by the memories the statue had evoked that she hadn't heard the priest approach her.

"Oh! I'm sorry!" she said as she composed herself. "I thought I was alone!"

"We are never alone in the house of God," said the priest with the confidence of a man who knew God personally.

Amalie nodded and smiled, not sure how to respond to such a statement.

"I'm Father Kreuger," the priest continued. "Can I help you in any way?"

"Yes, yes . . . I was wondering," Amalie began, but then decided to start over with her fabricated story, hoping to convince the priest to believe her. "My name is Liesl Kraus," she began.

"Kraus, Kraus . . . ," the priest repeated thoughtfully. "Are you a daughter of Artur Kraus from Simbach?"

"No!" Amalie shot back quickly, wanting to get on with her story so she could get it all out without giving the priest a chance to analyze each point. "I'm a reporter from Munich . . . with the *Tageblatt.* I'm doing a story on a man who was born here."

"A man?" the priest asked.

Relieved that the priest had asked a question about the story she was writing rather than questioning her credentials, Amalie continued.

"Yes, he's a politician now . . . in Munich. He's doing rather well and they . . . my editor thought it might make a good story, talking to his family, finding out what he was like as a boy and what might have contributed to his success."

"Very nice," the priest said. "There are so many terrible things in newspapers these days. It's a nice idea to talk about someone's success. Who is this man? I might know his family."

Amalie dug into her briefcase, holding it high, almost in the priest's face, as she pretended to go through notes looking for the name. "It's . . . Hitler. Yes, that's it. Adolf Hitler."

"Well, of course," the priest said pleasantly. "Alois' son."

"Alois? Does he still live in Braunau?" Amalie asked.

"No, I believe Herr Hitler passed on. I think it was . . . could it be twenty years now?" the priest asked rhetorically. "Let me check our records."

Amalie's heart leapt. This was what she was hoping for, and it had been so easy. It took everything she had to hide her excitement as she followed the priest to his office, where he began pointing at the labels of the record books on a shelf as he went from book to book, his lips moving as he silently read the names to himself. "Here we are!" he said triumphantly. "Hitler, Alois and Klara . . . née Pölzl. Ah," he said, clicking his tongue, "I had almost forgotten. The poor woman lost four children, four little lambs. First Otto, then the twins, and then Edmund." He shook his head sadly as he continued searching. "Yes, here we are, Adolf. Born April 20, 1889." As he turned the page, a piece of paper fell out of the book. "Ah!" said the priest with surprise, bending over to pick up the fallen note. "When a family leaves the parish, we generally don't keep further records on them, but I like to make notes on where they move to and anything else I might hear."

"So the family moved?" Amalie asked.

"Oh yes," the priest replied without looking up from the note as he tried to make out his own scribbled writing. "To Leonding. Before the war."

"Leonding?" Amalie said with surprise. Leonding was only a few kilometers from her mother's childhood home in Linz.

"Yes," the priest replied, still absorbed in the task of interpreting his handwriting and taking no notice of the tone of Amalie's voice. "Alois died there in ought-three. Klara died of cancer in December of ought-seven."

"Is there anything about his grandparents?" Amalie asked.

"No," the priest said, finally looking up from his papers. "I believe they came from Spital. The older records would be there."

Recalling that are three cities with the name Spital in Austria—one on the River Pyhrn, another on the River Semmering, and just to make things a little more confusing, a city called Spittal on the Drau River—Amalie asked, "Spital am Pyhrn or Spital am Semmering?"

"Am Pyhrn," the priest replied.

All of this was good news and bad news. The good part was that Amalie had gotten information on Hitler's family and a lead on the whereabouts of any remaining members. The bad part was that she now had to travel to Spital am Pyhrn and Leonding. She had no idea how she would she get to Spital, which was about a hundred kilometers southeast of Ried. Perhaps she could get her father to help by going to Leonding for her, but how could she involve Ethan in this without him becoming concerned about Gunther? Things could easily get out of hand.

Suddenly she thought of a plan. At the end of the week, she would suggest to Gunther that she might visit her father, since she was already going as far as Ried, and then she could make her side trip to Leonding and Spital over the weekend.

Amalie was worn out by the time she boarded the train for Munich. All of this plotting and planning and the accompanying anxiety had taken everything out of her. She pinned her ticket to her coat lapel and asked the conductor to make sure she didn't sleep through Munich. As the train crossed back over the Austrian border, she couldn't help thinking of the trip she had made three years before when she first went to Munich. Before long, she drew herself into the corner of the compartment and went to sleep, clutching her bright new briefcase on her lap under her coat.

Amalie made it to the apartment just a few minutes after eight-thirty to find Mrs. Haas asleep in the old overstuffed chair in the living room as Jakob, dressed in pajamas, played with his wooden toys on the floor at her feet.

"Mutti!" Jakob said exuberantly as he jumped up and ran into his mother's waiting arms.

Gertie was startled out of her sound sleep and put a hand to her chest, feigning a heart attack. "Gott helfen mir!"[9] she said with a little laugh and a heavy sigh, as she lifted herself out of the chair. "You almost scared me to death, Jakob!"

"I trust Jakob has been good," Amalie said, setting down her briefcase after Jakob returned to his play.

"As always!" Gertrude said in a cheerful tone. "He and Gunther have eaten, and Gunther, Friedrich, and Captain Grunewald have gone out."

"As always," Amalie said, commenting on the tendency of her husband to continually go out, even when there wasn't a pfennig to spare. Making a special effort to sound pleasant and friendly as she changed the subject, Amalie continued, "Well, Gertie, how are things going with you?"

"Well enough," Gertrude said briskly, brushing aside the question as she began to busy herself with picking up a dish and taking it into the kitchen.

Amalie sensed that Gertrude was feeling put out. Not really wanting to deal with a problem after her long day of work and travel, she found herself slightly annoyed at the older woman. Gertrude had been so willing to help when Amalie first asked her to stay with Jakob, especially when Amalie offered to pay her, but now she seemed upset. Amalie's annoyance was short-lived, though, as it occurred to her that perhaps taking care of Jakob all day and into the evening had been a little more work than Gertrude had expected. After all, taking care of a child is demanding enough when you're a young mother, but when your children are grown with lives of their own, and you've grown accustomed to your time being your own, suddenly having to take care of a child again for a long period can be quite a shock.

"He's a wonderful boy," Amalie said softly so that

---

[9]"God help me."

Jakob wouldn't hear as she entered the kitchen behind Gertrude, "but it takes a lot of patience."

"What?" Getrude asked, looking up from the dishes she was rinsing.

"You seem tired," Amalie said. "I thought Jakob may have been more of a handful than you expected."

"Oh no, really . . . Jakob was wonderful. We had fun today," Gertrude replied almost defensively.

There was a momentary pause as Gertrude continued with the dishes in silence. Amalie leaned against the counter beside her and stared at the floor, knowing she should ask what was wrong but not really wanting to get into a long discussion of Gertrude's problems. But Amalie had grown very fond of Gertrude, and it bothered her when Gertrude was upset.

"What's wrong?" Amalie finally blurted out, fairly sure that she would have to drag the information out of Gertrude.

"Nothing."

"Come now . . . I can tell that something's got you upset. I know you too well."

"It's nothing"

"Is it Jakob? Did he do something wrong?"

"No. I told you he was fine."

"Gunther?" Amalie asked, grasping at straws, watching Gertrude's face for a reaction as she ran through possibilities. "Friedrich? Klaus? Money?"

That last word hit a nerve as Gertrude looked as though she had been stung. She stopped washing dishes and leaned against the sink, adjusting her feet slightly, as though she needed to get better footing to hold herself up.

"Money?" Amalie repeated, moving a little closer and trying to look into Gertrude's downcast eyes. "Is it money?"

Gertrude said nothing and Amalie didn't know what to say. Amalie couldn't possibly offer her more money, because they could barely afford to give Gertrude what she was getting now. They barely had enough for food and rent, so there was nothing to say, and another silence filled the small kitchen, interrupted only by the sounds of Jakob playing with his toys on the floor in the living room.

Finally, Gertrude found the courage to speak, and in a labored voice, hoarse with emotion, she admitted sadly to Amalie, "I will have to leave my apartment."

Again, Amalie didn't know what to say.

"Manfred and I," the older woman continued slowly, keeping her eyes closed as she spoke, trying to fight back the tears. "We lived in that apartment for twenty years. We raised our two sons. We could never afford a house, but we always thought we would be able to get by. We were sure we would manage to get by, but now. . ." Gertrude was overcome by emotion. "There is no *we* anymore!" Finally the tears came. No sobbing, just the tears running freely from Gertrude's closed eyes, down her cheeks, tracing along the wrinkles in her face and sparkling in the light. "There's just *me*," she concluded, shuddering as she tried to stop crying but unable to hold back anymore.

Amalie could hardly stand to watch and felt the sting of her own tears as she gently put her arms around Gertrude, speaking softly and trying to comfort her.

"It's all right," she said, gently patting the older woman's back and holding her head against her shoulder as Gertrude continued to cry. "It will work out somehow . . ." But the truth was that Amalie had no idea what Gertrude might do, and she could imagine Gertrude out on the street with nowhere to go, just as so many others now found themselves. First they had survived the war, then the revolution, or "the war after the war," as they called it, and now they were falling victim to the inflation that ravaged the German economy, destroying their life's savings and robbing them of their homes.

They stood there for awhile until Gertrude stopped crying and eventually moved into the living room. Amalie convinced Jakob that it would be a good idea for him to go to bed a few minutes early. When Amalie rejoined Gertrude, she began to analyze the situation.

"Friedrich hasn't found any work yet?" she asked.

"No," Gertrude replied "He joined the army when he was only seventeen, and so he hasn't even learned a trade yet. He doesn't even seem to know what he wants to do. He talks about leaving Munich, as though it will be better in Berlin or somewhere else, maybe even out of the country. He's getting so desperate that it worries me. I feel like I don't know what he might do next. He says I'd be better off without him, but I can't imagine how he would think . . ." Gertrude let her sentence trail off, overwhelmed at the prospect of Friedrich leaving her.

"How long before you have to leave?" Amalie

asked.

"I think I should leave by next month. That should leave me with enough money to last another year if I can find a single room somewhere," Gertrude said dejectedly.

"Well," Amalie said slowly, "let's just think about this for a few days and see if we can't come up with something."

"Something?" Gertrude asked, a surprised tone in her voice. "Like what?"

"I don't know yet, but there must be something that can be done."

Gertrude took Amalie's hand. "Thank you, Amalie."

"For what? I really don't know if there's anything we can do."

"At least," Gertrude said with a half smile, "you've made me feel a little less alone."

"Well, that's something," Amalie agreed.

"I should be going now," Gertrude said, as she got up and started gathering her coat and bag. "I will see you and Jakob bright and early tomorrow."

It was only a little after nine o'clock, and Amalie knew Gunther wouldn't be home for at least another two hours. She hoped it wouldn't be much later than that, because she wanted to talk to him about going to visit her father and maybe even about Gertrude. The more she thought about it, the more she thought it might be possible to have Gertrude move in with them. It would be convenient to have a live-in babysitter, but what if they couldn't get along living in small quarters day after day? Suddenly the apartment seemed a little smaller than it ever had before.

It would mean Jakob would have to give up having a bedroom of his own, which he had done without for such a long time, and would have to sleep on the sofa again for God only knew how long. She decided to talk to Jakob and see how he felt about it first. That way, she might be able to diffuse Gunther's objections if he said Jakob shouldn't have to give up the room.

Amalie opened the door to Jakob's bedroom a little and watched his face in the light from the hallway as he lay on his stomach, pretending to be asleep. She could tell he was only pretending, because she could see his long eyelashes move when he blinked. He was obviously having difficulty keeping his eyes closed enough so that he would appear to be asleep while still being able to see what was going on.

"Jakob," she said softly as she went into the bedroom and knelt beside him. She lightly touched his shoulder, placing a gentle kiss on his forehead. "Jakob," she said again, and waited as Jakob carried out his charade of being awakened from a sound sleep.

"Mutti?" he asked, as though confused.

"Yes," she said. "Jakob, do you like Mrs. Haas?"

"Mrs. Haas?" he said, rubbing his eyes, not realizing for an instant who Amalie meant, but then making the connection. "Oh! Grandma Gertie!" he said.

"Grandma Gertie?" Amalie asked, a bit surprised and amused at his answer.

Thinking the tone of his mother's voice might be a rebuke, Jakob replied apologetically, "That's what she told me to call her."

"I see," Amalie said, smiling. "Then it's certainly acceptable. It's nice that you two are friends."

Amalie paused for a moment, stroking Jakob's hair, thinking that it was time for a haircut as she ran her fingers through the soft, brown strands that were starting to curl at the ends.

"Jakob, can you keep a secret?"

"Yes," Jakob said seriously

"You must promise not to tell anyone until I say you can."

"Even Vati?" Jakob asked.

"Especially your father," Amalie said quickly.

"Why?"

"Because this is something that I need to talk to him about, but I wanted to talk to you first because it also concerns you."

"What?"

"Jakob, Grandma Gertie needs our help."

"Because she has to go away?" he said, sitting up in bed.

Amalie was taken aback. "How did you know?"

Jakob averted his eyes and said nothing.

Amalie suddenly realized how he found out. "You were spying!" she said accusingly, but she couldn't help smiling a little at how well he had done it. She had no idea he had even left his room, and she usually heard his every move, or at least thought she did.

"I just heard you talking," Jakob finally said, still not able to look his mother in the eyes.

"My little spy!" Amalie said, letting out a short laugh and reaching over to tickle him under the arms. Jakob giggled, partly at being tickled and partly out of relief at not being punished for his transgression.

Amalie then tried to get serious, changing her expression and repressing her laughter. "Now, you know it's wrong to spy on people."

"Yes, Mother."

"We'll let it go this time, but don't do it anymore," Amalie said authoritatively, getting up to sit on the bed beside Jakob.

"Now, Jakob, what I have to say is very important. Grandma Gertie needs our help, and I thought it might be a good idea if she stayed here with us. All the time."

"That would be wonderful!" Jakob said excitedly.

"Yes," Amalie replied calmly, trying to quiet Jakob to make sure that he would consider the situation and not just respond out of excitement. "But there's something else. If Gertie came to stay here, she would stay in your bedroom."

"With me?" Jakob asked.

"No. You would sleep in the living room again."

Jakob was struck silent by this. He liked having his own room, and it would be hard for him to give it up, just as Amalie knew it would be.

"How long?" Jakob asked pragmatically.

"I don't know. A few months . . . maybe even a year."

Amalie watched Jakob's face as he knit his brow and pondered the situation, balancing his feelings for Grandma Gertie against how much he wanted a room of his own. Amalie studied his face—the blue eyes, the straight thin nose he had inherited from his father's side of the family—and watched as he sat there thinking hard about this grave problem.

"Ja!" he finally said with assurance, knowing that this was the answer he had intended to give all along. He knew how happy it would make Grandma Gertie.

"Thank you, little love," Amalie said, as she gave him a hug and laid him back down in his bed, pulling the sheet and blanket up around his face. "And remember, you mustn't tell anyone we talked about this until I've had a chance to talk with your father and Gertie."

"Yes, Mutti."

"Now go to sleep for real. Gute Nacht, Liebling. Schlaft gut!"[10]

She went to the front closet and got her briefcase, bringing it into the kitchen. Sitting down at the kitchen table and spreading out her papers, she began to map out her plan of attack, the method by which she would track down Hitler's family and his past. She spent the next few hours going over a map of Austria and train schedules and, finally, writing a letter to her father telling him that she and Jakob would be coming. She had decided it would be a good time for Jakob to see his grandfather again, and it would also give her a good cover so that no one would suspect it was anything other than a social visit.

At eleven o'clock, she put away all her papers and sealed the letter, then sat on the sofa in the living room reading the newspaper, waiting for her husband to come home. It was just a little after midnight when Gunther came in.

---

[10]"Good night, Darling. Sleep well."

"Amalie! You're still up."

"Yes. I was hoping you wouldn't be too late."

"What time is it?" Gunther asked. He seemed just a little drunk.

"Not too late," Amalie said, not wanting to challenge him since she needed to talk to him about the trip to Salzburg and also about Gertrude.

"It was a special night," Gunther began. "A farewell party."

"Oh?" Amalie said, feigning interest. "Who's leaving?"

"Friedrich," he said.

"What?" Amalie shot back.

"Friedrich has decided to try his luck in Berlin," Gunther said calmly, as he put away his hat and coat and walked into the living room. "He hasn't found a job, and he can't stand living off his mother. He says she can't support the two of them much longer."

There was a silence as Gunther sat down on the sofa next to Amalie, watching her face and waiting for her response..

"Gertie knew this might happen," Amalie said sadly. "We just talked about it tonight."

"Well," Gunther countered, "I told Friedrich that we would watch out for Gertie."

"Good," Amalie said thoughtfully. "Gunther . . . I want to ask you something, but I want you to think about it before answering. Just promise me you'll think about it."

"This sounds ominous."

"Gertie told me that she has to give up her apartment next month and find something cheaper."

"I didn't know it was that bad."

"Well, I thought perhaps . . . ," Amalie continued cautiously, then blurted out the rest. "If Gertie moved in with us, she could pay us a little rent and we could have a live-in babysitter for Jakob, and I talked to Jakob and he said he wouldn't mind sleeping in the living room . . . and we could all somehow get by together."

Gunther was stunned, not necessarily at the thought of Gertie moving in, but by Amalie's ability to say all that in one breath. "I guess we could try it."

Amalie was completely taken off guard by his sudden acquiescence. "We could?"

"Yes. I promised Friedrich we would watch out for her."

Amalie reached over and hugged her husband. "Sometimes I forget how wonderful you are."

"And then I remind you," he said with a smile, returning her hug. "Well, we'd better get to bed. It's late."

"One more thing," Amalie said, holding onto Gunther's hand to keep him from leaving the sofa.

"What is it?" he asked cautiously.

"I know we can't afford it, but . . ."

"Oh no. What can't we live without now?"

"No, really," Amalie said playfully. "Since I'm already going to Ried, and since Mr. Frieder is paying for that, I thought maybe I could take Jakob with me on Friday, and after I'm done working we could go on to Salzburg to visit Father."

"I suppose we could manage that," Gunther again conceded. "Is there anything else," he asked playfully, "or can we go to bed now?"

"No, that's everything," Amalie said, snuggling

close to her husband as they walked to the bedroom.

CHAPTER 7

Nineteen twenty-three was clearly the worst year of the runaway inflation associated with the Weimar Republic. The Germans had been consistently running behind on reparations payments until finally being forced to ask for a complete moratorium on reparations to give the German economy a chance to revive. The proposed moratorium made for a number of stormy meetings of the Allied Reparation Commission, which resulted in the departure of the British representatives. The French, left without opposition, issued orders for a military occupation of the industrialized Ruhr region of Germany, where they would have their own troops run the factories and deliver the finished products directly to French markets. The German government reacted swiftly to the military occupation by devaluing their currency even more, so that they could meet the French demands for reparations with virtually worthless currency rather than allowing the French to cripple German industry. But it was a Pyrrhic victory for the German government, as opposition to the new republic grew even stronger among an embittered German populace that was ultimately paying the price for the Weimar's desperate economic strategy.

Otto Maus, the author with whom Amalie was working in Ried, was not terribly comfortable with children, although he didn't dislike them. When he opened the door that Friday, he found not only Amalie, but her six-year-old son standing at her side looking up at him.

"Are you my Grandfather Ethan?"

"No, Jakob!" Amalie said with a bit of embarrassment. "I told you I had to do some work here first and then we'll be going to Salzburg. That's where your grandfather is."

Amalie smiled at Otto. "I'm sorry, Otto, but I had a chance to visit my father in Salzburg after we finish today, and I hope it isn't a problem that I brought my son Jakob. Herr Maus, this is Jakob. Jakob, this is Herr Maus."

"Guten tag, Jakob," Otto said as he bent over a little, taking Jakob's hand and shaking it lightly.

"Hallo," Jakob replied shyly.

"I'm sure he will be no problem," Amalie said apologetically. "He will be very quiet while we finish up."

With that, Otto ushered them into his home, leading Jakob into the living room. Like most of the other rooms in the house, it was filled with bookcases, but it was not like Sam Frieder's book-filled home, which Amalie had visited the month before. Otto's house was meticulously cared for, which Amalie found surprising, since Otto was a bachelor and she assumed that any bachelor's house would be a shambles.

"Do you read well?" Otto asked Jakob, as he placed a hand on the little boy's shoulder and directed him to a large, shiny leather chair.

"Yes, he does," Amalie answered for Jakob, who was now acting very shy, apparently overwhelmed by the luxurious surroundings.

The heavy leather chairs looked so new that they could just as well have come from a store that morning, and the lamps had shades of green- and almond-colored tiffany glass, all set on brightly polished brass bases. There was a deep blue carpet, thicker than the grass of the English Garden, which showed no wear at all and went from wall to wall of the room. Even the leather-bound books behind the cabinet doors, with their lead crystal windows, looked as though they had just been polished.

"He was reading when he was four," Amalie continued. "My father is a publisher, and he started me reading young, and we did the same with Jakob."

"Excellent!" Otto said, looking at Amalie and acknowledging her pride without question. He turned to one of the bookcases and unlocked the door, pulling out a book and then locking the door again. *What kind of man locks up all of his books?* Amalie thought to herself.

Otto knelt in front of Jakob, who was in danger of being swallowed up by the huge leather chair surrounding him.

"This is the first book I wrote," Otto began, as he opened it and paged through to the title page. "It did very well. Many boys about your age . . . well, maybe a little older . . . Well, I've gotten a number of letters from boys saying how much they liked it." Otto closed the book and tapped the cover thoughtfully as he looked out a window at the snow-covered street. *"The Tears of the Desert,"* he said absent-mindedly, repeating the title of the book out loud. "I was just starting then." He suddenly slapped the book against his other hand and turned back to Amalie and Jakob. "But that was a long time ago. You read it now while your mother and I do our work, and then you can tell me if you think it's any good." He handed Jakob the book and gave him a little chuck under the chin and a pat on the head before wandering off to his study.

Amalie stayed behind for just a moment until Otto was out of earshot, then turned to Jakob. "Now, Liebling, please don't touch anything. We should only be an hour or so, and please, please don't play with anything. We could never afford to replace anything here if you break it!" She gave him a quick kiss on the cheek and followed after Otto.

Jakob sat in the chair and opened the book, looking at the title page. *The Tears of the Desert,* he thought to himself. *What a dumb name!* The book smelled old and musty as Jakob glanced at a few pages, then quickly flipped through the rest, producing a fine dust that blew up and filled his nostrils. His eyes followed the dust particles as they floated into a sunbeam, creating a small cloud over his head. Looking up, he noticed a painting above the fireplace.

It was a picture of American Indians on a buffalo hunt, sitting astride their horses around a buffalo, aiming their arrows at its shoulder. Jakob climbed out of the chair and crossed the room to the fireplace. He had never even heard of Indians or buffalo, so he didn't really understand what was going on in this picture of half-naked men with arms outstretched, holding bows, riding on horses without saddles as they surrounded the huge, dark brown beast. Beside the fireplace mantel, he spotted a table that looked like a box with a glass top. Inside the box were little figures of men, some half-naked like the ones in the painting and the rest in blue uniforms. He couldn't have known that this was Otto's careful reproduction of the famous Battle of the Little Bighorn, but nonetheless he was fascinated by the little toys in the glass-covered box. He suddenly remembered his mother's warning about not touching anything, and even though he really wanted to open the box, he didn't. He dutifully returned to the big leather chair and opened the book, doing just as he had been told.

The next couple of hours passed quickly as Jakob found himself immersed in Otto's book about cowboys killing Indians in the Old West. He learned that the Indians had killed poor innocent settlers and little settler children, who hadn't done anything to make the Indians hate them. The story portrayed the Indians as mean and murderous, even the women and the children, and the cowboys as strong and good and determined to bring the Indians to justice.

Otto and Amalie were laughing as they came out of the study. "Jakob," Amalie called out, "we're going to leave now." Jakob continued reading without moving as Amalie and Otto continued talking.

"It's been a pleasure, Otto," Amalie said.

"Yes indeed," Otto concurred. "It has been very nice having such company."

"Well, I thank you for putting up with Jakob today."

"Oh, not at all! I never heard a sound out of him." Otto then turned to Jakob and smiled at the close attention the little boy was paying to his first published work. "You like it then, Jakob?" he asked.

Jakob, his mouth open as he continued to read, didn't even turn to look at Otto as he nodded his head.

"Jakob," Amalie interjected, "it's time to go now. Leave the book and come put on your jacket."

Once again, Jakob did exactly as he was told and closed the book, handing it to Otto as he passed him.

"No, Jakob, you take it. It's yours," Otto said.

"That's very kind of you," said Amalie. "Jakob, what do you say?"

"Thank you, Herr Maus," Jakob recited obediently.

"But there is something you can do for me in return," Otto quickly rejoined.

"Certainly, Otto. What is it?" Amalie asked.

"One last lunch together?" he asked in reply.

Amalie smiled. "Otto, you've been so kind. We couldn't possibly impose—"

"Amalie," Otto said, taking her hands in his, "I so rarely have guests, and all this week you've been like the first gentle breeze of spring here. Please do me the honor."

"Thank you, Otto," Amalie acquiesced graciously, and the three of them went around the corner to the small café where Otto always had his lunch.

Through the course of the lunch, Otto told Jakob about some of his experiences in the American West, although all of the information was only secondhand and Otto had merely been a tourist tramping around the old battle grounds and sites where unarmed Indians had been massacred by American troopers.

Otto actually had a fairly good grasp of the situation of American Indians and the disgraceful treatment the United States government had visited against them, unlike some of his contemporaries. Many other German writers of the same genre had never even been to America and so had little historical basis for the stories they wrote, but even though Otto had a good idea of what had really happened to the American Indian, he rarely told the truth in his books because he felt it lacked dramatic impact. Where was the nobility in trained, well-armed U.S. Cavalrymen riding down on unarmed innocents, slashing them with sabers and shooting them? Where was the glory in forcing the defeated Indian nations onto reservations where hunting tribes were suddenly supposed to metamorphose into agrarians, farming land that wasn't even fit to grow rocks? Where was the heroism in the great General George Armstrong Custer routinely delivering disease-infested blankets to reservation Indians in the hope of infecting them so that an epidemic would ravage the few remaining tribes? More important, how many books could he sell if he told of these things? So he simply ignored the facts and wrote books designed to make money, to excite the young boys who might buy them and create a great heroic myth of the American frontier, where white men were destined to tame and rule a savage land.

The mythology of the American frontier wasn't much different from the world view fostered by the rampant nationalism and Pan-Germanism that had permeated German society at the turn of the century and up through the early years of the war. Although that attitude certainly waned during the war and throughout the Weimar years, it would soon become stronger than ever, accompanied by the musical score of a new national anthem: "Deutschland über alles."[11]

Amalie slept for most of the trip to Salzburg while Jakob continued to read his new book. When they finally arrived, Amalie began to feel a bit anxious about the purpose of their visit. This wasn't just a happy reunion; this was to be a mission to coopt her father and convince him to join her in her strange plan.

Ethan Stein was waiting on the platform, watching each window as it passed, looking for his daughter and grandson. It had been such a long time, and such an important time for Jakob. How much he must have changed in almost four years. Was he already six years old? Or was he still five? Ethan was trying to remember Jakob's birthday and count off the years when he suddenly found himself face to face with his daughter as she leaned out the window of her compartment, almost close enough to kiss him, as the train kept going slower and slower until it finally gave one last rumbling shake before coming to rest.

"Father! Father!" Amalie called out just before ducking back into the compartment and gathering up the two old suitcases, the precious new briefcase, and of course, Jakob, and quickly working her way down the narrow passageway of the coach car. Dropping her bags unceremoniously in front of

---

[11]"Germany above everything."

Ethan, she wrapped herself around her speechless father and kissed him several times on the cheek. She then picked up Jakob and fairly threw him into his grandfather's arms.

"Look, Jakob," she said excitedly, "it's your Grandfather Ethan."

Ethan, usually a rather reserved and dignified man who wouldn't dream of making a scene in public, at first seemed taken aback by Amalie's effusive show of affection. But as he looked at the beautiful grandson he suddenly held in his arms, Ethan's face broke into a gentle smile and he hugged the boy tightly.

Jakob hadn't been sure he would recognize his grandfather. Back in Munich, when his mother had told him that they were going for a visit, Jakob had tried to picture him but couldn't really remember what he looked like. There was the photograph in the living room on the table, but it seemed so stiff and formal. But then he felt Ethan's arms tightening around him and suddenly it just felt right. The old man's touch. The smell of pipe tobacco. The gentle look in Ethan's eyes. Yes, this was Jakob's grandfather.

As they arrived at the front of the station, Amalie started to hail a cab.

"Amalie!" Ethan called out. "There's no need."

"Don't worry, Father," she said. "I can afford it. We don't need to take the trolley."

"No, Amalie!" her father protested again. "I've bought a motorcar. It's over here."

"A motorcar?"

"Secondhand," Ethan replied.

"Well! Things must be going nicely."

"Things are . . . well, they are going well enough now, but who knows about tomorrow?"

"Oh, Father. Always the pessimist," Amalie said, but as she said it she thought of how things were going in Munich, particularly the plight of Gertrude and Friedrich.

"It's not that," Ethan said as Amalie caught up to him as he headed to the parking spot where the small touring car waited. "I bought it because a friend begged me to. I feel as though I took advantage of him."

"Did you pay a fair price?" Amalie asked, knowing that her father would never intentionally cheat a man, no matter what the conditions.

"Yes, but still . . . " Ethan hedged.

"And if you hadn't bought it," Amalie continued "someone else would have who probably wouldn't have been fair."

"I suppose," Ethan acknowledged, "but I still don't feel good about it."

"You did the best you could, Father," Amalie said, understanding his ambivalence and trying to put his mind at ease as they loaded her luggage into the back.

Ethan turned out to be a good driver, which genuinely impressed Amalie, since she had never thought of her father as being mechanically inclined. When something broke in their house, even if minor in nature, it was either stored so that it could be repaired "someday" or thrown away and quickly replaced. She remembered thinking as a child that she must never break a bone or she might end up on the curb, waiting to be picked up by the rubbish man.

Amalie talked incessantly throughout the car ride. Unlike many other travelers, when Amalie slept on a train, she found it to be a restful sleep, so by the time they got to the house she was wide awake and filled with excitement at returning home. Jakob, on the other hand, was ready for a good nap, and Ethan showed him to his bedroom as soon as they arrived.

Father and daughter sat at the table in the dining room and talked for hours, catching up on family news and politics and discussing work and the state of the world. Ethan was pleased to find that his daughter had matured significantly in the time since she had left home just as the war was ending. He found it easy to talk intelligently with her about a wide range of subjects. She even seemed to have lost some of her childish prejudices against Judaism, which had been born during that period of rebellion all children go through as they begin to separate from their parents.

"I heard from Eleonore the other day," Ethan said, moving on to a new subject.

"Eleonore! My God, I can't believe how long it's been since I've seen her," Amalie exclaimed.

"Not since you left . . . almost four years ago now."

"How are she and her professor?"

"She's fine. Louis is almost tenured at the university."

"I always thought it ironic that my sister would marry someone on his way to becoming a botany professor, and she with her terrible hay fever."

Ethan laughed at the thought. "I remember how

she would stay inside for a whole month at a time."

"She lost so many boyfriends because she couldn't stop sneezing and blowing her nose," Amalie said, laughing along.

"I received a very unexpected letter just a few weeks ago," Ethan said, once their mirth subsided.

"From whom?" Amalie asked.

"Do you remember the Steins from Breslau?"

"Breslau?"

"Yes . . . in eastern Germany."

"Of course I know Breslau is in Germany!" Amalie said, as though her father was patronizing her. "I just don't remember hearing about the Stein family in Breslau."

"They're distant relations . . . third cousins twice removed or second cousins thrice removed," Ethan said in mock despair. "I can never keep those things straight. Anyway, the point is that I received a letter from Edith Stein, who passed on greetings from her mother as well as news of their family, part of which was something I found very strange indeed. She said that she was changing from a Jew to a Catholic."

"What do you mean?" asked Amalie, pretending ignorance, then adding facetiously, "Is she changing from one boyfriend to another?"

"No, Amalie," her father said as they both laughed again. "But I don't understand why someone would change from a Jew to a Catholic. It seems that both have their share of problems. I might understand changing from Jew to Protestant. Whoever heard of a pogrom against the Protestants?"

That brought another short burst of laughter

from each of them, but this time it was gallows humor. *Pogrom* is a Russian word meaning "devastation" that eventually came to refer to attacks on the Jews throughout Europe. The Jews had been persecuted since the Diaspora, the time when they were forced out of their homeland of Israel. Although some Jews remained in what would become Palestine, the majority traveled throughout the continent of Europe looking for new homes, and for centuries they were faced with pogroms ranging from the crusades to the inquisition and all the other lesser tortures visited against them from Vladivostok to Toledo.

"Where does Edith live now?" Amalie asked.

"Göttingen," Ethan replied.

"The university?"

"Yes."

"Is she a student?"

"She was. She graduated last year."

"What course?"

"Something strange. Some sort of philosophy called 'Phenomenology.'"

"What on earth . . . ?" Amalie asked, having no idea what Phenomenology could be.

"Well," Ethan began pensively, "as near as I can make out, some professor named . . ." He paused, trying to remember. "Husserl!" he said proudly, as though he had pulled the name out of thin air like a magician. "Yes, Edmund Husserl started it, and if I recall correctly, his theory is that an event that does not leave physical evidence can only be explained in terms of that phenomenon, a description of the event itself."

"It sounds like some sort of theological study," Amalie said

"Strange you should say that. That's exactly the way Edith put it. She says all her college study ties into the Catholic theology and their faith in miracles, and so on."

"Well," Amalie said, "you know I've never been much of one for religion."

"There might be something else behind it, though," Ethan said, as though just now making a connection from the rest of the information in the letter. "She said that she had been denied some sort of chair position at the university, and there wasn't much else that she could do with her degree other than teaching."

"You think she's converting because the university turned her down?" Amalie asked incredulously.

"Oh no," Ethan said, defending Edith's decision. "I wouldn't go that far. I wouldn't say that was the whole reason, but maybe it had something to do with it."

"Perhaps," Amalie allowed.

The conversation stopped for a moment, and Amalie thought this might be a good time to bring up her "mission."

"Father . . . there is something going on that I need to talk with you about. I need your help."

"What is it?" Ethan asked with a concern that matched his daughter's serious tone.

"First of all, I want to tell you that this might turn out to be nothing, and you can certainly say so if you feel I'm just being ridiculous."

"Yes, Amalie. Fine. Just tell me what it is."

"There is a political group in Munich that has me worried."

"Only one?" Ethan said, proffering his opinion about the confused state of politics in Munich since the war.

"Yes. One in particular."

"Which one?"

"They are called the German National Socialist Workers Party."

"I've heard of them," Ethan said as he tried to remember what they represented. "Right wing . . . anti-Semitic. They draw strongly from ex-soldiers."

"Yes."

"Why them? Why do they worry you in particular?"

"That's not important," Amalie said evasively.

"Well, there must be something that . . . Oh, my God," Ethan said, a stunned look on his face as he made the connection between ex-soldiers and his own son-in-law. "It's Gunther, isn't it?"

Amalie said nothing, trying to maintain a poker face, but then realized how ridiculous she had been to think that her father wouldn't have guessed.

Ethan persisted, a bit calmer now. "Gunther has joined these . . ." Ethan was at a loss for a derogatory epithet and finally rephrased his question in the most direct and accusing manner. "He's joined them, hasn't he?"

Amalie couldn't see any way to deny it. "It's not the way you think," she offered defensively.

"Then why are you worried? If it's not what I think, then why did you come all this way? That's why you came, isn't it? The real reason. There is trouble, and you need my help." Ethan's concern was obviously rising as he piled question on top of question, trying to get a straight answer but not giving his daughter a chance to speak.

"I just want to avoid trouble," she said quietly. "Gunther only joined because many of the soldiers he fought with in the trenches have joined. He joined because he had friends who joined, not because he hates Jews. He's a good man, a good husband and father who just needs to have his eyes opened."

There was silence as father and daughter sat facing each other. Ethan felt very frustrated. He had just been thinking how mature and intelligent his daughter was, and now here she was insisting that she should stay with a man who would join a political party of avowed anti-Semites.

Amalie also felt frustrated. She felt her father was just jumping to conclusions, assuming that this was all that there was to Gunther, assuming that he couldn't be saved . . . that he wasn't a good man.

"What do you want? What do you want me to do?" Ethan finally asked, staring down at the table.

"I want to find out about their leader. It seems as though he is the whole party. If he were discredited, the whole group might fall apart," Amalie said, finally revealing her plan and for the first time admitting to herself that her goal was to try to destroy the party.

"Amalie," Ethan said as he raised his head and made deliberate eye contact with his daughter. "These are dangerous people! They are extremists. Who knows what they are capable of, or what they might do to someone who interferes with them."

"I have to do this, Father. I don't know if I will find anything, but I have to try, and I need your help. I will do it with or without you, but I really hoped you would help."

Ethan was suddenly afraid for this headstrong daughter of his. That old attitude of hers was once again evident in the stubborn set of her jaw. But now there was something more. There was courage and determination in her eyes, and he knew she wasn't going to back down.

The next day Amalie made the trip by train to Linz, leaving Jakob in the care of her father. She had to change to a bus to get to Leonding from the Linz train station, and not long after she found herself at the foot of a small hill leading up to a Catholic church, where once again she decided to start by looking through the cemetery. She quickly came upon the stoic and forbidding image of Alois Hitler set in a weathered granite headstone. Blackened by the constant wash of chimney soot and dirt, the stone stood in stark contrast to the heavy snow that surrounded it. "Born 1837, died 1903," Amalie read to herself. Brushing away the snow, she found another portrait, this one of Klara Hitler with the inscription: "Born 1860, died 1907."

Amalie then went inside the church, and using the same story she had used in Braunau, succeeded in convincing the priest that she was Liesl Kraus, a reporter looking for information on a local man who had made good in Munich. She found out that Adolf and his mother and sister had lived in the house just past the wall of the cemetery for years after Alois Hitler had died. She also learned that in addition to Spital am Pyhrn, Spital am Semmering, and Spittal, there was yet another place named Spital, a small village near the town of Weitra, only about forty kilometers from Leonding. Contrary to what the priest in Braunau had told her, it was this small town where Klara Pölzl, Adolf Hitler's mother, was born and where she eventually met Alois Hitler, his father.

The trip to Leonding only took about three hours, and all during the return trip Amalie was planning for the next day. Should she take the train, or might she convince her father to drive her in the car?

When she entered her father's house, she found Jakob sitting on his grandfather's lap, holding a menorah in his hands. Ethan stopped speaking as Amalie entered, embarrassed by the fact that he was explaining what a menorah was to Jakob and not sure how she might react. He remembered how antagonistic his daughter was toward the Jewish religion by the time she had left for Munich, and he had no reason to believe she had changed her attitude. Jakob was Jewish by virtue of his mother being Jewish, so when Jakob asked what the funny candleholder was, Ethan felt compelled to explain the meaning of Hanukkah.

"So," Amalie said, a playful lilt to her voice as she broke the silence, trying to join in on their lesson. "I see Jakob found the menorah."

Ethan was intuitive enough to see that his daughter was giving him permission to continue, and so he cautiously resumed the lesson.

"Well . . . I was just telling Jakob how we start by lighting one candle, and then we light two, then three, and so on, so that as Hanukkah continues, each night we are bringing more light into the world."

"And did you tell him the rest?" Amalie asked as she knelt in front of her father and son, looking into Jakob's eyes. "Dreidls and Hanukkah geld and all the family coming for dinner?"

"I wasn't sure you remembered," Ethan interjected as his daughter attempted to create a fantasy of her childhood memories.

"I remember being a child," Amalie said pointedly to her father, "but I left childish things behind me."

"Now you're quoting the New Testament?" Ethan countered.

Amalie bristled at this remark, but she didn't want to get into it.

"What is the 'New Testament'?" Jakob interrupted.

"Well," Ethan began, turning his attention back to his grandson, "the first five books of the Bible are called the Old Testament, or the Jews call it the Torah or Pentateuch."

"The Jews?" Jakob said absent-mindedly as he looked down at the menorah his grandfather was still holding, saying it just because he remembered that he was a Jew.

"Yes," Ethan continued, "God chose the Jews to receive the Torah."

Jakob looked up at his grandfather. "Father doesn't like the Jews."

Ethan was struck by this much in the same way

that his daughter had been struck years before when Jakob had first questioned Amalie about what a Jew was. The child's situation was heartbreaking to Ethan. It was bad enough within the Jewish community to fear the outside world, but to have fear like that within one's own family.

Ethan looked up at his daughter, who appeared upset, as though her son had revealed a terrible secret. She took Jakob's hand and pulled him off his grandfather's lap.

"Come along, Jakob," she said, trying to pretend there was nothing wrong. "Let's make lunch together, you and I."

There was no more talk about it. Lunch consisted of sandwiches and small talk, and the afternoon drifted aimlessly until Amalie finally found the resolve to ask her father to make the trip with her to Spital the next day. He agreed without question. It was clear that he was with her. He now had some idea of what she faced at home, and knew that it must be hard enough on her, so he decided to let the past be and try to help however he could.

It was a Sunday morning in February when Ethan, Amalie, and Jakob arrived in Spital. Amalie was lucky that her father had offered to drive, since Spital was such a small village that there was no train station and bus service was unreliable. Amalie told Jakob that she was going to visit an old friend by herself, and as prearranged, her father drove past the small church and dropped her off a few blocks away. She wanted to make sure that Jakob didn't see her go into the church and start asking questions later. Ethan told Amalie not to worry, he and Jakob would just go riding in the motor car and be back in about an hour to pick her up.

It was in Spital that Amalie found the family history of Klara Pölzl, Hitler's mother, and traced her family, that of Johann Pölzl and Johanna Hiedler, to another small town about forty kilometers to the east called Dollersheim. Amalie had just left the church as Ethan pulled up with Jakob, and she told them they had to make one more stop.

The Austrian back roads between villages were rough and icy, with steep hills that made travel slow in the cold, open little car. Ethan was afraid the car might not make it up some of the steeper hills. It took two hours to travel from Spital to Dollersheim, a trip that under better conditions would have taken less than half that time. It was almost two o'clock in the afternoon, with only a couple of hours of daylight left. They had not yet had lunch, and even though they had eaten a large breakfast before taking off that morning, Jakob was beginning to fuss and complain. Once again Ethan dropped Amalie off, and Amalie said she would have lunch with her fictitious friend while Jakob and her father would find a restaurant.

Amalie was beginning to wonder if any of this was worthwhile until she finally saw the records of Alois Hitler. The entry under his birth listed him as Alois Schicklgruber, and at some point the name Schicklgruber had been crossed off and the name Hitler had been written in without any further notations. Finally she had found something curious, but what did it mean?

The priest she had been talking to was evasive at

first, then suggested that she might talk to the priest who had served the Dollersheim parish before him, Father Brumgart, who was now more than eighty years old and living in a monastery near Weitra.

"Did you have a good lunch?" Amalie asked a short time later as she got back into the car.

"Yes, we brought a sandwich in case you were still hungry," Ethan said, still sticking to the story that Amalie had been visiting an old friend.

"Thank you," Amalie said appreciatively as she quickly unwrapped the sandwich. "You know," she said thoughtfully between bites, "there is someone else I would like to visit . . ."

Ethan shot a glance at her, and from the look on Amalie's face, he could tell that she was on to something.

"Oh yes . . . your school friend in . . . where does she live now?"

"Weitra," Amalie said, swallowing a large bite of her sandwich.

"Yes, Weitra . . . but it will be getting dark soon. We could only just make it home before it starts getting really cold."

"I know," Amalie said. "I thought I might call Gunther and tell him we're staying one more day. I could go to Weitra by train. Is there any chance that Jakob could stay with you tomorrow?"

"I think so," Ethan replied. "I don't have much planned tomorrow, and I have a wonderful woman who comes in to clean every Monday. I think she and Jakob would hit it off for a couple of hours. Yes, I think we could do that."

By the time they got home, it was after dark and

the temperature had dropped to well below freezing. They all rushed into the house, and Ethan hurriedly began a fire that quickly filled the living room with warmth and the scent of pine as he threw a few pine needles into the blaze. He and Jakob watched the fire as the needles hissed and popped with tiny explosions of yellow flame.

Amalie had gone into the kitchen to check on their dinner, a venison stew she had started on a low flame in the oven before they had left that morning, and she soon returned to the living room to join her father and her son. Stopping in the doorway, she watched as the two knelt before the fireplace, where Ethan was allowing Jakob to throw a few of the pine needles on the fire by himself and warning him not to put on too many. It was a pleasant scene as she saw the wonder on Jakob's face with the light of the fire dancing about the room and her father with his hand on Jakob's shoulder.

It took a while, but Amalie finally managed to get a telephone call through to Munich after dinner. Gunther wasn't home, but Gertrude was there. She had made dinner for Gunther and was cleaning up, almost ready to leave. Gertrude took Amalie's message and left a note for Gunther that Amalie would be staying one more day, coming back early Tuesday, and she also agreed to call Mr. Frieder and tell him that Amalie would be a day late getting back to work.

The next day Amalie arrived in Weitra at eight-thirty in the morning, and about an hour later she found her way to the austere-looking monastery a few kilometers west of the city. Once again introducing herself as Liesl Kraus, she was able to get Father

Brumgart to agree to talk with her, but he seemed as cautious as the priest who had directed her to Weitra. Amalie at first thought that he was put off by her saying that she was a reporter, and that he wouldn't be of much help, but it soon became apparent to her that Father Brumgart's cautious attitude was more a product of his rarely having visitors than of his having anything to hide. He soon warmed up to Amalie and was happy to have a visitor who had come to talk just with him, someone who treated him as though he were important and interesting rather than just another resident of the monastery to be bathed, dressed, and fed.

Amalie let the priest talk a while before directing his conversation to Alois Hitler, and to her pleasant surprise, Father Brumgart remembered the occasion of the notation made in the birth records at Dollersheim.

"I don't tell you this lightly, Fraulein Kraus," the old priest began, pausing to look Amalie directly in the eye to make the importance of his point clear to her. "I will tell you this because I believe the truth is important. Father Strauchler was a good man, a good priest, and he only did what he thought was best . . ."

"Who was Father Strauchler?" Amalie asked, afraid that the old priest was getting lost in his reverie and wouldn't be able to give her any useful information.

"Father Strauchler," the old priest began laboriously, as though trying to keep the story straight while having to stop and deal with Amalie's interruption, "was the priest at Dollersheim when I arrived.

He was the one who actually dealt with . . . the problem."

Amalie was about to ask what problem Father Brumgart meant, but she thought better of it as the priest was apparently struggling to form the story into its proper chronology.

"They came to say that the boy, Alois, who was born a bastard, was now accepted as the son of Hiedler, but it was actually Alois' uncle who came to correct the name, since Alois' father was dead by then."

"Hiedler?" Amalie asked. "Don't you mean Hitler?"

"It's all the same . . . the same man," Father Brumgart said, waving aside the question as pointless.

"Father Strauchler spelled it wrong?" Amalie asked.

"Spelling wasn't important," said the old priest.

Amalie thought a moment and then checked her notes. Wasn't Hiedler the name of Klara Pölzl's mother? This was getting confusing. Adolf Hitler's grandfather on his father's side was named Hiedler and his grandmother on his mother's side was also named Hiedler.

"Was this the same Hiedler family from Spital?" Amalie finally asked.

"Yes, they were from Spital."

"Do you remember a woman named Klara Pölzl?" Amalie pressed on.

"Yes, yes," the old priest said with the hint of a smile. "I see why you look confused. The son . . . Alois . . . he married more than once and his last wife was . . ." Father Brumgart stopped a minute and squinted as he tried to remember the relationship between Alois and his last wife. "Yes, that's it! His third wife was his niece! Klara was Alois' wife and also his niece," the old man said with a smile and a little laugh at the scandal of it.

Amalie was careful to not react so that the old priest wouldn't think he had said too much. They went on to discuss the gossip he had heard about the family over the years. He told Amalie that Alois had left home when he was about thirteen, two years after his mother had died at their home in Spital.

"Father Strauchler," Amalie started her question as she looked over her notes, "it looks as though Alois' father's name was written in after his mother and father were both dead?"

Father Brumgart hesitated before answering, knowing that it was illegal to enter a change in those records without the proper documents, which should have included a statement from the mother. Such a statement would have been impossible in this case, however, since Alois' mother had died years before the Hiedler family had come forward to accept paternity. That was why the change in the church records hadn't been dated.

"Yes," the priest finally admitted after a long pause. "As I have stated, Father Strauchler was a good priest and tried to do what was best. What good would be served by denying the man his father's name?"

They continued talking for a while, but since Father Brumgart had no more information about the Hiedler family, Amalie tried several times to break off the conversation. It wasn't easy though, since it was apparent that Father Brumgart hadn't had any visitors for a long time and wasn't ready to let Amalie go.

When Amalie finally escaped, she determined that she had to go back to Spital again to see if she could find out anything more from other sources. It was almost ten o'clock that night when she finally returned home to find Ethan sitting in a chair in front of the fireplace, reading a book.

"My, my," Amalie said, obviously in a good mood as she hung her coat in the hall closet and breezed up to the fireplace to get warm. "I thought I'd never make it home."

"I was beginning to wonder myself. I was getting nervous," Ethan admitted. "I trust it was a successful trip."

"You'll never guess!"

"Skeletons in the closet?"

"His grandfather was Jewish!"

"What?" Ethan asked incredulously.

"Well," Amalie started as she sat down next to Ethan, calming a bit as she spoke, "I don't have any proof yet, but I talked to a few people in Spital after talking to the priest in Weitra and the . . . well, they say that Hitler's father, Alois, married his own niece, Klara. Alois was a bastard, and the rumor in Spital is that the father was a Jew, but it was covered up by the Hiedler family.

"Hiedler?" Ethan asked. "Where does Hiedler come into it?"

"Hiedler is Hitler," Amalie explained. "It was a misspelling in the church records. Hitler's father . . .

well, his grandmother . . . was named Schicklgruber, and for some reason a man named Hiedler said he was the father when this Alois, Hitler's father, was almost forty years old."

"Amalie, I don't understand this at all. Hiedler was Jewish?"

"It's all very confusing . . . I don't think Hiedler was Jewish, and the rumor seems to be that Hiedler wasn't Alois' father, even though Hiedler said he was the father, but he didn't come forward until Alois was middle aged."

"But if only the father was Jewish, then the boy isn't Jewish."

"Father, we're not talking about Halakah.[12] These people consider any Jewish blood a curse."

There was a pause as they both considered the implications of this revelation.

"Proof," Amalie said out of the blue.

"What?" her father asked, having been lost in his own thoughts.

"How do we get proof? What would be good proof, and just how important is this?" Amalie said, laying out the problem to her father.

"Well, I don't know how far he carries his anti-Semitic program," Ethan responded, analyzing the possibilities, "but I would say that the key is whether his anti-Semitism is just rhetoric, or if it's the foundation of their party. If this hatred of Jews is a large part of his program, then this information could be his downfall, but only if you have good, solid proof...

[12]A simple definition would be that Halakah is a Judaic legal code, but it is more than that, having to do with the oral tradition of the Talmud.

and if that proof is presented by gentiles, not by Jews."

"I have to leave tomorrow," Amalie said, once again seeming to pull a thought from out of nowhere, but of course this thought was the next logical step, because if there was proof to be found, it would most likely be in Spital.

"I know," Ethan replied.

"Is there any chance that you...," Amalie hesitated.

"Of course," he said simply.

"You don't even know what I was going to ask," Amalie said, pretending to be irritated at her father's presumption.

Ethan picked up his pipe from the small table beside his chair. "You want me . . . ," he began, then stopped to strike a match and draw on the pipe to light it, completing his sentence once the pipe began to produce its sweet-smelling smoke, ". . . to spend some time in Spital trying to find some foundation for these rumors."

"I think this might be important," Amalie said seriously.

"So do I," her father replied.

"Thank you, Father," Amalie said as she got up and gave her father a kiss on the forehead. "I'm going to get something to eat, and then I had better get to bed so we can catch our train in the morning."

As she a Jakob waited to board the train the next morning, Amalie felt sad at leaving, and yet she was happy she had come because she and her father had gotten past a very strained period in their relationship, one that had culminated in her leaving home in 1918. It seemed to her that he had changed so much, but when she thought about it, she realized that she had been the one who had changed, or at least she had changed the most.

Jakob wrapped his arms and legs around his grandfather in an expression of childish abandon, and Ethan held his grandson tightly, showing the same love in return.

Ethan recalled that he had not been so open and demonstrative with his daughter when she was a child. *Perhaps I've changed a lot since then*, he thought to himself, and he smiled as he let Jakob down.

"Take care of yourself," Ethan said seriously to his daughter as they embraced. "Remember what I said," he cautioned, "and be careful. These men could be dangerous."

"Oh, Father," Amalie said as an afterthought before getting on the train, "when you are looking for information on that matter we spoke of . . ." At this point, Amalie left Jakob standing by the steps of the rail car and walked back to her father, glancing around to make sure no one was within earshot. "I was using the name Liesl Kraus. She is a reporter for one of the Munich papers. I wanted to tell you . . . just in case you hear the name, you'll know it was me."

Amalie then walked back to the train and she and Jakob boarded, waving good-bye when they reached their compartment as the train started drifting away from the platform.

ABOUT A MONTH later, Amalie sat eating her Monday morning breakfast and rereading a letter from her father. She had received the letter just before the weekend, and there was one sentence that interested her in particular. Ethan wrote that even though he had made further inquiries, he had found out nothing more about "Aunt Klara." Amalie knew he was referring to Klara Pölzl, but Ethan wanted to make sure that Gunther wouldn't suspect anything in case he happened to see the letter.

Amalie hadn't found any new information about the Hiedler family either, and she was beginning to doubt that she had any chance of finding or proving anything that would compromise Hitler's standing in the party. Small towns and villages were always full of gossip and rumors. The rumors could have come about because someone felt they had been cheated by the Hiedlers at some time or another, or perhaps there had been an argument years ago and someone wanted a petty revenge.

Calling someone a Jew in the Waldviertel region in those days was considered an epithet, but to say that they were born a Jew, to make people believe through gossip and lies that the family was Jewish, that was a real revenge.

Amalie was beginning to think that she was on the wrong track as she picked up the newspaper, but then she saw the story at the bottom of the page:

NEWSPAPER REPORTER BEATEN TO DEATH

The battered body of Fraulein Liesl Kraus, a reporter for the *Münchener Tageblatt*, was found on the bank of the Isar River yesterday afternoon. Detective Dietrich of the Schwabing precinct, the officer in charge of the investigation, believes that Fraulein Kraus was attacked at some other location

> and then the body was left at the edge of the English Garden, where it was discovered early Sunday afternoon by a group of children playing in the park. Detective Dietrich went on to say that motives for the murder are unknown and that the victim had not been robbed or sexually assaulted. Relatives of Fraulein Kraus last saw her on Saturday afternoon, and the police request that anyone who may have seen her after that time, or anyone having any possible information regarding the murder, please contact Detective Dietrich through the Schwabing police precinct.

Amalie felt a strange heaviness in her chest as she read the story, and suddenly she couldn't seem to catch her breath. She couldn't believe what she was reading. It couldn't just be coincidence. It couldn't!

Her father had said these extremists were dangerous, but could they be this vicious? Could they have beaten this woman to death just because they had gotten information that a reporter named Liesl Kraus was checking into Herr Hitler's family history? If that were the case, then it meant that Amalie had caused this woman's death. The worst thing that Amalie had thought might happen was that Gunther might find out and divorce her. She never in her wildest dreams could have imagined this!

Amalie had to talk to someone.

No. She had to go to work.

She was shaking. She suddenly thought that she should call her father.

David. She could talk to David at work . . . or maybe his father Sam? Maybe she should talk to Sam.

Amalie just sat for a moment and tried to calm

down, finally deciding that she should go to work. She said a hurried good-bye to Gertrude, who had been helping Jakob gather his schoolwork just as he was ready to leave too. Jakob asked if they could walk together, and Amalie said yes, but Jakob knew as soon as they started out that something was wrong. His mother didn't usually walk so quickly, and all the while they were walking, Amalie didn't say a word.

"We're here," Jakob said as they almost passed the school.

"Oh! Yes, yes," Amalie said, trying to cover her impatience as she gave Jakob a kiss on the cheek and immediately turned back to the street, rushing off toward the trolley.

Jakob just stood a moment watching as she rushed away, wondering what was wrong, and then turned dejectedly toward the school as he made his way slowly along the sidewalk.

When Amalie got to work, David was about to say good morning when he noticed the strange, panicked look on her face.

"Amalie, is something wrong?"

"David. I have to talk to someone. It's . . ."

"Come into my office," David said as he put his hand on her elbow, guiding her to a chair and closing the door behind them.

They sat in silence as David waited patiently for her to begin, but after a few moments he finally asked, "Is it Gunther?"

"No, no. This is something terrible . . . ," Amalie said.

"What is it?"

"First, David, you have to promise that you will

speak to no one about this."

"Certainly. You have my word."

"In Linz, Leonding . . . that weekend when I was checking into things . . . I used the name of a newspaper reporter. I thought people might be more likely to talk to me if they thought I was a reporter, and they did. But David, this morning . . . they killed her."

"What? Killed who?"

Amalie started to speak slowly after she realized that he couldn't follow what she was saying. "I picked a name from the paper, the name of a reporter, Liesl Kraus. Her body was found yesterday. She was beaten to death."

"And you know who did it?" David asked incredulously.

"No, not exactly. I'm just afraid."

"Afraid of what?"

"I'm afraid I caused it."

"You think someone from the National Socialists did it?" David asked as he tried to follow Amalie's conversation.

"Yes," she said simply, suddenly making eye contact with David.

"Why? Because they thought she was asking questions?"

"She wasn't robbed . . . she wasn't raped," Amalie said, listing off reasons. "It's just like all the other political murders. Maybe a hundred people shot or beaten to death just in this city."

"Maybe she was investigating something else," David offered. "Maybe she found something completely different and she was killed for that."

"Do you have any contacts at the paper?" Amalie asked, trying to formulate a plan. "Could you try to find out?"

"I'll do my best," David answered.

Silence again filled the office.

"I guess there's nothing else to be done," Amalie said despondently after getting up from the chair. "I'd better get to work."

David got up and stopped her at the door as she was leaving. "You don't know what happened. Even if it was the National Socialists, you couldn't have known it would turn out this way."

"I keep thinking of Nietsche," Amalie said.

"Nietsche?"

"That old quote: 'He who fights with monsters might take care lest he thereby become a monster.'"

By the end of the day, David hadn't found out anything about the murder that would ease Amalie's conscience. Amalie was constantly unnerved by the incident as the thought of it kept weaving through everything she did—or more accurately, through everything she tried to do—since she didn't accomplish anything at work that day.

She forced herself to be bright and pleasant that night until she was alone, when she was finally able to make a telephone call to her father, warning him of the possible danger.

IT WAS several weeks before David finally came up with some information on the Kraus murder. He found out that Liesl had been working on a story about a particularly bloodthirsty Freikorps unit that had killed hundreds of unarmed civilians in Munich at the end of the revolutionary period, and even though all the Freikorps units had been ordered to disband after the final assaults on the revolutionaries in 1920, this particular group was still together. Apparently Liesl was going to name the men involved and tell about how they were still operating, despite their insistence that they were a just a political party and not a vigilante group intent on ridding Munich of all Communist influences. David even had a few names of likely suspects who may have actually carried out the assassination, and none of these men were directly associated with Hitler, although they and their party were considered sympathetic to Hitler's cause.

Amalie believed David when he told her there was no connection between her visit to Austria and Liesl's death, but still she had been so shaken by the experience that she determined to stop her search. She realized that even though Hitler hadn't had Liesl murdered, he could have. Amalie finally realized the kind of business her own husband was involved in, and it had a sobering effect on her.

The summer of 1922 passed quickly for Amalie. She was no longer aware of the days, the sunlight or warmth of the Bavarian summer. It all passed her by in a haze as she gradually became swallowed up by a state of depression. She began to wonder what the whole world was about, what it all meant. She was afraid of Gunther even though he had not changed much in that year. It was Amalie who had changed—in her perception of Gunther. She feared what he might become, as though he were some kind of monster, a werewolf who might become a killer with the change of the moon. Amalie began to spend more time at work, which she justified by talking about how bad the inflation was and how she had to work longer just to make enough to keep up, but the truth was that she was hiding.

Everything became strained around the apartment, as Amalie not only stayed away from Gunther, but also started to isolate herself from Gertrude and Jakob. It was a very dark period for all involved, but strangely enough, no one would come right out and ask what was happening or why. Gertrude began to think that maybe she wasn't welcome, but she was afraid to ask because she had nowhere to go. Jakob couldn't understand why his mother had stopped being his friend. Gunther's habit of avoiding Amalie when it looked like they might get into an argument was becoming increasingly worse. He didn't want to get involved in a fight because he found more and more that he didn't understand Amalie. He didn't know why she didn't like his friends, and he didn't know why she insisted on keeping her job. He didn't know why his marriage was so much different than he had expected it to be.

In the last week of September, David Frieder was sitting at his desk. It had been a particularly long week. He had gone begging and scraping to keep things afloat, negotiating with a printer and a book bindery on his latest project, a college-level textbook on geology that could potentially lead to more work with educational materials if he could bring the project in under budget. Under budget! Of course, when one talked about budgets these days, everything had to be indexed against the instability of inflation. Where he once talked about deutsche marks and pfennigs, he could now only refer to percentages.

"The price will go up," he would explain to the buyers from some university, "but the cost will be no more than 23.5 percent of your selling price."

It was almost eight o'clock in the evening as David lit a cigarette and exhaled audibly, as though he couldn't decide whether to sigh. He leaned back in his chair, propping his feet on the desk, something he rarely did.

After a moment, he found himself staring absentmindedly at the ceiling and suddenly felt that someone was watching him, and he self-consciously took a quick look out the open door of his office. No one was watching, but he could see a reflection in the window of the door. It was Amalie, still at her desk, her head almost buried in a stack of papers. David watched, suddenly fascinated by the intensity of her expression and the few strands of hair that fell about her face as she read through the papers in front of her. He realized that he and Amalie were probably the only ones left in the office, and that this might finally be a good time to talk with her. He had been meaning to speak with her for some time now, as he had noticed she was spending more and more time in the office even though there had been no significant increase in her workload.

Slowly, as though he were an old man, he slid his feet off the desk and righted his chair and stood, easing his lower back with one hand and carrying the cigarette with him as he casually walked out to Amalie's desk.

"Long day," he said as he stood beside her chair.

Amalie was startled. She smiled and nodded, then immediately turned back to her work.

David pursued the conversation. "Which one is that?" he asked, referring to the pages Amalie was reading.

"Proofing the copy for the pamphlet from the Department of Tourism."

"Tourists," David said with mild disgust. "American soldiers taking advantage of the inflation. What is it now?"

"I think about 7,200 marks to the dollar," Amalie answered. David took a puff from his cigarette, perplexed at Amalie's obvious attempt to ignore him, which certainly seemed ridiculous considering they were the only ones left in the office.

"You know everyone else has gone home?" David said in a tone that rendered the words half statement and half question.

"I'm almost finished," Amalie said in an appeasing manner.

"Amalie," David said as he pulled a chair from the desk next to hers and sat down beside her. "I couldn't help noticing . . ."

At this point Amalie was looking down at her desk, but David noticed she was no longer reading. He stopped in mid-sentence and broke off his gaze, but then suddenly found himself reaching out to Amalie and lightly touching her chin with the tip of his fingers, directing her to look at him. "What is it Amalie? What are you hiding from? Why can't you go home?"

Amalie pulled away, turning away from David as

tears misted up in her eyes. "I don't really know," she finally said.

"Amalie, I usually don't get involved in the lives of people who work for me. They have their lives and I have mine. But I consider you a friend, and I do get involved in my friend's lives."

Amalie was genuinely touched by this statement and found that she was able meet his eyes as she quickly brushed away the unwanted tears.

"I had a dream," she started slowly. "It keeps coming back. It started after that terrible murder . . . the Kraus murder."

"Well, it's no wonder," David offered sympathetically. "That must have been a terrible shock . . . under the circumstances."

"Yes, but the dream wasn't really about her, although she was in it. I dreamed I was running," Amalie began to gesture as she told about the dream, as though painting it on a canvas in front of David, coloring in all the pieces as she got caught up in the telling. "I was running from something, but I couldn't tell what it was. I ran into a house, or something like a house. It looked so small as I came up to it, almost like a doll's house. I looked behind me as I got to the door and it was all dark, and then I ducked into the house and suddenly it was a huge room. It was all dark, too, except for some small windows that I could look out, but the windows were too small for me to get through to escape. I started to panic because I could see a beautiful sunny day outside the windows, but there was no way I could get out, and I suddenly knew I was trapped by whatever had been following me. Then I found a door that seemed to come out of nowhere, and I went through the door into another room, and the doorway disappeared behind me and new doors suddenly appeared around the room. I ran from door to door, opening them, only to find that there was a mirror behind each door, like in a carnival funhouse. I kicked one of the mirrors and broke it, and I screamed because there behind the mirror was my mother's dead body blocking the doorway, and then I threw something that I had been carrying at another mirror, and when it shattered, there was the body of Liesl Kraus in the doorway."

Amalie's eyes filled with fear and she grew anxious as she told about her dream, and the tears returned. David was surprised by how emotional she was becoming at telling the story.

"And then I kicked the next mirror and Gunther appeared from behind it, and I thought I was safe and ran to his arms, but instead of holding me, protecting me, he suddenly grabbed me, stopping me from going through the door. He held me so tight that he was hurting me, and he turned me as he held me, forcing me to watch as the wall opened up behind me and the darkness began to swallow us up, and I screamed. Whatever it was that had been chasing me was there, and Gunther wouldn't let me go!"

Once finished, Amalie appeared exhausted. Telling someone about the dream was cathartic for her. David didn't know what to make of it all at first, mostly because he hadn't expected Amalie to be so emotional and his attention was distracted from the things she was saying.

He felt that he should hold her, comfort her, but

it was more of an intellectual impulse than an emotional response, and it showed in the awkwardness of his move toward her as he cautiously put an arm around her.

"I'm sorry to drop this all on you," she said. "You're the only one I've told about this."

"It sounds so frightening," David said softly. "Do you believe in dreams?"

"How do you mean?" Amalie asked, as though David had asked her if she believed in witches and fairies. "Do I believe that dreams tell the future?"

"No," David said in a clinical tone, rephrasing the question. "Do you believe in some kind of psychological basis for dreams?"

"Well," Amalie began as she turned a little toward David and his arm slipped naturally from her shoulder. "I suppose I believe there is some purpose. I believe there is something to Freud's approach."

"What do you think your dream means? Where did it come from?"

"Now that it's out in the open like this," Amalie said thoughtfully, smiling a little with relief at finally having someone she could talk to about it, "it seems pretty clear. I think it's about this whole affair with Gunther, and maybe I'm afraid of what Gunther . . . maybe I'm afraid that Gunther isn't the same man I married."

"Well, Amalie," David began, "I'm not a psychiatrist or anything, and I don't even know Gunther except for the few times we met here, but it seems your dream might be about something else."

David seemed to brace himself in the chair as he offered his thoughts on her dream. "Amalie, I think you're letting things you think might happen stop you from living now. I think you built the whole Liesl Kraus thing up in your mind, and even though you found out it had nothing to do with you, you never let go of it."

David paused to see how Amalie would react to his hypothesis. She seemed to consider what he was saying, but her expression didn't really give him a clue as to whether she accepted or rejected his explanation. David pressed on anyway.

"Amalie, you can't worry about everything that might happen as though it already has happened. You have to just deal with things as they come."

Amalie thought about what David was saying and finally replied, "You're right."

"I am?" said David, surprised at her sudden agreement.

Amalie laughed a little as she wiped her eyes a final time. "Yes you are," she said. "I was so afraid of what Gunther might do . . . afraid, I guess, that he might have been involved with Liesl Kraus's death . . . and I never let go of that fear, even after I was sure he had nothing to do with it."

"Well, that would certainly be a terrible thing," David said, "to think that Gunther might have . . ."

"But David," Amalie said, "I still don't know what to do."

"About what?" David asked.

"About the party . . . the National Socialists."

"Amalie, there might not be anything that you can do."

"But Gunther . . ."

"Amalie, you have to be realistic."

"Realistic?!"

"Amalie, admit it. There might not be anything that you can do about Gunther . . . or the party . . . or anything else. What is going to happen will happen. You just have to live with it. Look at yourself. Could things be any worse? You're obviously hiding here, and you go from one extreme to the other. You don't seem to know whether you want to change the world or hide from it."

When David finished talking, an almost overwhelming silence filled the room. David was afraid he might have gone too far—that he might have offended Amalie or hurt her. He didn't know what else to say, but he didn't feel he should take back what he had said either.

Amalie decided that David was right. She was tired. For all of her fears, nothing had happened in all that time since her visit to her father. She had been feeling that the world was closing in all around her, and now suddenly, with this simple conversation, she realized that the world had just gone on as it always had—without even noticing that Amalie Stein-Metzdorf was insisting to herself that it was ending.

"I think it's time to go home," Amalie said simply as she looked David square in the eye.

David smiled, and as Amalie gathered her things and stood to leave, he found himself putting his arm around her again, but this time it wasn't awkward or strained. A gentle squeeze, and then they said good night.

The conversation with David brought Amalie out of her isolation and started her thinking, and she felt an almost miraculous change as she rode the trolley. She began to see what she had been doing and how she had been running away, just like in her dream, running from the unknown.

She also felt sad as she realized that it wasn't only Gunther she had drawn away from, but Jakob too, and she thought how hard it must have been for her son over the past few months.

Gertrude was surprised to see Amalie before nine o'clock. "You're home early," she said.

"Actually, I'm late," Amalie countered.

"Well," Gertrude backtracked, "it's just after six and you've been working late for so long . . ."

"I think that's done now," Amalie said. "Things should be getting back to normal."

Gertrude wasn't quite sure what to make of that, but she didn't press Amalie. "That's good," she said. "You've seemed so tired lately."

"Well," Amalie said, stepping around Gertrude, "I'm going to put these away," and she went to the closet of the bedroom to put up her purse and briefcase. Then she went to look for Jakob in the living room, where she found him lying on the floor with sheets of paper spread around him, drawing with pencils. When Jakob first saw her, he flinched and started to gather the papers together, thinking his mother was going to be upset that he had made a mess, but instead Amalie knelt and started to spread the papers out again, and then lay down on the floor next to him.

"What are you drawing?" she asked.

Jakob's face lit up. "I'm drawing houses like father does!" he chirped, obviously happy to have Amalie there beside him like that.

"And so nicely," Amalie said admiringly as she held one of the drawings up in the light.

After looking at the other pictures for a moment, Amalie changed the subject. "Your birthday is coming soon."

"I know," Jakob said with a smile.

"Oh, you know, do you?" she said, tousling his hair. "Have you thought about what you might like for a present?"

"A little," Jakob said coyly.

"Well . . . what did you decide?"

"A dog."

"A dog?" Amalie repeated, thinking of all the difficulties of owning a dog, but apparently Jakob had no such concerns.

"Yes, like Mr. Scheiderman has down the hall."

"Mr. Scheiderman? The man with the big German shepherd?" Amalie asked incredulously.

"Yes," Jakob said with conviction as he nonchalantly went back to his drawing. "That's what I want for my birthday."

"I don't know," Amalie said as she got up from the floor. "We'll have to see what your father says about it."

Gunther was also surprised when he got home and found that Amalie was already there. She made up a story about business slowing down so that she couldn't put in any more long hours. Gunther was pleased, so pleased that he stayed home all evening, winding up the night by playing cards with Amalie and Gertrude and trying to teach Jakob the card game until it was time for him to go to bed. Amalie made a point of reading a story to Jakob and tucking him in, and Gertrude cleaned up the dishes and went to bed. Amalie and Gunther retired soon after.

"Jakob's birthday is coming up," Amalie said as she got ready for bed.

"My God . . . it's almost October already," Gunther responded.

"Two weeks. Seven years old already on the twelfth of October."

"That little boy is starting to make me feel old," Gunther said with a wry smile.

"And it's only going to get worse," Amalie countered. "I thought we might have a party on that Saturday."

"Saturday? The fourteenth?" Gunther said, trying to remember something. "I think Klaus said there's something going on that day."

"Something? Like what?" Amalie asked.

"A party function. Some rally out of town."

"A political rally? Must you go?"

"It's important. Especially now with things starting to happen."

"Like what?" Amalie asked.

"People are starting to pay attention. We're getting more and more interest."

"Some say it's only because times are bad. Once things improve, people will stop paying attention," Amalie said, taking a chance on contradicting her husband.

"They don't know. Those people aren't at the rallies. They haven't seen the way Hitler can embrace a crowd and lead them. No, the people who say Hitler is just a passing face aren't paying attention. They aren't listening to the streets."

"Well, as far as Jakob's birthday," Amalie began, attempting to work out a compromise, "I suppose we could have a little party on Thursday when you're here and then have a children's party on Saturday while you're at . . . Where is the rally?"

Gunther stopped in the middle of hanging his trousers on a hanger and looked up at the ceiling, trying to remember where Klaus had told him the rally would be held. "Ah . . . oh yes, Coburg."

"Well, that should be an all-day trip," Amalie said.

"Yes, we were thinking of going up on Friday night so we'll be fresh in the morning."

"I suppose Jakob will understand."

"Of course he will!" Gunther said, the thought never having entered his mind that Jakob would question his father's decision. Jakob, of course, would never bring up such a thing, but that didn't mean he wasn't hurt by the many times that his father wasn't there. Jakob just accepted that his father had many more important things to do.

"Oh," Amalie said as she remembered, "I asked Jakob what he wanted for his birthday."

"And what did he say?"

"He wants a dog. A German shepherd like Scheiderman's down the hall."

"We're already pretty crowded," Gunther said as he considered the possibility.

"That's what I thought," Amalie responded, pleased that Gunther was also against the idea.

"But maybe a smaller dog," Gunther continued, and Amalie was crestfallen. If Jakob wanted a dog, that was one thing, but if both Jakob and his father wanted a dog, then it was as good as done.

Jakob's birthday arrived quickly, along with a springer spaniel puppy named Honig that made Gunther a hero to his son, despite his going off to Coburg with Klaus on the following night. The following Saturday not only brought another birthday party for Jakob while his father was away, it also began a new phase for the National Socialists' plans for Germany.

Adolf Hitler and other members of his party had been very impressed by the political successes of a socialistic, anti-Communist politician in Italy. A former newspaper editor named Benito Mussolini had created a party based on the concept of ancient Roman rule, where one man led the government and directed all its authority. Mussolini derived the name for his party from an ancient Roman symbol of the emperor's power and the unity of the state, a bundle of sticks held in an eagle's claw. *Di Fascisti,* which literally means "bundle," soon became known in the English-speaking world as the Fascists, and eventually the name would come to refer to any similar form of totalitarian, anti-Communistic government.

Mussolini, in his drive against the Bolsheviks, had simply marched into certain cities in Italy, accompanied by his black-shirted troops, and laid claim to the towns in the name of the Fascists. There had been some resistance by Communist factions, but the Fascists received widespread support, including from the Vatican, which opposed the Communists because of their atheistic stand against all religions.

Leaders of the National Socialists in Germany

studied Mussolini's successes and decided to emulate them on that Saturday in Coburg. It was a grand show of bluff and bluster, complete with brass band and eight hundred fully uniformed storm troops, many of whom, like Klaus and Gunther, had paid their own way to Coburg for the "attack." There were jeers from the crowds and street fighting with rocks, fists, and sticks as the troops entered the town, but the street was soon cleared by the storm troops, and the next day when the National Socialists marched through the streets again, they were cheered by the crowds.

Amalie was shocked as she read in the Sunday newspaper that "Coburg was under the control of Hitler." This was Gunther's "rally," the takeover of a town by brute force. Suddenly, as Amalie read, a spark was rekindled in her. She had agreed with David Frieder's conclusion that she couldn't change the whole world, but at that moment, reading the story of Hitler's takeover of a single city, she determined that she would try to find something that could be used against him before he could take over the entire country. She had to reinstitute her plan. She had to decide how far she would go and what her ultimate goal was, and then commit herself to that goal above all else, and most frightening of all, she had to decide what she would be willing to lose in exchange for attaining that goal. Would she be willing to lose Gunther? For the first time, she began to think that instead of saving Gunther, the loss of her husband would be worth bringing Hitler down.

Amalie felt that her fears were more than justified when, only ten days later, Benito Mussolini rode the train into Rome and took over the Italian government without firing a shot. She knew this was Hitler's plan. He wanted to follow Il Duce's lead except for one important factor—Mussolini wasn't sending troops into the streets with money collection boxes labeled: FOR THE MASSACRE OF THE JEWS.

Christmas of 1922 certainly wasn't as bad as some of the other Christmases the Metzdorf family had experienced in Munich. It was certainly more materially festive than that first Christmas just after the end of the war. Even if the inflation made things difficult, at least this year there were some goods and food to be had, although still quite limited. This time Amalie, Gunther, Jakob, Gertrude, and Klaus used regular candles for the tree, and there was even a lot of talk about the new electric tree candles that appeared in several of the large Kaufhauses[13] near the Karlstor district, but the electric lights were still very expensive. The group repeated their traditional Christmas Eve gathering, begun in 1918, but this time Gertrude put a single candle in one of the living room windows as a remembrance of Friedrich, as she put it, "wherever he might be." Gunther and Klaus reassured her that even though she had received no word from him, no letter or message in almost ten months, he was probably doing fine and was just too busy to write.

There was a new addition to their group this year—Katrina Holzmann, a beautiful strawberry blond woman whom Klaus had met through his friends in the party. Katrina was nineteen, a few

[13]Department stores.

years younger than Klaus, who was now twenty-eight, but they seemed well suited to each other, and Amalie even noticed that Katrina seemed to have a calming influence on Klaus. Klaus had been seeing Katrina for several months, and Amalie hoped that Katrina might draw him away from the National Socialists, at least to the extent that he might become a bit less fanatical and possibly loosen his influence on Gunther. Amalie realized this was a lot to hope for, but she hoped nonetheless, and welcomed Katrina warmly whenever she came to visit.

It wasn't long after Christmas before a new crisis erupted in Germany. Things were not going well on the Allied Reparation Commission, the committee of French and English government officials who where deciding on the terms of the punitive payments demanded of the German government, and as a result, the English representatives walked out of the hearings in the first part of January 1923. The French, newly freed from the protests of their English counterparts, determined that they would take action against the Germans because the German government had fallen behind on the reparations payment schedule. On January 11, 1923, French and Belgian troops marched into the Ruhr region of Germany and occupied the area.

The rumors drifted in one on top of another. "The French had sent in Black Algerian troops." "German women weren't safe on the streets." "German women found on the streets after dark were raped." "The Algerians raided the zoos in the German cities of the Ruhr region and killed and ate the animals that were native to their lands."

The response of the German government was almost immediate. The Germans devalued their money so that the reparations payments would become a farce, causing the inflation of German money to go completely out of sight. Where the exchange rate against an American dollar was about 7,000 deutsche marks before the occupation, within a few weeks after the occupation, the exchange rate was 50,000 deutsche marks for a single American dollar. This was the final straw for the German middle class. Those who were still above water financially, who had not already been ruined and thought they might sneak by the inflation ebbing away their life's savings, were now swept away by a new tidal wave of inflation.

Within the next few months, the reality of the German economy became worse than anyone could ever have feared or imagined. One day Gunther was amazed as a fellow worker told him that he had missed the trolley to the bank, and in the time between the first trolley and the next, his paycheck was worth less than half of what it had been when he started out!

Large companies began to issue their own currency, notes for their employees to use in the small towns where the companies sponsored the stores. The Weimar government, unable to keep up with the incredible pace of the inflation, began to authorize the printing of larger denominations over smaller bills. A 10,000-mark note would have "eine million mark" printed over it in red ink, thus making it a 1,000,000-mark note. By the time Amalie was to travel to Ried again in April, when Otto Maus had specifically requested that David Frieder send her as David's representative, her train ticket cost almost a half billion marks.

In those four months between the beginning of the year and Amalie's return trip to Austria, she had finalized her plan. She felt she already had enough information to justify her continuing an investigation into Hitler's background, and beyond that, she decided to coordinate with others, people she trusted—like David and Sam Frieder and her father—to gather evidence wherever possible and build a history, a file as it were, that would one day destroy the party.

She made what she considered the most important decision in her plan, determining that the file must remain a secret until she had enough to bring the party down. She didn't want bits of information coming out that the party could simply downplay or deny completely. Amalie felt that she had to find information that would turn the members of the party against the party leaders, and that information had to be irrefutable. Furthermore, the file would have to be delivered from impressive sources in the world community. She knew that if it came from a Jew like herself, the party would simply pass it off as an unfounded and libelous attack by its mortal enemies.

The time for striking seemed to be closing in quickly as the inflation catastrophe moved more and more people to extremist views against the democracy of the Weimar government. The National Socialist German Workers Party, in particular, was growing faster than ever.

While Amalie was in Austria working with Otto, she again tried to find more information in the area around Spital and Weitra, and she managed to track a bit more of Hitler's family, but in so doing, she found a mistake in her earlier information. When the old priest told her that Hitler's father had married his own niece, it seemed to conflict with records that showed Hitler's father's third wife to be his cousin, not his niece.

During her time in Austria, Amalie thought about involving Otto Maus in her circle of confidants, but she decided that even though she liked him and he seemed like a good man, she didn't really know him well enough yet to risk it.

She found herself stymied in her investigation by the time she returned home. It seemed there was nothing more she could do without becoming far too obvious and drawing unwanted attention. She had to satisfy herself with just keeping up on newspaper articles and rumors and staying in touch with Sam Frieder, who had the time to pay close attention to the political scene and keep Amalie informed. Amalie decided that the best way to keep the information was to send it to her father. Now and again, Gunther would remark that he was surprised by the sudden increase in correspondence between his wife and her father, but he never really made much of it.

That summer was a good one for the family. Just as Amalie had made it a point to make a special Christmas for Jakob the year before, she wanted to spend more time with him during the summer. She wanted to make sure that Jakob wouldn't get caught up in it when things became strained between her and Gunther. She wanted to protect her son from the things she was seeing and from Gunther's politics.

The National Socialists had held many rallies during the summer and fall, and Hitler had been getting a lot of coverage in the newspapers for his aggressive challenges to the authority of the Bavarian government. The challenges had been fairly minor, something akin to a street tough trying to start a fight in a bar. He was constantly hurling insults, posturing, and making threats. It got to the point where his influence began to be questioned as more and more people came to believe he was a man of words but no real action. Amalie began to think she might have overestimated Hitler's role in the party.

"They changed the date!" Klaus said as he rushed into the apartment when Gunther opened the door. "It's tonight."

"Thursday?" Gunther asked in surprise.

"Yes. I just heard," Klaus explained. "Get ready. We've got to go. We can't miss this one."

Gunther looked at Amalie, who pretended not to be paying attention as she sat on the sofa reading her book. Jakob ran up to greet "Uncle Klaus," and Gertrude came out of the kitchen.

"What's this?" she asked good-naturedly. "Another for dinner?"

"I'm afraid not," Klaus replied. "We have to leave now."

"Right now? Not even time for a quick sandwich?" Gertrude pressed.

"No, really, we have to run," Klaus insisted.

"I'll get my things," Gunther interjected.

"What are you talking about? You've got to change here. We have to go directly to the Bürgerbräukeller,"[14] Klaus insisted.

"Well . . . it will take a while," Gunther said reluctantly, and then turned to Gertrude. "You might as well make a sandwich for me while I'm changing. I'm starved."

"It will only take a minute," Gertrude said, smiling as she went back to the kitchen.

Gunther was hesitant to change into his brown shirt and armband because he had never done so at home before. He knew that Amalie was nervous about the Nazis and didn't really understand what they were all about, so he tried to avoid upsetting her by never wearing his uniform at home, although it wasn't really a uniform since he wasn't a member of the Sturmabteilung. He was just a volunteer who helped support the SA at rallies, and sometimes he went along with SA troops to disrupt Communist meetings, and so on, but he certainly never told Amalie the details of these outings. It wasn't the sort of thing you discussed with your wife—going out and beating up leftists and Jews. She seemed especially sensitive about the Jews, even though he had tried to explain to her so often that these were a specific kind of Jew that had to be controlled. Gunther tried to keep a low profile at home, not out of fear or embarrassment, but more in the way that a parent tries to get a child to take castor oil, telling the child that it's certainly unpleasant, but once done with,

[14]A famous Munich beer hall.

everything will be better. Gunther knew that he was fighting for a better world, and one day his wife and son would thank him for having the strength to do the unpleasant things that must be done.

Gunther quickly pulled on his overcoat and was struggling to get his arm in the sleeve as he stopped at the kitchen to pick up his sandwich on his way out. Amalie glanced up from her place on the sofa just in time to catch a glimpse of the brown shirt and the red, white, and black armband sewn to the sleeve. Gertrude set the sandwich down as she took the sleeve and straightened it, helping Gunther get his coat on. Klaus smiled from the doorway as Gunther surrendered to Gertrude's assistance.

"Thank you, 'Mother,'" Gunther said sarcastically with a big grin, giving Gertrude a little kiss on the forehead. Gertrude laughed and gave Gunther a playful slap on the chest.

"Don't wait up," Gunther said to Amalie almost as an afterthought as he stuck his head into the living room. "This could be a long one." Jakob again ran up to his father and Klaus for good-night hugs, and then Klaus and Gunther were suddenly gone.

The glimpse of Gunther's brown shirt and swastika armband had made Amalie shrink back into the sofa involuntarily. She suddenly remembered back to an afternoon a few months before when she had seen three of the SA collecting money for the party. They had stood there with that look on their faces, that sneering contempt, the look that dared anyone to challenge them. And one man did. A stranger who just happened to be passing by stopped and told them to leave—that they had no right to do what they were doing—and the three suddenly set upon the man, punching him in the face and stomach. Once they had drawn blood from a blow to the face, they seemed to go crazy. In a frenzy, they knocked the man to the ground and kept beating him while he was down. A few people stopped and watched, but one of the three SA warned them to keep moving or they would be next.

That was one of the chief weapons of the Nazis. They were not afraid to use violence. On the contrary, many of the young Nazis enjoyed the power of violence, the power they felt in intimidating others. Gunther was certainly not in that class, whether Amalie really knew it or not. Gunther had the attitude of a soldier. He used the same techniques on occasion, but he used them as a soldier uses a weapon, a means to an end, not because he enjoyed it.

"From what I understand," Klaus began to explain to Gunther on the trolley, "they changed the date because Kahr is holding a meeting at the Bürgerbräukeller tonight."

Gustav von Kahr was the state commissioner of Bavaria under Bavaria's Minister President Eugen von Knilling. Kahr had announced that he would outline his plans for the future of the economy on Thursday, November 8, at the Bürgerbräukeller, the largest beer hall in the city with a main hall that could hold three thousand.

It was just after six o'clock as the trolley crossed the bridge over the Isar. Gunther and Klaus soon got off and made their way to the beer hall, passing through the huge wrought iron gates set in the arched gateway of the high wall around the beer hall grounds and through the large open area that served as a beer garden in the summer. Perhaps Gunther was just nervous, but the skeletons of the barren trees in the abandoned yard set against the cloudy sky seemed foreboding.

Von Kahr's meeting wasn't scheduled until eight o'clock, but Klaus had been told to get there early so that he and other party members would be sure to get key positions in the hall. Klaus wasn't sure exactly what was going to happen, but he knew there was going to be some sort of action. They kept their coats on so as not to give themselves away until the right time came.

"Hey, friend!" Gunther said jokingly as they sat down. "Can you spare a billion marks for a beer?"

"Only a billion?" Klaus said, playing along. "That's a bargain. I heard it's a billion and a half at the hotels."

Neither of them laughed, and Klaus went to the bar for the beer while Gunther looked around the room.

"What do you think?" Gunther asked as Klaus returned to the table. "Maybe we're just supposed to disrupt it?"

"No, I think it's something more," Klaus said nonchalantly, speaking into his beer mug as he took a drink.

"Do you know something you're not telling me?" Gunther asked.

"No. It's just the mood . . ."

"The mood?" Gunther asked as he tried to pin down his friend.

"I don't know . . . It just seems that . . . well, the SA leaders that I know have been saying that now is the time to make a move. They seem anxious."

"That could just be talk," Gunther replied.

"Perhaps."

Gunther suddenly had an uneasy feeling, as though he had just been told that the group at the next table had a loaded gun and he had no idea what they wanted or what they would do. The feeling was exhilarating but at the same time unnerving. Gunther and Klaus remained quiet for the next few hours, making small talk and keeping to themselves as they nursed their beers and waited.

The hall gradually began to fill, and by eight o'clock the room was packed. Klaus kept an eye on the door, waiting expectantly for whatever might happen next. Gunther settled in beside him as Kahr began his speech, which turned out to be a boring lecture on economics. After about a quarter of an hour, Klaus nudged Gunther's arm and motioned to the bar. There was Hitler in a black morning coat.

"Now things will get interesting," Klaus whispered to Gunther, and he had no sooner finished the sentence when storm troops pushed their way into the hall shouting, "Heil Hitler!" Klaus and Gunther threw off their coats and jumped to their feet, joining the chant of the storm troops. Hitler and other Nazis, brandishing pistols, pushed their way toward the stage as the storm troops at the door barricaded the exit. The crowd went into a panic and tables were overturned as some sought cover when the storm troops began beating people who tried to get out.

Suddenly Hitler climbed up on a chair and shouted for quiet, and when the uproar continued, he fired his pistol into the ceiling. Once the crowd had begun to quiet down somewhat, he shouted, "The national revolution has broken out! The hall is surrounded."

Gunther could hardly believe it. Klaus was right. Things were certainly getting interesting. The two compatriots stood in front of the stage while Hitler made his way through the crowd and onto the speaker's platform. Klaus smiled at Gunther for an instant, overwhelmed that their time was finally at hand, and then quickly turned back to the crowd with a menacing expression, ready to attack if need be.

Kahr was not the only member of the Bavarian government on the stage. Next to him was General Otto von Lossow, the head of the army in Bavaria, and Colonel Hans Ritter von Seisser, the chief of the Bavarian state police. When Hitler crossed the platform to speak with the three officials, Colonel Seisser's aide suddenly put his hand in his pocket, and Hitler immediately stopped and pointed his pistol at the aide, warning the major to take his hand out of his pocket. Hitler then ushered the three men into a side room, leaving the crowd to ferment.

The crowd soon grew restless, with many people making light of the affair and jeering the storm troops until Hermann Göring, one of Hitler's compatriots who had come in with the storm troops at the beginning of the event, emulated Hitler and fired another shot into the ceiling. Göring tried to keep the crowd calm until, finally, Hitler returned to the speaker's platform amid a renewed outburst and demanded silence, threatening to set up a machine gun in the hall.

Hitler then began to speak, and Gunther, still facing the gathering rather than Hitler, watched as the crowd became transformed. Hitler informed the crowd that the three members of the Bavarian government were going to support him and then went on to win over the crowd with his standard points of a strong Germany freed from the Weimar government and restored from the disgrace of the November criminals who betrayed Germany in her darkest hour, surrendering her to her enemies.

The crowd that had laughed at him and insulted and jeered him just moments before now cheered him. Gunther knew it would happen. He had seen it before. He had even been a part of the crowd once, another crowd from years ago that had been skeptical and then similarly swept up and moved, transformed not just by the power of his words, but by the power of his conviction, the power that he was. That man, riding the crest of emotion that surged within the crowd and the power of his rage at the world, became more than he was in the beginning. The demons within him seemed to create a greater him.

When Hitler finished speaking, the crowd roared out the words to "Deutschland über Alles."

That, however, was the high point of the evening. From there things quickly began to degenerate as the Nazis tried to coordinate their efforts with party members in other parts of the city. They also had trouble trying to convince Bavarian government officials that Kahr, Lossow, and Seisser supported the uprising and that they too should support the overthrow of the government. The coup began to collapse as Kahr and the others managed to get out word that their compliance had been forced and they did not, in fact, support Hitler's *Putsch*.

Another blow was dealt to the uprising when Hitler decided to leave the Bürgerbräu to personally settle a dispute between his men and some city engineers. General Erich von Ludendorff, who had been in on the plan to overthrow the government from the beginning but had not been informed in advance about the change of date, arrived at the beer hall in the meantime, and Hitler decided to leave the general in charge.

Soon after Hitler left, General Lossow convinced Ludendorff that he should be allowed to leave so that he could return to his headquarters to issue orders to his troops. Ludendorff, unaware that Hitler had been lying when he said that the three men supported the overthrow, agreed not only to let Lossow leave, but Kahr and Seisser as well.

Hitler was enraged when he returned to find that the three men had been allowed to leave. Ludendorff insisted that there would be no problem, as the three men had given him their word that they would not oppose the overthrow.

Gunther and Klaus knew nothing of this intrigue, of course. They only knew that things were becoming tense and tempers were flaring. They finally left at about two o'clock in the morning, when they were told to go home and get some sleep and return in the morning.

There was still much activity on the streets as they

made their way home. SA troops headquartered throughout the city roamed the streets looking for "criminals" to bring before hastily assembled tribunals. Socialist, Communists, Jews—anyone they considered an enemy of the party would be brought before the tribunal, and those found guilty of crimes against the German people would be sentenced to death.

Gunther decided to stay with Klaus that night rather than going through all the discussion and explanations with Amalie. They got about six hours' sleep, returning to the Bürgerbräu by ten o'clock Friday morning.

The atmosphere at the beer hall seemed even more strained than the night before. There was no euphoria of victory to be found there. It was obvious there had been complications during the night, and Klaus went about asking questions and then returned to Gunther, telling him about the Kahr, Lossow, and Seisser fiasco and that Ernst Röhm, the leader of the SA, was trapped at army headquarters with some of his troops. Gunther took the news stoically, although he was shaken. Just like Klaus, he had been waiting for this for a long time, and now it appeared to be falling apart. What were they to do now?

A few hours later, Hitler and Ludendorff decided to march through the city. Hitler told the men gathered in the hall that they would attract others to join them as they marched and make a popular success of their revolution by sheer numbers. When the march began, their direction was unclear, but then Ludendorff decided that they should head to army headquarters to rescue Röhm and his men. After a few blocks they were met by armed police, but when they found Ludendorff to be a member of the group, the police voluntarily turned over their guns. This success inspired the group as they continued the march, almost reaching the Feldherrnhalle on the Odeonplatz[15] before they were once again met by armed police, but these police were ready for battle.

One of the Nazis fired first, killing a police officer, and suddenly there was a hail of gunfire from the police force. Gunther and Klaus and the other former soldiers and storm troops instinctively fell to the ground, returning fire. It seemed to go on forever, but then stopped as suddenly as it had started. Hitler was one of the first men to rise. Gunther could see that he was hurt by the way he held his arm, but he didn't see any blood. The next thing Gunther knew, Hitler rushed past him and the other troops who were still lying on the ground and threw himself into a car that had appeared from nowhere. The car then sped away. Gunther couldn't believe it. Hitler had turned and run. He didn't care about any of his comrades who had followed him into this battle. He ran! When it became clear that the shooting was over and the cause was lost as the police began to round up the Nazis, Gunther grabbed Klaus and pulled him away from the crowd. The two of them disappeared down an alley and finally made their way to Klaus's apartment.

Neither of them talked as a cold, gray afternoon

[15]The German word platz refers to a "city square," and Odeonplatz is one such square.

wrapped itself around the apartment house. They threw their coats on the sofa, and Klaus started making a pot of coffee while Gunther sat at the kitchen table.

Klaus disappeared into the bedroom, leaving Gunther staring out the window, going over the morning's events in his mind. His trancelike state was broken as something landed on the table at his elbow.

"Here," Klaus said, motioning to the nondescript white shirt he had thrown at his friend, "you might as well change out of that smelly thing."

Gunther smirked as he pulled off his homemade swastika armband and traded his brown shirt for the white one.

"I'm going," he said as he finished buttoning up the shirt.

"Might as well," Klaus said with a certain paternalistic air, as though Gunther was asking permission to leave and Klaus was granting it.

The truth was that Gunther was confused. He wasn't sure what to make of what they had just been through. He picked up his coat and draped it over his arm as he walked to the door, then stopped with his hand on the doorknob, looking down at the floor as he addressed Klaus. "It's over, isn't it?"

"I don't know. All the cards haven't been played yet," Klaus responded thoughtfully, as though he knew some deep secret about what might happen next.

"You and your damn cards," Gunther shot back. He was tired and beaten, and he didn't want any of Klaus's dramatics at that point. "Do you think there's a chance?" he continued, wanting to know if there really was something Klaus knew that he didn't.

"For today? No."

"Then what are you saying?"

"Maybe this was just another battle. We won't know what's what until the smoke clears."

"Do you think many were killed?"

"Well, Adolf was in front and he survived."

"He ran," Gunther corrected.

"He retreated," Klaus euphemized. "You've been in a retreat before."

"Yes, I've seen a retreat before," Gunther said in a challenging tone. "He ran. He left everyone and ran to save himself."

"So did we," Klaus rejoined.

"After our leader!"

"The point is that we survived . . . he survived. That's why I say all the cards haven't been played yet."

"Well, I'd better go. I have to see if I still have a job."

"What?"

"The man I work for doesn't like Nazis. If he finds out I was at the Feldherrnhalle . . ."

"Well, good luck. I'm going to bed," Klaus said as he turned and walked away.

Gunther didn't even bother to tuck in his borrowed shirt as he put on his coat in the entryway of the apartment house. Turning up his coat collar, he stepped out into the cold, foggy afternoon, heading for home.

"Oh, my God!" Amalie said, her eyes filling with tears. "You're safe. You made it."

"Yes, we got away after the shooting. We went to Klaus's apartment."

"I didn't sleep at all last night."

"I didn't sleep too well either."

"Why didn't you send word? How could you let us go on, not knowing whether you were alive or . . ."

"Everything was crazy. There wasn't time to get word to you."

"Well," Amalie said, beginning to calm down, "what next? Are you home for good? Do you have to go out again?"

"I think . . . ," Gunther began, faltering, his voice breaking off as he forced himself to admit his unspoken fear, "it's over."

Amalie's heart leapt. She was at once astonished and overjoyed, but she kept silent for a moment, composing herself, afraid that she would incite Gunther to rage if he could see that she was happy that the Nazis had fallen. She wanted to appear sympathetic, but first she wanted to be sure of what her husband meant. Did he mean this was a setback, that the *Putsch* had failed, or had he given up on the Nazis altogether?

"What's over?" she asked, as Gunther leaned wearily against the doorjamb.

"Everything."

"What everything? You and me, we're not over," Amalie insisted to her husband.

"No, of course not," Gunther said as he began to take off his coat. "You and Jakob . . . I feel like you're all I have left." With that, Gunther put his arms around his wife.

Amalie was a little frightened by this. She began

to wonder if this was like a little boy running home to his mother after a bully had beaten him in a fight. Gunther had been so distant when he was immersed in the party, and now, with the battle lost, he had come back to her. She was confused. Here was Gunther, without the party and holding her in his arms, something she thought she had wanted more than anything else, and now she wasn't so sure. *Damn it!* she thought to herself, wondering what was wrong with her. She questioned everything. She couldn't seem to ever just let herself be happy with things as they were. *Just for this moment*, she thought to herself, *I will be happy*, and she continued to embrace her husband.

After a few moments, Amalie looked up at him. "I called your office this morning when you didn't come home . . ."

Gunther suddenly tensed in Amalie's arms, as though he had just been hit with an electric shock. He assumed that Amalie had told his employer where he had gone the night before, and now there was certainly no way that Gunther could talk his way out of losing his job. His eyes flashed at Amalie, but before he could say a thing, Amalie put a finger up to his lips.

"I told them you had a bad case of influenza and wouldn't be in Friday, and maybe not even on Monday," she said peremptorily.

Gunther managed a tired smile. "You did that on purpose," he said in a teasing manner.

"Did what?" Amalie asked innocently.

"You know what," he said as he gave her a swat on the backside.

"Gunther!" Amalie said with a little laugh, and just then Jakob heard them and Gertrude also realized Gunther had made it home, and suddenly the apartment was in an uproar as everyone tried to speak at once.

The next few weeks found Adolf Hitler in jail, having been tracked down to the country house of one of his Nazi party comrades and arrested. He was soon sent to Moabit prison, and by whatever sense of political hierarchy existed within the prison, he occupied the same cell that had held Anton Graf Arco-Valley, the man who had assassinated Kurt Eisner some four years before. Arco Valley was moved to a new cell.

Amalie thought everything would become very quiet after that, but she was mistaken. Klaus proposed to Katrina, the girl he had been seeing for more than a year, and Gunther, Amalie, and Gertrude were swept up in the planning. Klaus had decided they would get married the week before Christmas because that would be the greatest Christmas gift he could ever wish for. Gunther was to be the best man and Amalie one of the bridesmaids, while Gertrude offered to help Katrina's mother with the reception dinner.

It was a fairly small wedding, about seventy-five guests, and Amalie had never seen Klaus smile so much. Jakob sat beside Gertrude in the huge Catholic church that seemed to swallow up the small party of friends and family. He watched the priest in his white robes and listened, not understanding the Latin liturgy of the wedding ceremony. The whole thing was very confusing to him. Jakob had never been to a wedding, and he had never been in a Catholic church before, but this was certainly not like the first time Amalie had been in a Catholic church just a year or so earlier. Being raised as a Jew, Amalie had endured many childhood taunts and threats that caused her to be uneasy, to almost fear Catholic churches.

Jakob was overcome by the church, as any little boy would be sitting within the huge structure towering over him, with its spires and stained glass windows and somber-looking statues in every corner. All the saints in heaven looked down on him as he gazed up at the ceiling, his mouth wide open, taking in the enormity of the church.

That Christmas was the best Gunther, Amalie, and Jakob had ever known as a family. It was as though they were now freed from the weight of the world. Gunther spent a lot of time at home since Klaus was now "occupied" with his new wife. The only thing that could have added to the festivities of that Christmas Eve would have been Friedrich coming home, but there was still no word after all that time. Even though everyone tried to reassure Gertrude that she would hear from her son soon, she didn't talk about it as she once again lit a single candle and placed it on a table in front of the living room window.

The greatest gift of that holiday didn't come until the first day of the new year. None of this group of friends had ever heard of Hjalmar Schacht, the new Reich Commissioner for National Currency before that day, but it was on New Year's Day of 1924 that he established the Gold Diskont Bank.[16] It was through a number of loans from banks of other nations that Schacht established a new German economy based on gold and issuing currency in pound sterling. It was a coordination of the British empire currency and German currency that solved the most pressing problem facing the German people. With the signatures of a few German banking officials and some foreign banking representatives, the inflation problem in Germany was ended.

We've won, Amalie thought to herself. Hitler's *Putsch* had failed and Hitler was in jail. The economy was restored, and that had been one of Hitler's greatest focal points in arousing the people who came to his rallies. Her husband had become disillusioned with the leader who abandoned him when the bullets started to fly, and this led Gunther to leave the National Socialist German Worker's Party. It seemed certain to Amalie that the vicious little man who came from nowhere was destined to return to anonymity.

[16]Gold discount bank.

CHAPTER 8

The period from 1924 to 1928 in Germany was marked by a major change in the pattern of political unrest when Friedrich Ebert died in 1925. It is no small thing to note among the web of political assassinations in Germany that Ebert, first leader of the Weimar Republic and the man marked by the right wing extremists as the worst of all the November criminals, died of natural causes. The event that actually marked a change in the violent unrest in Germany, though, was the election of General Paul von Hindenburg to the office of president as the successor of Ebert. Here was a man who represented a political compromise between the right and the left. He was elected president, which meant that Weimar would stand, satisfying Germans of the moderate left, and he was a military man with a history reaching far back to the days of Imperial Germany, which satisfied most of the moderate right. The extremists on both the left and right, however, were still constantly agitating. The Communists and the Nazis still pursued their now common practice of street fighting, especially in Berlin, where Joseph Goebbels was trying to perfect his skills at demagoguery through his new vision of political propaganda fostered by his mentor, Adolf Hitler. When Adolf spewed his rambling and bitter commentary of hate, Four Long Years of Struggle with Ignorance and Stupidity, *a title that was later shortened to* My Struggle, *he stated outright that the common people would easily be convinced of anything if it was "handled" properly. "The big lie" became part of the party's propaganda policy from that time on.*

Anna giggled as she watched Lissa stick out her tongue. The old priest holding out the wafer paid no attention, but Anna could hear Sister Angelina making a clicking noise with her tongue. When Anna turned to look, Sister Angelina pointed a finger and made a cross face, which told Anna that her First Communion was no time for giggling. Anna quickly turned back toward the altar, looking straight up at the statue of the Virgin Mary

Once Anna had been properly chastised, a little smile crossed Sister Angelina's face as she confided to Edith who was standing close beside her, "Lissa does look silly the way she sticks out her tongue. One might think she was trying to catch a fly!"

"Sister Angelina!" Edith whispered back with mock indignation.

After a moment the two women found themselves transfixed as they took in the warmth and gentleness of the scene. "This is one of my best memories of teaching," Edith said in a hushed and emotional voice. "All the preparation and then . . . the looks on their faces, the feeling in the chapel. It made the rest of the problems worth the trouble."

"I remember my white dress," Sister Angelina reminisced, "and all the excitement, even though I didn't really understand how important it was."

"I was much older," Edith explained. "I was over thirty when I made my First Communion. It was a completely new life for me."

Sister Angelina knew that Edith had converted

from Judaism, but she had never broached the subject even though it interested her. "Why did you do it?" she asked after a brief pause.

"Convert?"

"Yes, why did you convert? Wasn't it hard to change from being Jewish to being a Catholic?"

Edith didn't hesitate with her answer because she had been asked so many times before and had long ago had to answer that same question for herself.

"No, not at all. It was as if I had been looking for something all my life, and then some people—some friends of mine at the University in Göttingen—introduced me to Catholicism, and it seemed to be the thing I had been looking for all my life and just didn't know it."

"All your life?"

"It's hard to explain, but when I really bean to have an interest in Catholicism and accepted Jesus as the messiah and savior, it just felt right, as though that was how it should have been for me all along."

"That must have been comforting."

"It felt like a homecoming."

"How did your family accept it?"

"Some well, some not so well," Edith said with a note of sadness. "My mother has come to accept it, but my father still seems to hope that I'll come to my senses and give it up. Some of my relatives haven't spoken to me in . . . it's almost six years now."

"I'm sorry to hear that."

"That's just the way it is, I guess. Some people only accept you if you are what they want you to be."

"That's the philosopher in you coming out again," Sister Angelina noted with a smile. "I understand you're lecturing tonight," she continued, changing the subject.

"Yes, my first. I've been offered a chance to speak on educational issues. I'm a little nervous, especially since I have a relative coming to hear me speak."

"Your mother?"

"Oh no! She's in Breslau. It's a cousin that I've only met once when we were little girls. She works as an editor for a Munich book publisher, and she sent me a letter saying she would be coming to Speyer on business."

"A woman editor?" Angelina asked.

"I was surprised too. I started corresponding with her when I heard that she was in Munich. It's been interesting and friendly, especially since she accepts my new faith."

"Oh, how nice."

"She's a wonderful letter writer. It will be good to meet her face to face after all these years."

Amalie was impressed with the city of Speyer. It was one of the cities on the Rhine that had been occupied by French troops in 1923, and it was this event that had prompted Amalie to begin corresponding with Edith. There had been many rumors of the mistreatment of Germans by the French occupation troops, including stories that German women couldn't walk the streets at night because they would be raped by French soldiers. There were also strange rumors that the Black African groups in the French occupation army had taken animals from the zoos that were indigenous to their homelands and killed and eaten them.

Edith had written to Amalie's father that she was moving to Speyer to teach in a Catholic girls school, and Ethan had passed on the information to Amalie, who started writing directly to Edith to find out what was really going on.

Edith didn't have much to say, except that she had never personally seen anything that would substantiate the rumors. The letters were a little awkward at first, as the two of them were really strangers to one another, but after a few letters their correspondence became less formal and each began to get a better picture of the other's world.

Amalie was not only interested in Edith's conversion, but also Edith's study of the methods and nature of education. Edith, on the other hand, was impressed that Amalie was an editor with a publishing firm. It was such an unlikely profession for a woman in 1928, especially a married woman with a child.

Amalie had gotten an early start that morning, so she had time to stop occasionally and scrutinize the old churches as she walked through the city on the way to her meeting. The city was older than Munich, and the architecture reflected the strong influence of the Holy Roman Empire, with many churches of Romanesque style as opposed to Munich's Gothic cathedrals. The buildings were certainly less ornate, but they were more substantial, almost as though they were part of the earth. They were like mountains that a selective volcano had caused to erupt on chosen sites as earthly reminders of an eternal prescience.

Amalie continued to wander for a while until she

found herself in front of a tiny synagogue nestled within a row of bleak-looking buildings. The Hebrew school had just let out, and a group of boys rushed by her, laughing and shouting as they made their way down the street. She thought of Jakob. He had just turned thirteen, the traditional age in Judaism when a boy goes through the ceremony to become a bar mitzvah[17] and accepts the responsibility of learning Torah, but of course this wouldn't happen with Jakob. The subject of raising Jakob in the Jewish faith, to any degree, was taboo with Gunther. Yet Ethan had written a letter so full of anticipation and hope asking that Amalie might consider the possibility that she found herself torn.

"No," Amalie said to herself. She knew it would hurt her father, but she couldn't talk about it with Gunther, and worse yet, she couldn't bring it up to Jakob. She had a much greater problem than the question of a bar mitzvah, though. Jakob was turning away from her. It was probably just his age, and it wouldn't have been such a terrible thing in and of itself, since it's normal for a boy as he enters puberty to seek out his father more as he tries to develop into manhood, but Amalie was afraid that he was also being molded. Gunther had once again become sympathetic to the Nazis, and it was clear that it would not take much to move him back to the party. Amalie was terrified that he would take Jakob with him.

It was a moment of reckoning for Amalie as she saw this terrifying possibility for her son. She desper-

---

[17]Literally, son of the commandments."

ately wanted to turn him away from it, and just then she realized how her father must have felt as he saw her turning away from him so many years before. The irony of generations. All the promises we make to ourselves about not making the same mistakes with our children that our parents made with us. That feeling of déjà vu as we watch our children struggling through their lives, and we try to shout out that we know the answer to this problem or that because we went through it and survived, and yet so many times our children can no more hear us than we could hear our own parents. We find ourselves only able to look on, as though encased in glass, unable to be heard. Everyone feels that their situation is different, insisting that they really do know the answer or that they really can tell what will happen next, but Amalie's complaint was more specific. She had wanted to save her husband and then decided that she might have to let him go in order to meet an even greater crisis, but how could she ever even think of giving up on her own son?

There was nothing unusual—or interesting, for that matter—about Amalie's meeting, and she had plenty of time to get back to her hotel, get some rest, and freshen up before going to Edith Stein's lecture.

The lecture was mercifully short, only about forty-five minutes, and it was well laid out and easy to follow, even for a layperson such as Amalie. It was only about nine o'clock when Edith finished and Amalie went up to introduce herself and compliment her cousin, inviting her to go for a cup of coffee so that they could have a chance to talk.

The conversation was mostly small talk, centered around the Stein family, until Edith began talking about when she first came to Göttingen from Breslau.

"Of course, everyone looked down on me at first," Edith stated as a matter of fact.

"Because you were Jewish?"

"Worse. I was a Jewess from the east. They all assumed we had come from Poland."

"Oh yes, of course that would be worse," Amalie said with an air of disgust at not just the German prejudice against Jews, but even the prejudice of German Jews against Polish Jews. Before the word *kike* became a common slur against all Jews, it was originally the word German Jews used for the Russian and Polish Jewish ragpickers. "It seems that everyone is always looking for someone to look down on," she said, completing her thought.

"That was the most difficult part of attending the university," Edith continued. "Things would be going along nicely, and then someone would make some stupid remark and all the hatred and stupidity would be right there again. Another kike from Galicia . . ."

"It's all part and parcel of the same thing," Amalie said angrily. "Scratch a German and find an anti-Semite."

Edith was taken aback by the damning statement. "You don't really think it's that bad, do you?"

"You don't know?" Amalie said, staring at Edith defiantly. "Certainly you've heard of Hitler. I thought they were done with him, but I was wrong. As soon as Hitler got out of jail, he addressed a crowd at the same beer hall where he started the *Putsch* in twenty-three, and so many people came that they were turned away at the door. Thousands of them, just waiting for him to return." Amalie stopped for a moment to compose herself as she realized how upset she was getting.

"The Nazis are rebuilding. There aren't many of them, but they're spreading out, expanding into other parts of the country. Hitler is just waiting to try again, and he hates us more than ever. Have you read his book?"

"His book?" Edith asked.

"Yes, he started it while in prison. He says he will send all the Jews out of Germany, and even more, he wants to take the East for Germany and throw all the Jews out of those areas, too."

"But he's a madman. No one takes him seriously," Edith countered.

"I don't think so. They can't seem to stop him. There is something about him . . . something he touches in the soldiers who fought at the front that makes them fanatical about him. And even worse, people who lost all their money during the inflation are starting to listen."

"But how can all these people believe . . . ?"

"The Jews have always been a target."

"But that comes and goes. It doesn't stay for long."

"No one I've heard of has ever worked so hard at it before. He doesn't just want the land of the Jews or their money, he wants them gone forever. He's started talking about Darwinism in his speeches more and more."

"Darwinism?"

"They call it 'Eugenics' or 'social Darwinism.' The talk has been around for some time. They say survival of the fittest applies to mankind as well as the animal kingdom, and that man with his intelligence and reasoning should 'assist evolution' for people. He says man should conscientiously remove inferior people from society so that society can improve faster than if things were left to natural selection."

"Well, it's just talk," Edith said with resignation in her voice. "We just have to trust in God and hope for the best."

Amalie was stunned. *Trust in God?* she thought to herself. *Hope for the best?* Was this what it meant to be a Catholic? She changed the subject, realizing that she might get carried away if she kept dwelling on the Nazis, and she and her cousin spent the next hour talking about family before they finally said good-bye and Amalie made her way back to her hotel.

Amalie had been careful over the past years to cultivate her conversation so that she would not casually betray her feelings about the Nazis. She was determined not to be outspoken because it would make her conspicuous in Gunther's circle of friends, and she decidedly wanted to hear all she could about the progress and direction of the party. As it was, Gunther's friends in the party—Klaus, in particular—knew that she had no taste for the particulars of what the Nazis did, but Klaus just dismissed it as a woman's aversion to the necessity of violence rather than opposition to Hitler and his party. After all, it was the same sort of attitude that his wife Katrina expressed, but Klaus had always enjoyed shocking people with his stories of demonstrations and beatings and other such actions in the war for control of the streets.

Klaus had remained a member of the Nazi party throughout the time when Gunther had gone through his crisis of faith after the beer hall *Putsch* in 1923, and now Klaus was more adamant than ever that Adolf Hitler was destined to lead the German peoples to their own great destiny.

Katrina hadn't calmed Klaus as much as Amalie had hoped she might. Granted, in the four years they had been married, Katrina had managed to improve Klaus's manners a bit, but she would never dream of contradicting him in public and she had no desire to engage in conversation about current events or politics. She was content to have babies and be a good housewife. Katrina had already dutifully presented her husband with three sons. After being childless for the first two years of their marriage and beginning to fear that something might be wrong, it suddenly seemed as if she hardly made her way out the front doors of the hospital before announcing to all her friends that she was expecting "another little gift from heaven," as she was so fond of saying. Her lack of political awareness was more than made up for by her prolific nature regarding heirs to the throne.

Amalie returned to Munich the day after meeting with her cousin Edith. It was June 6, Amalie's thirty-fourth birthday. She realized that she had been living in Munich for ten years now, and thought about how happy she had been in the past few years at finally having gotten Gunther back from all the distractions of the world. She laughed to herself as the thought crossed her mind that a world war and a revolution should be considered something more than just "distractions," but she felt as though all those other great dramas had closed in on the world of her family, and when the crises were finally over, she, Gunther, and Jakob at last had time to be a normal family.

Thirty-four! Not that thirty-four was old, but she couldn't help but wonder where those years had gone. For the first time in her life she had vivid memories of things that happened twenty years before! That sounded like something her grandfather would say . . . "Why, I haven't seen old 'so and so' in over twenty years." She now had a teenage son who was taller than she was.

Thirty-four. It didn't even sound good. Turning thirty wasn't so bad. Thirty was an accomplishment, but thirty-four was just carrying it too far.

When Amalie arrived home, her lugubrious attitude was obvious to Gertrude. The past five years had been rather good to Amalie and Gunther financially. Gunther's boss had taken a liking to Gunther and had even helped him go to school while still working, so that he could become a qualified architect. Amalie had been promoted to an editor position with Frieder and Son Publishing, and before long Gunther and Amalie were able to buy a small house in the Fürstenried district, coincidentally not far from Sam Frieder's house. Gertrude had moved with them as though she were a member of the family. Amalie and Gunther had insisted on taking her along when they went to find a house and had listened to her opinions on each property, and they all—including Jakob, of course—were in on the final decision as to which home they would buy.

"Don't tell me the birthday girl is feeling sad," Gertrude said as she stood in the kitchen doorway watching as Amalie unceremoniously dropped her briefcase and overnight bag in the living room.

"Don't remind me," Amalie said as she plopped into a chair.

"Well, you'd certainly better not expect me to cry for you!" Gertrude said good-humoredly as she headed back into the kitchen. "I turned sixty-two this year, so don't talk to me about thirty-four! You're still a child. You probably only finished packing away your dollies a few months ago."

This made Amalie laugh a bit, and she got up and went into the bedroom to change.

"Are you off for the day?" Gertrude asked, since it was only a little past noon on Friday.

"Yes. David said I should take the weekend and have a good birthday."

"Will you?"

"What?" Amalie called back, as she had been slipping her blouse over her head and hadn't heard what Gertrude said.

"Are you going to celebrate?"

"Well, right now I'm going to take a long bath."

"In the middle of the day?" Gertrude asked, wondering how someone could disrupt their schedule by taking a bath in the middle of the day. After all, normal people just wash at the sink before going to bed, or in the morning before going to work, but take a bath in the middle of the day? Never.

"You should try it some time," Amalie called back. "A little change in routine . . . you could shake things up a bit."

"You're crazy," Gertrude said, laughing as she poured batter into a pan for Amalie's birthday cake, which she planned to serve after dinner that night.

"Gertie, we've known each other a long time, and I at least thought I'd taught you that."

"Taught me what?"

"A little craziness . . . It's good for the soul."

Gertrude laughed louder this time as she started to clean up the kitchen.

Amalie slid slowly into the bathtub, but then realized how stuffy the bathroom seemed and she got up again, opening the window over the tub and then quickly re-submerging herself in the warm, soapy water. She sighed heavily as a fresh spring breeze suddenly floated into the bright, white bathroom, bringing with it the scent of recently opened blossoms from the plum tree outside the house. She closed her eyes just for a moment and smiled, not even aware that she was drifting off to sleep.

"Mother, please!" came the voice through the door as Amalie bolted awake, splashing water over the side of the bathtub. "I really need to get in there!"

At first Amalie was confused and couldn't figure out what was going on, but then she realized she had fallen asleep and it was Jakob at the door, needing—rather desperately it seemed—to relieve himself.

"Just a moment," she called out as she clambered

out of the tub and put on her robe. Her skin was all wrinkled from soaking in the water for so long. She hated how the robe felt against her wrinkled fingers, but forced herself to move quickly for Jakob's sake.

Jakob quickly brushed past her as soon as she opened the door and rather pointedly closed the door behind him, almost hitting Amalie as she stood in the hallway.

"You're welcome," she said curtly.

An image suddenly flashed through Amalie's mind. The river. She hadn't been near the river that day. When was it? Why had she suddenly remembered standing by the river's edge? The thought seemed to panic her as she tried to remember. It must have been a dream. She looked at the clock in her bedroom. It was almost three o'clock. She had been sleeping in the bathtub for more than two hours.

"Happy birthday, Mother," Jakob said as he stuck his head in the bedroom doorway, startling Amalie.

"Oh! Thank you, Liebling," Amalie said, then called out to Jakob as he continued down the hall, "Stay close to home. Your father will be home early tonight."

"I will," Jakob replied without breaking stride. "I'll be next door with Karl."

Amalie finished getting dressed and went into the living room, leaving the traces of an incomprehensible dream behind and picking up the morning newspaper from beside the chair where Gunther had left it before he had gone to work.

"Did you enjoy your bath?" Gertrude asked puckishly.

Amalie just looked up from her newspaper with a slow burn. "You let me sleep in there for two hours!"

"And it wasn't easy," Gertrude laughed. "I didn't think I could hold my water that long!"

"That wasn't very nice."

"I know, I know . . . but I just couldn't resist."

Just then Gunther came home from work, catching the tail of the conversation as he came into the living room. "Couldn't resist what?" he asked.

"Gertie's being mean to me, and on my birthday, too."

"Gertie! How could you? But don't worry, dear, your present will make up for anything that might have gone badly today."

"Oooh, that sounds promising. What is it?"

"It's a surprise, of course."

"And a pretty good one. I've been looking around for a week."

"That's what I figured, so I made sure it wasn't in the house. I'm having it delivered tonight at seven."

"During dinner?"

"Just before."

"Not even a clue as to what it might be?"

"I promise you'll love it."

"I'll hold you to that."

The afternoon passed quickly as everyone pitched in to get things ready for the birthday dinner. Klaus and Katrina would be coming with all three children, and even though Klaus had his sons regimented into strict obedience, Amalie wanted to make sure there was nothing breakable within three feet above the floor.

Jakob soon came home from his friend's house

with Honig, the spaniel Gunther had gotten him for his eighth birthday, close at heel, and Klaus and Katrina arrived soon after that. Jakob and the boys played with Honig while the adults talked and Gertrude put the finishing touches on dinner.

At one point, Gunther caught Amalie glancing anxiously at the clock and laughed, letting Klaus and Katrina in on the joke. Amalie felt like a little girl as she anxiously awaited seven o'clock, and then finally, a few minutes before the magic hour, they all heard a car drive up and park in front of the house. Amalie started to get up, but Gunther jumped up and raced her for the door, the two of them laughing as they almost crashed into each other. Gunther pressed his wife against the door and put his lips to her ear. She thought he was trying to kiss her and pushed him back playfully, laughing all the while. "Not now!" she said, "First the present and then the kisses."

Everyone in the room was laughing by now, as Gertrude came in to watch the excitement. Gunther put up his hands to quiet Amalie. "No," he said, unable to stop laughing himself, "I'm not trying to kiss you this time! I have to tell you something!" Amalie stopped struggling as he drew close. "There's more than one surprise," he said softly. "Whoever is at the door, don't say anything until he comes in." Amalie looked very confused, but she nodded in agreement. Gunther reached for the doorknob, making sure to obstruct the doorway from everyone's view as he slowly opened the door.

Amalie was dumbfounded. It was Friedrich—Gertrude's Friedrich! None of them had seen him for almost six years. He had gone to Berlin to make a living and had all but disappeared for nearly two years, until finally Gertrude had gotten a letter at Christmas in 1925. It said that he was doing fine and that she shouldn't worry, but the fact that he made no mention of visiting and gave no mailing address made it clear to Gertrude that he was struggling to get by. Gertrude took it in stride and never complained to her friends.

Over the next few years the letters became more frequent, one arriving every few months until finally there was a very special letter. It had a return address. That little note at the end had made Gertrude very happy because it meant that Friedrich was doing better. If he couldn't come home, at least he had a place of his own. Then it turned out that he was becoming involved with politics. There was a lot of effort to strengthen cells of the Nazi party in the north, and Berlin was the territory of Gregor Strasser and his new assistant, a short man with a club foot named Joseph Goebbels. Friedrich's connection with the first days of the party in Munich and his experience with the Freikorps had put him in a position to make good contacts, which eventually got him work as a clerk and chauffeur at the small headquarters of the Nazi party in Berlin. He also managed to supplement his income with part-time work for businessmen who were sympathetic to the party and therefore willing to allow him to work his schedule around party duties.

Gunther took Amalie's arm and guided her, moving aside so that Gertrude, who had been smiling at their antics and standing behind them, could see her son. The smile drained from her face as she looked into the smiling eyes of her long-lost son and broke into tears. It was as though her feet couldn't move as she opened her arms to Friedrich, who swept into the room and embraced his mother. Gunther and Amalie smiled as they looked on, and Amalie slipped her arm around Gunther's waist, pulling him close. Klaus explained to his wife that it was Gertrude's son, returned from Berlin after many years away, and their three little sons looked up at Gertrude as she cried, not understanding what was wrong. Jakob quickly moved in and corralled the little boys, spending the next few minutes trying to explain that "Grandma Gertie" was crying because she was happy.

Why didn't you tell me you were coming?" Gertrude finally said through her tears.

"I wanted to surprise you," he said, still embracing her. All of the problems from years ago had been swept away, and Friedrich was overcome to see her and his old friends again. The others finally came over and greeted Friedrich, too, welcoming him back home.

"This really is the most incredible surprise," Amalie said excitedly as she stepped in to give Friedrich a hug.

"Oh, Amalie," Friedrich said, "I almost forgot it's your birthday! I'm not the present, I'm just the delivery boy." And with that he headed for the door with Amalie in tow. "There," he said. "It's yours."

"What?" Amalie asked as she looked out.

"The car, of course. Gunther's gone and bought a car for you."

Once again Amalie stood dumbfounded as everyone else poured out of the house in the dwindling light of the early spring evening to get a closer look at the used touring car.

"Oh, Gunther . . . " was all Amalie could manage to say. Jakob immediately jumped behind the steering wheel and pretended to drive as Gunther and Klaus looked the car over, discussing the engine and how far it could go on a full tank of gas, and so on. Jakob startled everyone as he honked the horn, and it was Gertrude who reprimanded him, telling him he shouldn't do that because he might wear out the car before his mother even got a chance to ride in it. After a few minutes, Gertrude wiped her eyes, still wet from the emotional reunion, and insisted that they all come in for dinner, and everyone started to file in slowly, Gunther and Klaus, followed by Katrina and then Gertrude and Friedrich, until Amalie and Jakob were alone as she looked the car over admiringly.

"Is it really ours, Mother?" Jakob asked dreamily.

"No, it's mine. Your father gave it to me," Amalie said playfully.

"Won't you even let me ride in it?"

Amalie smiled and gave Jakob a hug, struggling as she managed to pull him out of the driver's seat. "Ja, Elch-kind,"[18] she replied as they walked toward the house, Jakob standing a full two inches taller than his mother.

When they joined the others at the dinner table, Gunther told his wife that Friedrich had a wonderful suggestion, that they should all pack a lunch and

---

[18]"Yes, moose child."

take a long drive to the mountains for a picnic the next day. Klaus said he would drive and they could take both cars, so that everyone could go.

"And Friedrich can show me how to drive," Amalie added.

The three men exchanged amused glances without saying anything, but Amalie caught on immediately.

"Now you all stop that. I'll be a good driver!"

"Yes, I think she will too," Katrina added supportively, taking Amalie by surprise.

"Thank you, Katrina," Amalie acknowledged with a nod.

The meal was delicious, and made even better by the unexpected presence of Friedrich, whose adventures in Berlin fairly dominated the conversation throughout the evening, not by Friedrich's choice, but by virtue of the continuing stream of questions from everyone else.

The time that Friedrich had been in Berlin had been a particularly decadent period in the history of the city. Friedrich was careful to use euphemistic terms in his descriptions of the night life, in consideration of the attentive presence of the women and children. Katrina felt a little out of place, not having met Friedrich before and not having much interest in the terrible things going on in Berlin, so she ended up in the living room with her sons, playing with them and keeping them occupied.

It was almost midnight when Klaus got up, declaring it was time to leave, and went into the living room to gather up his sleeping wife and children.

"We'll be at your door at ten o'clock tomorrow

morning, so you should all be ready to go or we'll leave without you," Klaus declared.

"But you don't even know where we're going," Friedrich said with a laugh, since he was the one who had mysteriously suggested a spectacular picnic location without revealing where it was.

"No matter," Klaus said boastfully. "We'll just drive south until we see a mountain."

"Katrina," Amalie said, "maybe you should drive home tonight . . ."

"No, I'm so tired that I don't care where we end up. It's up to Klaus where we go."

Everyone managed to help Klaus and Katrina gather up toys and children's jackets and blankets, and all the rest, and get them on their way in under half an hour, which was no small accomplishment. There was a collective sigh of relief once they had gone, and only then did Gertrude think to consider where Friedrich would sleep.

"He can sleep in my room," Jakob said excitedly, pleased that he had something to offer the great adventurer. "I can sleep on the floor and you can use my bed," he continued, addressing Friedrich directly.

"I wouldn't want to put you out of your bed," Friedrich replied with a laugh.

"No, really, I wouldn't mind," Jakob insisted.

"You might as well," Gunther agreed, and Friedrich went out to the car to get his bag.

When Gertrude and her son met in the hallway a short time later, she got up the courage to ask him how long he would be visiting.

"I think I might be moving back for good," he

said, and once again Gertrude couldn't help but embrace him.

Her first thought was that everything could be the way it was, but she quickly dismissed that as an old woman's fantasy. Nothing could be like it was before. Nonetheless, it was a wonderful feeling, knowing that he would be living in Munich again.

The house finally quieted down as everyone went to bed. In the eerily brilliant moonlight that drifted in through the window of his room, Jakob looked over at Friedrich.

"Friedrich?" he whispered. "Are you awake?"

"Yes," Friedrich mumbled as he lay on his stomach with his face in the pillow. "What is it?"

"Tonight . . . ," Jakob began tenuously, carefully choosing his words, "when you were talking . . . What's a 'lady of the evening'?"

Friedrich lifted his head and looked over at Jakob. "How old are you?"

"Thirteen . . . and a half."

"Thirteen . . . " Friedrich repeated as he considered his response.

"And a half," Jakob repeated, hoping to get Friedrich to give him a man's answer rather than the answer a man would give to a little boy.

"Well . . . it's a woman who offers herself . . . who agrees to stay with a man if he pays her."

"A whore?"

Friedrich smirked as the unexpected reply registered. "If you knew what a whore was, then why did you ask?"

"I'd never heard them called 'lady of the evening' before."

"Oh."

"Did you ever . . . ?"

"Pay for a woman? No," Friedrich lied.

In truth, when Friedrich first arrived in Berlin and was all alone in the city, he found that he could get a room and a girl for almost nothing. Soon afterward he was using the proceeds from some black market transactions to avail himself of such accommodations. He certainly didn't think that was the sort of thing he should reveal to Jakob. As a matter of fact, as it turned out, Friedrich would never speak to anyone about such particulars of those days in Berlin.

"How old were you when you first . . . " Jakob pressed on cautiously.

"You shouldn't think of such things," Friedrich admonished sanctimoniously. "When you get married, you will . . ."

"Are you married?"

"No, not yet."

"Are you going to get married soon?"

"I don't know, but there is this girl . . ."

"In Berlin?"

"No, she lives down here."

"Munich?"

"No," Friedrich said, and then after a short pause he asked Jakob if he could keep a secret.

"Yes," Jakob replied earnestly. "Absolutely."

"Tomorrow's trip . . . we're going to see her."

"What's her name?"

"Angela . . . but everyone calls her Geli."

The next day, true to his word, Klaus and his family drove up in front of the Metzdorf home at ten o'clock, honking the horn. It was a perfect Bavarian spring day, and everyone was ready to go. At the last moment Jakob insisted on bringing Honig so that she, too, could enjoy a romp in the fresh mountain air, and even though Gunther protested, Amalie sided with Jakob and Honig's passage was secured. It was a tight fit, but Honig rode on Jakob's lap while he and Gunther sat in the back seat and Amalie and Gertrude sat in front, with Friedrich driving. Amalie watched carefully as Friedrich worked the clutch and shifted gears, and he tried to give her instruction on the shifting pattern of the stick as they went along.

They soon drove through the small village of Grunewald and laughed as Klaus started honking and waving as they passed through the town that bore his last name.

They had driven for almost an hour when Friedrich suggested they stop and all get out and stretch their legs in the town of Rosenheim. Gunther wanted to visit the house his grandfather had owned, so Friedrich followed his instructions and stopped across the street from the simple cottage.

"It seems so much smaller," Gunther said as he got out and looked at the house. Jakob put Honig on a leash as everyone else got out of the car, and Honig immediately began to bark at another dog in one of the yards.

Gunther was lost in thought as he crossed the street and walked up to the front yard of the house. It needed painting, but the yard was well kept and planted with flowers.

"Ten . . . eleven years . . . ," Gunther wondered.

"Eleven now," Amalie said as she stood beside him, confirming how many years it had been since his grandfather had died.

"This was one of the places that got me through, during the war," Gunther said thoughtfully. "You and Jakob . . . my mother . . . and here. I never said it before, but I loved him more than I loved my father."

"I know," Amalie said as she took his hand and squeezed it gently. He didn't think it had been that obvious and was surprised that she knew. He put his arm around her and they walked back across the street to the car, by which time Klaus and Katrina and the boys pulled up and Klaus asked why they had stopped. Gunther had told Klaus about his grandfather during the time that they were together at the front during the war. Gunther went on to tell a couple of the funny stories the old man used to tell over and over, like the first time they saw a train locomotive, and the stories about being a stable boy for a baron when he was a boy.

When it was time to get going again, Klaus and Friedrich insisted that Amalie take the wheel and try to get them out of town. Amalie tried to perfect letting out the clutch at the right time while pulling out into the street and then shifting into second and third gears. After a while she managed to get them to the edge of town, where she turned things back over to Friedrich.

It turned out to be a rather long trip, eventually stretching out to more than two hours and several more rest stops before they reached the small town of Berchtesgaden at the foot of the mountains.

"I want to say hello to someone," Friedrich said unexpectedly as he pulled up to the driveway of one of the mountain villas. Klaus pulled his car up beside them and got out, once again asking why they had stopped.

"We must be close. We certainly don't want to go up any farther. It's still awfully cold up in the mountains," Klaus said.

Just then Friedrich came down from the house with a pretty young woman with light brown hair, both of them smiling and laughing. Klaus looked at the two of them walking toward the car for a moment and then turned to Gunther with a big smile. "So this is why we drove for two and a half hours. The perfect picnic spot, eh?"

Gertrude shifted in her seat, suddenly feeling uncomfortable as she watched her son and the strange girl walking toward them.

"I had to stop since we were so close," Friedrich said when they got to the car. "I thought maybe Geli would like to come on the picnic with us, if it's all right with everyone."

"Geli?" Klaus said in a tone meant to needle Friedrich, as it became apparent that this had been Friedrich's plan all along.

"Oh . . . yes. This is Geli. Geli, these are my friends. Klaus, Gunther, Gunther's wife Amalie, their son Jakob, and this is my mother, Gertrude." It was apparent that Friedrich was uncomfortable as his transparent plan was exposed, and he wasn't very good at covering his embarrassment.

Amalie seemed to be the only one willing to let

him off the hook as she held out her hand to Geli. "Hello, it's nice to meet you. You're certainly welcome to come along. We have plenty, don't we?" she said as she turned to Gertrude.

"Yes," Gertrude said curtly. "We have plenty."

Geli agreed, saying she just needed a moment to tell her mother she was going. Friedrich explained to everyone that there was a terrific picnic area on the Königssee, just a few kilometers to the west.

Geli was very talkative and pleasant as they drove, explaining how she and her mother had just moved from Austria to take care of the villa for her Uncle Alfie.

"Uncle Alfie?" Gunther asked from behind her.

"Yes," she said as she tried to turn enough to make eye contact. "He's some sort of politician in Munich."

"Adolf Hitler?" Gunther asked in an odd way that made the question sound like a statement.

"Yes! Do you know him?"

"We're from Munich. Everyone in Munich has heard of him."

"I knew he was popular, but I didn't realize he was that important," Geli said.

They soon pulled into the picnic area by the Königssee, where everyone's first instinct was to get out and stretch. Amalie and Gertrude started to unpack the food while Jakob unleashed Honig and ran to the lake. Katrina started getting the boys out of the other car, and the men gravitated together.

"Hitler's niece?" Gunther queried with a smile.

"What!" Klaus shot back, as Friedrich just smiled. "You're trying to seduce the Führer's[19] niece?"

"I wouldn't say that," Friedrich said impishly. "I met her a week ago and she said I should stop by sometime."

"Do you think she really meant it?" Gunther asked.

"If she didn't, she certainly covered well when I showed up at the door," Friedrich replied. "She seemed really happy to see me."

"Come over here!" Gertrude suddenly called out to the three men. "It's time to eat. Everything is ready."

Gunther yelled to Jakob, who had taken off his shoes and rolled his pant legs up and was running along the shore, splashing in the cold water of the Königssee as Honig chased happily beside him. Both of them turned and ran toward the picnic site when they heard Gunther calling. Just before they reached the blankets Amalie and Gertrude had carefully laid out for everyone to sit on, Jakob called Honig back and leashed her to a tree about twenty meters from the cars, so that she wouldn't bother anyone while they were eating.

The weather had held up nicely all morning. It was fairly warm for early June in the mountains, with just a light breeze. The conversation was pleasant, with Klaus resisting the urge to embarrass Friedrich in front of Geli and Geli managing to hold her own whichever way the conversation turned. She talked very casually about how her father had died and her mother had welcomed "Uncle Alf's" offer to come

---

[19]The term *Führer* translates at "leader," but *Der Führer,* or "the leader," was a term reserved strictly for Adolf Hitler.

and keep house for him at the villa he rented in Berchtesgaden. She had met Friedrich just a week before in Munich, when she had gone visiting with her mother. Friedrich explained that he had actually been in Munich for more than a week, but he had had a bit of trouble tracking down Gertrude until he caught up with Klaus through some of the Nazi party members, and Klaus had then gotten in touch with Gunther.

They had just finished eating and everyone was either lying back and relaxing or cleaning up when Amalie noticed the dog out of the corner of her eye. It moved slowly and tiredly, straying from place to place in the sparse pine trees near the picnic ground. It didn't seem out of place; in fact, Amalie's first thought was that it must belong to one of the other families that were out enjoying a picnic along the lakefront.

When the dog got closer, Amalie could tell it was a Doberman, and it suddenly occurred to her that Honig was tied out between the Doberman and the picnic area, and she told Jakob to go get Honig so that the two dogs wouldn't start fighting. After all, she assured herself, the strange dog wouldn't come near the family.

Amalie turned back to what she was doing as she packed dishes in a basket, but looked up just in time to see the strange dog as it caught sight of Jakob running over to Honig. The dog's head jerked up as though it had just noticed the people, even though the whole group was less than twenty meters away. Honig suddenly started barking at the Doberman and the Doberman charged. Amalie sat frozen. It was as though everything was moving in slow motion as the dog charged toward Jakob and Honig. She finally managed to break from her trance and reach out to Gunther.

"My God! Look!" she shrieked as she shook Gunther. "It's going to attack!" Gunther immediately jumped up, but by that time the Doberman had already pounced on Honig, immediately clamping down on her throat and lifting her off the ground, flailing her body as it tried to break her neck. Jakob was only a few steps away, and he jumped on the Doberman, knocking it sideways and reaching his left arm around the dog's torso while clutching at the its throat, trying to force it to release his beloved Honig. The dog let go of the mortally wounded Honig and turned on Jakob, slashing at his forearm with a twist of its head and then biting down on the fleshy part of his hand between the thumb and index finger. At that moment Gunther's foot came up and kicked the Doberman in the back, just below the neck. The dog suddenly turned on its new attacker and Jakob fell off, writhing in pain and holding his right hand and forearm against his chest. The Doberman, now back on all fours, was about to lunge at Gunther as their eyes locked. The dog hesitated for an instant for some unknown reason as his muscles tensed, and then he sprang. The Doberman didn't even see the tree limb as it struck him to the ground short of his prey. Klaus had run over to the trees and found a fallen limb, and was using it as a weapon, continuing to beat the Doberman after it had fallen. It was as though he had gone crazy, hitting the bloody corpse again and again.

Amalie hadn't even heard herself shrieking and screaming as the attack occurred. It wasn't until the others had run over that she realized she was hoarse. Once Klaus and Gunther were sure the dog was dead, Gunther walked over to his son. Jakob was crying uncontrollably. He was petting Honig's bloody fur and repeating over and over, "Oh, Honig, Honig . . . Meine schones Honig."[20] Gunther picked up his son and held him tightly against his chest as Amalie rushed toward them, with Geli and Gertrude close behind. "I know the way to the doctor's house in town," Geli offered, and she helped as Gunther got into the back seat of the car, still holding Jakob across his lap. Friedrich got in front to drive while Geli got in on the passenger side to navigate, and they sped off down the road.

Those remaining just stood by in disbelief as they watched the dust billow up from behind the car. "I'll have to take the dog in," Klaus said quickly as he walked over to the dead Doberman and wrapped it in one of the blankets, then threw it into the trunk of his car. He hoped he could catch up with the others because he didn't know where they were going.

"I'm going with," Amalie said. It was natural for her to want to be with Jakob, but the others had left so quickly that she'd had no chance to get in the car.

Katrina came up to the door just as Klaus was going to take off. "What about us?"

"You and Gertrude and the boys wait here. Once I find out where they are, I'll come back and get you." He then stepped on the gas, throwing up dirt and

[20]"My beautiful Honig."

rocks behind the car as he began the race to catch up with Friedrich.

Gertrude stepped back and finished gathering everything up. A few moments later, she turned and caught sight of Katrina's sons standing in a row, staring at Honig, lying bloody and still, and she began to cry. Katrina called the boys away and then walked over to Gertrude and embraced her.

"WHY DID YOU let him bring the dog?" Amalie asked herself in a low voice between clenched teeth as she and Klaus raced down the road after the others. Klaus didn't say anything, and Amalie repeated the question, not wanting to ask the other question. She knew the answer, but for some strange reason she had to have Klaus confirm it.

"Rabies," he said without looking at her. Nothing more was said as they drove into town.

Amalie was numb by the time they caught up with Jakob and Gunther at the doctor's office. The doctor did what he could to clean up the wounds, but told them they should take Jakob to the hospital in Salzburg for the best care. Klaus pulled the doctor aside to explain that he had the body of the dog in his trunk, and the doctor told him it should go to the same hospital so that they could run tests and get results as soon as possible.

Klaus took Geli home on his way to get Gertrude and his family, telling Katrina and Gertie what had happened and suggesting they might as well go home to Munich.

Anger flared in Gertrude's eyes. "If you think I'm going back to Munich while little Jakob . . . ," she started. "Klaus Grunewald, I've loved that boy as if he were one of my own for as long as I've known you, and I will walk to Salzburg before I leave him lying hurt in a Salzburg hospital. He needs his Grandma Gertie as much as he needs his mother and father!"

Klaus looked at the expression on Katrina's face as she held his own youngest son in her arms, and he knew they had to go to Salzburg with the others.

It turned out that the Doberman was not rabid—just an old dog that had apparently wandered away and gotten lost in the woods. The doctor said the dog was probably so old that he could barely see, and from what Gunther explained about the incident, the doctor thought it was most likely the movement of Jakob's running and the other dog's barking that prompted the attack. In short, it seems that Honig and Jakob just got in the way of a lost and confused old dog as it lashed out in its last fit of energy and rage at a foreign and frightening world.

Even though the dog was not rabid, and the doctor in Berchtesgaden had done a good job of cleaning Jakob's wounds, there was still a great danger of infection, as with any animal attack, and the doctor insisted on keeping Jakob there until the following Wednesday. Since they were in Salzburg, Amalie called her father and told him what was going on, and he immediately came to the hospital.

Klaus and Katrina, feeling they had done all they could, decided to leave after a couple of hours.

"I think I'm going to leave with Klaus," Gunther said to Amalie as they stood by Jakob's bed.

"Please don't go," Jakob interrupted.

Gunther turned to his son, taking his hand. "You'll be fine now. I've got to get home to work. Your mother and I can't both take off work. She'll stay."

"But I want you to stay, too. I . . ."

"No, I'm sorry son, but it's best I go. You just have to understand."

Jakob did understand. Other things always came first for his father. This was just one more time when Jakob was an inconvenience to him.

Amalie called David Frieder at home to tell him that she would be staying. Gertrude and Friedrich both decided to stay too, Gertrude because she wanted to be with Jakob and Friedrich because he knew Amalie wasn't able to drive the car by herself yet. Ethan offered to put them all up in his home.

The days passed quickly as Jakob returned to good spirits and the feared infection never materialized. He knew his bandages and the scars they covered would impress everyone at school, and he wore them proudly as proof of how he had fended off a wild beast in the woods with his bare hands. He became very quiet as they passed through Berchtesgaden on the way home, thinking of Honig and wondering if she was still lying out in the forest somewhere by the Königssee, but he couldn't bring himself to ask if it was true.

Gunther was already home from work by the time the group arrived. They were all glad to be home again to familiar beds and back to their normal routine. No one spoke of Honig or the attack. Gertrude went about making dinner after changing into clean clothes, and Amalie walked over to the apotheke[21] to get the bandages and ointments necessary for changing the dressings on Jakob's wounds. Friedrich immediately monopolized the telephone as he began to call his party contacts so that he could find work and move back to Munich for good.

Jakob disappeared into his room, lying on his bed and reading the latest book by Otto Maus. Otto hadn't forgotten Jakob, and whenever he finished writing a book, he made sure to send an autographed copy to his young fan. Jakob found the books to be light reading, but he respected that Otto considered him a friend and dutifully read each one as though it were an obligation.

Gunther looked in as he walked by his son's bedroom. "Jakob, if you have a moment, I'd like you to come outside with me," he said in a way that caught Jakob off guard. It sounded like a request, a marked contrast to Gunther's usual draconian tendencies.

Jakob immediately sat up on the bed, quickly marking his place in the book before following his father out to the back yard. It was a very small yard, just large enough to hold the little vegetable garden that Gertrude tended and a garage.

"I guess we'll have to clean up the garage now that we have a car," he said offhandedly as they walked. Gunther stopped short of the outbuilding and turned toward the garden, where there now stood a little rhunic marker, a stake with a gabled roof on it and the inscription: HONIG, TREU KLEINE FREUNDIN.[22]

---

[21]Apothecary or drug store.

[22]"Honig, true little friend."

Jakob was speechless as he stood and stared at the marker. His father had taken the time to bring Honig home and bury her there. It was something he never would have expected. He didn't think his father had cared about the dog, and suddenly Jakob realized that he hadn't even known how much his father cared about him until they took that panicked ride to the doctor's office. His father had held him so tightly, so close, as though he would never let go and never let anything hurt him.

What a confusing time it is to be thirteen. A boy thinks that he has begun to know certain things. He identifies and passes judgment on people in his life, and thinks he is well on his way to being a man, singular and independent. Then things happen that make him feel like such a child again, so frightened and helpless. People constantly surprise you, for better and for worse.

"You brought her home," Jakob half whispered.

"She was a good dog," Gunther pronounced, putting his arm around Jakob's shoulder. "We couldn't just leave her there."

Jakob turned under his father's arm and hugged him, surprising Gunther. Gunther then turned back to the garage as though that had been their true destination all along, as though he had only intended to discuss cleaning out the garage so that the car could be stored there and they had only happened upon the little grave next to the garden by accident.

CHAPTER 9

It wasn't long after Adolf Hitler's release from prison that the Nazi party began to grow again, soon becoming even larger than it had been before the failed Putsch *in Munich. The trial had generated enormous publicity for Adolf Hitler throughout the world, transforming the Nazi party into a growing national movement.*

As with any political group, the leaders of the Nazi party tended to socialize within their own ranks, and a result of this was the formation of a youth association for their children based on national socialist political views. The Nazi youth organization, called the "Hitler Jugend," or "HJ" for short, was developed along the lines of other groups such as the Catholic and the Communist youth organizations that had been around for quite some time by then.

Eventually, when the Nazi party and Adolf Hitler came to power, membership in the Hitler Youth would become obligatory for both boys and girls from the ages of ten to eighteen. Over time the HJ would split into different age group and gender subdivisions, while other youth groups would be outlawed in Germany. The evolution of the Hitler Youth programs paralleled the development of the Nazi party within Germany. The HJ would become a forum for the political indoctrination of those who were being forced to join. Ultimately, as Germany moved past the rearmament period and toward seemingly inevitable military confrontations, the Hitler Youth programs became paramilitary training grounds for the young people of

Germany. The HJ and its related programs would virtually deify Adolf Hitler in the minds of these impressionable children.

"YOU KNOW she was born close to there, don't you?"

"Who?"

"Geli, of course!"

"Friedrich, why is it that whenever I talk to you these days, you always manage to turn the conversation around to that girl?"

"Well, I guess I just think about her a lot."

"That's pretty obvious!"

"But don't you like her, Amalie?"

"Of course I like her, but I like a lot of people."

"But don't you think she's something special?"

"Special?"

"Yes . . . almost like you would think she was a princess or something . . . if you didn't know better."

"Oh, Friedrich! You really do have it bad!"

"Please don't joke with me Amalie. She's making me crazy! She seems to like me well enough, but nothing ever happens. Even when we've gone out alone once or twice, it's as though I'm just an escort that Uncle Alf has arranged because he's too busy to go himself."

"I hate to be the one to say it, but hasn't it occurred to you that she might just be flirting with you? Have you ever just come out and said how much you like her?"

"No, not really."

"Well, then, what's this all about? Why would you expect her to pay any real attention to you if you never even declare yourself?"

"I'm afraid she doesn't feel the same about me and I'll just embarrass myself."

"Can that be any worse than torturing yourself like this?"

"Yes!"

"How? How could it be worse?"

"Amalie, if I tell her how I feel and she rejects me, she could tell Uncle Alf that I'm annoying her. That would be terrible. Who knows what he might do? He's very protective of her."

"Friedrich, I don't want to be the one to hurt you . . ." Amalie said, fumbling with the words as she tried to find a delicate way to explain the situation, "but there are certain things . . . Friedrich, a lot of people are saying that Geli and her uncle are . . . 'involved.'"

"Oh, Amalie, you can't believe all that talk. Geli has even told me she's heard what they're saying and it's just not so."

"Well . . . I guess people will always talk. Especially when it involves someone so well known."

"Yes, that's it . . . It's just talk. Amalie, I need someone to help me."

"Help you? How?"

"I thought maybe someone might ask her if she cares about me. Someone who could save me from making a fool of myself. I couldn't stand it if she laughed at me. I need someone to find out if there's even a chance . . ."

Amalie couldn't hold back a smile as she asked the question for which she already knew the answer. "Who?"

"Well, I thought maybe you might . . . you seem to like her . . ."

"I hardly know her. We've only met a couple of times."

"That's the beauty of it. You're going to Vienna on business, and she told me that she wanted to go back there for a day or two to pick up a few things from her mother's house. You could go together."

"Well, I guess I could . . . if she wanted to . . . ," Amalie said hesitantly.

"Excellent! When are you going?"

Amalie told him about her plans to visit Vienna. David Frieder had entrusted her to negotiate a financial agreement with a retired archeologist there who had written a book in connection with several excavations in Egypt, including his very limited contact with the men who eventually uncovered the tomb of King Tutankhamen. The book was only significant in that the author had a number of contacts in the teaching community who had committed themselves to using it as required reading for beginning archeology courses in universities across the country.

The commitment by the author's friends was just a ploy to give the old man a little something extra for his retirement income, but David only cared that he had a product with a guaranteed market. Thus, he looked upon it as a chance to continue Amalie's education in the publishing business with the rare opportunity of a learning experience with limited variables. In other words, there was no chance of Amalie making any big mistakes that could ruin the company while she still had the latitude to make a good deal for the publisher if she worked at it.

After Friedrich left, Amalie began thinking about the implications of Geli accompanying her to Vienna. She wondered to herself how it might help the cause she had abandoned almost five years before, when she had been investigating Hitler's background and couldn't find any leads for evidence of anything that might hurt the party.

She decided to take a quick trip to Sam Frieder's house. Maybe she would start looking around again, but this time with the assistance, albeit unwitting, of a member of the Hiedler family.

Sam was now sixty-seven years old, but there was no sign of him slowing down in his hobbies and clubs.

"Amalie," he said warmly as he opened the door, "how are you?"

"Very well, Sam. And you?"

He thought about it for a moment and then smiled. "Pretty good. Yes, I'm doing all right. So," he continued as he motioned for Amalie to sit, "what brings you out so far to see David's crazy old father?"

"Oh, it's not so far now. Didn't David tell you that my family has moved out here? We're practically neighbors now. I only live a few blocks away."

"Well, that's nice news."

"Yes, it's a very nice neighborhood."

"That's good . . . very nice . . . So, how are things at the office?"

"Business is good. Hasn't David talked to you? He says he calls every week."

Sam smiled at this and cupped his hand to his mouth, delivering a stage whisper. "I'm checking up on him."

Amalie laughed and reassured Sam that things were going very well for the company, and then her expression changed as she brought up her reason for visiting. "Sam, do you remember when we first met, and we talked about . . . an investigation."

"A what . . . oh yes. You were checking up on Hitler. Well, things certainly have changed since then. Most say he'll just fade away pretty soon."

"I've heard that too, but I don't believe it."

"Why?"

"I know it might sound foolish, but it's my husband. He supported Hitler in the beginning, until the *Putsch*."

"That's what got you started in all this," Sam asked.

"Yes. Well, Gunther let it all drop after Hitler was arrested, but lately he's started listening again. It seems that Hitler has changed his approach. He's not as . . ."

"Reactionary?"

"Yes. I think he's just changed tactics to appeal to more people. I'm not really sure, but that's the feeling I get when I listen to Gunther's friends."

"So what is your question, Amalie?"

"Sam, I can't tell you everything, because I just think that the fewer people who know what I'm doing, the better. Not that I don't trust you . . ."

"I take it you're going to start looking into things again."

"Yes, but this time there is a difference. I think I may have a connection in Hitler's family. He's always gone to great lengths to keep his past under wraps...

Have you read his book?"

"I tried, but it was such meandering drivel . . ."

"Absolutely," Amalie concurred, "but I forced myself to read it all, and he never talks about his family except for brief mentions of his mother and father."

"So you think he has something to hide?"

"I'm hoping."

"What do you want from me?"

"I need some advice. When I went out before, all I had to go by was gravestones and church records."

"Did you find anything?"

"There was one discrepancy in particular . . ." Amalie stopped, realizing how easy it would be to tell everything to Sam, but he noticed the look on her face as she stopped.

"Never mind," he said. "It's not important that I know the details. What advice do you want?"

"Sam, what would be considered proof? Do you have any idea what I might be looking for?"

Sam laughed at this. "You can't tell me what you've found so far and now you want me to tell you what you're looking for."

Amalie smiled weakly at the paradox but didn't comment.

"All right then," Sam said thoughtfully as he stroked his chin and looked up at the ceiling. "As near as I can figure, you must be talking about some scandal in his family . . . perhaps heredity. Well, if you're looking for his family, I can only think of a few sources that would go back more than two generations. You mentioned headstones and church records. Beyond that, the only sorts of records for that time would probably be a family Bible or, if there was any land ownership, a will. If the family was important, there could be city records, but if they lived in a village or small town, chances are there would be no reliable town records. There might be tax records . . . other than that, I wouldn't know."

GELI RAUBAL did accompany Amalie on the trip to Vienna on a Friday morning some two weeks later. Geli went directly to her mother's house while Amalie met with the retired archeologist.

Everything in the Raubal house was covered for storage, so Geli took a room at a small hotel nearby for her and Amalie to share that night. Amalie arrived at the house some four hours later, and when she knocked on the door, it swung open and she just walked in, looking around until she heard Geli singing and slowly followed the sound to one of the two small bedrooms upstairs. Geli was startled when she looked up at the doorway to see Amalie standing there.

"That didn't take very long," she said pleasantly.

"No," Amalie said with a hint of defeat in her voice.

"Didn't things go well?"

"They went well enough...," Amalie admitted. "I just took one look at this old man who had never written a book before and probably never will again..."

"You think you gave in too easily?"

"Maybe a bit."

"So," Geli began facetiously, "you probably should have pushed his face into the ground and forced him to take half of what he wanted."

"You're absolutely right!" Amalie said with a laugh as she pointed a finger at Geli to punctuate the point.

Amalie sat beside Geli as she went through her things. They discussed Geli's treasures, Amalie asking about various items as Geli set them aside and explained the history behind them. This came from the fair in Linz, that was a gift from the first boy who ever kissed her, and so on. It was clear that Geli planned on staying with Uncle Alf for quite a while and wanted to bring her prized childhood mementos back to Germany to make it more like home.

"Are we going to try to take everything with us?" Amalie asked.

"Of course," Geli rejoined.

"I mean, why don't you get some boxes and pack it up to ship as freight to Berchtesgaden?"

"That sounds like a good idea," Geli agreed. "Let's go get some crates now so I can pack things as I go through them."

"If you don't mind, I'd really like to just take off my shoes and sit for awhile," Amalie said as she dropped a shoe and started to rub her foot.

"You wait here then. I'll be back in a few minutes."

When Amalie had visited Spital years before and asked about Alois Hitler, Adolf Hitler's father, the local people pointed out a house there and mentioned Alois' daughter and son-in-law. Angela Raubal, Geli's mother, was that daughter. She was Alois' daughter by his first wife, and she had married Leo Raubal. They had moved to Vienna some time after that.

Amalie hadn't had a chance to get into the house in Spital, but now she felt that if such a record as a family Bible existed for the Hitler family, she might be able to find it in this apartment in Vienna. That was why she had contrived to have Geli leave the house so that she might search the apartment.

Amalie started methodically going from room to room, checking for any books at all. Geli had to go to a couple of places looking for boxes and ended up walking to the train station, where they had crates for sale at the freight window. It was a little awkward carrying the boxes back to the house, and all told, Amalie had about an hour to go through the house uninterrupted, but even so she couldn't find what she was looking for.

Geli didn't suspect anything as she cheerfully pushed her way into the house, letting the boxes fall about her. She started recounting her adventure of finding them as she went into the kitchen and started digging under the sink for a hammer to pry open the empty crates. Complaining how stuffy the house was after being closed up for several months, she opened the door off the kitchen to let in some air. When she started walking back to the living room, a breeze caught the door and slammed it shut, so she went back to open the door again, this time reaching up to a shelf in the closet near the door and pulling down an old box, which she used to prop open the door.

Amalie helped Geli pack up her things in the boxes and then nailed the lids on as Geli finished labeling the boxes for delivery.

"There! That's all done," Geli said as she fumbled through her pockets for keys. "I suppose we'd better lock up."

"Don't forget the kitchen," Amalie said, reminding Geli of the other door.

"Wouldn't that be a joke! Take the time to lock the front door and leave the back door wide open," Geli said as she breezed into the kitchen.

"Mother would kill me if she saw that!" she called out to Amalie in the other room.

"Saw what?" Amalie asked, humoring Geli as she rattled on.

"Using that old Bible to prop open the door."

Amalie just smiled, but her heart leapt as she took a couple of quick steps toward the kitchen just in time to see Geli pick up the old, handmade wooden box and put it back on the shelf in the closet.

"Well, I have some friends I promised to meet," Geli said as they both headed for the front door. "Would you like to come along?"

"No, I promised my sister I would stop by."

"Oh, you have relatives here?"

"My sister and brother-in-law and their daughters."

"Do you come often then?"

"No, not at all. As a matter of fact I haven't seen my sister in ten years."

"Ten years?"

Amalie was a little embarrassed. It had really been more like twelve years, but she thought it sound sounded better just saying ten. "I know. It sounds terrible, but after our mother died when we were young, we grew apart. Eleonore left home when she was seventeen to marry and . . . well, months become years, and before you know it, it's been five and then ten."

"I always wished I had had a sister."

"There are no guarantees, Geli."

"What?"

"I wish my sister and I could have been more . . . I wish we could have gotten along, but it just didn't work out that way. Just being sisters wasn't enough to make us best friends."

"Don't you like her at all?"

"Certainly . . . I mean, she is my sister. I love her like a sister, but she just isn't the sort of person I'd choose as a friend if we weren't related."

"Ten years!" Geli repeated with a note of astonishment. "Well, I hope you have a good reunion. I'll see you later at the hotel."

This was the first time Amalie had been to Vienna since the war. She had visited Eleonore and Louis soon after they had married and moved into a dingy little apartment there. It had been an awkward visit. Amalie had expected she would stay with them for the two days, but Eleonore insisted there wasn't enough room and told Amalie very pointedly that she must find a hotel room. The visit ended on an even more unpleasant note as they got into an argument, which culminated in Eleonore shouting at Amalie that Amalie was her sister, not her mother. Even though apologies had been exchanged and the two corresponded regularly, there were still buried resentments between them. After all, it wasn't just that Amalie hadn't visited Eleonore in ten years; Eleonore hadn't made the trip to Munich either.

Amalie mentioned in a letter that she would be in Vienna on business, and Eleonore had written back and said it would be the perfect chance for her to stop by. Amalie had never even seen Eleonore's daughters, three-year-old Rachel and five-year-old Sophie.

"Amalie!" Louis said as he embraced his sister-in-law in a great bear hug. Amalie couldn't help staring. He had lost a great deal of hair and put on considerable weight since she had last seen him, but even so he looked better than when he was younger. He had looked so strict and humorless back then, with his large black-rimmed eyeglasses perched on top of a triangular face, his wiry black hair growing out of control. Now the features had softened as they expanded, and the brass of his wire-rimmed glasses complemented his slightly tanned, pinkish complexion.

Louis and Eleonore's apartment was much nicer than the one Amalie had visited ten years earlier.

"Louis . . . how are you?"

"Wonderful. Things are wonderful. Come, you've got to meet the girls."

"Where's Eleonore?

"You just missed her. I'm surprised you two didn't run into each other on the stairs. She went out for coffee. We don't drink much, so she forgot to check, and when she went to make some, we were out. She'll only be a minute. It's funny . . . she said you'd come while she was gone."

"It's always like that . . . a watched pot," Amalie interjected, trying to slow down Louis's rapid-fire ramblings.

"Yes, that's right," he continued as he ushered Amalie into the living room. He stopped in the doorway and drew in a loud breath. "Well," he said as he smiled proudly, "here are the girls."

It was obvious that the pretty little girls had been told to sit and wait quietly until their Aunt Amalie came, as though they were prized possessions on display. Seeing the two girls fidgeting as they waited for inspection reminded Amalie of herself and Eleonore when they were young girls.

"This is Rachel," Louis bubbled as his daughters stood up, "and the oldest there is Sophie. Come, girls, give your Aunt Amalie a kiss."

Eleonore came in just as Amalie knelt and took the two girls in her arms, in more of a gathering gesture than an embrace, and Rachel and Sophie offered up their obligatory kisses. "So, you've met my little darlings."

"Eleonore!" Amalie said as she abruptly stood up, leaving Rachel and Sophie in mid-kiss. She was stunned. Her sister had put on weight too, but that wasn't what shocked Amalie. Eleonore looked just like Ruth, just like their mother had looked in those happier days so long before.

BACK IN MUNICH, Friedrich, Klaus, and Gunther were having a reunion at the Sterneckerbräu on Herrnstrasse.

"Here's to your return!" Klaus said as he raised his beer stein to toast Friedrich.

"It's been a long time," Gunther mused. "Remember that night we first met the Führer?"

"Of course. How could anyone forget?" Friedrich

replied. "Just about ten years ago now . . . You were with him in twenty-three, weren't you?"

"Yes," Klaus said. "That was when this one left!" he continued, referring to Gunther's departure from the party.

"I thought it was over," Gunther said defensively. "The police and army against us, Hitler in jail, the deutsche mark stabilized . . . It just didn't seem to make a difference anymore."

"Just wait," Klaus replied, "the time will come again when it will make a difference."

"Are you thinking of rejoining?" Friedrich asked Gunther, ready to sell him on the party and its war against Bolshevism.

"I'm older now. I choose my battles more carefully. It's not enough to fight just for the sake of fighting."

"It sounds like you've grown fond of the republic," Klaus said with an air of contempt.

"Oh, come now, Klaus! Having Hindenburg as president is not like having Ebert or Eisner running the country."

"But it's still a republic. A confused, pathetic, rambling collection of committees," Klaus declared with a finality that just left Gunther exasperated at his friends intransigence.

"Can't we talk about something else?" Gunther asked.

THE NEXT morning, a bright and sunny Saturday morning, Amalie and Geli got up at about nine o'clock and had a leisurely breakfast at the hotel before getting ready to catch the train home.

"So . . . how was your sister?"

"Good. Very good. It was probably the nicest visit we've ever had. She has two darling little girls, and her husband has become . . ." Amalie paused as she searched for an explanation.

What?" Geli asked impatiently.

"I don't know. He just seemed so happy to see me, and they were all so nice. Now I wish I had gone sooner."

"You see! People can change," Geli said triumphantly.

"I'll tell you what," Amalie began, changing the subject. "Let's split up the work. You go to the station and send the freight man out, and I'll go to the house and wait for him and then ride back to the station with him."

"That sounds fair enough," Geli replied. "Here's the house key. And for God's sake, don't forget to lock up like I almost did."

Amalie hurried off down the street to Geli's house. Once she got there, she found she was much more nervous than she thought she'd be. She went directly to the back closet in the kitchen, where she took down the box and opened it. There was the old Bible, just like Geli had said. It was stuffed with papers, and there was something that looked like a family tree in the front pages, but she didn't have time to go over it. She had thought about it the night before and decided that the best thing to do was to send it off to her father in Salzburg, where she could go over it in her own time when she managed to get away for a weekend to visit him. That way, it would be safe, and hopefully, with the Raubal home unoccupied, it would be some time before it was even discovered that the book was missing.

Things went well when the freight man came. He had a number of packages on the wagon already, so even if Geli somehow saw the wagon come into the station, the extra package wouldn't be noticed, and he also asked for payment when he picked up the packages, which allowed Amalie to pay for the extra package out of sight of Geli.

"Did everything go all right?" Geli asked when she met Amalie walking into the train station.

"Yes. I made sure everything was locked up. Here's the key."

BACK IN Munich on that Saturday morning, the house was quiet. Gertrude had made breakfast, done her marketing, and then gone off to visit friends for the day. Gunther sat reading his newspaper while Jakob lay on the floor with the parts of the newspaper his father had discarded. When Gunther finished, he put the paper down and watched his son. Jakob was intent on an article about a soccer game as he chased the story from one page to the next, and Gunther watched his every move.

The incident in Berchtesgaden had surprised Gunther. It had awakened in him something intangible about the passage of time and how he had taken things for granted. These were the good times, and he just assumed they would always go on like this, but with the attack on Jakob, with the frightening thought of losing his son, he began to think about a lot of things. Who was his son?

Wasn't it odd? It had all seemed so clear to him

before. You grow up, get married, have children, and then they grow up and get married, and so on. A neat, clear-cut line of succession of the human race. But now he suddenly began to wonder who his son was and who he might become. It was almost like an identity crisis, except that the crisis was Gunther's and the identity was Jakob's! Gunther was just beginning to realize his changing role in his son's life and his son's changing role in his life. Jakob was turning into a different and distinct person who would become more and more separate from his father, and Gunther was just awakening to that inevitable truth.

None of this is any great revelation to those who have thought about it, but at that moment it was stunning to Gunther. Gunther's father had been cool and distant, and Gunther grew up thinking that was just how fathers were supposed to be.

Another thought hit Gunther as he sat there watching his son. It had been eleven years since Gunther had left his father's home, and he had never heard from his mother or father since. He couldn't remember ever bringing up the subject of his parents in conversation in his home. It was as though they were dead, and Gunther realized that he wanted something different than that for himself and his son.

Many of Gunther's childhood memories were unpleasant. His father was strict and unyielding toward him and his brother and sister. They lived in fear, knowing that any transgression brought swift and cruel retribution. Gunther swore as a child that he would not be like that, and he had done well to keep his promise. He had rarely raised a hand to Jakob, and on those occasions when he felt he had to spank his son, it never amounted to more than a couple of swats on the backside with his hand.

"So . . . what do you have planned for today?" Gunther asked.

"Nothing special," Jakob said as he looked up.

"We could do something together . . ."

"Like what?"

"Let's go out to the park and just see how it goes," Gunther answered.

Jakob smiled and popped up from the floor, picking up the newspaper. This was a bit unusual, but he liked the idea of spending the day with his father, just the two of them. He started for the front door, thinking they would walk the few blocks to the park near their house, but Gunther called him back.

"Let's go out this way," Gunther directed as he headed for the back door.

"Are we taking the car just to go to the park?"

"I thought we'd go to the English Garden for a while and then pick up your mother. Her train will be arriving at about two o'clock."

They talked of superfluous things as they drove—the weather, sports, and things they saw along the road as they passed. Before they knew it, they were pulling up next to the park. They walked for a while until they unexpectedly came upon Klaus Grunewald.

"Klaus!" Gunther called out. "What brings you out? Where are Katrina and the boys?"

"They're at home," Klaus said as he gave Gunther a good-natured slap on the back. "I'm here with that group," he continued, pointing to several boys about the same age as Jakob. "It's my turn to watch over them."

"Who?" Gunther asked.

"The youth group . . . Hitler Jugend."

This didn't mean much to Jakob as he looked on, watching the other boys as they were moving bales of hay and unrolling some kind of small banners. "What are they doing, Uncle Klaus?"

"Well, this week we're going to set up an archery range."

"Archery?"

"Yes. You know," Klaus insisted, "bow and arrows. They shoot at targets on the hay bales."

"Bow and arrows! Like the Indians in America?"

"Now you have his interest," Gunther said with a smile as he put his arm around his son's shoulder. "He's been reading those books about cowboys and Indians for years."

"Of course, the Indians weren't the only ones to use bow and arrows," Klaus said professorially. "The bow and arrow have been in use in Germany for well over a thousand years."

Jakob took Klaus's declaration as gospel and was eager to try shooting a bow and arrow. "Can I try it, Uncle Klaus?"

"I don't know, Jakob . . . I mean, since you aren't a member of the group."

Gunther knew what Klaus was aiming at. He wanted Gunther to rejoin the party, and then Jakob could enroll in the Hitler Jugend.

"I suppose we could let you try . . . at least today," Klaus continued teasingly, and with that Jakob ran over to the group of boys and immediately blended in with the cacophony and motion.

"Should we help?" Gunther asked, watching as one of the bales of hay fell over for the third time and several of the boys tried again to make it stand up so that they could tie the target onto it.

"No, no. That's the point," Klaus said passively as he watched. "They're supposed to do it themselves. Youth leading youth. I'm just here to make sure nothing goes wrong."

When the targets were finally set up, the boys separated into six squads of three. The other boys told Jakob that they had done this before, explaining that they gave each ring of the bull's-eye a different point value, just like on a dart board. Each boy got three tries, and then the scores of each squad were compared. Jakob was teamed with two boys named Johann and Thomas.

Thomas was the first to go on their squad, and Jakob watched closely as he slid the arrow down the grip until it came to the bowstring and then fit the fork at the end of the arrow on the string. Even though it was the first time he had ever been this close to a bow and arrow, Jakob noticed how awkward Thomas was with the bow as he held it across his chest, completely unaware that the arrow was aimed dangerously down the line of other boys while he tried to line it up, taking a long time as he got ready to shoot. When Thomas was finally ready to shoot, he drew back the arrow quickly, and the string seemed to slip out of his fingers as the arrow arched up and over, not only missing the target, but completely missing the bale of hay and stabbing into the hill beyond.

Thomas was not the only one to suffer this embarrassing fate, as one of the other boys down the line also overshot his target, but Thomas grimaced and stomped his foot, swearing under his breath. He then followed the same ritual of slowly setting the arrow and quickly sending it off, this time catching the outermost ring of the target and raising his arms in a silent victory cheer. Inspired, Thomas then quickly dispatched his third arrow, hitting the bale of hay just below the target.

Once Thomas was done, everyone waited until the other boys on the squad finished shooting their arrows, so that the first set of archers could all go out and retrieve the arrows for the second group.

Johann was a bit shy and was more than willing to let Jakob go next. Learning from Thomas's failings, Jakob decided that the other boy's downfall had been his impatience. He thought of his Indians on horseback as he made sure to aim the arrow at the ground when he slid it across the bow's grip and then pulled it up, lining up the shaft of the arrow with an imaginary line that he drew in his mind's eye, linking himself to the bull's-eye. Before he let go, he thought of how the arrow had arced downward when Thomas had shot and decided to raise his aim slightly. The bow was hard to pull, forty pounds of draw, but he forced himself to pinch the fork of the arrow and hold the string as long as he could until he was sure that he was lined up. Then he quickly released the arrow, as quickly as one might snap one's fingers. The arrow suddenly took flight, but not like Thomas's arrow. This arrow didn't arc high up into the air and then slip lazily into the bale of hay. It drove straight and hard into the very center of the bright red bull's-eye!

Jakob was surprised, and yet he wasn't. He somehow knew instinctively that his was the right way to do it, but having never shot an arrow before, he hadn't really expected to succeed at the first try.

Gunther, who was talking with Klaus and only watching Jakob out of the corner of his eye, suddenly tapped Klaus on the shoulder, and Klaus, who had his back to the boys, turned to see what Gunther was pointing at just in time to see Jakob release a second arrow with a deadly accuracy that put it just slightly below the first but still securely within the red bull's-eye. Before the two men could walk over to Jakob, he had mechanically repeated his performance with his final arrow, setting it above the other two, almost in the bull's-eye in the next ring.

Johann and Thomas, especially Thomas, were stunned at the display, and finally Thomas managed to comment, "You must have been shooting for a long time!"

"No," Jakob said coolly, "this was my first time."

"The mighty Orion!" Gunther said as he tousled his son's hair.

"Excellent, Jakob! Excellent!" Klaus said.

"I didn't get the last one all the way in the bull's-eye," Jakob said apologetically, at which point Klaus and Gunther laughed.

"Jakob!" Gunther said. "Don't be so hard on yourself! This is incredible for your first time."

Jakob looked up and smiled meekly, and Gunther couldn't help but wrap his arm around his son, pulling Jakob close. By that time everyone else was done shooting and a number of the other boys had gathered around Jakob's target as Jakob went out to retrieve the arrows for Johann.

Gunther was proud of his son in a way that he had never been before. Both Gunther and Jakob realized that this was something different between them. An acknowledgment by Gunther that his son was not just a child, but there was a person there, a person Gunther could like, could actually love. And Jakob craved this love and acceptance from his father and would do anything to achieve it.

"You should really join us," Klaus said to Jakob. "Hitler Jugend could help you develop your talents and make you even better and stronger."

Jakob looked up at Gunther. Gunther knew that his son didn't understand everything that this suggestion entailed. He wondered if Jakob had even made the connection between Hitler Jugend and the Nazi party. Gunther knew Amalie could never accept it, and he knew that the Hitler Jugend would not accept Jakob if they knew his mother was Jewish.

"Do you think he could get in?" Gunther asked Klaus.

"It could be arranged," Klaus said thoughtfully, for he was certainly aware of the difficulties involving Amalie, "but you would have to become a member of the party again."

Jakob wasn't really sure why he wasn't supposed to tell his mother about Hitler Jugend, but it seemed like a grown-up thing between his father, Klaus and himself. The kind of confidence that men would keep among themselves, for whatever reason.

"I can tell Mother about the bull's-eyes, right Vati?" Jakob asked later as they sat in the Hauptbahnhof waiting for Amalie's train to come in.

"Yes," Gunther said as he watched the crowd milling about them in the station, "just don't mention the club. Just say we came upon a couple of boys and they let you try your hand."

Amalie was traveling alone after Geli changed trains to go to Berchtesgaden. She hadn't expected to be met at the station and nearly shouted when she felt someone tugging at her overnight bag, until she realized it was Jakob. He had seen her getting off the train and ran to help her with her things.

"How was everything?" Gunther asked.

"It went well."

"And Geli?"

"Fine. It was nice having someone to talk with on the train. And what did you two do last night?"

"This morning I got to shoot a bow and arrow!" Jakob interrupted.

"You did?" Amalie said, matching her son's excitement the way a mother does when she sees that spark in her child's eyes.

"Yes," Jakob continued. "Some boys in the park let me shoot."

"He made a bull's-eye," Gunther added.

"Two!" Jakob corrected. "Almost three!"

"Just like Orion," Gunther rejoined.

"Who is Orion?" Jakob asked his father as they began to walk out of the station.

"Orion was a great hunter in Greek mythology. When he died, he became a constellation of stars."

"How did he do that?"

"I don't know. That's just the way the myth goes," Gunther said, hoping to avoid a long line of questions.

"Let me see . . . ," Amalie began, taking over from Gunther as she tried to recall the legend. "Orion was blinded by . . . Oenopion, I think it was. And then he had a child lead him back to the light of the rising sun, and there he regained his sight."

"Why did he blind him?" Jakob asked.

"Who?" Amalie asked, as Jakob had broken her train of thought.

"Why was Orion blinded?"

"Oh. Orion had attacked Oenopion's daughter."

Jakob let the subject drop as they got into the car. Amalie was surprised when Jakob jumped into the front seat with his father instead of getting in the back with her, but she didn't say anything about it.

"The trip reminded me how long it's been since I visited Father," Amalie said as they turned onto Goethestrasse. "Jakob, maybe we should take the train to Salzburg next weekend."

Jakob just looked at Gunther without answering, as though he wanted his father to rescue him.

"Well," Gunther started hesitantly, "I think Jakob has an appointment at the park next Saturday."

"Oh, I see," Amalie said with a hint of disappointment, "maybe the week after."

When the week had almost passed, it became obvious to Amalie that Jakob didn't want to go with her to visit his grandfather, although he never came right out and said as much. He just kept avoiding the subject and coming up with excuses until Amalie finally decided to go alone to Salzburg two weeks later.

"Did you get the package?" were the first words Amalie spoke to her father when she got off the train. She had written a note and put it in the box on top of the Bible, asking Ethan not to go through the book because she wanted to be the first to do so. She also explained that they couldn't discuss it in any way through letters or telephone conversations.

"It arrived almost two weeks ago."

"Good," Amalie said breathlessly as she rushed Ethan through the train station, suddenly stopping when they got outside as she realized she had no idea where the car was parked.

"This way," Ethan said dryly after waiting to see how long it would take his daughter to see that she would have to follow him instead of leading him. "The car is over here. Now, what's this all about? Where did you get this Bible, and why is it such a secret?"

"I stole it," Amalie answered, letting her words land heavily over the muffled roar of the car's engine.

Ethan didn't take this admission easily. It seemed so foreign coming from Amalie, and yet she said it with a defiance meant to convey it was necessary. "You stole it? From whom? Why would you steal a Bible?"

"I'm not sure, but I think it's what I've been looking for in this Hitler affair. I didn't get a chance to go over it. I sent it off as quickly as I could. Right under her nose."

"Whose nose?"

"Geli. Hitler's niece. I found it at her house while

she was packing, and I don't think they'll notice it missing for quite some time."

"Well, I'd say you're taking quite a chance, but then again, it is just a family Bible. Even if they did trace it to you, what would they do?"

"That depends on what I find. It may mean everything."

There was little conversation after that. Even when they got to her father's house, Amalie immediately put her bag in her room and then silently cleared the table in the dining room. Retrieving the box from Ethan along with a stack of writing paper for notes, she sat down and prepared to go through the book. A short time later Ethan stopped on his way through the dining room when he noticed Amalie just sitting and staring at the box. She hadn't even lifted the cover yet. She just sat there with the note paper and pencils and the box in front of her.

"Is something wrong?" Ethan asked.

Amalie looked up at him and tried to smile. "I don't know why I'm so nervous." She then looked back at the box. "Yes I do," she rejoined. "This might be what I've been looking for all these years. Success or failure. And I'm not sure I'll know one from the other."

She then let out a deep sigh and took the lid off the box, carefully lifting out the book and all the papers that had been pressed into the pages from one generation to the next.

The cover was once a bright red that had aged to a dull reddish brown. The Bible had aged as it's owners' had, but instead of wrinkles, there were cracks in the cover and binding, and the edges of the pages were withered, brown, and brittle.

The first pages showed the names of family members, starting with Annaliese and Edmund Hiedler, who were married in 1818, and their children: Johann Georg Hiedler and Johann Nepomuk Hiedler. The next generation showed Johann Nepomuk's daughter Johanna, who married Johann Pölzl and had a daughter named Klara Pölzl, but that page ended with that generation and seemed to show only one side of the family. Amalie tried to figure out why Geli's parents would have had this Bible, and then she turned the page. The next page started with Johann Georg Hiedler and Maria Schicklgruber, married on May 10, 1842, and below them was Alois Hiedler without a birth date. It showed Alois' marriage to Franziska Matzelsberger in 1883 and their children, Alois Jr. and Angela. Angela married Leo Raubal and had two children: Angela's daughter, who was also named Angela and nicknamed Geli, and Leo Raubal Jr.

This was the sort of thing that one could look at over and over again, trying to draw lines between the two parts of the family on those two separate pages. The name Klara suddenly hit her. "Of course," she thought to herself, "Klara! Adolf Hitler's mother."

How strange that Alois and Franziska were on one page and Klara, without mention of Alois as her husband, was on the other. The family must not have wanted to acknowledge Alois' multiple marriages. Amalie suddenly realized, after studying the entries, that the first page clearly had different people making entries from one generation to the next, as there were obvious differences in the writing styles, but the second page, although different inks were used from generation to generation, was all written by the same person.

"Why?" she silently asked herself.

Since she had stolen the Bible, she couldn't ask anyone in the family about the discrepancies. She called out to her father.

"What is it?" Ethan asked nervously as he quickly came into the room. "What's wrong?"

Amalie realized that she wasn't the only one on edge. "Nothing serious. I just had to ask you a question." She then went over the pages and the different generations and explained how she thought one person had made all the entries on the second page.

"My guess would be," Ethan said thoughtfully, "someone omitted some skeletons in the family closet and then someone else tried to put together the missing pieces." He then arched his left eyebrow as he looked up from the Bible. "It sounds just like what you're trying to do."

"Oh, Father! Don't do that!"

Ethan was caught off guard. "Do what?" he asked.

"That thing you do with your eyebrows. It looks like two unfriendly caterpillars wrestling on your forehead."

This was a fairly recent development in Ethan's physiognomy, as he was now fifty-six years old and his eyebrows had suddenly seemed to start growing out of control and becoming excessively bushy.

"I don't think that's relevant to the subject at hand," he said.

"I know," Amalie countered with a smirk, "but I

think you're right. That must be it. If I were to guess, I would say it was Geli's mother, Angela, who filled in that second page. After all, the Bible was in her house, and that page shows her side of the family."

"That makes sense," Ethan said as he turned back to the Bible. "What are these other papers?" he asked as he started to page through the book.

"I don't know, I haven't gotten that far yet."

"Would you mind if I helped?"

"No. That would be fine . . . but let's go slowly. I want to check each piece of paper."

They started going over every page of the Bible and each piece of paper. Amalie wanted to make sure there was no writing in the Bible, no clues written on the pages of text or in the margins, and they looked over each piece of paper as they came to it. There were tax receipts and letters—letters from sons to mothers and mothers to their mothers, letters about the weather or about births and deaths—but there didn't seem to be anything monumental. They were halfway through when they came to the thickest letter, still in its original envelope, in the same place where it had been for many years and where it had caused the most severe crack in the binding of the book. It was addressed in a beautiful, elaborate German script: *"To be delivered to Alois Hiedler solely upon the death of Johann Nepomuk Hiedler."*

The look Amalie shot her father contained a mixture excitement and trepidation. Could this be it?

"A will?" Ethan offered.

Amalie gently opened the envelope, handling the pages as if they were the petals of a fragile flower. The text of the pages was written by the same careful hand that had addressed the envelope.

"The following document represents the deathbed confession of Johann Nepomuk Hiedler as told to Brother Marcus of the monastery at Weitra in November of 1881," Amalie read aloud to her father.

"He had his confession written down and addressed it to his son?" Ethan asked in confusion.

"Alois wasn't his son," Amalie corrected. "He was his nephew."

"Perhaps not," Ethan said slowly. "Maybe that's the confession."

Amalie was clearly surprised by this suggestion and quickly immersed herself in the papers, handing each page to her father so that he could read them as soon as she finished.

The document started by relating a rambling litany of Johann Nepomuk Hiedler's recent sins in business dealings and other small affairs, and then, as he apparently became lucid for a period of time, he began to talk about his mother and father. His father was from the Waldviertel, but his mother came from Graz. He made it clear that he was only doing this so that Alois would know and then Alois could do whatever he wanted with the papers. Johann just wanted to get it off his chest, to tell the truth before he died. His mother Annaliese was a Jewess. Her maiden name was Frankenburger and she came to Spital from Graz after running away from home when she was seventeen.

Annaliese was unhappy with her home and had thought about running away many times, but it wasn't until the maid, Maria Schicklgruber, was leaving that she got up the courage. Annaliese and Maria had become friends, and when fifteen-year-old Maria decided to return home to the Waldviertel district, Annaliese went with her. Eight years later, Annaliese married Edmund, Johann's father.

Amalie read all this with interest, but there was nothing shocking until she got to the fourth page. It was there that Johann Nepomuk Hiedler said that when he was seventeen years old, he and the woman who was once his mother's maid, Maria Schicklgruber, who was twice Johann's age, "knew each other," as the monk who was taking the notes so delicately put it. It was during this single episode that Alois Schicklgruber was conceived. Maria agreed to raise the child alone with the assurance of her friend Annaliese, Johann's mother, that Annaliese would give her money on a regular basis to help her raise the boy. Annaliese had been an only child and had inherited a substantial amount of money upon her father's death in Graz, even though she had run away from that home so many years before, and it was this money that she shared with Maria.

Later, when Johann Nepomuk Hiedler married, he convinced his brother Johann Georg Hiedler to marry Maria so that she wouldn't be alone and Alois wouldn't be without a father. In consideration, Johann Nepomuk agreed to forego his share of the remaining inheritance from his mother when the time came. Maria died five years after she and the brother married, and Johann Georg wandered off a short time after that, leaving Alois to live with the family of his real father, Johann Nepomuk, even though Alois didn't know the truth. Alois ran away from home when he was thirteen, leaving house number thirty-six in Spital, never to return, never to retrieve the confession after Johann Nepomuk Hiedler's death.

It had been Johann Nepomuk Hiedler who, as an old man, pressured church authorities to legitimize Alois Schicklgruber as Alois Hitler, in the name of Johann Georg Hiedler, when Alois was in his late thirties. Alois apparently never knew the real motive for Johann Nepomuk's actions, thinking that since he had become somewhat successful as a customs official, the old man only wanted to claim him as a member of the family for the aggrandizement of the family name.

Amalie came up for air. She had gotten so immersed in each turn of the document pages that her head was swimming by the time she was done reading. This was the key! This was the explanation that tied the two parts of the family together. Hitler's father, Alois, had in fact married his own niece, as one of the rumors had suggested when Amalie first went to Spital so many years before. It was the confusion over Alois' paternity that gave rise to the contradicting rumor that his third wife had been a cousin, not his niece. But here was proof, and now the other rumors, the rumors of Jewish blood, were clear. They had said that Maria, Alois' mother—Adolf Hitler's grandmother—had worked for Jews in Graz and that the son of her employers had gotten her pregnant, but it was Annaliese who had come with Maria to Spital and then had a son, Johann Nepomuk, who got Maria pregnant. So the rumor was true! Johann Nepomuk was, on his mother's side of the family, the son of the Frankenburger Jews from Graz who had gotten Maria Schicklgruber pregnant!

And this confession was the only proof of all this. A single piece of paper, a deathbed confession unregistered with any legal authority, written by a monk almost fifty years before. Below the well-crafted script of the monk from Weitra, it was signed by the shaky hand of the dying man: "May God forgive me my sins and have mercy on my soul. Johann Nepomuk Hiedler, September 14, 1881."

"I don't know what all this means," Ethan said to Amalie when he finished the final page and she sat considering her next step.

"By itself, not much," Amalie started to explain, "because it speaks only in terms of Alois and his place in the Hiedler family. This only becomes important when you go to the next generation, to Adolf Hitler. Hitler and Hiedler are the same family."

"Yes, you told me that before," Ethan interrupted.

"The importance," Amalie continued, "depends on how important anti-Semitism is to the Nazis. They seem to have eased up. This document, along with the other things I've found, says that not only did Adolf Hitler's father have a Jewish father, his mother also had a Jewish grandfather, and they were both the same man." Ethan still looked confused, so Amalie tried rephrasing the declaration: "Johann Nepomuk Hiedler, the son of Annaliese Frankenburger of Graz, who was Jewish, was both Hitler's maternal great-grandfather and his paternal grandfather, and this confession is proof of it."

Suddenly Ethan's eyebrows started challenging each other again as he began to understand the significance of Amalie's discovery.

They sat without speaking, going over the pages once more until Ethan finally broke the silence. "What are you going to do with it?"

"I'm not sure. . . . What do you think?"

"The newspapers?"

"No," Amalie said quickly, as she had considered it before and dismissed the idea. "That would just be a splash on the front page that Hitler could brush away."

"Then what?"

"It might be worth more as a weapon."

"You mean blackmail?"

"His fear of what this might do to his career might be greater than any actual damage if it were made public. After all, he's the one who's the fanatic."

"That sounds like quite a gamble," Ethan said with obvious concern in his voice. "How would you approach him?"

"That's the catch. The timing . . . and the messenger. I don't think it's necessary now. It may never be necessary," Amalie mused. "He's lost a lot of popularity. Some say he's already finished in politics."

"That's what I've heard," Ethan said, finally speaking his mind. "I know this meant a lot to you before, but I keep hearing that since the *Putsch* he's just faded further and further into the background. He's just a caricature . . . a joke. A novelty whose time has gone."

Amalie felt belittled by her father's outburst.

Ethan saw the look in her eyes as he continued.

"Amalie, I love you and I care deeply about you . . . maybe now more than ever, and I just feel I have to tell you that you might be *obsessed* with this beyond reason. Maybe it was your trouble with Gunther in the past that kept you searching, but even that's over, isn't it?"

Ethan waited for his daughter to answer.

"Isn't it? You told me he walked away from them years ago."

"Yes," she said quietly.

"Then what is it? Why would you go on about this?"

Amalie said nothing. She did something she had never done before when she and her father had a disagreement. She just got up and walked away, without a word, going up to her bed and lying down to rest.

Ethan didn't know what to make of it. When he used the word obsessed, he meant it in a casual way, like someone who plays cards too often or gets too engrossed in a hobby, but this behavior seemed even more serious. It seemed like an obsession that no one could challenge, and that frightened him.

Ethan watched his daughter go up the stairs and, not knowing what else to do, went in and made dinner for the two of them.

Over dinner they talked about publishing and Jakob and any other subject they could think of that would keep them clear of talk about the papers still spread out on the table in the other room.

The next day, Saturday, Amalie got up early and packed the papers and the Bible in the box, keeping out the confession. She had coffee with her father and then went into town, hoping to find a photography shop that might be open. She was lucky. She stopped at the window of a shop that was closed but saw someone inside brush past the window, so she knocked at the door. A bespectacled eye peeked out from behind the drawn shade on the door, on which the word *Geschlossen*[23] was painted in green, descending from the upper left corner of the window to the lower right. The man's finger then appeared, pointing emphatically at the sign on the shade.

"Please!" Amalie said to the eye in the door. "It's very important."

The eye and finger disappeared and Amalie knocked again, this time more loudly as she called out again, "Please!" She stopped knocking as she heard the lock being turned on the door. This time a face appeared as the door opened slightly. The bespectacled eye sat with its partner below a very large, bald forehead and above a full beard and mustache. From a small mouth lost somewhere in the whiskers came a strained, high voice: "Es tut mir leid, Meine gnädige Frau,[24] but we are closed today. I am only finishing up some work on my own."

"But please," Amalie said, expressing her desperation with her eyes. "I just need this document photographed."

"Yes, well, we will be open on Monday."

"But I have to leave tomorrow!" Amalie interrupted.

The man sighed and looked down at the thick envelope, and suddenly Amalie knew that he would

[23]Closed.

[24]"I'm sorry (*literally*, it does me pain), my dear woman."

agree.

"It's only ten pages . . . just a document . . . black ink on paper," she said, trying to convince him that it would be an easy job.

"When do you need it?"

"I need the papers today."

"No, I mean when do you need the prints?" the man said with a note of exasperation.

"Oh yes, of course. I don't know. If you can mail them . . ."

"Yes. How about two weeks?"

"That would be fine," Amalie said as the man opened the door and let her enter. "I'd need the negatives, too."

"Of course," the man said. "We always send the negatives."

"Yes, well I just wanted to make sure in case I need more prints later," Amalie added as she tried to cover her anxiety.

It took about thirty minutes to set up and photograph Johann's confession, and Amalie had the photographs sent to Frieder and Sons in her name. She thanked the photographer profusely for accommodating her and gave him an extra fifty schillings, causing him to smile for the first time during her visit.

"Thank you," he said as she walked toward the door. "The fact of the matter is," he added with a smile, showing gratitude for the extra consideration as she waited while he unlocked the door for her, "I think maybe I can send these to you in one week instead of two."

"I appreciate that," Amalie said as she offered her

hand and then left for her father's home. When she got there, she put the original of the confession in the box with the other papers and asked Ethan if there wasn't some place to hide it. He assured her that he had a safe place and then disappeared into the cellar.

That night and the next morning passed without incident, and Amalie was soon packing for the trip home when Ethan came in.

"I have something for Jakob," he said cautiously, not sure how Amalie would feel about the gift. "It's a watch," he continued as he took it out of its box.

It was a gold pocket watch with the inscription: "To Jakob on his 13th birthday, from Grandfather Ethan." Below that was the Hebrew spelling of the word *sch'ma,* the first word in one of the oldest and most important prayers in Judaism. Amalie said she was sure Jakob would love it. She knew that it had been meant for the bar mitzvah that never took place. Ethan had sent Jakob money on his birthday instead. Amalie guessed her father hadn't sent the watch because he thought it might be inappropriate, and now he was having second thoughts.

The ride to the train station was quiet and tense. Amalie didn't say a word until Ethan parked the car, and they both sat there in silence as Ethan obviously struggled to say something.

"Thank you for your help, Father," Amalie said before Ethan could speak. "I hope you're not too angry with me."

Ethan smiled. "Amalie, I'm not angry. I love you. I care about you as if you were still my little girl. I'm just worried."

"I know," Amalie said as she cast her eyes downward, pretending to inspect her handbag, which she held in her lap.

"Please promise me," Ethan continued, "that you won't do anything drastic without talking to me first."

Amalie looked up into her father's eyes. "Yes, I will, but you must promise me that you will tell absolutely no one about the Bible."

"Of course not!" Ethan said defensively. "I know what this means to you." They didn't talk much once they were at the platform, but as Amalie was about to get on the train for Munich, she turned back and hugged her father before boarding.

GERTRUDE WAS the only one there when Amalie got home. She informed Amalie that Gunther and Jakob had been gone all morning with Klaus, and she didn't know where they were or when they would be home.

What a difference from the last time she came home. It was a long ride on the trolley from the Hauptbahnhof, and it was hours before Gunther and Jakob came home. They rushed in full of laughter and good spirits.

"You two must have had a good time," Amalie said, trying to match their enthusiasm.

"We played soccer!" Jakob said excitedly.

"We?" Amalie asked, at which point Gunther smiled sheepishly. "They didn't have enough boys, so Klaus and I were the goalkeepers."

"Father blocked them all," Jakob said with pride.

"Really, Gunther, you should have let them win at

least a few," Amalie admonished.

"I know. I got carried away. It wasn't like I was playing against the boys. It was more like playing against Klaus."

"Well, at least you had fun together."

"Absolutely," Gunther affirmed.

"Let's do it again next weekend," Jakob piped in.

"We'll see," Gunther said, "but tonight, let's go out to eat." By that time Gertrude had come into the room. "What do you say, Gertie?" Gunther continued. "A night out of the kitchen? We could try one of those Chinese restaurants near the Hauptbahnhof."

"Chinese?" Gertrude asked incredulously. "I've never eaten Chinese food. I've heard it isn't good for you."

"Isn't good for you?" Amalie exclaimed. "Why, Gertie, it's just vegetables and meat cooked a little differently."

"Yes, Gertie," Gunther agreed. "You should try it at least once. Let's go early and avoid the crowds."

It took longer than expected for everyone to get ready since both Gunther and Amalie felt they needed a bath, Gunther after his soccer game and Amalie after her train trip from Austria, and so the streets were crowded by the time they drove up Goethestrasse. It had been an extremely hot July day in the city, and as the sun drifted downward to the Munich skyline, the early evening brought little relief from the heat. The gentle breeze streaming in through the car windows was a welcome benefit as Gunther spent almost twenty minutes looking for a place to park. His tenacity was finally rewarded as he came upon a car pulling away from the curb, right in front of a dimly lit sign advertising: "Yen Chi Loo Restaurant." Gunther quickly and expertly maneuvered the car into the parking space.

"What is 'Yen Chi Loo'?" Jakob asked. He had gotten out of the car first and stood under the sign, waiting for everyone else to catch up with him.

"I'm sure it's some strange Chinese concoction," Gertrude said, once she had struggled out of the car and stood looking apprehensively at the sign above her. "Probably made with opium."

"That's the name of the owner," Amalie said with a smile as she took Gertrude's arm and led her down the stairs from the sidewalk to the restaurant entrance below street level. "I can't believe you've never eaten at a Chinese restaurant," Amalie continued as they entered the restaurant, which was as dimly lit as the sign on the street had been.

A waiter called to them in a strange accent, asking how many there would be, and then seated them at a table over which was a large hanging lamp. The lamp, with its wide paper shade and tassels made of bright red string, hung down almost to eye level, obscuring everyone's view. Jakob reached up and brushed his hand against one of the tassels as Gunther sat down beside him.

Gunther watched with amusement as Jakob carefully studied the drawing on the lampshade. It was a stylized oriental rendering in red and black ink of oriental men and women, with only a single line slashed up at an angle on either side of the nose to depict eyes. All the human figures were dressed in kimonos, with their black hair drawn up into a ball on top of their heads.

"How come we've never come here before?" Jakob asked of no one in particular as he again stroked one of the tassels from the lamp, still staring in fascination at the shade.

"We did," Amalie said as she unfolded her napkin and put it on her lap. "A few years ago. But you put up such a fuss that we haven't been back since."

Jakob looked at once disbelieving and ashamed of the forgotten incident, as though he had denied his mother entrance to such an exotic place by his bad manners. "I'm sorry," he said.

"I didn't mean it like that," Amalie answered. "It's just that sometimes young children are so sure they won't like something different even before they try it . . . We shouldn't have brought you then. Now that you're so much more mature, I'm sure you'll find something you like."

Jakob smiled at the compliment, even though it came in such a roundabout way, and then looked up as the waiter came to the table.

"You ready order now?" the young man asked in broken German. Gunther looked at the others, noting that they needed a few more minutes, and asked the waiter just to bring tea for now.

"Tea?" Jakob asked. "But Vati, you always drink coffee."

"It's customary," Gunther replied. "We always drink tea in a Chinese restaurant."

Jakob seemed satisfied with that answer, but all the while the question had been asked and answered he had kept his eyes on the waiter as he walked away. "Did you see his eyes?" he asked quietly of his father in the tone a young boy would use when telling a dirty joke for the first time.

"Come now," Amalie said, not so much as a scolding, but more in disbelief. "You've seen a Chinaman before."

"No, I haven't," Jakob contradicted as he shot straight up in his chair, turning toward his mother, as though his sudden improvement in posture would put his statement beyond reproach.

Amalie just looked at her son, and the look was enough to cause Jakob to qualify his remark. "Well, not in real life," he said thoughtfully, as though making an effort to search his memory for the truth. "I've seen them in movies and pictures, but not a real person like this."

"Well," Amalie chastised in a whisper, "you certainly know it's not polite to stare."

"Yes, of course," Gertrude piped in supportively, even though she had done her own fair share of staring, making a close inspection of the waiter's face when she thought he wasn't looking.

"But Vati, why do they look so strange?"

Gunther felt that Jakob was putting him in the middle and cast a quick glance at Amalie to see if she was going to correct their son again, but when Amalie didn't say anything, he decided he might educate the boy.

"Well," he started slowly, "first you have to understand that man is a kind of animal." Gunther knew that in a discussion like this with Jakob, he would have to allow plenty of time for questions, as Jakob had been full of questions ever since he first learned to speak. So Gunther paused and waited, but Jakob also waited in silence.

"And there was a man named Darwin who studied animals for a long time and learned that over the course of time, animals change. He called it evolution." Gunther paused again, but this time only for an instant, as though lending weight to his declaration rather than waiting for possible questions. "And man, like the animals, has gone through evolution, and some of the former stages of man still exist today along with modern man."

Amalie's stomach turned as she listened to Gunther's lesson in the development of man.

"Some people say that the differences in man relate to the place he lives," Amalie interjected, surprising Gunther, who had expected that Jakob would be the only one to interrupt him.

"Only to a point," Gunther countered. "Different lands do not account for the difference in intelligence and industry."

Amalie suddenly envisioned a loud argument developing as Gunther recited Nazi party line about social Darwinism. It was at this moment that she knew for sure he was back in their clutches. They had him. Worst of all was that now, even right in front of her, he was teaching it to her son.

"Like the Jews?" Jakob asked innocently.

The effect that simple question from Jakob had on Amalie can hardly be described in words. It took the breath right out of her. She had been betrayed. Jakob had been stolen from her. She couldn't believe it, and she tried to remain outwardly calm as she found herself forced, almost against her will, to ask her son: "What do you mean?"

"The way the Jews have to live off other people," Jakob said without any idea of how the statement affected his mother.

Everyone was silent at the table. Gertrude was embarrassed, and Jakob didn't know what he had said wrong. Gunther just didn't want to talk about it, not because he thought his son was wrong, but because he knew how unreasonable Amalie could be in these matters.

Amalie couldn't speak.

Just then the waiter returned to the table and Gunther ordered several different items, pretending to be jovial to distract everyone from their uneasiness and insisting that they would all try a little of everything. "It will be an adventure," he said with a smile, winking at Gertrude, who also wanted to gloss over the awkwardness of the moment.

Silence overtook the table again once the waiter left, until Amalie finally spoke. She had suddenly made the connection between Klaus and Gunther and soccer, and realized what was going on. "Jakob, who are the boys you played soccer with today?"

Jakob looked at Gunther, uneasy because of the accusing tone of his mother's question and not knowing what to say, since his father had told him that his mother shouldn't be told about the youth group.

"It's just a group of boys who meet in the park on the weekends," Gunther said, answering for Jakob and trying to casually brush the question aside.

"A group? A youth group?" Amalie asked.

"Well . . . yes," Gunther said, still trying to avoid a messy argument. Gertrude watched nervously as they talked, and Jakob, who was sitting between them, sat silently and uncomfortably looking down at the table.

"Is it the youth group that Klaus talked about? The one for the children of party members?" Amalie asked in a final accusation that caught Gunther in his lie of omission.

Gunther knew there was no way out and found himself getting angry at being trapped. "Yes," he said defiantly after a brief hesitation.

"But Darling," Amalie said sarcastically, trying to keep her voice from shaking, "I thought you weren't a member of the party anymore."

"I only did it for Jakob," Gunther countered with a resolve that came across as little more than pathetic, as he blamed the lie on his son. "He wanted to play with these boys, and I had to be a member before he could join."

"But," Amalie said again, this time holding up her index finger as she made her point, "how can he join when his mother is a Jewess?"

This time Jakob looked up, and hoping to comfort his mother and show her that he and his father had thought of that and taken care of everything, he said, "It's all right mother. We didn't tell them."

Amalie just looked at Jakob. She knew he didn't understand, but that couldn't stop the tears. It occurred to her that this was just what she had done so long ago. Just as she had cast off being Jewish when she came to Munich, so Jakob now denied his mother so that he could belong to the Hitler Youth. She could almost hear her father's sad laughter in her ears, see him shake his head at the irony of it.

Amalie couldn't bring herself to continue talking about it, and mercifully, the food arrived. She quickly dried her eyes with her napkin and busied herself with dishing up for Jakob and Gertrude, explaining what was what as she put small portions of each item on their plates.

The dinner conversation was sparse after that, and Jakob contented himself with studying the surroundings, taking in the exotic smells and trying the different foods while the three adults tried to avoid a scene in public.

Amalie was especially quiet on the ride home while Gertrude tried to make conversation about how nice the restaurant was even, though it was so strange. Amalie was thinking not so much about how hurt she was, but about what she might say to Jakob later, or if she could even bring herself to talk to him at all about it. She carried on the hypothetical conversation in her head, trying different approaches and phrases, but she realized she had no notion at all of what he might say. What did he understand about all this? What did he think was going on? She had thought that her father had won him over in the course of their visits to Salzburg in the past few years. Jakob seemed interested when Ethan would tell his stories and teach him about the Jews, but it must not have been enough. Maybe it was just because that's the way children are at this age, feeling the need to reinvent themselves in some way, trying to create someone to replace the child they were such a short time before.

"Well? What do you think?"

Amalie was caught off guard as she snapped out

of her trance and suddenly realized that Gunther was talking to her.

"What?" she asked.

"You haven't heard a word I've said, have you?" Gunther said with a smile as he tried to make up with her.

"No," Amalie said quietly. "I was just thinking. What did you say?"

"I said we should do something together tomorrow. It's been a few weeks, and the summer goes so fast."

"Yes, fine. Whatever you think," Amalie said without emotion.

"An outing on the Isar. You haven't been to the English Garden in quite a while, have you?" Gunther asked as he tried to keep the conversation going.

"No, not at all this summer," Amalie said, still maintaining a quiet monotone, forcing Gunther to work at the conversation.

"Good! I'll call Friedrich and we'll all meet there."

The next day, Gunther called Friedrich and invited him to the park. He also called Klaus to tell him about the confrontation with Amalie.

"Don't worry about it," Klaus said, lacking any real sympathy for his friend. "Maybe I'll see you tomorrow at your picnic. We'll be down at the park again with some of the older boys from the HJ."

It was a hot day in the English Garden, without a cloud in the sky. Amalie hadn't had a chance to talk with Jakob about the incident at the restaurant, so she resigned herself to waiting for a better time and decided to try to make the best of their outing. She couldn't help thinking of the last picnic as she and Jakob got out of the car, and she found herself subconsciously scanning the park, looking for possible danger.

"You made it!" Gunther exclaimed as Friedrich walked up to thc car. "But you're alone! I thought you were going to ask Geli to come."

"I did," Friedrich responded with a note of despair in his voice as he pointed to a car pulling up to the curb about a half block away. "She insisted that Uncle Alf should come along."

Gunther watched as Geli floated playfully out of the car. She reached back inside the car and pulled at someone's hand, and suddenly there he was, Adolf Hitler walking toward Gunther and his family picnic.

"He's going to join us?" Gunther asked incredulously.

"Yes," Friedrich said, "a chaperone. I'll never be alone with her."

"He's going to eat with us?" Gunther asked, ignoring Friedrich's lament.

Gertrude and Amalie were paying no attention to the event unfolding by the car as they laid out the blankets and food. "Hello," Klaus called out as he walked up to them.

"Klaus!" Gertrude replied with surprise. "What brings you to the Garden?"

"I was here with the boys and I saw you. So . . . where is your husband?" Klaus asked with a smile, addressing Amalie.

Her hands full, Amalie nodded casually toward the car, looking over just in time to see Adolf shaking hands with her husband as they were being introduced by Geli.

"Well, this is certainly unusual," Klaus said, transfixed by the scene yet trying to be nonchalant, but not doing very well at it. "He rarely comes down here. It's so . . . public."

"Who?" Gertrude asked, turning to see what Klaus was talking about. "My God!" she said. "It's him . . . with Friedrich and Gunther. They're coming over here!"

It was Geli who made the introductions, doing very well to remember everyone's name and identifying Amalie as the one who had been so kind as to go with her to Austria when Adolf had been so busy. Adolf made a point of addressing Amalie and Gertrude with a gracious acknowledgment and a genteel kiss on the hand, which completely won over Gertrude in an instant.

Adolf had asked his chauffeur to bring along some folding deck chairs, and they were quickly set up around the blanket as the politician proceeded to hold court under the shade of an elm tree. One of the boys from the youth group had come looking for Klaus, and once he found that he was in the company of the Führer, word soon spread to the other boys, and they quickly joined the gathering. Klaus, acting like the leader of a platoon, immediately took control of the situation and organized the boys so that they could meet Adolf one by one.

Adolf soon loosened up in the company of these people who revered him, and he was clearly impressed when Klaus dispatched the group of boys to serve as a sort of guard unit to keep people away as they sat and talked.

Jakob, Gertrude, and Amalie sat quietly and listened as the others talked, Jakob because he was too young to join in, Gertrude because it was the thing to do, and Amalie because she felt like a spy who had managed to get into a secret meeting. The men talked politics as they ate sandwiches and drank beer from dark brown bottles.

"Jakob," Klaus called out during a lull in the conversation, "bring us another beer, would you?" Jakob dutifully got four bottles and began handing them out until he came to Adolf, who politely refused.

"I don't drink much," he said by way of explanation as he glanced at the bottle, noticing the scar on Jakob's forearm. "What's this?" he asked, pointing at the four-inch scar. "An old battle wound?"

"That's from a dog attack," Gunther explained as Jakob stood silently while Adolf held his wrist and examined the scar. Jakob was uncomfortable at being the center of attention and didn't know what to do.

"It looks recent," Adolf said with the authority of one who had seen many scars and wounds.

"Only . . . what is it? Two months now?" Gunther asked as he consulted Klaus.

"Yes, about that," Klaus confirmed. "But our Jakob, he took it like a man."

Our Jakob? Amalie thought to herself. Perhaps Klaus felt that Jakob should have two fathers . . . and no mother.

Adolf soon turned the conversation to the early days of the party, and Friedrich piped in with his story of how they had met Adolf so long ago at the

Sterneckerbräu, and Adolf smiled.

"Are you a party member?" Adolf asked of Friedrich.

"Absolutely!" Friedrich said proudly. "That was how I came to meet Geli," he stopped to cast a smile in her direction before continuing. "Through party members."

"Good, good," Adolf said as though anyone who joined the Nazi party was to be considered of the highest character. "I'm happy that Geli has the right kind of friends here in Munich. So what work do you do?"

"I'm an inventory foreman at a factory here. The owner is a party member."

"The party is growing steadily," Adolf said in a way that defied contradiction, as though the party were inevitable and, so, its victory.

"Yes, even in the factory, some of the men are joining."

"But only the best of them, right?" Adolf said, like a lawyer asking a question for which he already knew the answer.

"For the most part . . . ," Friedrich said evasively.

Adolf was surprised at this equivocation when he had been so sure that the young man would say exactly what his Führer wanted to hear. "The most part?" he asked, prompting Friedrich to explain.

"Yes, well, there is one other party member in my department at the factory . . . I mean, a man who is ready for anything, but he does have one shortcoming."

"What's that?" Klaus interrupted as his curiosity got the better of him.

"Well, I'll give you a hint," Friedrich said with a smile. "His nickname at the factory is 'Zeigel.'"[25]

"I see," Klaus said with a broad smile, and even Adolf couldn't hold back a laugh. As Uncle Alf laughed, he suddenly broke wind in a most convincing manner, bringing the conversation to a sudden halt as everyone found themselves at a loss. What does one say when the Führer passes gas?

"I know what you mean," Adolf said, forcing a smile and getting the conversation going again while completely ignoring the embarrassing situation. "But it's important to remember that strong backs are just as important to the party as strong minds. Maybe even more so!"

The rest of the men agreed wholeheartedly, as once again there was a pause, and Klaus and Gunther exchanged pointed glances as each took a drink of his beer. Gunther had been amazed that Jakob, or any of the other boys, for that matter, hadn't said anything or laughed at Uncle Alf's indiscretion.

"Those first days in the Sterneckerbräu . . . We went through a lot," Adolf finally said to his bottle of mineral water in the way that any soldier would reminisce about a hard battle from the past.

"Well, to be honest," Gunther said quietly, somewhat ashamed as he dared admit his terrible failing to Hitler himself, "after the . . . ," he faltered for an instant as he tried to find a suitable euphemism. "After the 'trouble' in twenty-three, I left the party."

Adolf didn't comment, and there was an awkward

[25]"Brick."

pause until Gunther perked up a bit as he continued, "But I'm back in now. I've just rejoined."

This resolution brought a smile back to Adolf's face. "To tell you the truth," Adolf said as though confiding to a close friend, "I felt like leaving the party, too, after that fiasco at the Feldherrnhalle." With that, he started to laugh, and everyone else joined in, relieving the tension and showing Gunther that all was forgiven—forgiven by the Führer himself.

"But I learned from that mistake, and now we have rebuilt the party and will continue to make it stronger, for we cannot afford to abandon the cause of Germany's resurrection. I've said before that the will of the German people was as strong as steel, but I was wrong. . . . The spirit of the German people is stronger than steel. But like steel, this spirit must be tempered, it must feel the heat of that passion which would rebuild Germany to be great again, in fact to be greater than it has ever been before."

By the time Adolf had finished, even though he had spoken calmly and quietly, using the old orator's trick whereby the listener must listen closely to hear what is being said, it seemed to Klaus and Gunther and Friedrich as though their leader had been shouting from some gilded podium at the head of a great crowd. Amalie had listened, too, but her perception was of how easily Adolf's invectives fell upon the ear, how he swept them up without his message of hatred. She suddenly realized what was meant when some of his followers called him a genius—coarse and vulgar—but still a genius in his way. This captured Amalie's imagination. She stared at him as one might watch a primate in a cage at the zoo, amazed at how much it was like a human but fully aware that it was certainly not.

Klaus caught Amalie's eye as she stared at Adolf, and he smiled to himself thinking how incredible a personality Adolf Hitler was that he could even captivate a Jewess like Amalie.

The conversation soon turned to more mundane topics as thoughts floated about, caught in midair, light and elusive, caustic and amusing, not tied to one another, but chasing and rolling like dogs at play on a warm summer's day. After a half hour or so it became apparent that Adolf was restless. Throughout the time the group had been eating and talking, a few people had recognized him as they strolled through the park or sought to lay out their own picnics nearby, and they had come over to meet him, but the sixteen- and seventeen-year-old boys of the youth group followed their orders and stood their ground, refusing to let anyone approach the Führer. After a while, though, Adolf began to feel exposed in the public park.

"It has been a pleasure meeting you all," he said abruptly, interrupting Klaus in mid-sentence as Klaus went on about something his three boys had gotten into, "but I'm afraid we must be going now."

Having said that, he stood up from his chair, and his chauffeur immediately snapped the chair closed and waited behind Adolf. Adolf then offered his hand to Geli, who was still sitting on the ground, talking with Amalie and Gertrude in a conversation separate from the men. "Come, Geli," he said as he waited for her to take his hand, but Geli wasn't ready to leave and there was just the flash of something in her eye. Perhaps it was anger at being summoned to his side and expected to immediately come to heel, but whatever it was, it passed just as quickly.

"Can't we stay just a bit longer?" she asked. "It's so nice out today."

"No, it's almost three," he said as he looked impatiently at his watch to confirm his statement. "We have an engagement tonight, and we'll need the time to get ready."

"Well, why don't you go and send the car back?" Geli suggested. It was clear, especially to Amalie, who was sitting behind Geli in a place where she could see Adolf's expression, that Geli was testing his patience, and worse yet, she was embarrassing him in public by not doing as he wanted.

He apparently decided on a tactical retreat, as he quickly agreed, and he and his chauffeur started for the car. Klaus and Gunther followed behind with the other two folding chairs, using them as an excuse to have a final word or two with Adolf along the way.

Geli went on talking with Gertrude as though what had just happened was nothing but a pleasant exchange between her and Uncle Alf and not a test of wills. Amalie thought to herself how interesting it all was. The rumors of something going on between Geli and her uncle must have been true, although she wondered just how far their "something" went. After all, she had found out that Hitler's mother was his father's niece . . . maybe it was a tradition in their family. The thought struck Amalie as amusing.

"Your uncle is so charming," Gertrude said in a way that schoolgirls might talk about a new boy in their school. "And those eyes . . . they look right through you."

"Yes," Amalie agreed, rejoining the conversation. "They *are* piercing."

If Gertrude had known Amalie better—that is, if Amalie had let Gertrude know her better—Gertrude might have wondered how, or why, Amalie sat through the entire afternoon in such company without raising a word of objection. Especially in light of the trouble in the restaurant the night before. But Gertrude wasn't thinking in those terms. She thought the issue at the restaurant was about Gunther keeping a secret, not about the content of the secret, and so it never occurred to Gertrude that Amalie hated Uncle Alf.

Amalie felt even more like a spy as she tried to find out more about Adolf through his niece.

"Wasn't that horrible?" Geli asked rhetorically a few moments after Adolf had left.

"What?" Gertrude asked.

"The way he . . . the way Uncle Alfie makes such a noise and a smell and everyone has to pretend that nothing happened."

"Oh, don't be silly," Gertrude answered unconvincingly. "It's natural . . . he must just be having stomach trouble. It's not like he did it on purpose."

"But he does it all the time. All the time! We've even been to formal dinners where he has . . ."

Amalie couldn't help but laugh out loud as Geli went on.

"Amalie!" Gertrude scolded. "The poor man can't help it."

"I know, I know, but I just had a picture of him in

evening dress bowing to some bejeweled dignitary's wife when . . ." She was unable to complete the sentence as she laughed even louder. Geli joined in laughing right along, and even Gertrude couldn't hold back a little chuckle.

Geli said that she was very fond of her uncle, but he only thought of her as an escort, someone he could call on at a moment's notice to accompany him to social functions. When she said this, Amalie wondered if Geli didn't feel something more for her uncle than fondness, since she was beginning to sound like a wife who felt she was being taken for granted.

Gunther, Klaus, Friedrich, and Jakob soon returned to the blanket under the elm tree, and Friedrich strategically placed himself between Geli and Amalie.

"So," he said as he made himself comfortable, "what have you girls been talking about?"

He was so obvious about insinuating himself between Amalie and Geli that neither could resist laughing. Gertrude glared disapprovingly at her son as he sat helplessly, disarmed by the other women's laughter.

CHAPTER 10

If Germany had listened closely, it might have heard a bell tolling in the distance on that crisp afternoon of October 24, 1929. It was a historical day on the American stock market when the prices of stocks began to fall faster and farther than they ever had before. The plunge culminated in a week-long stock panic that sent the market crashing to undreamed of lows, destroying family fortunes in a matter of minutes and driving many stock speculators to suicide. The 1920s had been an unprecedented period of growth in America, as always seemed to happen in that country after a war, but there was always a leveling. However, 1929 signaled more than just an economic leveling, as Black Thursday became the final call, not just for the American economy, but the global economy as well. The economic depression would soon reach out to touch virtually every industrialized nation on earth.

The faltering Weimar economy offered incredibly fertile ground for the seeds of a new revolution—a national socialist revolution—but this time it would not be Adolf Hitler in the midst of a street fight in Munich. Though there would certainly be countless bloody street confrontations between the Nazi Sturmabteilung and the Communists, this time Hitler and his followers were biding their time. They sat comfortably in the belly of their Trojan horse known as the Berlin Reichstag, waiting as the German Mittelständers[26] *began one by one to take the horse's reins and pull it into the courtyard, where Germany would finally be taken from within.*

Joseph Hubert was just a passing acquaintance of Amalie's. A boyhood friend of David Frieder's, he often dropped by the publisher's office when they were going out for lunch. They had invited Amalie to go along a few times, and she had come to look forward to Joseph's visits.

When he entered the office, the receptionist would smile and deliver the reflexive "Grüss Gott," but Joseph would only smile and give a slight nod, heading straight for Amalie's desk and launching into the setup for a joke that, no matter how well executed, would never make up for the content. But Amalie was always polite enough to muster a good laugh.

"Are you coming with us today?" Joseph asked with a smile.

"Am I invited?" Amalie countered with a flirtatious smirk.

"Let's ask the boss," Joseph said as David joined them. "Is Amalie coming with us today?"

"Well, that's up to her, but I certainly don't think I should leave the two of you alone together."

"No. Much too dangerous!" Joseph concurred.

"Yes, like storing the matches with the gunpowder," Amalie played along.

"Ratskeller?" Joseph asked in the shorthand one uses among friends, asking if Amalie and David wanted to go to the Ratskeller restaurant in the basement of the Neuen Rathaus for lunch.

They nodded in agreement and began gathering

---

[26]Midsize businesses falling between small family-run businesses and large multinational companies; a sort of middle class of the German economy.

up their coats as Joseph started in on another joke that had been around for years. "Did you hear about the Nazi rally the other day?" he asked as they made their way down the stairs from the office. "Hitler went into one of his rages and shouted, 'And who is to blame for the troubles of Germany?' and a little voice from the back of the crowd called out, 'The bicycle riders.'" Joseph continued, even though Amalie and David appeared inattentive. "So Hitler gets a confused look on his face and finally calls back, 'The bicycle riders? Why the bicycle riders?' and the voice from the back of the audience calls back, 'Why the Jews?'" Joseph laughed heartily at the joke while Amalie and David only smiled politely. "I guess you heard it," he finally said with defeat in his voice.

"Everyone's heard it," David said as he opened the door onto the street.

It was a cloudy day, and a cool, late September wind filled the hallway as the trio started toward the new city hall, just as the Glockenspiel in the tower began dutifully chiming off the arrival of midday, its brightly painted statues dancing out their farewell to the morning. Marienplatz was filled with people milling about from store to store, many of them people from the country who had come to Munich for Octoberfest and were now window shopping and passing time as their vacation drew to a close. It seemed as though everyone stopped to watch the clockwork action as the Glockenspiel chimes sounded.

As they entered the square, Amalie couldn't help but smile to herself at the sight of all those people stopped in their tracks, staring up at the spectacle in the tower. She wondered if everyone in Munich was a tourist that day, as she and her companions made their way to the Ratskeller, which was as crowded as the square had been.

"Order what you like," Joseph said, once they had been seated at a table and began looking over the menu. "I'm buying lunch today."

"Oh, my God," David said, "is it the end of the world already?"

"No," Joseph replied as he picked up his napkin and unfolded it, drawing out the word as though it had more than one syllable. "It is a celebration . . . or perhaps, more accurately, a party. A farewell party."

"Farewell party?" David asked. "What are you up to now?"

"Yes," Amalie interjected. "What sort of crazy scheme is it this time?"

The question went unanswered until they had all placed their orders with the impatient waiter, and then Joseph continued as the waiter slipped away through the crowded room. "It's not a scheme, just the decision of a lifetime. I have decided to seek my fortunes elsewhere."

"Oh, God," David said as he rolled his eyes, "not that nonsense about Berlin again! You have the same chances of making a living here as you would in Berlin."

"Not Berlin," Joseph said as the waiter came to the table with their beers.

"Then where?" David pursued.

"America."

"Oh, Joseph!" Amalie exclaimed before David could respond.

"America? Why America?" David asked with a certain abrasiveness. "Do you even know anyone in America?"

"I have . . . ," Joseph began defensively, faltering as he tried to find a proper description, "distant relatives."

"What does that mean?" Amalie asked, turning to David for a translation.

"That means," David said, staring at Joseph, defying his friend to contradict him, "that they might let him stay with them for two days, but they won't lend him any money."

Amalie laughed, but neither David nor Joseph joined her.

"Do you even know what you'll do there?" David asked. "You've tried everything here from publishing to radio to salesman."

"You were in radio?" Amalie asked.

"A little while," Joseph offered weakly.

"Two weeks," David corrected.

"Two and a half weeks," Joseph retorted defensively.

"I just don't understand," David said with frustration in his voice. "If you have all these problems finding work here, where you have family and friends to support you . . ."

"I just think that a new start, a new country . . . ," Joseph tried to explain, and then his eyes suddenly lit up as he remembered the old cliché. "A land of opportunity!"

"Where the streets are paved with gold," Amalie said with a laugh that was meant to point out what a ridiculous proposition it was, but Joseph took it as a sign of support.

"Yes," he said, "streets of gold."

"Amalie," David scolded, "don't lead him on with this idiocy."

Amalie nodded. "Joseph, he's right," she said. "It's not easy to get into America, and if you do, you'll need money to get by, and it is best to have family or friends who can sponsor you and help you get started."

"I have some money," Joseph said, still on the defensive.

"But passports, immigration, visas . . . all of this takes time, and you have to show—"

"That's all done," Joseph said defiantly.

"Done?" David shot back in surprise. "When are you going?"

"The week after next."

"Two weeks? It's all done and settled?"

"Yes."

David looked at Amalie, who didn't know what to say.

"Why didn't you tell me earlier?" David finally asked after a long pause.

"I didn't want you to try to talk me out of it."

"Oh, Joseph," David said sadly. There was another long pause as the waiter brought them their food. "You know I just worry about you as a friend."

"I know."

"Is there anything I can do?"

Suddenly Amalie's head popped up from eating her lunch. "Otto!" she said, trying to address both David and Joseph as she looked quickly back and forth between them. "Otto Maus . . . He has a brother in New York. Brooklyn, New York."

"Yes," David agreed. "The writer from Ried. He once told me that if I ever got to New York, his brother would put me up for a week. He's a . . . Damn, I can't remember what he does. He runs some kind of factory."

"He owns it," Amalie corrected."Otto told me his brother owns a factory that makes . . ." Amalie stopped in mid-sentence, unable to remember what it was that Otto's brother made either. "Ice boxes!" she finally proclaimed as the answer popped into her head. "That's it. He makes ice boxes for homes."

"Yes," David agreed. "Joseph, at least let me call Otto and see if he won't send a letter of introduction for you."

Joseph agreed, and they finished their lunch, with David eventually wrestling the check away from Joseph, insisting to his friend that he would need every pfennig he had for the journey. The Ratskeller was still packed as they left the restaurant, and would likely become even more so as the afternoon wore on. David's good-bye to Joseph at the door leading up to the office had added meaning as prelude to the farewell that would see Joseph off to America a few short days later.

It was the tenth of October in 1929 when Joseph Hubert boarded the train for the north of Germany, where he would then board a ship for America. He didn't really understand the significance of the stories he heard a few weeks after arriving in New York, tales of stock brokers jumping out the windows of tall office buildings, but he was not alone. He was about to be enrolled in the same school of economics as the rest of America, as they all learned the lessons of Black Thursday.

BLACK THURSDAY in America fell about a year and a half after Friedrich had introduced Geli Raubal to his friends. It is hard to say whether Friedrich was an eternal optimist or just blinded by infatuation, but he held out hope that he and Geli might get together long after it was obvious to everyone else that Geli's attention was somehow reserved for her Uncle Alfie. The exact nature of her involvement with her uncle was the topic of conversations all over Munich.

Adolf and his party had made gradual but significant advances across the country in the five years since his release from jail, and he was once again considered to be an important man in Germany, especially in Bavaria. Geli was living in Uncle Alfie's nine-room apartment on Prinzregentenplatz, with her bedroom right next to his, while Adolf had sent his half sister, Geli's mother, to keep house at his mountain retreat in Berchtesgaden.

Amalie, seeing the advantages of being Geli's friend in order to get any possible information on Hitler, had made a point of appearing to be the loyal wife of a devoted party member whenever she was around Friedrich, and especially Geli. Gunter was pleased, thinking he had finally won his wife over and she had put aside her unreasonable criticisms of the party. It was becoming obvious to Amalie that Uncle Adolf was closing Geli off from the outside world. Apparently Geli was to escort Uncle Alf to parties and other events, but she wasn't allowed to go out with other men. Amalie was sure, however, that being shut off from the rest of the world, Geli might confide more in the few people who were sanctioned by Adolf as suitable friends, so Amalie went out of her way to appear to be one of those suitable friends, to be on the perimeter of Adolf Hitler's inner circle.

It is an interesting aside that Klaus Grunewald never once referred to Amalie as a Jew to anyone close to Hitler. It is an insight into Klaus's character that it never even occurred to him that Amalie, as a woman, as the wife of a Nazi party member, could ever in any way pose a threat to the party or Hitler. Perhaps even more significant to Klaus, with his cynically political nature, was the importance of having Amalie as an ally, since she was a friend, and apparently quickly becoming a confidante, of Hitler's beloved niece. It made sense, therefore, that since Klaus wanted to become part of Hitler's inner circle, he would not compromise Amalie's position as his possible link to that inner circle.

In spite of all of these intrigues, life went along smoothly for the next few months; in fact, things around the Metzdorf house were the picture of bliss since Amalie had managed, seemingly overnight, to change her opinions of the party.

Jakob, who turned fifteen in November of 1929, had matriculated from the JV, the Jungvolk division of the Hitler Youth, which accepted boys from age ten to fourteen, into the actual Hitler Jugend program, which accepted boys from age fourteen to eighteen. The youth group had been growing steadily along with the membership in the Nazi party, and by 1929 the Hitler Jugend had enlisted more than ten thousand boys across the country. Along with this growth, the group was also becoming more organized and restrictive, developing a much more militaristic nature as Hitler, in particular, began to see the value of indoctrinating children into the ways of national socialism long before they were actually of age to join the party.

Jakob was still known by the nickname "Orion" among his friends in the HJ, the name his father had given him on that day when he had displayed his natural talent for archery in the English Garden. Jakob was prized by his friends as a natural marksman, and as the group progressed to small-caliber rifle competitions, Jakob adapted to the new medium easily. Some of the older boys even suggested that Jakob might be good enough for the Olympic team from Germany that in a few years' time would compete at the 1932 games in the city of Los Angeles in America.

In the spirit of the Olympics, it was proposed that some of the chapters of the Hitler Youth should get together for an intramural competition in the summer of 1930. By the time summer came, it was all too obvious that the economic problems of America were sweeping across Europe, and the unemployment rate in Germany, in particular, was rising dramatically. Many of the parents saw the games as a pleasant escape, and so the attendance was expected to be high. The interest level became so high that some of the other boys groups, such as the Catholic Youth League, asked if they might also participate. Suddenly the competition was becoming an event, one that even warranted an appearance by Hitler himself.

Adolf was not worried about the economic crisis that Germany was facing as 1930 wore on. He saw it as an opportunity to discredit the German Republic and win even greater support for the Nazi party as he worked to get ready for the Reichstag elections to be held that autumn.

When the day of the competition finally came, the event was held in a recently harvested farmer's field outside of Munich, which volunteers had spent weeks preparing. Hitler made his speech, a "volkish" speech in which he admonished his listeners to look at how the Italians, under their fascist government, had managed to withstand the depression, and how Germany too could survive and even prosper under the auspices of German national socialism. The Nazis in the crowd went wild as the speech concluded, but the others merely offered up polite applause. Polite applause, however was quite a change from the bloody confrontations Adolf and his followers had met with when he spoke in years past. Polite applause meant that he had been accepted as a candidate entering the political mainstream; it meant that perhaps victory was not so terribly far away.

Once the competition was under way, Jakob won the archery contest with little serious challenge from any of the other groups. Hitler stayed to observe the excellence of his Hitler Jugend. Geli, of course, was at his side when he arrived, but when Adolf had to leave unexpectedly, as he always did, Geli remained with Amalie and Gunther to watch the rest of the games. When everything was over, Gunther and

Jakob went off to talk with the other fathers and sons about the races and contests while Geli and Amalie stayed in their seats in the small bleacher section.

"It looks like it might rain," Geli said, looking up at the growing cloud cover, trying to make conversation.

"And it was so nice this morning," Amalie said, keeping up her end of the chatter. "That's always the way in Munich at this time of year. The weather can change so quickly."

"It's so nice to have an afternoon away," Geli sighed.

"A break from your busy schedule?"

"No . . . it's not that. I just can't . . . Adolf doesn't like me to be away from him. We're always together. Always."

"Is that so bad? I mean, having someone who cares about you that much?"

"Yes, in a way."

"But?" Amalie asked.

"What?" Geli asked in response.

"It seemed as though you were going to say something else."

Geli looked down at her feet and then back up at Amalie, making eye contact momentarily and then quickly looking away, as though ashamed.

"Can I trust you? I mean . . . could you promise not to tell anyone if I told you something?"

"Yes."

"I mean really not tell anyone . . . your husband or family or anyone. It might even be dangerous for you if you did. Maybe you don't even want to hear it if that's what it means."

"Geli, I've known you for quite a while now and I consider you a friend . . . and love you as a friend . . . and I've noticed how you've changed since we first met. If you need someone to talk to, a friend to confide in, I can be that friend. I *am* that friend. If you don't want me to tell anyone something, then you can be sure that I will keep it to myself."

"I have to talk to someone."

"What is it?"

"Well . . . Uncle Alf . . . Adolf and I . . . we . . . spent a night together."

Amalie was careful not to react. She had to know if there was something else about the man that could be used against him. What could he possibly be doing that would cause Geli to change as she had? Geli was still very good in public. She kept up the appearance of the outgoing, carefree, beautiful girl, but those who knew her sensed that something was going wrong, that this—whatever it was that she had with her uncle—and his overprotectiveness were taking a toll on her.

"We . . . " Geli started, but then stopped, once again staring at her feet.

Amalie felt an unexpected shudder move through her. Was it guilt? She suddenly felt incredibly sad for this young woman who sat beside her, so obviously in pain, and here she was waiting to use her. Amalie had to remind herself what a friend might say, how a friend might comfort another friend at a time like this. She guessed that since Geli and her uncle had had sex, Geli was having trouble dealing with the incestuous aspects of the relationship.

"Geli," Amalie said, gently taking Geli's hand, "it's

not such a terrible thing if you might have . . . you shouldn't feel bad . . ." Amalie didn't know what else to say until it finally dawned on her that it might have been more than just a sexual encounter, that Adolf might have forced Geli. It was certainly in keeping with Amalie's opinion of Adolf that he might have raped his niece. Amalie suddenly shifted in her chair to face Geli and took her other hand too. "Geli, did he force you? Did he rape you?"

A single tear ran from Geli's eye, trailing along her nose and falling to her lap as she continued staring down as though unable to raise her head.

Amalie bent down a little, trying to make some eye contact as she softly asked the question again. "Did he rape you, Geli?"

Suddenly more tears came and Geli began to sob. Amalie instinctively put her arms around Geli and began to pat her back softly, whispering into her ear, "It's all right Geli . . . It will be all right."

Even as Amalie said it, she knew it was a lie. It was the sort of thing you say to calm a frightened child, whether it was true or not. Amalie knew Geli was trapped, and it wasn't just a man, a jealous lover, it was the party too—it was all of these fanatical men. What would they do to a woman who cried rape, pointing a finger at their Führer?

"It's worse," Geli finally blurted through her sobs. "It was disgusting, degrading . . . It was like a nightmare . . ."

Amalie was still holding Geli tightly against her shoulder. She could hardly understand what Geli was saying through her sobbing, but she didn't interrupt her. When Geli's tears finally slowed, Amalie pulled away a bit and gently lifted Geli's face, reaching into her purse for a tissue and wiping away a couple of tears before handing the tissue to Geli.

"If he raped you, he can still be arrested, even if he is Adolf Hitler."

"That's not it," Geli finally said, looking around as she talked, still unable to maintain eye contact with Amalie. "I wanted to . . . be with him, but I never thought he would . . ."

Amalie was dying to find out what the girl was so reluctant to tell her and wanted to shout, "What? What did he do?" But she kept her calm, waiting for Geli to say what she had to say in her own time.

"He . . . he . . . ," Geli tried again, but stopped. She wiped away another tear as quickly as it appeared, then shifted in her seat, straightening up as she prepared to say it at last, to make it real by admitting it to Amalie. "We started by kissing. He said he loved me . . . and needed me. Only me." Geli suddenly drew a deep breath, and there was a strangling noise, as though she were having trouble breathing, but she forced herself to continue. "He picked up that whip, the one he carries all the time . . ." For the first time, Geli looked directly at Amalie, and Amalie suddenly saw the sad, haunted look deep in her eyes as she continued, "He wanted me to hit him, to beat him with that whip, to pull off his shirt and beat him." This time it was Amalie who looked away, but only for an instant. She didn't want Geli to think that she was turning away form her. "And that's not the worst of it," Geli continued. "He wanted me to. . . ," she began, and then stopped again. "Oh, God," she said, bending forward at the waist and burying her face in her arms. "He wanted me to urinate on him."

Amalie said nothing. She didn't know what to say. She just waited until Geli raised her head again.

"He's sick," Geli said. "Maybe he just needs someone who loves him, who really loves him. Maybe he can forget about this. Don't you think?"

Amalie was stunned by the question at the end of Geli's string of rationalizations.

"Don't you think?" Geli asked again.

"I don't know," Amalie said after a moment's hesitation. "I think you should . . ."

Amalie was interrupted in mid-sentence by Gunther calling to her as he headed toward them. "Amalie! We're ready to go."

Amalie was relieved at the interruption and turned immediately to answer Gunther rather than trying to finish what she was saying to Geli. "All right. We're coming." Then, turning back to Geli, she tried to think of what to say but realized there wasn't anything to be said. "We'll have to talk about this later."

"I feel better just telling you about it," Geli said as she got up and wiped her eyes again, asking Amalie for another tissue so she could blow her nose.

The ensuing car ride was dominated by Gunther and Jakob rehashing the details of the competition. Amalie got out and walked Geli to the front door of the apartment building on Prinzregentenplatz, reassuring her once again and giving her a quick hug before leaving.

"What was that all about?" Gunther asked as Amalie returned to the car.

"Nothing. Geli and Adolf just had a little argument, and we were talking about it after the games."

Gunther accepted the explanation, and he and Jakob soon returned to their discussion of the games. When they finally made it home to Fürstenried, Amalie tried not to be obvious as she quickly excused herself and went to the little writing desk in her bedroom. She hurriedly wrote out a description of the day, along with a transcription of her conversation with Geli, which she quickly sealed into an envelope and labeled: "Confidential conversation w/Geli Raubal - 29/10/'30." Hearing steps approaching, she slipped it into the small drawer in the desk just as her husband came into the room, pulling out a clean sheet of writing paper in the same motion, hoping that Gunther hadn't seen the envelope.

"What are you up to?" he asked as he passed by.

"Writing a letter to Father about Jakob winning the archery shoot."

"Good news travels fast," Gunther said with a big smile, glowing with pride in his son, as though he had taught Jakob everything he knew.

The letter Amalie wrote to her father, the letter she made sure was mailed that evening, did include the news of Jakob's victory, just in case Gunther might someday ask Ethan about the event, but it also included instructions to store the enclosed sealed envelope with the family Bible she had stolen from Geli's apartment in Vienna.

IT WAS JUST a week later that Gunther's boss called him into his office. Gunther felt himself tense up a little, particularly the muscles at the base of his neck. He felt he had a fairly good relationship with Herr

Lange, although certainly not like Amalie's relationship with David Frieder. Amalie had invited David and his girlfriend of the moment for dinner on a number of occasions, whereas Gunther had never met socially with Herr Lange. Perhaps it was because Herr Lange was in his late sixties, much older than Gunther's thirty-five years, but nonetheless Gunther felt they had the kind of friendship that develops out of mutual respect. They were both good at what they did. Herr Lange was a good administrator and Gunther was a good architect. Despite his confidence, however, Gunther was concerned about being called into the office like this.

Every other time he had been invited into Herr Lange's office, there had been some kind of prelude. Stopping by Gunther's drawing board, Herr Lange would say, "We need to talk about the Borchard building. Come to my office tomorrow after lunch." But this time it was Herr Lange's pretty secretary who had walked over to Gunther's drawing table and stopped. Waiting for Gunther to finish the line he was drawing, she brushed aside the few strands of red hair that had swept down over her right eye.

"Herr Lange would like to see you in his office."

"Now?" Gunther asked, surprised at the breach of the traditional twenty-four hour notice for such an appearance.

"Yes. He says it's important."

Only after Gunther left that day would he figure out that even she knew what the meeting would be about. Herr Lange stood up and motioned to one of the heavy, dark wooden chairs as Gunther entered the office. Once they were both seated, Herr Lange stared out the window and began to speak in a monotone. Gunther watched the expensive fountain pen in Herr Lange's hand, which he used alternately as a pointer for imaginary charts and as a baton leading an invisible orchestra, as he droned on about business matters. Finally he turned his swivel chair to face Gunther, resting his elbows on the large wooden desk

"And so, because of these canceled contracts, and because of the stock market problems that are affecting so many companies these days . . . ," he said, stopping to take a deep breath before continuing, "we have to reorganize our little company. This is going to be hard for all of us. I'll have to go back to actually drawing plans . . ."

"And me?" Gunther finally asked, the first words he had spoken since entering the office.

"I'm afraid . . . I am terribly sorry . . . terribly sorry, Gunther. You're a fine draftsman, very competent . . . an artist, one might say, but we have to let you go."

Gunther had known as soon as Herr Lange had started talking about the economy and canceled contracts that this was where the conversation was leading, but still, when the words were actually spoken, he felt a sickly panic rise within him. There was a long pause until he was finally able to ask, "When will I leave?"

"Well . . . I would understand if you were upset and wanted to leave immediately, but if you could finish the project you're on now, I do have a couple of small home projects I could send your way if you want to do them on your own."

"Yes," Gunther said, trying to be practical rather than insulted. "I would appreciate that. I should be able to complete the changes on the Reiger building by next Wednesday."

Herr Lange got up and walked around his desk, extending his hand as Gunther rose. "I can pay you through the end of the month, and I'll have Trudi get you the information on those house projects."

Gunther reflexively returned the handshake and almost found himself saying thank you for the two-week severance pay and the other job references, but it caught in his throat and he said nothing as he turned for the door. Herr Lange put a hand on Gunther's shoulder, stopping him as he turned away.

"If there was any way, Gunther, any way that we could keep you on, I hope you know that I would."

Gunther softened at this last gesture. "Yes, Herr Lange. I . . . I would like to thank you for all that you have done. You helped me get started, and I am grateful for that."

"I had hoped we could part as friends," Herr Lange said, smiling weakly as he gave Gunther a pat on the back. Gunther even managed to return the smile.

Gunther had a hard time telling Amalie about losing his job. He waited for three days before he finally told her after they got into bed, waiting until she turned out the lamp on the bedside table. It wasn't that he was afraid to tell her. He knew she wouldn't turn away from him. It was the way that he felt about himself that bothered him, as though he had somehow failed. He remembered the time after the war when he had gone without work for so many months, and how he felt when Amalie had started working for Frieder and Son. Could he make it on his own as an architect? Would there be enough work if the economy kept going the way it was? How bad would it get? He suddenly thought of the inflation years and shuddered at the question.

Within a few weeks of Gunther's losing his job, opponents of the Nazis were shocked at the huge gains the party had made in the national elections. Even the party leaders were surprised as the Nazis suddenly became the second-largest political party in Germany, with 107 seats in the Reichstag.

While Gunther was happy with the advances made by the party, his main concern was making a living. He kept busy for the next few weeks by finishing up at the firm and bidding everyone good-bye, never to see any of them again, and then starting work on designing the houses for the two clients that Herr Lange had referred to him as a token gesture.

He bought a used drawing board and set it up in a corner of the living room. The huge board seemed to dominate the small room, and he thought about taking over the garage as an office, but these plans were always overshadowed by his fear of not being able to make it as a freelance architect when the economy was so bad.

It seemed so strange, watching Amalie go off to work and Jakob leaving for school each day, trying to work in the house as Gertrude went about her chores. When Gunther and Gertrude had lunch together, it was usually in silence. Gertrude was so used to eating lunch alone that she had nothing to say, and Gunther was simply in no mood to talk.

One day Gunther found himself standing at the window after lunch, staring out at nothing in particular, as the postman suddenly passed in front of the window, breaking his trance. Even that seemed strange. Gunther had never brought in the mail before. By the time he got home, it was always sorted out in the small rack on the wall in the kitchen—the bills in one slot, personal letters in another, and business correspondence in the third. He stood in the doorway, forgetting to close the door as he leafed through the few pieces of mail.

It felt as if he had stared at the letter for ten minutes before opening it. It was from his mother. Gunther had not been to Elsbethen in fifteen years and had not heard a single word from his father's house since their last argument on the subject of his marriage to Amalie, when he had gone home on leave during the war. What could possibly move his mother to write after all this time? His father must be dead. When he finally opened the letter, he learned that his father was ill. Oskar Metzdorf had been diagnosed with lung cancer at the beginning of October.

Gunther's first thought was of himself. It wasn't bad enough that he had lost his job, and now to find out that his father has cancer. Bad luck comes in threes. Isn't that what they say? What would happen next?

"Are you going?" Amalie asked as they sat down to dinner that night.

"Going?" Gunther asked, caught off guard, lost in thought about how fifteen years had passed since he had spoken with his father.

"Are you going to see your father?" Amalie persisted.

"How come we never visit them?" Jakob asked on top of his mother's question.

"Why?" Gunther asked, as though in some kind of daze, yet with the kind of incredulity that inferred that Jakob should have known why Gunther never talked with his parents.

"They had a fight," Amalie interjected, answering Jakob.

"Yes," Gunther concurred, "a fight. Because I married your mother."

Jakob didn't know how to respond to his father's statement, so he quietly went back to eating his dinner.

"Do you really think I should go see him?"

"Yes," Amalie said, cautiously venturing an opinion. "We've certainly changed. Maybe they've changed too . . . After all, they did write."

"I suppose that's something," Gunther admitted grudgingly. There was a pause as he thought about it. "I certainly have the time now," he finally said.

It only took a few days for Gunther to finish up his work on the house plans, and he soon found himself on a train to Salzburg, where he would catch a bus to the small town of Elsbethen, some ten kilometers to the south. The last time he had been to Salzburg was when they had taken Jakob to the hospital there after the dog attack. He had thought of going to see his parents' house back then, just to drive by, but he hadn't. He hadn't even mentioned it to Amalie.

The house was an uphill walk of about thirty meters from the bus stop. Gunther stopped a moment before opening the wrought iron gate at the foot of the red-brick steps that led up to the front door. The house had aged noticeably. The yard was still immaculate. The flowers had lost their bloom, the brown stems struggling to stand against a late October wind while a few still stubbornly refused to let go of the remaining petals of what was once a rose or a chrysanthemum.

The thick varnish on the heavy oak door had been baked by the sun, cracking the once-shiny finish into little brown bumps that should have been scraped away years before, but this was how the house had grown to such a sad state. A loose tile here and there, cracking paint on window trim . . . everything was still in place but not quite right. How do you knock on a door you haven't seen in fifteen years? Do you approach it as an old friend who has been away, or should you be formal, not taking the chance of being embarrassed because you're too friendly when the door can't quite remember who you are?

He didn't have to knock. His mother opened the door as he stood there thinking about it. She must have been waiting for him. Maybe she saw him from the window as he came up the steps. Had she been waiting all morning for him? Had she been waiting all these years for him to walk up those steps?

Marie just looked at him, searching his face for some sense of who he was now. Then she looked him up and down. He was a bigger man now, not fat, but filled out, changed from the boy of nineteen to the man of thirty-five. Gunther didn't move. He didn't smile. He didn't reach out, although a part of him wanted to raise a hand to touch her face. Marie stepped out onto the front stoop and put her arms around her son, around arms that didn't move from his side. She had her head against his chest, resting against the warmth of his woolen overcoat, as Gunther finally managed to put his arms around her.

"I've come home . . . to see you . . . and Father . . . to see if there's anything I can do."

Marie finally released him from her embrace and took his hand, leading him inside. The smell of the house brought a kinescope of memories flashing through Gunther's mind—pictures of holiday gatherings, birthdays, school friends and relatives he hadn't seen for so long. He was also caught off guard by the physical change in the house. It had become such a small house! The stairway was shorter and more narrow than it had been when he and his Realschule[27] friends would come charging down from his bedroom and out into the sport arena that was the back yard. The dining room couldn't possibly have held all the aunts and uncles and cousins who would stop by during the week between Christmas and the beginning of a new year.

Still holding Gunther's hand, she pulled him into the small den where Oskar Metzdorf sat wrapped in a colorful Afghan that Marie had made years before. His hands rested on his oversized stomach. God! Even his father had shrunk!

"I told you he would come," Marie said softly, with an emotional edge to her voice that said her hus-

[27]German equivalent of grammar school.

band hadn't believed, but she knew that Gunther would not ignore his father in such a time of crisis.

The pipe Oskar held produced a steady, thin line of sweet-smelling tobacco smoke that spread out and dissipated as it rose above his head while he stared silently at his son.

"Should you be smoking?" Gunther asked after a pause of many years.

Oskar was shocked to hear his son speak. Here he was standing in front of him, and now he was even talking to him. There was an involuntary twitch as Oskar tried to decide what to do. Should he reply? Would it be that easy after all this time, just to start talking? Was small talk enough? He thought all of this in an instant and looked down at the pipe.

"Oh no . . . I don't smoke it. I stopped cigarettes. I just light this to . . ." Oskar fumbled around as he gestured at the pipe during his explanation, trying to rationalize how seeing the smoke from the pipe was part of how he stopped smoking cigarettes.

Calmer now, he caught Gunther off guard as he smiled and brushed the Afghan aside, standing up and walking over to his son. "How have you been?"

Oskar looked at his son in much the same way that Marie had moments before, trying to see who he had become, and Gunther smiled and laughed a little at the casual question. In an uncharacteristic gesture, Gunther actually put his arm around his father and gave him a couple of quick pats on the back. "Good, Father. I've been good."

The conversation between father and son was strained as Marie brought in coffee and then left them to talk. The talk quickly turned to the common ground of architecture, and Gunther was surprised to find that his father not only knew where he worked, but that he knew Gunther had been working there for years.

"We went to a dinner party a few years ago . . . twenty-three or twenty-four," Oskar explained, "and there was Ethan Stein. Well, your mother had to find out . . . She asked him how you were doing."

Ethan, Marie, and Oskar had all met when Gunther and Amalie first started seeing each other as teenagers. It seemed it was tolerable to Oskar for his son to go out with a Jewish girl, just as long as he wasn't serious about her. "Wild oats" and all that sort of thing. It wasn't until Gunther announced his intention to marry Amalie that Oskar showed his true colors, denouncing Amalie as a Jewish slut trying to better herself by stealing away his son. Gunther had known that his father had no Jewish friends, and Oskar would occasionally make an anti-Semitic remark or tell a vulgar joke, but it wasn't until the engagement that Oskar's blind anger and resentments boiled over, driving his son away. This made Gunther even more determined to marry Amalie, to spite his father.

Then there was the chance meeting at the dinner party. It had been five years since Marie had heard anything about her son, and with everything that was going on in Munich, she couldn't stand it anymore. She had to know if Gunther was all right, and so she walked over to Ethan, who had expected that Amalie's in-laws would ignore him. He was caught completely off guard when he turned from talking with one of the guests to find Marie Metzdorf standing beside him.

They began by exchanging pleasantries, and then, with the expression of concern so characteristic of mothers everywhere, Marie asked about her son and his family. They talked for quite a while as Oskar kept an eye on them, seeing how Ethan reacted to Marie, pretending to be interested the conversation in some of the other clusters of guests around the room. Eventually, when he had made a complete circle of the room, Oskar found that he too was standing with Ethan. There was a tension between the two men that wasn't there between Marie and Ethan. While Gunther hadn't given a complete report of Oskar's reaction to Amalie and her father, he did make it clear that his father had no interest in associating with Jews. It was an awkward alliance that night as Oskar asked about Gunther and Jakob and, as an afterthought, a politeness, also asked about Amalie.

It was after this clumsy reintroduction that Ethan and Oskar began to keep in touch, with the understanding that Amalie and Gunther shouldn't know at that time. As with so many family disagreements and misunderstandings, the conflict had taken on a life of its own. One irrational act leads to another until no one can actually give a sound reason for their actions. Gunther assumed that his father wanted nothing to do with him, and Oskar assumed that his son felt the same, so neither would risk his pride by taking the first step toward reunion.

The relationship between Oskar and Ethan was the strangest result of the problems between Oskar and his son. It's much easier to sustain mindless bigotry when you don't know anyone from the community whom you hate, and conversely, of course, it is not as easy to believe the lies of hatred when you have . . . a friend. Thence came the paradox of Oskar's anti-Semitism driving his son away while it was his son's absence that eventually drove his anti-Semitism away.

The conversation between Gunther and his father on that afternoon in late October of 1930 certainly didn't cover all of that history, though. Oskar only touched on his friendship with Ethan and then shocked his son by saying he had been wrong.

"I even have a Jewish doctor!" Oskar said with a laugh, as though that were the ultimate sign of reform.

The declaration suddenly reminded Gunther of the reason for his visit, and his manner changed as he asked his father how things were going with the doctor.

"The cancer?" Oskar said as a preface, letting Gunther know that it was all right to say the word *cancer.*

"He says it is as good as can be hoped for. It seems the cancer is in just one area."

"He's absolutely sure?"

"As sure as he can be."

"What next?"

"He says they have to operate, to remove part of my right lung."

Gunther looked as if he had just been slapped in the face. For some reason he hadn't expected that, but then he couldn't say what he had expected. Maybe he had hoped that it wasn't really cancer, that the diagnosis had been wrong. "When?" he asked after a pause.

"I'm going into the hospital tomorrow."

"Tomorrow? So soon?"

"Well, the diagnosis was made a couple of weeks ago. Dr. Rosenau wanted me to go in the same week that he told me it was cancer."

"Why didn't you?"

"I . . ."

"Did you try another doctor?"

"No. I can't really explain it. It doesn't make sense, but even though I believed the doctor, I still couldn't really . . ."

"You were afraid," Gunther stated with both sympathy and confrontation.

Oskar sighed and looked down at the floor. He felt ashamed even though he had no reason to be ashamed. "It's not easy facing your fears when you've spent most of your life insisting that you're not afraid of anything."

This was very difficult for Oskar to admit. Gunther knew at this moment that his father had changed. He had become more human. Oskar then began talking in a way that Gunther had never heard before. He began talking to his son as a man, two men discussing life.

"I can hold a picture from some time of my life in my mind's eye," Oskar said as he looked at the pipe in his hand, which continued to send its steady stream of smoke rising to the ceiling. "I can even picture myself as though I were an observer of my own life, a bystander watching as the dreams were dreamt and the sins committed and the joys consumed and the pains endured." Oskar stopped for a moment and then looked at his son. "I'm not the one to tell someone how to live their life. I never took risks. I haven't chosen well . . ."

Gunther didn't know how to respond. His father certainly had reason to be depressed. "It isn't like that," Gunther said, doing his best to sound convincing without actually coming up with any specific contradictions. "We all make mistakes."

Just then Marie came in, telling them it was time for dinner and they all went into the dining room and, after quickly saying grace, began to eat.

"It all started . . . ," Oskar said, suddenly interrupting himself with a noisy slurp as the spoonful of venison stew he was trying to eat turned out to be hotter than he had expected. "It was just a bad cold," he said, once he had swallowed. "Then it got worse, and the doctor, the one Ethan recommended, was afraid it might be pneumonia. He made a photograph . . ."

"They used the X-ray machine on him," Marie proclaimed in the awkward phrasing of someone who wants to sound well informed but doesn't really know what they're talking about.

"Yes," Oskar acknowledged as he smiled at his wife, "the X-ray machine. Well . . . Dr. Rosenau said it was bronchitis, but he said he had found something else and he needed another picture. Then a week later he told me I had lung cancer, but that it was early."

"If the doctor hadn't made those pictures . . . ," Marie interrupted, at the same time reaching over to touch Oskar's hand, which rested on the table as he clenched the spoon.

"I wouldn't have known until I got really sick,"

Oskar continued, finishing Marie's statement, "and by then it would have been too late. Rosenau says I'm lucky that they only have to take part of a lung. Any later and there wouldn't have been anything they could do."

Gunther forced himself to smile as though he believed it would be just a matter of a simple operation, but he knew it was much more dangerous. This would be a major operation, and even if everything went well, there would be a great chance of infection. During the war, Gunther had known a lot of men who had survived battles with relatively minor wounds but had ended up dying from an infection they got in an army field hospital.

Oskar went into the hospital as scheduled the next morning, with the operation scheduled for the morning of the day after that. Gunther and his mother sat in a waiting room of the same hospital where Gunther had brought Jakob after the dog attack years before.

A fly kept making its rounds of the small room, always coming back to rest on Gunther's hand. It became a game, with Gunther holding his hand still, waiting to see it the fly would actually find its way back, and then when the fly landed, he would shake it off, sending it back on its journey around the room. It had been two hours since the operation began, and when it was almost noon, Gunther's stomach growled and Marie looked up with a start. Gunther just smiled and shrugged his shoulders.

"Maybe we could get something to eat," he said.

Marie, with an anxious look, just shook her head.

"They said even if it went well, we could expect it

to take at least another hour," Gunther continued, trying to change Marie's mind.

"I don't know . . . ," Marie said, her shaky voice showing just how nervous she was. "I think we should wait."

"Come. We need to go for a few minutes. It will take your mind off things for a little while."

Marie looked up with eyes that clearly searched for reassurance.

"Come," Gunther said again as he got up and helped his mother on with her coat. They stopped at the nurse's station on the way out, and Gunther told the nurse where they were going, saying that they would be back in just a few minutes.

It was a gloomy, rainy day as they walked out the front door, and Gunther couldn't help thinking what a fitting day it seemed for a funeral. He quickly chased the thought away as he tried to convince himself that there was nothing to worry about. His father would be just fine. But he just couldn't keep his mind from wandering. What would happen to his mother if his father died? Did they have any money? Gunther didn't have the slightest idea what his parents' fortunes had been since he last saw them. What would it mean to Gunther if his father died?

Marie barely touched her lunch, so Gunther rushed through the meal so that they could get back to the waiting room. Their absence from the hospital hadn't taken Marie's mind off the operation at all, as she spent most of the time in the café staring out the window at the third floor of the hospital across the street. Their timing couldn't have been better as it turned out. Just as they came out of the elevator, they ran into Dr. Rosenau, who walked over to Marie and took her hands in his. "We're finished," he said. "Everything went well, and now we just have to watch closely to make sure there are no complications."

"It's over?" Marie said as she finally let a tear run down her cheek. "He'll be all right now?"

"We have to watch him closely for the next few days. After an operation like this . . . We just have to be extra careful."

"I want to see him."

"No, that wouldn't be a good idea right now. He's still under the anesthetic and he needs rest."

"Please," Marie persisted.

Dr. Rosenau looked at Gunther and then back at Marie, then gave in with a sigh. "I could let you go in for just a moment, but I want to warn you that he doesn't look good right now . . . and he's asleep. He won't even know you're there."

"He'll know," Marie said, as though she knew something that the doctor didn't.

Gunther just stood by as his mother went to Oskar's bedside and lifted his hand, gently placing it on top of her own and then covering it with her other hand. She looked at him tenderly as a few more tears rolled down her face, but she didn't make a sound as she slowly leaned over and kissed him on the forehead. Gunther put his arm around her as she turned away from the bed and moved toward the door to leave.

It was a long night for Marie as she slept alone in the bed she had shared with her husband for more than thirty years. She woke in the middle of the night to the deafening solitude. She missed Oskar's snoring. She lay there staring at the ceiling, telling herself over and over again that it would only be a few days before her husband was back home again. Eventually she got up and went down to the kitchen for a glass of water. On her way back to her bedroom, she stopped at the open door of Gunther's room. It had been Gunther's bedroom as a boy and now it was the guest bedroom, but she and Oskar had always referred to it as "Gunther's room," even during all those years of Gunther's exile. She watched her son sleep, listened to his breathing, trying to understand how everything had gone by so quickly. Finally she went back to bed, only managing to fall asleep after an hour of staring out the window at the cold and distant stars.

Marie was up early the next morning making breakfast, just as she always did, and she and Gunther struggled to make small talk while they ate. Afterward they bundled up against the cold and made their way to the Elsbethen train station, eventually arriving at the hospital in Salzburg just before eight o'clock.

They were allowed in to see Oskar, but still only for a short time. He was still asleep, and once again Marie held her husband's hand, but this time his eyelids fluttered and he was suddenly awake and smiling weakly as he looked into his wife's eyes.

"There you are," Marie said softly, as one might speak to a child.

"I made it through," Oskar replied weakly.

"How do you feel?" Gunther asked.

"It hurts," Oskar said with a grimace. "Dr. Rosenau says that's to be expected. He says I'll feel much better in a few days."

"We came in yesterday to see you but you were asleep," Gunther went on, trying to keep the conversation going and the mood light. "The doctor said you wouldn't even know we were here, but Mother insisted that somehow you would!"

"But I did know," Oskar said as he squeezed Marie's hand.

"Your mother held my hand and kissed me on the forehead. Your mother isn't as foolish as you think," Oskar continued. "You should believe in her more."

The three of them talked for a few more minutes, until Marie said it was time to go before the nurse came and told them they had to leave. Marie was content now and willing to leave so her husband could rest. She'd had to be there early that morning to make sure that he was all right. She was afraid he might be too "down" or too "up."

She knew from her experiences with other friends and relatives who had been hospitalized that sometimes you could tell a lot about how a person would recover by how they acted. If they were sad or overly worried, they might not make it, and strangely, she had known people who were really happy and bright after an operation, but who had died suddenly in the night. Oskar seemed to be the same as always, not too happy or too sad. From his mood, she knew that Oskar would do the best he could and the rest would be up to the doctors.

Just as they were about to leave, Oskar called Gunther back, asking Marie to leave them alone for just a minute. Marie left them without asking why, because she knew what Oskar wanted to say. He wanted to make things right with his son. Oskar had told his wife that he wanted to talk with Gunther before the operation because he honestly didn't know if he would live through it, but in all the confusion, the right moment just didn't present itself then.

"I just wanted to thank you for coming," Oskar began. "I just thank God that I have the chance . . ."

"It's all right, Father," Gunther interrupted. "We've both changed . . ."

"Yes, but I just wanted to say . . ." Oskar paused as he tried to reach for one of the eloquent phrases he had rehearsed in his mind but never said out loud, and now none of them seemed right. "I'm sorry."

Gunther smiled at the way his father had searched so hard for two such simple words, but of course, these were not simple words between the two of them. Terrible things had been said many years before when father and son had parted company, but these two simple words at this time in Gunther's life meant more than perhaps anything else his father had ever said.

"Me too," Gunther replied.

"No, no," Oskar insisted with a grimace. "It was all my fault, not giving you a chance, not giving Amalie a chance."

"We all make mistakes," Gunther said. "I shouldn't have run away like that. We might have worked it out if..."

There was an awkward pause as they both became lost in thought for a moment. "It's all that asinine business about the Jews," Oskar finally said. "After I got to know Ethan Stein . . . and this Dr. Rosenau saved my life! I just feel like I was such a fool."

What was the old man saying? Gunther thought to himself. *From one extreme to the other? First he hates all the Jews and now he loves them all?* But of course this was not the issue at hand. This was about a father and son healing old wounds, and Gunther wanted that as much as his father did.

"Well, now it's time for you to rest. Mother and I will be back tomorrow afternoon."

Oskar smiled, and Gunther reached for his father's hand, not sure how to touch him. A handshake didn't seem right, so he just held his father's hand as he said good-bye.

Marie was waiting in the hallway by the door as Gunther came out.

"Is everything . . . ?" Marie ventured cautiously.

"Everything is fine," Gunther said as he took his mother's arm.

Gunther called Amalie from a public telephone the next day to tell her that everything was going well and that he would be staying for another two weeks, until Oskar was out of the hospital. He also told her about the clandestine communications between her father and his. Once she was off the phone, Amalie thought to herself that this was a good sign. If her father could keep this secret from her for all these years, she felt better about the confidences she had entrusted to him about Adolf Hitler.

CHAPTER 11

It was in 1930 that Josef Goebbels invented the myth of Horst Wessel. Horst Wessel was a young pimp who was a Nazi on the side. A girl Horst wanted was also involved with another young man who happened to be a Communist, and when the two men eventually fought over the girl and Horst was killed, Goebbels said that Horst had been killed fighting for the Nazi party against the Communists. From this incident came the "Horst Wessel Lied," the song that became the classic marching song of the Sturmabteilung as they fought other political factions, especially the Communists, in the streets of Germany, saying that they would not be happy "until Jewish blood came spurting from the knife."

Meanwhile, as the SA was making its presence known in the streets, the Nazi party surprised even its own leaders by winning 107 seats in the German Reichstag, compared to only 12 seats won in the elections of 1928. This made it the second-largest political party in Germany, confounding Hitler's opponents and changing the face of the Reichstag as the new representatives chose to attend in full SA uniform, answering the roll call with a loud "Present. Heil Hitler!"

Gunther had managed to get a three-day pass from the front to go home at Christmas just after Jakob turned one year old in October of 1917. That was the last Christmas Gunther had spent with his mother and father. It was the Christmas when his father had gone into a rage about his son marrying a Jew and had told Gunther that he was never to come to the house in Elsbethen again.

The Christmas of 1930 saw Gunther, his Jewish wife, their son, and even Ethan Stein coming to spend Christmas Day with Oskar and Marie.

Not only was this the first Christmas that the immediate family had spent together in fourteen years, it was also the first Christmas since the end of the war that Amalie, Gunther, and Jakob didn't spend with their adopted family, Gertrude, Klaus, and Friedrich.

It was a strange get-together, with Oskar and Marie lavishing all their attention on Jakob, whom they hadn't seen since he was a baby, while everyone else expressed concern about Oskar and asked how he had been since the operation. Everyone wanted things to go well, and so the day was pleasant enough, but the happiness seemed forced. It had been such a long time since Ethan had seen Gunther and since Oskar and Marie had seen Amalie that none of them knew each other anymore, and it would take time before they could be more natural with each other. After all of Gunther's expectations, Christmas seemed anticlimactic.

New Year's Eve was spent back in Munich with Klaus and Katrina, Gertrude, Friedrich, and Friedrich's latest girlfriend. Klaus went on at length about the Reichstag elections and how it was only a matter of time before Adolf Hitler would be head of the government. Amalie shuddered at the thought but joined in with the rest as they toasted the possibility of Adolf's ascension with champagne.

Amalie began to worry even more about Gunther as the new year began and he was still unable to find work. Even though she made enough money for them to get by, Gunther felt that he had to be the one who brought in the most money, that he had to support the family. The tension at home grew, and Amalie found that she was glad each day when she would leave for the office so that she could get away for a while.

Amalie found herself spending more time with Geli as they both tried to get away from their uncomfortable situations at home. A few months into the year Geli had managed to convince Uncle Alfie that they shouldn't take any chances of improprieties between them, now that the Nazi party had become so much more prominent and he was in the national spotlight. She had been very careful in her approach, as she was afraid that he might fly into a rage at the mere mention of their sexual encounter, but instead he was quiet. He couldn't even look at her. She had shamed him. She felt sure that he was relieved when she suggested that they not ever repeat the episodes or even mention them again.

Soon after that, Geli became secretly engaged to Adolf's chauffeur. When Adolf found out, he blamed everything on Emil, the chauffeur, and fired him on the spot, but that didn't stop Geli from trying to break away.

Later in that summer of 1931, Geli confided to Amalie that she had met someone during her last visit to Vienna. She was in love with a painter in Vienna and had managed to meet with him a number of times, even though Uncle Alfie still kept a close watch over her.

Amalie was worried and tried to convince Geli that she was playing with fire, that she couldn't get away with playing Adolf for a fool, but Geli only laughed. Geli had recognized that moment when Uncle Alfie couldn't look her in the eyes. That moment was power. She felt that things were turning now and that it was just a matter of time before she could get everything she wanted, and she was willing to bide her time.

Amalie was also biding her time. She began to wonder if now was the time to attack Adolf. She thought that since the party had gained power, this might be the right time—just as Adolf came into the spotlight—but instead she decided to wait, as there were some strange developments coming out of London.

The American newspaper syndicate owned by William Randolph Hearst had come upon a young man in London named William Hitler. William Hitler was Adolf's nephew, the son of Adolf's half brother, Alois Jr., who was Alois Hitler's first son, his illegitimate son by the woman who had eventually become Alois Hitler's first wife. Geli had met William one day when Uncle Alfie had called a family meeting. Adolf had paid for William's and Alois Jr.'s passage from England and then summoned Geli and her mother Angela so that the whole family could be addressed. Geli swore Amalie to secrecy as she prepared to tell her what the meeting was about.

"I've never seen Uncle Alfie so mad!" Geli began.

"I told you that you have to be careful," Amalie

said, trying to warn Geli again about her secret affair.

"Ja, ja . . . but Cousin William, you won't believe what he said!"

"What?" Amalie said with a smile, becoming more interested in the gossip.

"He said that the reporters were very interested when he mentioned that he thought there were Jews in the family!" Geli said with a laugh at the possibility of scandal in the family tree.

Amalie's eyes grew large, but Geli only took it as surprise at what she had just been told. Amalie was considering what this might mean to her. The Bible! Did Adolf know about Angela's family Bible?

"Remember," Geli cautioned through her laughter, "you promised not to say anything."

"No, of course not. Was it true?"

"I don't know, but Uncle Alfie was shouting that none of us should ever say anything about our family. He was furious. He said that there were a lot of people just looking for things to use against him, and even a rumor about things like that could hurt him."

"Well," Amalie said, trying to appear the loyal follower as Geli's laughter subsided, "I'm sure it's not true."

"Oh, I'm sure you're right, but it shouldn't really matter." Geli replied.

"But haven't you heard what he says about the Jews?"

"Yes, but that's just politics," Geli said, brushing the comment aside. "Politicians say all sorts of things that they don't really mean."

"Geli, just because you have a Jewish boyfriend, don't think it doesn't matter to others. If Uncle Alfie knew that you had a Jewish friend in Vienna he'd go crazy."

"Do you think so?" Geli asked coyly.

"You are playing with fire," Amalie said slowly, scolding Geli and trying to impress on her again how dangerous her game was.

"You worry too much," Geli retorted, using the same scolding tone.

Neither Amalie nor Geli could have known that Adolf was so concerned with William Hitler's insinuations, and the rumors that Adolf himself had heard when he was younger about Jews in his family, that he sent Hans Frank, his lawyer, to the Waldviertel region to investigate.

When Frank returned to Munich after completing his investigation, he was concerned about how his client would react to the findings. Not only did Frank come to the conclusion that there was Jewish blood in the Hitler family, throughout his investigation he kept running into people who said that a reporter, a female reporter from Munich named Liesl Kraus, had been there a few years earlier asking the same sort of questions. While Frank's information was slightly incorrect in that he said it was a son of the Frankenburger family in Graz who had gotten Marie Schicklgruber pregnant, when in fact it was a grandson of the Frankenburgers, he had come to much the same conclusions that Amalie had. The only thing that differed in the investigations was that Amalie had Angela Raubal's family Bible and the confession from Johann Nepomuk Hiedler.

Adolf was, just as Frank expected, enraged by the report, denying it, saying that it was not possible. He then went on to say that he wanted Frank to track down the reporter he had mentioned. Neither Adolf nor Frank said it out loud, but they both knew that Liesl Kraus would not live long after she was found. She would just disappear some night, never to be heard from again. Frank would hit a dead end a few days later when he learned that Liesl Kraus had been murdered almost ten years before, but he couldn't shake the feeling that somehow there was more to the story.

It was September when Geli decided to make her move. She knew that she held all the right cards, that she could control Uncle Alfie and get away to Vienna. She had lunch with Amalie on the sixteenth and told her that she was leaving for Berchtesgaden the next day to say good-bye to her mother and that she would leave for Vienna from there. Amalie knew that it would be a long time before she would see Geli again, so she embraced her as they were about to part company.

"Remember," Amalie said pointedly, "you must write to me. Let me know how things are going."

"I will," Geli assured her. "You've been a real friend. It hasn't been easy in Munich." Geli then surprised Amalie with a kiss on the cheek before she pulled away and smiled, giving a little wave as she hurried down the street.

That afternoon Amalie managed to get out of the office in time to get down to the Hauptbahnhof and see Geli off as she boarded the train to Berchtesgaden. Amalie was relieved once the train was under way. She was happy that Geli had made it, that she had managed to escape from Uncle Alfie. Amalie had been so worried about Adolf somehow finding out about the family Bible from Vienna and managing to trace it back to her, but she wasn't only worried about herself. She was sincerely concerned about Geli, and so she smiled to herself as she walked through the Hauptbahnhof away from the train platforms and down to the U-bahn, boarding the subway for Fürstenried station.

"YOUR UNCLE called," Angela told Geli when she got to the villa at Berchtesgaden. "He says you are to go home immediately."

"I am going home," Geli replied curtly to her mother.

"He wants you back in Munich."

"I told him I was going to Vienna."

"Then you had better talk with him."

"We did talk. I don't belong to him. He can't stop me."

"He can," Angela said as a matter of fact. "He said that if you don't come back on your own, he will send someone to bring you back."

Geli's eyes flashed at hearing this threat. "He said what?"

Angela said nothing as Geli fumed for a moment, but then tried to regain her composure.

"I'll go talk to him," Geli finally said with anger in her voice. "I'll talk to him and then we'll see who will stop me from going to Vienna!"

On Friday morning Geli took the train from Berchtesgaden back to Munich. She left her suitcases by the front door of the apartment, and when the housekeeper asked if she should have someone take them up to Geli's room, Geli replied coldly that they should be left right where they were, that she would not be staying long. She started for her room, but then stopped on the stairs to tell the housekeeper that when Uncle Alfie got home, he should be told that she was waiting to talk to him. She put a particularly ominous emphasis on the word "talk," which alerted the housekeeper that there would probably be another of the shouting matches that had become more and more common in the apartment over the past few months.

Adolf was scheduled to attend a meeting of Nazi officials in Hamburg on Saturday morning, so he only intended to stop at the apartment long enough to get ready for the trip. He arrived in the late afternoon with Friedrich Haas and Heinrich Hoffman. Friedrich had done some driving for Adolf after Emil, the chauffeur who had been involved with Geli, had been fired.

Adolf smiled a little as the housekeeper told him that Geli had returned and was waiting in her room to "talk" with him. Adolf enjoyed having power over her. She had treated him badly many times, humiliated him, but when it came down to it, he owned her. She would do as she was told.

"She can wait," Adolf said, making sure that she heard that he was home, letting her know that she could just wait until he was ready to discuss matters, to lay down the law.

Adolf leisurely went about checking his bags and making sure everything was in order as he supervised the new chauffeur loading the car. After about an hour, Adolf finally walked to Geli's room.

Geli was sitting at her writing desk, working on a letter to a girlfriend in Vienna, writing that she would soon be coming to see her. Geli looked up and stopped writing in midword, turning to face her uncle.

"You wished to speak with me?" Adolf said, as though he had no idea what was on Geli's mind.

"I wanted to tell you something," Geli countered immediately, every word ready and waiting for her uncle. This was to be her declaration of separation and independence.

"And what is that?" Adolf asked patiently, sure that he was in control, no matter what his niece said.

"I am going to Vienna."

"You are not going to Vienna," Adolf corrected.

But Geli persisted. "I am going to Vienna, and you are not going to stop me."

"What makes you believe that?" Adolf countered, thinking he would give Geli enough rope to hang herself.

"Because I don't think you want me here."

"Don't be ridiculous. Why wouldn't I—"

"Because I might be an embarrassment," Geli said pointedly.

Adolf felt his control of the situation quickly slipping away. "An embarrassment?" he said with just the slightest, almost imperceptible, creak in his voice—a creak that Geli instantly recognized as the sound of the knife she was wielding at his back.

Geli was not stupid, although at times she was a bit too headstrong, but she recognized this in herself, and she quickly tried to back off a bit to appease her uncle. "I love you, Uncle Alfie, but I really want to go back to Vienna to live."

"How would you . . . ," Adolf began, but he stammered a bit as he took a step toward Geli while he formulated the question, his voice rising as he went on. "What do you think would embarrass me?"

Geli stood up from her chair and stepped away from the writing desk, trying to keep distance between her and Adolf. "I just want to leave," Geli shouted back.

"But you just said you love me!" Adolf said angrily.

"Not like that!" Geli shot back.

"Then who, you slut? Is it the new chauffeur? Some delivery boy? Some ragpicking Jew?" Adolf reached a crescendo on the word *Jew.*

Geli began crying as her uncle became hysterical, and she lashed out at him. "Yes! A Jew! In Vienna . . . I love him. I love him! Something you wouldn't understand you sick . . . sick pervert!"

"A Jew?" Adolf was now flailing his arms in wild gestures and screaming so loudly that he became hoarse. "A damned Jew!!"

Friedrich, who was sitting in the kitchen with Heinrich and the housekeeper, could no longer ignore the shouting as it became animal-like in its ferocity. "I'll see if I can't calm them down," he said as he headed toward the sound of the fighting. He arrived at the door of Geli's room just as Adolf lunged at her with his fist, striking Geli on the bridge of the nose, producing the sickening sound of cartilage being crushed as the blow connected. Geli was almost unconscious as she flew backward, landing on the floor just beside the writing desk, bumping the desk and knocking over a glass vase, which fell to the floor near her hand. Geli managed to recover herself just enough to pick up the vase and throw it blindly at her uncle. The thought of Geli fighting back at him when he was so justified in beating her pushed Adolf over the edge into an uncontrollable rage. Just as the vase smashed against the wall, he pulled out his pistol and fired at Geli, the sound of the gunshot coinciding with that of the breaking glass. She crumbled to the floor from her sitting position. She was killed instantly as the bullet entered her heart.

Friedrich stood at the door, unable to comprehend the reality of what he had just seen. Adolf stood motionless as the pistol slipped from his hand and fell onto the thick carpet at his feet. Friedrich broke from his trance and ran to where Geli lay on the floor to see if she was still alive.

Friedrich didn't know what to do. Kneeling, he cradled Geli's head for a moment, thinking of how much he had loved her and how she hadn't loved him. Gently placing Geli's head back on the floor, he looked up at Adolf. There was no need to tell him that she was dead. Adolf knew it. Friedrich felt like panicking, but he fought to stay calm as he tried to think of what to do. He stood up slowly and walked to the door, checking to see if the key was in the lock, then went to Adolf and took him by the shoulder.

"She's gone," Friedrich said softly. "There's nothing to be done here." Friedrich then led Adolf back to his own bedroom and sat him down on the edge of his bed.

"I . . . ," Adolf began, sounding distant and hazy. "I didn't . . ."

"I know it was an accident," Friedrich said, "but we've got to think of you now. Just wait here a minute."

Friedrich then went back to Geli's room. He quickly picked up Adolf's Walther pistol and pressed it into Geli's hand. He tried to make it look as though she had been seated in the chair of the writing desk and had fallen out when she shot herself. He didn't know what else to do, and he didn't have the presence of mind to think out anything more elaborate, although he did try to straighten up the room a bit so that it wouldn't look like there had been a fight. He finished up by locking the door to Geli's room.

"We've got to leave now," Friedrich said as he returned to Adolf, who was still sitting on the bed, staring blankly at the wall. "We have to stay on schedule."

"Leave?" Adolf asked as Friedrich's words finally got through to him. "What about the police? There will be questions. An investigation."

"We'll take care of that later. Right now we have to leave for Hamburg. We can still make it to Nuremberg tonight."

Friedrich helped Adolf up and managed to get his coat on him. "You've got to get hold of yourself," Friedrich said, staring directly into Adolf's blank eyes, and suddenly Adolf was there.

"Yes," Adolf said, "yes . . . we'll go to Hamburg."

Friedrich helped Adolf to the stairs but let him walk down to the car by himself, then went to the kitchen. Sending Heinrich out to start the car, he somehow managed to put on a good show for the housekeeper, telling her that Geli was upset and that she had thrown them out of her room and locked the door. "You'd better just leave her alone," he said smiling. "You know how she gets." The housekeeper nodded with a wry laugh and followed him to the door to bid them a good trip.

Friedrich felt better once they were on their way and putting some distance between them and the apartment. He rode in the back with Adolf, telling Heinrich to stop at the first place where they could make a telephone call, once they were out of the city.

"I'll call Max," Friedrich confided to Adolf. "We know a couple of sympathetic policemen."

Once they got to a small inn with a telephone booth, Friedrich called Max and told him to go to a public phone and call him back. He didn't want to take any chances that someone might be listening in on their conversation.

"There's been an accident," Friedrich said, once Max had called him back.

"Where?" Max asked cautiously, wondering what Friedrich was up to.

"At the apartment."

"The apartment?"

"Adolf's."

There was a pause as Max began to realize that this must be important. "What do you need?" he finally asked.

"You've got to stay by the phone. I'm . . . we're on our way to Hamburg."

"The telephone at Adolf's?"

"No, no! Your telephone! Don't go to the apartment. I'll call you in about four hours. Wait by the telephone at your place."

Friedrich then hung up the phone and returned to the car, getting in on the passenger side in front with Heinrich, leaving Adolf alone with his thoughts in the back as the car sped away from the small inn toward Nuremberg.

They were on the road for quite a while before Friedrich finally spoke to Heinrich, but it wasn't because he didn't trust Heinrich. Heinrich had been with Adolf from the start, and everyone knew he would give his life if necessary to protect the party, and to him, Adolf was the party.

"We have a problem."

Heinrich looked concerned as he glanced up from the road, only taking in Friedrich's sullen profile, since Friedrich couldn't look Heinrich in the eye as he began to plan out a course of action.

"Back at the apartment," Friedrich continued quietly, as though Adolf would not hear him. "There was an accident."

Heinrich again looked over at Friedrich, and this time Friedrich looked him in the eye. "Geli was . . . ," Friedrich began, trying to think of how best to say it but unable to come up with anything other than the horrible truth. "She's dead," he finally blurted out, quickly averting his eyes and sinking back into silence.

Heinrich was astounded but kept his composure. "When? How did it happen?"

"She shot herself."

"When?"

"In about an hour from now."

"What?"

"We have to be in Hamburg before word gets out. Adolf has to be seen in Hamburg at the hotel."

"Who knows about this?"

"Only us. We have to be careful. I need your help in working it out."

Heinrich thought for a moment, realizing that Friedrich was asking him how they could best cover it up, obviously to protect Adolf. Automatically glancing in the rear view mirror to see how Adolf was reacting to all of this, he saw that he was slouched over against the door, staring at the back of the front seat with an empty and confused look on his face.

"What do you have in mind?" Heinrich asked as he glanced at Friedrich for an instant before turning his attention back to the road.

"It looks like a suicide, but we need do everything we can to make sure that all the pieces fit."

"How?"

"I called Max Amann when we stopped back there. He's waiting for me to call when we reach Nuremberg."

"What are you going to tell him?"

"I'm not sure."

"Well, the longer we wait, the better our alibi," Heinrich said as he shrugged a shoulder back toward Adolf in the back seat, indicating that by "our alibi" he meant Adolf's.

"We can't wait too long."

"How long do you think?"

"She has to be discovered in the normal course of the day."

"The housekeeper?"

"Yes, Frau Winter. She would call her down for breakfast."

"What if Geli is found now?"

"That shouldn't be a problem. Her door is locked and she asked not to be disturbed."

There was an uncomfortable pause as Friedrich's statement made it clear that this was not just speculation. Geli was really dead and the coverup was already begun.

"Will she cooperate? Frau Winter, I mean. Will she do what we say?" Heinrich asked.

"I'm sure of it. Her loyalty, along with money . . . We have to make sure everyone keeps this as quiet as possible. Max . . . Frau Winter . . ."

"And Frau Reichert?"

"The landlady? I suppose . . . She's been with Adolf for years, and he's taken good care of her."

"What about the newspapers? The police?"

"That's what I have to discuss with Max," Friedrich said as he rubbed his eyes wearily, feeling the stress of the situation, anxious to get to Nuremberg and work out the details with Max. "Max knows a couple of policemen, and we have to work out a story with Frau Winter and Frau Reichert. There must be matching testimony that everything was fine long after we left."

The road to Nuremberg seemed to stretch out forever. Friedrich called Max as soon as they checked into the hotel, and once again Max went out to a public phone to call him back. Friedrich laid out the whole story, along with his plans to protect Adolf. Friedrich was relieved when Max told him that he thought he could take care of the coroner and have the body sent quickly to Vienna for burial. The rest of the story fell into place once Friedrich checked with Adolf to make sure that there was money available to ensure loyalties and hold it all together.

The story would be that there had been no argument between Geli and Adolf, and that she had been extremely pleasant as she bid Adolf and his escorts a good trip. There was a strange sound in the middle of the night, it would be said, and when the housekeeper knocked on Geli's door in the morning and she didn't answer, the housekeeper called Max, who went to the apartment and broke open the door. The speculation would be that Geli had committed suicide because she wanted more than anything to be a singer and was distraught over an upcoming concert. The coroner would do a cursory examination, and the body would be on its way to Vienna for burial within hours of being discovered.

Several newspapers ran stories suggesting that the circumstances of Geli's death were highly questionable, but they had nothing to go on. There was no autopsy. The body was out of the country, and the party had worked hard to put out their version of what happened to any paper that would print it.

It wasn't until days later that Friedrich allowed himself to feel anything. He spent the night drinking in a quiet beer hall, then went for a walk in the English Garden. A gentle breeze seemed to carry distant whispers, voices from long ago and far away.

He found a park bench where he sat watching the river. It was past two in the morning, and the silver wash of a bright September moon was spilling over the trees and grass and into the river. He sat for a while with his legs stretched out, hands locked behind his neck, looking up at the stars, at the few sparse clouds illuminated by the moonlight. Then he suddenly sat up straight and looked out at the river as the silvery water rushed by. And he cried.

Amalie cried too when she heard. She knew what had really happened, although she wasn't privy to the actual events surrounding Geli's death. No one in the inner circle was talking. She had tried to warn Geli how dangerous the game was, and she had hoped that somehow she could save her young friend. Amalie had thought Geli was safe when she had left for Vienna, and she didn't even know Geli had come back to Munich until she heard the news of her death. She knew that Adolf was somehow responsible, but she didn't know how. She was deeply depressed, feeling that Geli had slipped through her fingers.

Then she began seeing the newspaper stories that Adolf's people were feeding to the press about Geli committing suicide. Everyone in the Nazi inner circle was holding their breath, waiting to see what might happen. Would the authorities believe it was suicide?

Amalie was so angered by the reports that she even considered going to the press herself with the information she had on Adolf, but then thought better of it, deciding that what she knew wouldn't be enough to ensure that he would be brought down.

The scandal of Geli dying in Adolf's apartment and all the rumors that went with it swirled about Munich for months. Adolf was genuinely grieved by Geli's death. He secretly went to Austria to visit her grave, even though he was under threat of arrest, since the Austrian government had outlawed his Nazi party and declared him persona non grata in that country.

Even though Friedrich assured Amalie that Adolf had been devastated by Geli's death and insisted that such sincere grief was proof that Adolf had had nothing to do with the tragedy, Amalie was not convinced. Amalie knew the beast and his nature, but she had made her decision to wait, and so she was forced to appear sympathetic to poor Adolf.

This, however, was not to be the most difficult event with which Amalie had to contend that September of 1931. Gunther's period of unemployment had been hard on him and the family. He tied his work to his value as a man, and being without work made him feel as though he had failed his family. Even though they managed well enough on Amalie's salary, he became sullen and withdrawn. It didn't take much for him to start an argument with any member of the household, especially Jakob, who was now at an age when children are naturally rebellious, and so life in Fürstenried became quite uncomfortable.

One evening after dinner, as the two of them sat reading in the living room, Gunther told Amalie that he had decided to join the Sturmabteilung division of the party. With his wartime experience, and with Klaus's and Friedrich's recommendations, he assured her, he should have no trouble starting out as a group leader and quickly moving up. Gunther made it clear as he spoke that the matter was not open for discussion—that he had been thinking about it for quite some time and had come to a final decision.

Amalie wasn't really in a position to discuss it anyway. She had abrogated her right to protest when she had gone out of her way to become Geli's friend and to be accepted by the Nazis as the wife of a devoted party member.

The conflict between who she was and who she had pretended to be robbed her of sleep that night. *What now?* she kept thinking to herself as she lay awake, staring at the ceiling, as Gunther snored contentedly beside her. *What now?* She looked over at her husband and wondered who this man was beside her. They had been together for seventeen years, but still she found herself asking, *How could he be so stupid?* Part of his "declaration" that night, his justification for deciding to join the SA, had been that the whole Jewish thing was now past. All she had to do was listen to his speeches and read the newspaper stories, he had insisted, to see that Adolf Hitler had changed.

It was obvious to Amalie what was happening. She knew that Adolf was only doing and saying what was needed to win elections. The changed she could see was that he had gone from being a fanatic with political aims to being a politician with fanatical aims.

Her problem, it seemed to her as she lay awake analyzing her life, was that she tried to be too smart. *Maybe it's time for me to leave,* she thought to herself.

Divorce? Start over again? Where? What about Jakob? The more she thought about it, the more she began to feel trapped. She couldn't leave Jakob, and she didn't know if he would go with her. The only solution she could come up with as far as a place to live was going back to Salzburg to stay with her father, and the thought of that didn't appeal to her very much. Trapped!

LEAVING THE house the next morning, Gunther looked at his watch and saw that he had almost an hour before he had to meet Klaus, so he decided to walk to the Braunhaus rather than taking the U-bahn. Strolling casually down Residenzstrasse on his way to Briennerstrasse, he soon found himself at the edge of Max-Joseph-Platz. As he stood for a moment, it suddenly struck him as ironic that here he was on his way to join the SA and had ended up within a few meters of where he and Klaus had lain when the police started shooting at them back in '23. It was the exact spot where he had seen Adolf jump up from his place in front of his troops and run to the car that waited to drive him away to safety.

Gunther began walking again, rationalizing to himself that all of that had been a long time ago. Things had changed. Adolf had changed. He knew now that Adolf hadn't been running to save himself, that he hadn't been afraid. He had run to save the party. He had known the party would someday save Germany and . . .

Gunther wasn't paying any attention to the people he passed or where he was going as he stared down at the sidewalk. He was too busy convincing himself that he was doing the right thing. He looked up to find that he had passed Briennerstrasse, and ended up having to go back two blocks before turning off Residenzstrasse. He was still twenty minutes early, and rather than going inside, he waited on the bench out front for Klaus.

It was less than a minute before Klaus suddenly went by in a rush, not even noticing Gunther as he flew up the steps of the headquarters.

"Klaus!" Gunther shouted.

Klaus looked around to see who was calling, then smiled as he walked over and sat next to Gunther. "I thought I was late. You caught me off guard."

"No," Gunther said, "there's still a little time. I hate to seem too eager."

"Right," Klaus agreed. "There's no time to get nervous when you arrive just on time."

"I'm not nervous," Gunther said confidently.

"No, of course not," Klaus said, hesitating for a moment before going on, not sure how Gunther would take what he was about to say. "Whatever you do," he continued, "don't mention that Amalie is Jewish."

"Of course not!" Gunther replied. "But how far will they go to check?"

"Since she's Austrian, they may not be able to follow up as well as they would in Germany. Make up a maiden name. Say that both her parents are dead."

"Brunner," Gunther said abruptly, deciding on a new maiden name for his orphaned wife.

"Where did you get that name?"

"One of the men at the front. Joseph Brunner. He always talked about how important his family was, rich and famous."

"Maybe that's not such a good idea then if the family was well known."

"No," Gunther said with a smirk, "it turned out it was all lies. He was killed, and I wrote to his family. From the letter his mother wrote in return, it was clear that they were just working people."

They laughed as they got up and headed for the building, but fell silent once they entered. It was a sacred place, like a church, the embodiment of the party, a symbol of how far the party had come from those nights when they would sit in the back of the Sterneckerbräu arguing and drinking watered-down beer.

Klaus, always in control, went up to the desk where a young man in uniform sat typing. As he started to tell the young man about Gunther's appointment, he was interrupted by an officer who strode into the lobby and began asking the young man about the letter he was working on and another letter that he had yet to begin. The officer was tall and blond with a long, thin nose, but he looked a bit strange because, although he was thin, he had broad hips, almost like a woman's. Klaus was annoyed at the interruption, but as the officer began to speak in an odd high-pitched voice, Klaus recognized who he was. Once the officer had finished giving the young man his instructions, he turned back toward his office, making brief, cold eye contact with Klaus without a word of acknowledgment, as though daring Klaus to say anything. He then strode quickly back to his office and shut the door.

"Was that him?" Klaus asked the young man once

the officer had closed the door. "The new head of security?"

"Yes, SS Obersturmbannführer Reinhard Heydrich," the young man recited as he made notes on a letter that Heydrich had just corrected.

"From the navy? Naval intelligence, right?" Klaus pursued.

"Yes, naval intelligence. Wilhemshaven. Are you a reporter?"

"No, no," Klaus said as though insulted. "I was just curious. I've heard about him, but never met him before."

"You still haven't met him," the young man said with a patronizing tone.

Klaus gave him the sort of smile that said he would just as soon have hit the young man as smile at him, then asked where he and Klaus had to go to see Ernst Röhm, the head of the SA.

Their acquaintance with Adolf, along with Klaus's aggressiveness when it came to his social and political standing, got Gunther right to the top as far as joining the Sturmabteilung. It wasn't as though he were about to enlist in a military organization; it was more like Gunther was being interviewed for a special job in a successful company.

Röhm was a nasty little man. It was common knowledge that he was a homosexual, and he would often comment in casual conversation that terroristic violence was a necessary means to further the party's interests. He had been a soldier who enjoyed war and had the scars to prove it, including an obvious one on the bridge of his nose that showed in profile where a bullet had cut out a distinct notch.

The interview went on for almost two and a half hours, with Klaus sitting in as a character witness for the first hour before being asked to leave Gunther and Röhm alone to continue their talk in private. Klaus alternately sat in the hallway and paced along the wide corridors. He could have left—Gunther had even suggested it—but Klaus wanted to know what went on as soon as Gunther was finished.

Gunther only allowed his exhaustion to show after he had left the office and Röhm had closed the door behind him.

"Well?" Klaus said in an excited whisper, keeping his voice low because everything echoed in the large hallway. "How did it go?"

"Well enough, I think," Gunther said with a tired smile. "He seemed to like me."

"Watch out for that!" Klaus said with a laugh, referring to Röhm's reputation as a homosexual.

"No, not like that," Gunther shot back. "I mean he seemed impressed with my record."

"Yes, they like men who worked their way through the ranks rather than those who got their commissions through family connections."

"Yes, that's exactly what he said."

"What else?"

"He took a lot of notes. I think they're going to do a thorough background check."

"Did you tell him 'Brunner'?"

"Yes," Gunther said, but just as he was about to say something else, they came into view of the reception desk and stopped talking until they had passed the young clerk and left the building. "I must call Father and tell him about this Brunner thing . . . make sure he and Mother don't say the wrong thing."

It was only a matter of three weeks before Gunther heard that he had been accepted as a group leader. There were no questions about any of the information he had given, including the references to Amalie Brunner.

Jakob was very proud of his father. His circle of friends in the youth program were very impressed that his father started off as a group leader. Everything was growing—the youth group, the party, the SA—and it looked like Adolf Hitler would soon be one of the foremost leaders of Germany. More and more, Jakob's world became focused on the Nazi party.

He was fifteen years old now and beginning to feel more confident in his social world. It all seemed clear and well defined. He knew who to like and who to hate, and he knew that he was part of a group that would always be on his side. It was like having two families. He was no longer an only child, since he now had his brothers and sisters in the Hitler Youth programs.

He would often attend the dances set up through the youth group, but he was still very shy among the girls, even though he was becoming more and more interested in them. He tried very hard not to think about sexual things, since the youth groups were often addressed by speakers who would explain how destructive sex could be. He tried hard not to masturbate, having been warned about the terrible things it would do to his mind and his body, but every now and then he would give in to the temptation and then feel terrible guilt at being so weak.

There was one girl in particular that Jakob was interested in. Ingrid Schmidt was the daughter of one of the men who worked at the party headquarters in Munich. A year younger than Jakob, she had long blond hair that she always wore in smooth braids. She smiled easily at anything Jakob would say when they ended up talking at one of the youth group parties, and she always seemed to want to touch him. She would reach for his hand or touch his arm when making a point in conversation, and he found that he liked it, yet at the same time it made him feel uncomfortable because he wasn't sure what it meant.

The other boys would often sit around after some group-sanctioned activity and talk about girls, but Jakob had no way of knowing that most of what they said was exaggeration. They would tell stories about things they had seen or how far they had gone with a girl, or how much girls wanted sex, although they couldn't come right out and say it, and this was the first time Jakob had even heard of such things. By this time he knew the mechanics of sex, but he had never actually seen a girl or a woman with her clothes off. After the first few discussions with the other boys, however, Jakob started to make up his own tales and did his best, as did all the other boys, to establish a reputation that would preclude him from being embarrassed by the often heard chants of "virgin," which were accompanied by laughs and finger pointing when the boys began to pick on someone in the group.

One of the boys he had met on the first day he joined the group had become a good friend.

Thomas was the only one to whom Jakob would confide that he was still, in fact, a virgin, despite his protestations to the rest of the group. Thomas was in the same position, but he felt that the two of them were a team, and if one somehow succeeded in losing his virginity, the other would become anointed by virtue of their friendship. One would live vicariously through the other's great achievement, and so he would often try to push Jakob into situations where it looked like there might be good prospects for success, and Jakob would do likewise for him.

"She wants you," Thomas whispered into Jakob's ear as he discretely pointed at the at doorway across the room. They were at one of the group parties in August of 1931, and at last it seemed to Jakob that Thomas might know what he was talking about. Ingrid had just arrived and was smiling invitingly at Jakob.

"No," Jakob replied, just to be contrary. "We're just friends. We just like each other."

"That's how it is sometimes," Thomas kept whispering in a monotone. "They try to be friends just to get close, but really she wants you to rip off her blouse and lick her tits."

Jakob began to blush violently, unable to retreat, since Ingrid was making a beeline toward him across the dance floor, just as the tinny music of an old phonograph began playing softly. She was kind enough not to mention the obvious color in his cheeks as she stood in front of him, ignoring Thomas as she boldly asked Jakob if he wasn't going to ask her for the first dance.

"I don't dance very well," Jakob said apologetically.

"That's all right," Ingrid replied with her characteristic smile. "I've had lessons. I can help you." And with that she took Jakob's hand and led him to the edge of the dance floor.

Jakob felt awkward and clumsy as he waited for instructions from his teacher.

"Put your right hand here," Ingrid began as she took his hand and reached it around her, placing it on her lower back, "and hold my left hand out like this." Jakob could feel that he was still blushing, since his face was just as hot as it had been the moment before, especially when Ingrid put her right arm around his waist and gave him a gentle pat on the bottom as she did so.

"Now hold me closer," she continued as she pressed tightly against him. Jakob felt himself becoming aroused and began to blush even more, embarrassed that she must be feeling his erection pressing against her, but Ingrid said nothing about it. She just kept smiling and instructing him how to waltz. "Now move your feet in rhythm to the music. One, two, three, four. One, two, three, four. You're doing fine!"

Jakob finally realized that Ingrid must be aware of his erection, but she obviously didn't care. She didn't say anything, but just kept smiling all the while, eventually even resting her head on his chest as they circled around the floor. He hadn't ever noticed the smell of her hair before, and the way it caught the light as they moved. He began to feel more at ease, and once the music stopped, he even managed to ask her for the next dance.

After their third dance, Ingrid decided they

should take a break and suggested they go for a short walk. Thomas made a face and smiled as Jakob glanced over at him, and Jakob responded by smiling back as he took Ingrid's hand, escorting her out of the hall.

The dance was in a building within a block of the west bank of the Isar, a ways north of the Deutches Museum. The night was warm and bright, and it was natural that they would walk toward the river to stand on the Maximiliansbrucke[28] in the moonlight. They watched the river flowing beneath them for a while and then headed to the walking paths that led down to the landscaped banks of the river and eventually to one of the ornate black iron benches, obscured from view by the dense shrubs and undergrowth.

"A nice dance tonight," Jakob said as they sat down.

"Yes," Ingrid agreed without much conviction, as though her mind were on something else. "They usually are nice."

"Usually they're so bright," Jakob continued, trying to keep up the small talk.

"What?"

"The dances. Usually the chaperones have the lights so bright."

"Oh . . . yes, you're right"

"But tonight they were just right, like a glow in the room."

"Jakob," Ingrid interrupted, "do you want . . . would you kiss me?"

---

[28]The Maximilian Bridge.

Jakob was caught off guard. He had been trying to figure out how he might steal a kiss. He reached over and kissed her, surprising himself as he put his hand on her breast, pressing against the stiffly starched cotton of her blouse and the rigid seams of her brassiere. He deftly undid a button on her blouse while still kissing her, fully expecting she would pull away, but she didn't.

He felt encouraged and slid his hand under the white blouse, gently pressing on her breast, but he didn't know how to get the brassiere off. He had never done anything like this before, and so he contented himself with sliding his hand down to the warm soft skin of her abdomen and then slowly up and down her side as they continued to kiss.

He didn't even notice as Ingrid undid another button on her blouse and reached back to undo the hooks of her brassiere. He suddenly felt the brassiere sliding down over his hand and was dizzy from breathing so heavily, as though he couldn't catch his breath. He reached up to hold her small breast in his hand and stopped kissing Ingrid as he looked down to see what he held.

Her skin was flushed pink, and Jakob put his face to her chest, pressing his cheek to her breast and then turning to kiss it lightly, feeling the heat radiating against his cheek. Ingrid didn't move. She didn't make a sound. She didn't tell him to stop.

Thomas was right! he thought to himself excitedly. *She did want me.*

Just then Ingrid put a hand on Jakob's head and stroked his hair, and then turned on the bench as Jakob moved with her until he was sitting with his back against the bench. Ingrid slowly pulled away from him, looking into his eyes and making no effort to cover her breast.

She caught him off guard again as she suddenly slid her hand down the front of his pants. Jakob had been erect since they were dancing, and certainly nothing had changed that since they had left the party. Ingrid's fingernail accidentally jabbed at him as she ran her hand down his hard stomach toward his thigh, and he jerked back instinctively, afraid of being hurt. Ingrid stopped for a moment and whispered "Sorry," but his only response was to stretch out his legs and spread them apart so that she would have room to explore.

Ingrid smiled and continued slowly, feeling her way down, lightly running her hand over his body. "It feels so strange," she murmured as she gently moved his testicles from side to side until they started to draw up tightly. Jakob was unable to talk. He had never touched himself before in quite that way, lightly, gently, He had never had a sexual encounter before, and had no idea how it could feel, and now that this beautiful girl was touching him like this, it sent shock waves through his legs and started his head swimming.

Ingrid then moved her hand up, barely touching it, feeling how big it was. She lightly moved her hand over the skin, up and down, until Jakob couldn't stand it anymore. He quickly undid his pants and reached down, putting his hand over hers and forcing her to grip him firmly. Ingrid giggled because he seemed so frustrated, and she liked the thought that she excited him so and made him lose control.

"Harder," Jakob finally managed to whisper, but as he gripped her hand and forced her to pump up and down, Ingrid suddenly became frightened. Things were going too far, and this wasn't just playing anymore.

She tried to let go of him, but that only made Jakob hold her hand even tighter. "Stop it!" she cried. "You're hurting me!" She tried to pull away, but Jakob still held her hand.

"Oh, God!" he gasped. "Please don't stop. Please don't stop now!" Ingrid kept trying to pull away, standing up and almost breaking free, but Jakob jumped up and wrapped his arms around her, his pants falling down around his ankles as he began pressing himself against her, desperately, uncontrollably rubbing himself against the coarse fabric of her skirt.

Ingrid began crying and saying "No, no," but Jakob felt out of control, unable to stop himself. He reached down for her skirt with one hand while still holding her tightly, and pulled it up, at last finding skin to rub against. He didn't even try to enter her as he thrust over and over again against the soft skin of her thigh, quickly coming to orgasm.

Once it was over, it felt like coming out of a nightmare. He couldn't believe what had happened—couldn't believe what he had done—that he had been so out of control. Ingrid was crying and frantically trying to brush his semen off her leg, as though it were acid burning her skin.

Jakob struggled to pull up his pants. He knew he had to do something, but he didn't know what. What could he say? He felt like running away, but where could he go? She knew his name. He had hurt her. He had terrified her, and now he had to face the consequences.

"I'm . . . I'm sorry. I couldn't . . . ," he stammered, looking down at the ground, ashamed. How could he have done such a thing? How could it have happened? "I couldn't stop," he offered lamely.

Ingrid stopped crying for a moment and stared at him, and even in the darkness he could see the contempt and disgust, the hatred.

"I'm sorry! I'm sorry," he continued, sounding almost as though he was going to cry too.

"You bastard!" Ingrid finally spat out at him. "You sick bastard. You're a disgusting animal." She took a long swing, slapping him as hard as she could, so hard that her fingers left red marks on the cheek that only moments before had rested against her breast. Then she turned and ran off toward the party.

"Wait!" Jakob shouted as he took off after her. "Please."

Ingrid stopped as he came after her, recoiling as he reached for her. "Don't you dare touch me. If you touch me, my father will kill you."

"No, Ingrid, please . . ."

"What?"

"Please don't tell anyone. I'll do anything . . . give you anything. Please, just don't say anything."

Ingrid's eyes narrowed with contempt, but she didn't say a word. She knew she was in control again, and she reached behind herself to fasten her brassiere and then slowly buttoned up her blouse, continuing to stare at Jakob with an expression that dared him to say anything or to move toward her. She finally turned and walked slowly back to the party. Jakob turned and walked in the opposite direction, toward the U-bahn station, frantically wondering what would happen next. Would Ingrid tell? Would her father come to kill him? Maybe the police would come for him. The ride home was mind-numbing as his imagination ran wild.

He got home before his mother and father, who had also gone out for the evening, and fell into bed with his clothes on, pulling the covers up over his head and crying quietly, ashamed of what he'd done and wishing he could somehow take it all back, afraid of what the morning would bring.

When his mother and father asked about the dance the next morning, he just said everything was fine and left it at that. He was grateful for the reprieve the weekend offered, that he didn't have to worry about whether Ingrid had told everyone at school. But the weekend flew past, and he soon found himself walking down the halls of the school, wondering each time someone made eye contact with him if they somehow knew about what happened.

But Ingrid knew she didn't need to confront Jakob or tell his friends. She knew that part of her revenge would be making him sweat, making him wait to see what she would do to get back at him. She also knew within hours after the incident how she would take her revenge.

HELMUT PUPPENSPIEL was the leader of Jakob's youth group section. In keeping with the policy espoused by the Nazi party that the Hitler Youth groups should be led by young people, Helmut was just nineteen.

Ingrid found Helmut at the Alten Rosenbad restaurant in the Schwabing district, which was frequented by party members and had, in fact, been a favorite meeting place of Hitler himself in the early days of the party. Helmut was laughing with two friends as Ingrid walked up to his table.

"Herr Puppenspiel?" she asked with authority, although it only barely covered the apprehension the fifteen-year-old girl felt as she addressed the youth group leader four years her senior.

"Yes?" he answered with an air of superiority as he looked up at the girl.

"I need to talk to you about one of the boys in your group."

"Someone caught your eye?" Helmut shot back with an arrogant smirk.

"There is a serious matter that we need to discuss," Ingrid rejoined resolutely.

Helmut realized it must be some sort of trouble, and he had strict orders to make sure there were no problems or scandals within the youth group. These suggestions came from the party leaders, who were beginning to realize the potential of indoctrinating and training soldiers long before they actually became soldiers. Helmut asked his friends to leave for a few moments so that he and Ingrid could talk privately.

"Now, then," Helmut began, motioning Ingrid to sit beside him, "what is it?"

"Jakob Metzdorf."

"Jakob? What's wrong with Jakob? He's one of our best . . ."

"He tried to rape me."

Helmut stopped in mid-sentence.

"Jakob?" he asked after finding his voice again. "But Jakob is a quiet, shy—"

"He did it," Ingrid interrupted.

"When?"

"Last Friday. At the dance."

"At the dance?"

"We left to go for a walk."

Helmut thought for a moment as he took in the information. "Did you tell the police?" he finally asked.

"No."

"Why not? Why are you telling me? Why did you wait to say anything?"

"My father works at the Braunhaus. I don't think the Hitler Jugend should be embarrassed. I just want Jakob Metzdorf out of the HJ so that I won't have to see him ever again."

"You want him thrown out?"

"Yes."

"And you want me to tell him why?"

"No."

"I suppose you want to tell him."

"Yes. I want to tell him because I know how much he loves it. I want to be the one to tell him why this is happening."

Helmut tried not to show any change in his facial expression as Ingrid's plan sank in. *Hell hath no fury . . .* he thought to himself.

"This assumes that I take you at your word that

everything happened as you say," Helmut said slowly as he analyzed the developing situation. "It would be a cruel joke if it wasn't as you said, if you had some other reason to dislike Jakob and just wanted to—"

"Herr Puppenspiel," she interrupted, "I could just tell my father and he would take care of it, but you should know that it would be a big mess. This way, only you, I, and Jakob would have to know."

And you get to drive the knife into his heart yourself, Helmut imagined saying to the pretty young blond girl, but he only managed a wry smile at what a neat package she had made of everything.

"Very well," Helmut conceded, "I'll see Jakob tomorrow afternoon. I'll tell him then."

The next day Helmut sat waiting for Jakob outside the Neue Realgymnasium in Sendlingertores district just as classes let out for the day. "Jakob!" Helmut called out from across the street.

"Helmut?" Jakob said with surprise, not expecting to see his friend there since they were going to see each other in just about an hour at the HJ meeting. "What gives? Aren't we meeting this afternoon?"

"Yes, but there's something we need to talk about."

It made Jakob a little nervous that Helmut was so serious.

"Like what?" Jakob managed to squeak out.

"Let's sit," Helmut said, motioning Jakob over to a bench. "Someone came to talk with me yesterday."

Jakob's face was eager with anticipation at what Helmut might say next. Helmut always joked about Jakob going to the Olympics because of his talent in archery, or could it be word of a promotion? Jakob knew he was well liked in the group. He did well at all the sporting events, and he participated in planning the social events. Maybe he would be asked to lead a squad.

"They . . . this person . . . told me there was . . . an incident," Helmut continued, stumbling through his little speech as Jakob began to tense up. This no longer sounded to Jakob as though it would be a pleasant talk. "An incident at the party last Friday night," Helmut finally finished up in a rush of words, punctuating the accusation by looking Jakob in the eye for the first time since they sat down.

"I . . . what kind of . . . ," Jakob stuttered, as he instantly switched from wanting to offer an explanation to wanting to pretend that he didn't know what Helmut could possibly be talking about, but Helmut pushed ahead, leaving no room for Jakob to confirm or deny what was about to be said.

"A girl says you attacked her," Helmut stated, looking straight out across the street rather than looking Jakob in the eye. He spoke in a monotone as he handed down the sentence. "I'm afraid there is no place for that sort of behavior in the HJ. You have to leave . . . resign. Because I like you, I'll let you do it yourself rather than letting the other men know."

Jakob was crushed. The HJ was everything to him. All his friends, the sports, the respect he had earned, it all centered around the youth group. He stared down at the gray sidewalk, fighting to keep from crying as it started to sink in. He was deeply hurt, but there was nothing he could do about it. He had made a mistake, and now he had to pay for it.

"Did she tell the police?" Jakob finally managed to

ask in a half whisper.

Helmut was caught off guard by this. He had expected Jakob to stand up for himself, to call the girl a liar, to say that nothing of the kind had happened.

"No," Helmut replied, realizing that Jakob was beaten.

"Will she?"

"I don't think so. She seemed to just want you out of the group."

Jakob was relieved a bit, but then he realized that this was punishment enough. She must have known that. She had taken away everything he had.

Helmut felt sorry for Jakob and managed to put his arm around him for a moment, pulling away with a quick pat on the back. "You'll be all right, Orion. It could have been much worse. I understand her father is some official at party headquarters. Consider yourself lucky that she handled it herself."

Helmut then got up and walked away, quickly disappearing around the corner of the block.

Jakob sat alone on the bench for a while, not knowing what to do next. What would he say to his friends in the HJ? How would he explain it to his mother and father?

It was no coincidence that Ingrid came by at that moment. She had seen Helmut waiting by the school, and she was sure that he was waiting for Jakob. She had hidden and watched as Helmut and Jakob talked, and when she saw Jakob's head fall, she knew that was the moment Helmut had told him. She felt an incredible rush of excitement at that instant, like a marksman watching his bullet bring down the quarry. Her bullet had hit home.

When Helmut left, she began to walk toward Jakob. He didn't even notice her until she stood in front of him and spoke. "A pig like you doesn't belong in the HJ."

"I'm sorry," was all Jakob could manage to say into the hate-filled face that confronted him.

"Now you're sorry!" Ingrid shot back before storming off down the street.

GERTRUDE WAS surprised when Jakob came into the house. "You're early!" she said with a smile, looking up at the clock. "And late."

"I had something to do at school," Jakob replied, but the truth was that he'd spent the previous hour and more coming up with reasons that he could use to explain to his friends and family when they found out he had resigned.

"Well, you're late for after school, but didn't your boys group meet tonight?"

"Yes, I decided not to go."

Gertrude let the issue drop at that. "Dinner won't be ready for another hour."

"I know. I've got some reading to do."

"Are you all right?"

"Yes, everything is fine," Jakob lied as he headed to his room. It seemed like only a few moments later that his mother and father came home and Gertrude was calling him to dinner.

Amalie had had a good day and for the first few minutes of dinner dominated the conversation telling them about a book she had bought for Frieder and Son by outbidding another publisher.

Gunther, on the other hand, had had a rather bad day full of petty bickering and unreasonable requests. When the conversation lulled, he asked Jakob how his day had gone.

"Good."

"Anything new?"

"Not really," Jakob replied, but then decided to casually bring up leaving the HJ, thinking it would be better to tell his parents himself before they had a chance to find out through anyone else. "I decided to leave the Hitler Youth program," he said, his eyes riveted on his dinner plate.

Amalie, Gunther, and Gertrude were all shocked, knowing how deeply involved Jakob had been in the group.

"When did you decide this?" Gunther asked.

"I've been thinking about it for some time now," Jakob replied as he began moving his food around the plate with his fork.

"Why?" Amalie asked, trying not to appear too eager since the news pleased her so.

"A lot of things," Jakob said evasively, which began to frustrate Gunther as he tried to understand what could possibly make his son want to leave the HJ.

"Things like what?" Gunther pressed.

"It's getting too . . . ," Jakob began. "It's like being in the army."

"But that's good!" Gunther insisted. "It teaches you discipline."

"But it's so much. It's not as fun as it used to be," Jakob whined.

"Everything doesn't have to be fun!" Gunther said, raising his voice. "Sometimes the things we don't like are good for us in the long run. We learn through adversity."

"What else?" Amalie asked, interrupting Gunther and urging Jakob to keep talking before Gunther got carried away.

"They're talking about the Jews," Jakob finally offered, as though his mother had pulled it out of him, but in reality he knew this was something that would gain her support against his father.

Gunther listened intently as Amalie probed this new reason.

"What kind of talk?" she asked.

"They say the Jews should be killed. They're talking about Grandfather Ethan!"

"You didn't tell them about your grandfather, did you?" Gunther asked, trying to cover his panic. After all, it would not take long for a connection to be made between Jakob's having a Jewish grandfather and a father who was a member of the Sturmabteilung. Amalie stared angrily at Gunther, clearly annoyed at his reflexive response to this threat to his job, and Jakob knew he had won his mother over. Jakob continued his attack.

"They sing that song . . . 'When the blood of the Jews is running down our knives, then we all will be happy.'"

"It's just a song!" Gunther said loudly. "I keep telling you it's just talk!"

"I think that's enough," Amalie countered, surprising her husband with the finality in her voice. "Jakob seems to have made up his mind."

"But what will they say if my own son leaves the..."

"This isn't about you," Amalie said calmly.

"He's my son!"

"And what does that mean? That you own him? That he has to do exactly as you do and believe only what you believe?"

Gunther hadn't seen this side of Amalie for quite some time. She had been so agreeable, but now that seemed to be changing, ever since . . . If he had to put his finger on it, it seemed that it was just about the time Geli Raubal killed herself when Amalie started to change. Gunther didn't respond to his wife; he just went back to eating his meal in silence.

Jakob also finished his dinner in silence, but not because he was feeling angry or frustrated. He was relieved that his tactic had worked. He had succeeded in turning his mother against his father and keeping them from finding out the real reason for his leaving the youth group.

Now if he could just make something like that work with his friends in the HJ, but he knew that would be much harder. They couldn't be played one against the other like his parents could. Jakob did have an idea, though, that he could somehow use the argument he had tried to pass off on his parents about the HJ becoming too much like the army. He would tell them he had quit because didn't like being told what to do all the time. He would play the rebel—an individualist who was born to lead rather than follow. It was far from the truth, and Jakob wasn't sure if he could pull it off, but he didn't think there was any other way.

CHAPTER 12

Even though the Nazi party had won enough Reichstag seats to make it the second-largest party in the country in 1930, Adolf Hitler lost the presidential election of 1932 to Paul von Hindenburg and then in November of 1932 the Nazis lost 34 of their Reichstag seats. It once again looked like Adolf Hitler and his party would fade away, but the Nazi representatives still remaining in the Reichstag continued to make their presence felt, disrupting the proceedings whenever things went against them.

There were also continuous intrigues regarding the office of Reichschancellor as Hitler tried to get Hindenburg to appoint him to the second-highest office in the Weimar government. Hindenburg would have none of it, as he personally disliked Hitler. Eventually, however, as three different Reichschancellors came and went, due in large part to the intransigence and disruptive practices of the Nazis in the Reichstag, Hindenburg was convinced by a number of advisors that Adolf Hitler was the only man who could hold the government together. The eighty-four-year-old Hindenburg grudgingly appointed Adolf Hitler Chancellor of Germany on January 30, 1933, although he never asked Hitler in person if he would accept the position, as he had done with the other Reichschancellor appointees.

Paul von Hindenburg could not have imagined the consequences of his action at that time, and he probably looked upon it as only a temporary political expedient. He clearly underestimated the former Gefreiter[29] *and couldn't have foreseen the road down which Adolf Hitler would lead Hindenburg's beloved fatherland. One can only wonder if it was just coincidence that the old man died within moments of Adolf Hitler's passing a law that combined the offices of Reichschancellor and president. Thus it was that Hitler became Germany's Führer instead of a Reichschancellor under the president's thumb. The Nazis celebrated that day with torchlight parades throughout the country, and a new oath was issued to Germany's military forces, an oath in which they no longer swore allegiance to the Weimar constitution. Now it was Adolf Hitler alone who demanded their allegiance, for Adolf Hitler had become the state.*

The RSHA section of the SS, the Reichssicherheitshauptampt[30] *of the Schutzstaffel,*[31] *was where Reinhard Heydrich worked in Munich as head of the party's security police, known as the SD,*[32] *one of seven departments within the RSHA. The organization of the Schutzstaffel was still being developed, including the creation of an office known as the Geheime Staats Polizei,*[33] *which would soon become known all over the world by its shortened name: Gestapo.*

Ernst Röhm, the leader of the Nazi Brownshirts, had only returned from Bolivia in January of 1931 after a self-imposed exile brought on by conflicts between Hitler and him as to how the party should be run and the role of the Sturmabteilung

---

[29]Corporal, the rank Adolf Hitler had held in the First World War.

[30]National Central Security Office.

[31]Guard detachment.

[32]Sicherdienst.

within the party. This conflict between Röhm and Hitler was not limited to just those two men.

The rank and file of the Sturmabteilung, especially in Berlin, also had problems with the direction national socialism was taking in Germany. The talk in the SA was that the Nazis were becoming just another political party, another group of weak men forced to compromise with other interests rather than strong-willed leaders who would take the nation by force and bring about the resurrection of the fatherland through national socialism.

"GOOD MORNING, Rebecca. Please come in," Gertrude said, a note of pleasant surprise in her voice as she opened the door.

"Good morning, Gertie."

"And what has you up and about so early on a Saturday morning?"

"I . . uh," Rebecca stammered as she inched past the doorway at Gertrude's invitation.

"Did you need something?"

"Well, Frau Haas . . ."

"Frau Haas? Suddenly you're so formal. It must be important."

"Maybe I was silly to come over," Rebecca rattled off as she turned for the door.

"Nonsense!" Gertrude said, putting a hand on Rebecca's shoulder. "Now tell me what you need."

"Well . . . ," Rebecca started, her eyes darting nervously about the floor. "Mother's out . . . and I don't know where Max is . . ."

"No wonder," Gertrude said sympathetically. "Your brother is just like my boys used to be on Saturday mornings. They were always out of the house before

I even had a chance to ask them about their chores."

"Yes," Rebecca continued, a little more at ease. "Like I said, Mother's gone and I can't find Max, and I'm supposed to . . . put some things in the attic, and I hoped that maybe . . ."

"You wanted Jakob to help you?" Gertrude said, finishing Rebecca's thought but refraining from comment on the obvious ploy to be with Jakob.

"Well, yes," Rebecca answered, still nervous and trying to avoid eye contact.

Gertrude and Rebecca had become friends since they had first met months before, and Gertrude had suspected for some time that Rebecca was interested in Jakob, but they never discussed it. Rebecca and her younger brother Max were latchkey children. Their father had died in the Great War and their mother had to work, and so Rebecca would stop by to see Gertrude almost every day. Rebecca was a bright girl who often amused Gertrude by talking about her interest in Freudian psychology. It seemed like such an odd interest for a young girl, especially when she tried to explain the strange things psychology taught. Just thinking about the day that Rebecca, the fifteen-year-old girl, tried to explain to Gertrude, the sixty-six-year-old German housewife, about a theory called "penis envy" would continue to inspire fits of laughter in Gertrude until the day she died.

"I'm not sure," Gertrude said sympathetically. "Jakob has been . . . he hasn't been feeling well lately, but I'll go ask him."

Jakob had been having a hard time since leaving the Hitler Youth. He had been almost sixteen when he dropped out, an age when it seems more important than ever to fit in, and the worst of it was that he had been so popular one moment and then suddenly ostracized the next. Contrary to what Shakespeare said about love, Jakob thought that it would have been better if he hadn't been popular in the first place.

Gunther reacted to his son's isolation with a mixture of hostility and frustration. He had taken a lot of pride in his son's achievements, and it seemed to him that Jakob had quit without any good reason. He tried to talk with Jakob, to understand his reasons, but after a few weeks of Jakob's withdrawal, Gunther accepted it and ended up becoming more involved in his work. The inevitable result was that he and Jakob began to drift apart. Perhaps he was more concerned about how these events affected him than about how Jakob was doing.

Amalie tried to help, but Jakob pushed her away too, afraid that somehow she might find out the horrible truth. He would shrug his shoulders whenever she tried to talk about it and say that the HJ just didn't suit him anymore. Amalie certainly didn't want to press him to go back, since she had never approved of his membership in the HJ in the first place, but she knew it was hurting him. In the long run, all she could do was write it off to the difficulties of adolescence. Perhaps it was just a phase of rebellion against Gunther. She noticed that it had affected their relationship, but she couldn't decide if that was something Jakob wanted or just an unexpected side effect. Whatever the cause behind it, Amalie worried about Jakob's isolation and the hours spent by himself reading or just laying on his bed with the door to his room closed, saying only that he wanted to be left alone.

The knock on the door startled Jakob, who was only half awake. "Jakob!" Gertie sang, "May I come in?"

"I'm still sleeping," Jakob called out, at which point Gertrude opened the door just enough to put her head in.

"Gertie! What if I hadn't been covered?" Jakob said sleepily from under the bedding that almost covered his mouth.

"I used to give you baths. You haven't changed that much."

"I hope I have," Jakob said indignantly.

"Come, Jakob, it's time to get up."

"Why?"

"I've volunteered you."

"What?"

"Yes, I'm tired of you laying about the house all day. Rebecca needs some help, and I said you would."

"Without asking me?" Jakob said, maintaining his indignation.

Gertrude surprised Jakob by sitting on his bed, something he couldn't ever remember her doing before, and then she reached out and brushed the long unruly hair out of his eyes.

"I'm worried about you . . . You seem so—"

"I'm all right," Jakob interrupted. "I just—"

"Please," Gertrude said, interrupting Jakob in return. "I would consider it a personal favor if you would help Rebecca put some things up in their attic."

Jakob almost said no, but then he noticed the look of concern on Gertrude's face and nodded yes. "It will take a few minutes to wash up and get dressed."

"Thank you, Liebchen, that's very nice of you."

By the time Jakob appeared in the kitchen dressed and ready to go, Rebecca was just finishing a hard roll and a piece of ham that Gertrude had given her for breakfast.

"Where's mine?" he said, as though he had been left out on purpose.

"Goodness, you have atrocious manners young man," Gertrude scolded as she took a plate of sliced ham out of the refrigerator and offered it to him.

Jakob smiled as he grabbed a slice of ham with his fingers and stuffed it in his mouth, chewing a couple of times with his mouth open.

"Jakob!" Gertrude scolded again. Clamping his mouth shut but otherwise ignoring her, Jakob shoved a roll in his coat pocket, then took another one and made himself a sandwich. Then, barely acknowledging her presence, he motioned to Rebecca to follow: "Come on, Becca."

Rebecca dutifully scampered after Jakob, turning to smile at Gertrude as she left.

When they were about halfway across the yard, Jakob looked at Rebecca.

"Aren't you going to get in trouble?"

"For what?" Rebecca asked, looking puzzled.

"The sandwich."

"What?"

"The sandwich . . . you ate a ham sandwich."

"So what?"

"I thought you were Jewish."

"Oh, that," Rebecca said with a blend of indignation and just a hint of embarrassment. "Jakob, you're Jewish, too!"

Jakob kept looking straight ahead as he walked. "Only half," he said curtly.

"According to Jewish law," Rebecca instructed, "you are a Jew because your mother is Jewish. The Jews don't believe like the Nazis do that you are part this and part that. You are either a Jew or not a Jew."

"I am a German."

"So am I," Rebecca said defensively. "My family has lived in Germany for almost six hundred years. My father was killed in the war, fighting for Germany."

Jakob thought about going back on his word to Gertrude and leaving Rebecca standing there at the front gate of her yard, but instead he coolly opened the gate, allowing Rebecca to go first, and then followed her into the house.

"These boxes over here," Rebecca pointed out as she breezed through the house. Climbing up on a chair she had placed under the access panel, she pulled down the door.

"One of us needs to climb into the attic while the other one hands up the boxes."

"I'll go up," Jakob volunteered.

"Good," Rebecca said with a smile. "I think there are bats up there. I hate going up."

"Thanks a lot," Jakob replied sarcastically.

"Are you afraid of bats?"

"Let's just say I don't care for them much."

"I thought all boys liked bats and mice and snakes and—"

"I thought all girls were quiet and shy," Jakob said as he jumped up and caught the edge of the door frame, showing off as he swung his feet up to the opening and vaulted into the attic.

Rebecca didn't miss a beat in the conversation, but she was impressed. "What do you mean? I'm shy," she insisted.

"Like a pit bull.

"That's not true. At least when I first meet someone, I'm shy."

"Like when you first met me?" Jakob challenged as he climbed into the attic, disappearing into the small hole until he turned around and stuck his head out, then his arms, ready for the first box.

"You wouldn't even remember the first time we met," Rebecca challenged.

"Of course I do," he said as she handed him the first box and he disappeared into the attic again, packing the box away in a corner and quickly returning to the opening in the ceiling. "It was on my way to school one morning, and there was a downpour, and you offered me half of that silly pink umbrella."

Rebecca smiled at the picture of Jakob crouching under the tiny umbrella with her as they made a dash for the U-bahn station.

"No," she replied simply.

"Of course it was," he protested. "That was the first time I ever saw you."

"No, the first time was when I was over at your house talking with Gertie, and you raced in from school and changed into your HJ uniform and ran out again."

"You make it sound like I didn't even see you."

"You didn't."

"Well then, we didn't really meet."

"I met you . . . Gertie introduced you as you rushed out the door."

Jakob didn't know how to reply to this, so he just ignored it and reached for another box.

"Are you an anti-Semite?" Rebecca asked from out of nowhere.

"That's a silly question. You just told me I'm a Jew and now you want to know if I hate 'em?"

"It's not like some people aren't both."

"Well, I'm not."

"Not which?"

Jakob smiled as he pulled a box out of Rebecca's hands.

"Neither," he said.

"How did you get into the HJ?" Rebecca asked with a look of earnest curiosity. She wasn't challenging Jakob this time; she was just curious how someone with a Jewish mother could get into the Hitler Youth program. Jakob said nothing, but that didn't stop her from asking more questions when he returned for another box. "Why did you drop out?"

Again there was silence as he quickly took a box and disappeared.

"They say you got a girl pregnant," she said loudly enough so that he could hear her no matter how far he retreated into the attic. It took a moment before he reappeared at the access door and looked down at her.

"Any more?" he asked with anger in his voice as

his temper grew short.

"Questions or boxes?" Rebecca asked, working hard to hold back a smile as she realized that she was getting to him, getting through to this stranger who lived only five houses away, the one she had wanted to know for so long.

"Boxes."

"No."

Jakob then made an equally physical display of exiting the attic as he had made of his entry, landing squarely on his feet in front of Rebecca.

"Would you like some toast and tea?" Rebecca offered.

"Tea?" Jakob tossed back as though insulted, since only women and ridiculous young girls drank tea.

"Coffee, then?" she amended.

"Thank you," he said smugly, thinking she should have known in the first place that, being an adult, he would drink coffee. He even managed a smile as Rebecca drifted into the kitchen. For some reason she found herself thrilled at the prospect of making toast and coffee for Jakob. She imagined herself as a woman entertaining a gentleman caller instead of just a neighbor offering something to the boy who had helped put up boxes in the attic.

Rebecca and Jakob were in the middle of their domestic episode when they heard the front door slam and someone hollered, "Becca!"

Oh no, Rebecca thought to herself as her friends Kurt and Jürgen flew into the living room and through to the kitchen, *I hope they don't try to pick a fight with Jakob.*

"Metzdorf!" Jürgen said with surprise as he fell

into one of the chairs at the kitchen table and started eating a piece of the rye toast without even asking, as though it were his own home.

"Hassler," Jakob acknowledged casually between a bite of toast and a sip of coffee. Jürgen was also from the neighborhood, and he even went to the same school as Jakob, but he wasn't in the same circle of friends that Jakob had known. Jürgen had, for whatever reasons, made a point of staying clear of anyone involved in the Hitler Youth programs.

"Look, Kurt," Jürgen said, using the piece of toast to point. "It's Jakob Metzdorf."

"Who?" Kurt asked innocently.

"Orion. The golden boy of the HJ," Jürgen said defiantly as he stared at Jakob, daring him to say anything.

"You're HJ?" Kurt asked with an edge to his voice, confronting Jakob and then looking at Rebecca, wondering why she would have someone from the Hitler Youth in her kitchen.

"I was. I'm not anymore. They're getting out of hand," Jakob said, as though he had been a pagan who had finally come to see the way of God.

Kurt seemed satisfied with the statement, but Jürgen pressed on. "Getting thrown out for getting a girl pregnant isn't the same as leaving because you object to their politics."

Jakob's eyes flashed anger, but he controlled himself. "That," he began slowly, "is a lie they spread to discredit me."

"Prove it," Jürgen challenged.

"How do you prove something didn't happen? Where is this pregnant girl? Where is the baby?"

Jakob was calm as he spoke, still finishing his toast and the last of the coffee as he summed up his case. "They didn't want anyone else to leave, so they had to make up some lie about why I left."

After a pause while Kurt and Jürgen thought about Jakob's version of the story, Rebecca smiled and said she knew it had all just been rumors.

Kurt and Jürgen weren't as quick to accept Jakob's explanation, but it was obvious to them that Rebecca had a crush on him, so they were willing to give Jakob the benefit of the doubt.

Kurt, Jürgen, and Rebecca were a group of friends on the outside. They hadn't quite fit in at school when they were younger, and all three had gone on to higher schooling rather than trade education when they were fourteen. Their career plans all seemed to give insight as to how they dealt with people. Kurt planned on a career in scientific research, and he kept trying to qualify and quantify the emotions and motives of others, as though he might someday work out an equation of human nature. Jürgen on the other hand was a superior mathematics student who seemed to have chosen to try to understand numbers rather than people. Jürgen was thus quite a social contrast to Rebecca and her pursuit of Freudian psychology.

"Well . . . ," Jürgen said, changing the subject, "are we still going to the museum?"

"That's right!" Rebecca said as she turned to Jakob. "There's a new exhibit at the Deutches Museum. Do you want to come?"

Jakob looked at Kurt to see if he would "uninvite" him, but Kurt surprised him by deferring to Rebecca and agreeing that he should come. So the four of them stopped by Jakob's house on the way to the U-bahn to let Gertie know where they were going.

"The museum?" said Gunther as he overheard his son on the way out the door. "Good! It's about time you started getting out of the house."

Gunther had given up trying to do things with Jakob on the weekends and had settled on getting more involved with his work in the SA. But things hadn't been easy since he had joined, and he rarely talked about his work when he was home. On the one hand, he had been with the party from the early days, so there were a lot of familiar faces among the ranks in Munich, but on the other hand, he had left after the *Putsch* in '23, which caused some resentment among those same old comrades. Then Gunther had had to contend with the momentous defection of Jakob from the Hitler Youth, which seemed to bring these conflicts right into Gunther's own home.

Gunther was annoyed with Jakob's assertion that the youth group was turning against the Jews. He tried to tell Amalie that the song Jakob mentioned was just a song, and that all the talk about Jews was just rhetoric. He had even talked to some of the SA troops from Berlin, where Hitler himself had told the SA that they shouldn't bear arms against the Jews and Communists in the streets.

Amalie countered that Hitler had only issued such orders because elections were going on at the time and any fighting in the streets might hurt his chances of being elected. She said that Adolf obviously wanted to appear to be more liberal, a middle-of-the-road candidate who could appeal to Social Democrats and members of the Catholic Centre party so that it would be a simple choice between Hitler or the Communists. She was clearly more astute at the nature of politics than her husband, as Gunther believed in some kind of mystical alliance where national socialism embodied a paradox of a dictatorship that actually represented the will and spirit of the individuals within the nation. A group of people willing to give up their individuality to be free individuals, willing to hand over all power to the state, to its government, so that they might themselves be powerful. It was a form of Nazi mysticism that each of these things would naturally follow the other. You had to leave critical thinking behind in order to truly be swept up in the dogma of national socialism. Give up everything to the Nazis and everything will come to you.

Amalie saw through the pretense. She knew it wasn't an oversight that Adolf forgot to mention the elimination of the Jews from his new Germany. There was even a group called the Jewish National Union that supported a proposal by Hitler to deny Jews from Eastern Europe entry to Germany. The German Jews believed that Hitler's shouts of Germany for Germans meant them too.

The most disturbing thing to Amalie, though, occurred just a few weeks before Jakob had upset his father with his announcement. On July 31, 1932, the day of the Reichstag election, a Vienna newspaper ran a headline that read "Heil Schicklgruber" with a story about Adolf's father being illegitimate. The story didn't mention Jewish blood in the family, but

Amalie was shocked to see it in print and waited to see what kind of reaction there would be to a story that revealed a number of things that had turned up in her own research.

Hitler had lost the election that year for the office of president, but he had come very close, finishing just behind Paul von Hindenburg and far ahead of the other candidates in total number of votes. Apparently, a recently published newspaper article revealing correspondence between Ernst Röhm and a psychiatrist in which Röhm acknowledged that he was a homosexual, along with other stories directed against the Nazis, had very little effect on the popular vote. This was greatly disturbing to Amalie, who began to question whether anything she uncovered would ever make any difference as Adolf became more and more popular.

Through the end of 1932 and into 1933, political intrigues developed one after another in the new cabinet, with Hindenburg going through three Chancellors—Bruning, Papen, and finally, General Kurt Schleicher—until at the end of January of 1933 it was Adolf Hitler's turn, as leader of what had become the largest political party in Germany, to become Chancellor under President Paul von Hindenburg.

It was a bleak day at Frieder and Son Publishing when the news came in. David and Amalie had pursued many political discussions during the presidential election and the subsequent run-off election between Hindenburg and Hitler, and finally the Reichstag elections that followed soon after the presidential election. Throughout all those months

Amalie and David assured each other that with each failure Hitler faced, it meant another nail in his coffin, that the German people would see through the charade, and soon all of those ridiculous Brownshirts marching in the streets with their flags and slogans would be a thing of the past. They had had their moment and it was just about to pass, but then Hitler somehow managed to sneak in the back door.

David had been a sounding board for Amalie through all that time. She had discussions with him that she could never have had with Gunther, and now David would share her sense of foreboding while Gunther would be out celebrating the party's victory.

The day that Adolf's ascension to the office of Chancellor was announced, David suggested that he and Amalie should go out for whatever it was that one might call the antithesis of a victory celebration . . . perhaps a lunchtime wake for democracy in Germany. It was a quiet meal in a small café, and David uncharacteristically ordered a bottle of wine with the intention of making it two or even three bottles as the opportunity presented itself. It seemed that David had managed to choose just the right place, one with a similarly minded clientele, because none of the other patrons seemed overjoyed that day, even though if they had chosen to strain their ears, they might have been able to detect the distant strains of a blaring brass band playing at the Braunhaus a few miles away.

"The dumplings are a little tough today," David said in passing as he took a bite of the liver dumpling from his soup and glanced over toward the door.

Amalie must have caught something out of the corner of her eye, because she looked up at just the right moment up to see the amazed expression on David's face, as though he had seen a ghost—a welcome ghost.

"What?" she asked as she turned to see what he was looking at over toward the door.

"Joseph!" David called out, causing a few of the other diners to look at him.

Joseph Hubert smiled as he caught sight of David and Amalie and quickly made his way over to their table.

"What on earth are you doing here?" David asked as he stood up and took his friend's hand, but then decided instead on a great hug.

"I've just now gotten into town," Joseph said when David finally let go and Joseph reached over to give Amalie a quick peck on the cheek.

"How long are you staying?" Amalie asked as Joseph pulled up a chair from the table next to them and sat down.

"For good!"

"What?" David exclaimed.

"That's right," Joseph said with a smile. "Uncle Max died about a month ago, and the dear old man left me something in his will."

"So why didn't you ever write?" David asked.

"Well, before that all I had was bad news, and I couldn't see writing you just to complain. I did all that to Mother . . ."

"What bad news?" Amalie interjected.

"No money, no job . . . things in America are awful now."

"What about that factory? The one Otto Maus owned. Didn't you get a job there?"

"Sure. Old Otto was as good as his letter of reference, and I worked for almost a month until the factory went out of business."

"Oh no," David said sympathetically.

"Yes," Joseph said emphatically, as though David was questioning the truthfulness of his statement. "A while later I got a job selling radios, but then even that slowed down, and they kept the long-time employees and let a lot of us new ones go."

"That's terrible!" Amalie commiserated. "But Joseph, things are just as bad here."

"No, that's the great part! Not only did uncle Max leave me enough money to come home, he also left me a majority interest in a textile mill in Dresden, which his lawyer assures me is still paying dividends."

"But money's not the only thing," David said, lowering his voice. "Haven't you heard? Hitler's just become Chancellor."

"Why are you talking like that?"

"Like what?"

"Like you don't want anyone to hear you. Don't they know Hitler is in?"

"Yes, they must, but don't you get what that means?"

"In America they said things are starting to settle down here."

"Joseph, I've heard that they're already rounding up all the Communists in Berlin and sending them off to prison. There are even rumors of executions."

"What does that matter? You're not a Communist, are you?" Joseph smiled as he repeated the question. "Are you?"

"My God!" David went on, still speaking in hushed tones after glaring at his friend for a moment. "Are you really that thick? Hitler has always said that the Communists were directed by the Jews. If he's rounding up the Communists today, you can be sure he'll come for the Jews tomorrow."

"There's the problem," Joseph said with a note of triumph, as though he finally figured out the flaw in David's logic. "You're afraid for yourself, but don't you see? We're Germans. When Hitler rages against the Jews, he's talking about the kikes . . . the Russian and Polish Jews."

David was stunned and turned to Amalie for help in convincing Joseph that there was trouble ahead, but Amalie said nothing. She had already banged her head against the wall too many times trying to make that same argument in her own home.

"Just mark my words," David finally said, "within six months there will be some sort of *pogrom* in Germany."

"Against the Russian Jews," Joseph insisted.

"Against all the Jews," David corrected.

There was an uncomfortable pause as David and Amalie went back to eating and Joseph thought about what had been said until he finally turned back to David in a conciliatory gesture.

"There may be trouble for all of us, but surely once all the Communists are taken care of, things will settle down and Hitler will leave us alone. We're an important part of the community."

David just kept on eating.

"Oh, come now . . . I'm sorry we ever got started on this political shit," Joseph whined. "God knows, politics never have been an aid to good digestion."

David managed a weak smile. Joseph could be incredibly frustrating at times, but David could never stay mad at his friend for long.

"We were already upset about this whole thing when we came in," Amalie said, trying to help David explain.

"Oh, and then I add fuel to the fire," Joseph said, finishing the thought, showing that he was willing to let it all pass.

"Let's talk about something else," Amalie piped in. "Tell us more about America."

Joseph went on for almost an hour about the buildings and the enormity of New York City, telling them all about the Guggenheim Museum and Harlem and Manhattan. Joseph had also made a trip to Washington, D.C., one weekend with a girlfriend because they wanted to see the Smithsonian Institute, but other than that he had spent all of the last couple of years in New York.

He had managed to get by well enough on his broken English, especially since there was a strong German community in the city, and he had had several different girlfriends during his time there, but they were all German expatriates like himself. Thus, he said with a certain air of superiority, he didn't feel he could really say what American women were like.

Amalie found it amusing that if Joseph had had an American girlfriend he would then have felt qualified to pass judgment on all American women, but that was the kind of man Joseph was.

By the time they got back to the office, it was almost time to call it a day, especially since neither of them was in the mood to work anyway. David went off with Joseph, and Amalie headed for the U-bahn to catch the next train to Fürstenried.

When Amalie arrived home, she was informed by Gertrude that Gunther had called to say he would be working late. In reality, he was out with Klaus and Friedrich. It just so happened that on that same day, Klaus Grunewald retired from the army, at the rank of major, on the anniversary of his twenty years of service to the cavalry and immediately signed up as a member of the RSHA section of the SS.

The RSHA was a recent division in the Nazi party hierarchy. A department of the SS, the RSHA included the security division of the SS known as the Sicherdienst, or simply by the initials SD. The SD was the department headed by Reinhard Heydrich.

Klaus, ever the social climber, saw Heydrich as an important man in the party, mostly because of the way that Heydrich seemed to have come out of nowhere to lead his department, but also because of the rumors floating about that Hitler was impressed by Heydrich. Klaus, therefore, wanted to get to know Heydrich and hoped to get on his good side, but not so much that he would consider serving in the SD under Heydrich's command.

Klaus saw himself strictly as a fighter, so he chose the Waffen SS as the section to join. He was quickly accepted by virtue of a record that included his continued membership in the party since its beginning, his status as an officer in the regular army, and his personal contact with Adolf Hitler in the early days of the party and later through Amalie's and Friedrich's friendship with Geli Raubal. He was one of the loyal party members from the *Putsch* of '23 who had stuck by Adolf through thick and thin and was therefore expedited into his new position.

The news of a Hitler Chancellorship, which was defeat for Amalie and David Frieder among others, was cause for great celebration for Gunther, Klaus, and Friedrich. Actually, it was just another evening spent in a beer hall, like so many before and so many yet to come, as the three friends raised their large beer mugs in a toast.

"Our time is here at last! To the future!" Klaus said as he swung his mug close to the others without making contact.

"To the future," Friedrich agreed.

They were all in uniform, Gunther dressed in the "Brownshirt" uniform of the SA and Klaus and Friedrich both in the black uniforms of the SS. Friedrich was now a clerk in the SD, helping out with the massive task of putting together files on all of the new party members who had swelled the ranks as a result of Hitler's impending rise to the Chancellorship and his promises of prosperity for Germany and an end to Communist aggression.

"It's been fifteen years now," Gunther said after they had downed most of their beers. "It seems like a hundred. Wearing a uniform again . . . When I close my eyes, it doesn't take much to hear a master sergeant calling out a marching cadence."

"A twenty-year retirement!" Klaus added, trying to outdo his friend. "How's that for old?"

"I remember many times during the war when I never thought I'd live to be thirty years old," Gunther continued. "Now thirty is just another lost memory."

"Well, at least the things we fought for are about to happen," Klaus continued.

"How are things going at the Braunhaus?" Gunther asked, turning to Friedrich. "They say Heydrich sets up his files in cigar boxes!"

"It sounds good in the newspapers," Klaus said, answering for Friedrich and gesturing as though holding up a newspaper and reading an imaginary headline out loud. "The struggling party exists on the pfennigs donated by its members and other sympathetic working people, and so on."

"I've heard some of the money even comes from America," Friedrich said, chiming in with Klaus's propaganda.

"I've heard that too," Klaus answered, "but never at headquarters. Lips are tight."

"I wouldn't be surprised," Friedrich added. "There are a lot of people outside of Germany who would like to get rid of the Communists and would gladly pay us to do it."

"You make us sound like mercenaries," Klaus countered, a challenging edge to his voice.

"No, no," Friedrich said emphatically. "I just meant that they would help supply us so that we can do the job that must be done."

"Well, it's best not to talk about such things," Klaus said, and even though he said it with a careless lilt, Friedrich took it as a warning. Operations at the Braunhaus were very secretive, and any casual remark might be scrutinized if the wrong person overheard it.

"Speaking of rumors," Klaus continued, turning to Gunther, "I understand you've been doing some talking."

"Talking?" Gunther responded nonchalantly, feeling that his friend was already getting carried away with his new position.

"Yes . . . Gunther, you're playing a dangerous game," warned Klaus. Friedrich watched in silence as Klaus and Gunther got caught up in their conversational duel, as though he weren't even there.

"What the hell are you talking about?" Gunther asked with rising anger.

"Rumors."

"There are always rumors. What rumors?"

"You've been telling the new men that the Jews are not the enemy."

"But Adolf himself said—"

"He didn't say that!"

"Yes, he did."

"No, he said that there should be no incidents during the elections."

This remark hit home with Gunther because it was exactly what Amalie had said when they had argued before.

"This is not a good time to start trouble," Klaus continued. "Remember Walter Stennes in Berlin. The SA almost revolted there. Things are too tense."

"But I haven't said anything—" Gunther started, attempting to minimize his personal campaign of tolerance for Jews based on his "good Jews and bad Jews" rationalization, a campaign that had been affected mostly by Amalie's influence, but also by the Jewish doctor who had saved his father's life.

"We understand," Klaus interrupted with a gesture between himself and Friedrich, cutting Gunther off in mid-sentence. "We know it's Amalie, but you can't let that confuse the issues! There is an uneasy feeling in the Braunhaus, rumors of a possible revolt of the Sturmabteilung here in Munich."

"No," Gunther protested. "There's nothing like that here."

"Don't you see?" Klaus shot back with frustration. "It doesn't matter whether it's true or not. The problem is that some people think it may be true. You've got to make sure that you don't stand out for any reason."

Friedrich's eyes widened like a student's who finally understands the reasoning behind a difficult math question. "You mean that if they think something might be wrong," he interrupted, trying to clarify what Klaus was saying, "they'll look for anyone who—"

"Yes," Klaus continued, interrupting Friedrich's thought. "Just like in the trenches. The snipers only got the men whose heads showed over the wall."

The reference to snipers in the war brought a nervous laugh of recognition from both Gunther and Friedrich, a bit of graveyard humor that made its point.

Gunther finally agreed that it would be best not to say anything that could be taken wrong, and Klaus, who had only spoken out of genuine concern for his friend, was relieved. They then got down to the business of celebrating Klaus's retirement and subsequent enlistment in the SS, continuing to party until long into the night and early morning of the next day.

FEBRUARY 27, 1933, was an uneventful day for the Metzdorf family. Gunther made it home in time for dinner, which had been the exception rather than the rule since the beginning of the year. Just as Amalie and Gunther were about to go to bed, there was a report on the radio that the Reichstag building in Berlin was in flames. It was already being declared an act of arson by Communist agents.

The announcer seemed on the verge of hysteria, reporting that it was believed that one of the men responsible was already in custody. Neither Amalie nor Gunther knew what to make of it, whether it was a single act of violence or just the start of another period like several they had lived through at the end of the war. Whatever the case, they went to bed hoping that everything would be under control in the morning.

The next few days signaled a new reality for Germany—a frightening new reality. Marinus van der Lubbe, a Communist from Holland, had been arrested in connection with the Reichstag fire, but that would certainly not be the end of it. There would be far-reaching consequences stemming from the act of arson on the night of February 17.

Chancellor Hitler used the incident to exercise emergency powers, issuing a decree the next day that effectively canceled free speech and freedom of the press, along with many other civil rights that one would expect to find in a democratic state. The decree went on to remove the seal of privacy from mail service and telephone communications, freeing government agents to intercept both forms of communication without just cause, and the police were now also allowed to enter private homes without cause.

Many people, rather than being alarmed by these actions, applauded Hitler's efforts. They knew these actions weren't directed against them and felt it was worth giving up such rights in order to stop the Communists, who were now being arrested in large numbers, along with suspected Communist sympathizers. Just as David Frieder had presaged a month before, the rumors of executions didn't arouse popular public opposition.

"He just needed an excuse," David Frieder said in a low voice that frightened Amalie as she sat in his office, listening as he read from the newspaper.

"What do you think it means? Are we next?" Amalie asked.

"We? We as Jews?"

"That, too, but I meant as a publishing house."

"Well, I think we're in for something either way. If he suspends newspapers, it's just a matter of time before he sends someone out to check on all the publishers."

"But isn't it just temporary? An emergency decree?"

"There's always a chance of that, but I think he was just waiting for something to happen. Any incident would have worked for him. Maybe I'm just an alarmist, but I think this is only a first step."

David spoke with the air of a fortune-teller, believing in the future he predicted and speaking as though the vision appearing before him was so real to him that he might actually reach out and touch it. Amalie knew that it was only an opinion, that David could just as easily be wrong about what might happen, but his mood of impending disaster made her extremely uncomfortable.

"What do you think we should do?" Amalie asked. "I mean, for the firm."

"We might want to review our current projects . . ."

"You mean we should censor ourselves?" Amalie asked with surprise, as it seemed to her that David was going to compromise everything he believed in at the first sign of trouble.

"To an extent."

"What extent?" Amalie asked, her voice rising.

"Amalie, it's important in life to choose one's fights. You cannot possibly win every battle. We have to go through the books we're working on and see which ones we really believe in, and balance that against the distinct possibility of the government closing us down."

Amalie wanted to argue the point, but it seemed self-evident. They could try to go on just as they had been, but what good would it do if Frieder and Son was closed down like some of the newspapers?

"I suppose I'd better get a list together," Amalie said with defeat in her voice as she rose from her chair. "Should I call a meeting for tomorrow to go through everything?"

"I don't think so," David answered. "I think I'm going to have to do this myself. These will be hard decisions, and I don't think a committee could do it fast enough."

The month of March saw Frieder and Son drop almost a third of its book production schedule. David lied to a number of authors and printers, using any excuse he could come up with to try to "cleanse" the publishing firm of some of the more left-wing projects to which it had committed itself. David's actions were a substantial financial drain on both the company's and his own personal assets, and there were legal considerations that required him to buy off several authors. He also managed to transfer some works to other publishers whose interest in their profitability outweighed any concern about politics. David was not proud of what he had done, but felt certain that a Jewish publisher would soon be targeted by a government that seemed each day to be leaning more and more toward the goals of the Nazi party, which everyone had kept insisting would never be in complete control.

On April 1, 1933, Amalie became convinced of David's prescience when it was announced that because of "atrocity propaganda" by foreign newspapers, there would be a boycott of all Jewish businesses throughout Germany.

It was the Sturmabteilung that was sent out to stand at the entrances to all Jewish businesses across the country and remind anyone who approached that they were owned by Jews and that true Germans should take their business elsewhere. The boycott was not violent except for a few isolated incidents. Even many of the new young Brownshirts didn't take the boycott very seriously. They felt that the Communists were the enemy, not Feldstein the butcher down the block, where their mothers had bought meat for years. It was up to Adolf Hitler to educate them.

Amalie and Gunther, and for that matter Gertrude and Jakob, didn't mention the boycott once in the three days it lasted. What was there to be said? Gunther went out each day to organize troops, directing them to different sections of the city with the names of stores to be boycotted, while Amalie went to work each day wondering if her own husband would appear at the door of Frieder and Son, shouting at clients that this was a Jewish business and they should consider taking their business to a good German publisher.

It seemed that there was some new decree or law every week restricting rights, especially the rights of the Jewish community. Jews were forced out of the civil service, and their numbers were restricted in universities. After a huge May Day celebration when a new national labor organization under government control was announced, all other labor unions were outlawed in Germany.

Meanwhile, the trouble that Klaus had been talking to Gunther about in the ranks of the Sturmabteilung was continuing to develop. The SS was mobilized in Munich on March 9 when a regional commander—or Gauleiter, in the parlance of the Nazi party—by the name of Adolf Wagner appeared along with Ernst Röhm at the office of the Bavarian Minister President, demanding that he appoint General Ritter von Epp as a general state commissar.

This was not only a clear challenge to Adolf Hitler's authority over the entire operation of the

SA, but also a challenge to the national government's authority over the region of Bavaria. The demands were not taken seriously, and Röhm and Wagner ended up withdrawing without having accomplished anything except antagonizing Hitler and the other party leaders.

Hitler had made promises to leaders of the regular army, the Wehrmacht, that they would be the sole military arm of the nation, not merely a force in conjunction with the SA, as Ernst Röhm had hoped.

Gunther started to spend more time with Klaus. Between the discomfort of the situation at home and the long days of work, he found it easier to talk with his old friend rather than face his problems with his family.

Klaus had never been much of one for spending time at home anyway. Katrina took care of the boys, and that kept her occupied, so Klaus fairly well did as he pleased. Not that he was ever unfaithful to his wife. It was more like she was a possession that he kept on the shelf at home—pretty to look at and fun to take out every once and again when he felt like it—but not to worry, she would always be there.

Strangely enough, it was a fairly accurate assessment of their marriage from Katrina's point of view as well. They had gotten married because they felt that they should be married—that was just the way things were. Katrina wanted children, and Klaus wanted boys as heirs to the throne and family name. It was all very convenient, and the situation was hardly ever shaken by conflict because they rarely ever interacted on any meaningful level, so there wasn't anything to get upset about. They went to great pains to fit into each other's lives and stay out of each other's way.

That was why Klaus looked upon Gunther's life as a sort of comic opera. What else could one expect when one married out of one's race? How could Gunther have ever considered marrying a Jew? Now he would have to reap what he had sown, but Klaus, uncharacteristically, decided not to rub salt in Gunther's wounds. They kept to safe topics as they wasted their hours downing beer and commenting on the passing parade in the beer halls, fighting their way through to the next day.

Amalie never questioned Gunther about where he had been or why he had been out so late. She kept herself busy, too, spending time working at home and writing letters. One letter was to her cousin Edith in response to a letter Edith had written to Amalie in which she told of being forced to leave her post as a lecturer on pedagogy at Göttingen University because of new legislation against Jews in teaching positions. She had decided to become a cloistered nun and work on her writings, which combined Catholic theology with the study of phenomenology.

Amalie also wrote to her father, taking care to censor what she wrote and making only subtle comments on the way things were going in Munich, afraid that her letter might be opened and read by some government clerk. She went on to say that she would like to visit soon. She knew it was time. She and Gunther were about to celebrate, or at least acknowledge, twenty years of marriage, and she knew in her heart that she could no longer keep trying to make it work. She could honestly say she loved him, even as she knew she had to leave him, because things would not get better and they would certainly get worse.

The rest of the year and the beginning of the next was a dreamlike paradox as the noose of Hitler's quest for power tightened, yet life had an eerie sense of normalcy for the Metzdorfs. The tension in their household was gradually becoming more pronounced as each member of the family had to work harder and harder to pretend that nothing was wrong. Gunther began taking constant trips out of town on the weekends and working later during the week, until it seemed that he only came home to have a late dinner and sleep before going back to his SA duties.

It was a time for daydreaming for Jakob as he became more involved with Rebecca, and the thought of her swept him onto newfound waves of passion, taking him to places he had never been before. On the one hand, Amalie saw it as a good thing that Jakob was getting more involved with Rebecca and her friends, as it had drawn him out after he left the HJ; but on the other hand, Jakob, like his father, was hardly ever home. Amalie was concerned about how far Jakob was pulling away from the family, but at the same time she was relieved that Gunther wasn't home to drag Jakob back into the Nazi fold.

Christmas of 1933 was forced and bleak. Gertrude spent the day with Friedrich, and Klaus and Katrina went to visit Katrina's family for the holidays, leaving Amalie, Gunther, and Jakob to exchange meaningless gifts and eat a large Christmas dinner replete with long, awkward silences and obligatory compliments to Amalie for being such a good cook.

It was about a month later, one of those dark January afternoons when the sun disappears just after four o'clock and the night seems even darker because the light abandons the earth at such an early hour, that Amalie ran into Jakob just as he was about to leave.

"Leaving already?" she asked as she unloaded her briefcase and a couple of manuscripts onto a chair so that she could take off her coat.

"A play tonight!" Jakob said with a smile, clearly anxious to be on his way but considerate enough not to walk out in the middle of the conversation.

"Where?"

"It's a school play . . . some of Rebecca's friends."

"Oh, Rebecca," Amalie said with a smile. "You two are seeing a lot of each other."

"Silly little kike won't leave me alone," Jakob said with a smile, talking about Rebecca as though he were irresistible to her.

Amalie's eyes flared, and she reached over and slapped Jakob hard in the face. "Jakob Metzdorf, you may think you're all grown up and practically on your own, but don't you ever say anything like that again in my presence."

Jakob's face smarted and he felt a tear form in his right eye, but he quickly brushed it away. He thought he had made a good joke. He had never used the word kike before and had only used it jokingly to shock his mother, and now he felt terrible that she had taken him seriously.

Amalie stormed out of the room and into the kitchen, where she went to the sink and drew a glass of water. There was a twitch in her shoulder, residue of her anger, as Jakob appeared in the doorway. She saw the redness around his eye and took an offensive posture as she stood in front of the sink, half expecting him to start spewing some vile Nazi rhetoric like his father.

"I'm sorry, Mother. It was just a joke . . . a very bad joke."

He couldn't look her in the eye as he apologized, and she melted as he said the words, walking over to him and taking his hand.

"Jakob, I'm sorry I hit you, but that was such a terrible thing to say."

"I know," Jakob said, still looking at the floor. "And the strange thing is that I really like Rebecca."

"Maybe you're just afraid," Amalie said, bending slightly as she tried to look into his eyes.

"Afraid?"

"Maybe you're afraid that you like her more than she likes you, and so you pretend not to care."

Jakob thought about it for a moment as they stood there silently. He felt uncomfortable talking about a girl with his mother.

"You can talk to me," Amalie said as she gently touched his chin and raised his face to look at her. "I was a girl once. I might understand more than you think."

Again there was a strange silence as they stood looking at each other.

"And Jakob," Amalie continued, "I love you very much. Don't ever forget how much I love you."

Jakob suddenly realized how long it had been since his mother had said that to him—since he had given her the chance to say it. The strain between mother and father, father and son . . . all of that had driven him away from her. It bothered him that he couldn't say it back. For some horrible reason he didn't feel that he could tell his mother that he loved her too, as though he had drifted so far away that the chance to say it was lost. He managed to give Amalie an awkward hug and then turned for the door.

Amalie watched him as he went. She was afraid for him. She worried about how he shut himself off. Had it really been a joke? Was that why he couldn't say that he loved her? He seemed so lost, and she didn't know how to reach him.

IT HAD BEGUN to seem as though the gray and snowy winter would last forever when it finally gave way to spring. It had been hard for Frieder and Son Publishing that winter, as David's fears proved well founded. A number of publishing houses had been closed down and some confiscated by the government under the Chancellor's emergency power decree, and most of those targeted were owned by Jewish families. So far, those efforts had been directed mainly at large concerns in Berlin and other parts of northern Germany. Not that Munich would be ignored—everything would happen in its time. There was no need to rush. Now was the time for the Nazi majority to consolidate its power through the measured pace of legitimate government process rather than fanatical revolutionary destruction.

"Jakob," Amalie said one Monday evening just after dinner in May, "I need to talk with you."

Jakob was uncomfortable with the ominous tone his mother was using and immediately sat up, laying the book down on the bed beside him.

"Jakob, you're just about to get your school certificate," she said, referring to the certificate of maturity that all students get after passing a final examination from secondary schools before going on to a university. "The way things are going, though, I'm afraid you might not be able to go to the university here."

Jakob knew what she was talking about, but he had put it out of his mind for some time now, ignoring the fact that he might be subject to the new limitations on Jewish students at the university. Somewhere in the back of his mind he was sure that he could just lie about his mother being Jewish, as he had done to get into the Hitler Youth.

Amalie continued, since Jakob said nothing in response. "And I thought . . . now that you've decided on the law instead of medicine . . . Well, I thought you should consider going to stay with Grandfather Ethan in Salzburg. There are two universities close by where you would be sure to be accepted."

Jakob didn't know how to respond at first. "Leave Munich?" he finally said, as though it were inconceivable.

"That might be best," Amalie said reassuringly.

Panicky at the thought of having to leave Rebecca, he stammered, "But I . . . I guess I just never thought of it. Leaving you and father." This last he added in a desperate attempt to inspire her to help him find a way to attend the University of Munich.

Amalie kept her eyes locked on the floor as she prepared to deliver another shock. "I was thinking that I would go to Salzburg too." Jakob could make no sense of what he had just heard because it seemed to come out of nowhere. He knew there had been tension between his mother and father, and they didn't talk much, but he just thought that was the way all married people acted when they got as old as his parents. He thought most of the trouble was because of the way he had acted, the way he hurt his father by leaving the HJ and the way he hurt his mother by lying about her being Jewish.

Amalie still couldn't look up as she made her confession to her son. "You know your father and I... you know we don't talk. We hardly even see each other... and that seems all right with him... and so I thought..."

"You're going to leave father?" Jakob asked incredulously. He didn't know anyone personally whose parents had gotten divorced. The subject only came up in the context of dirty jokes among his classmates about sexually desperate divorced women or men freed from the bondage of a frigid wife.

Amalie looked up. "Jakob, please don't say anything. Don't say anything to anyone until I've had a chance to talk to your father."

"You haven't told him yet?" Jakob asked with the same tone of disbelief.

"This is not easy for me," Amalie said with a heavy sigh. "It's a hard decision to make. I don't know how to do it 'right.'"

"Maybe if you just talk to Father . . ."

"I don't think that would do any good."

"Have you tried?"

Amalie felt exhausted as she looked into Jakob's eyes and saw the hint of fear—fear of the unknown, of what this might mean to him.

"Promise me you won't say anything. Promise me that you'll think about a university near Salzburg, and I'll promise you that I'll talk with your father."

"When?"

"Soon, but don't worry. If it did come down to us leaving, it wouldn't be for some time yet. When is your last examination?"

"The end of July."

"Well, don't worry about it. I didn't want to upset you, but I thought you should know."

"Before Father?"

Amalie was surprised, as this sounded like an attack. She thought about ignoring it, but then she thought better of it. "Jakob, I know this is hard to understand, but if you think about it, can't you see how far apart your father and I have grown. Haven't you noticed how different things are? And do you think he doesn't know these things are happening?"

"And I guess I didn't help much . . ."

"What do you mean?"

"I know how disappointed Father was when I . . ."

"Oh, Jakob! I'm sorry to tell you this, but this isn't about you. This is between your father and me. I'm sorry if you feel like you're in the middle, but you really aren't." Amalie couldn't hold herself back as she moved closer and pulled her son to her, hugging him and giving him a kiss on the forehead. "I know this is a hard thing to understand . . . and I'm sorry," she said as she let go and stood up, not knowing what else to say, leaving Jakob alone to think about what had been said and to imagine what might happen.

"THEY THINK there might be trouble tonight. We need to go out and patrol," Klaus said as he stood in the doorway of Gunther's house.

Months had passed since Amalie and Jakob had had their talk, but Amalie still hadn't brought it up to Gunther. She wanted to wait until the last minute so that if it turned out that she would be leaving, Jakob would be done with school and ready to leave. She stood frozen for a moment as she watched Gunther in his SA uniform join Klaus, who was also in uniform. It seemed so foreign to her, seeing these two storm troopers in her house.

"We'll probably be late, so don't wait up," Klaus said with a smile to Amalie as they left. She merely nodded and went back to reading her newspaper.

It had been raining on and off throughout the day and continued to do so into the evening on that night in late July. The Sterneckerbräu had already become a shrine since Adolf had become Chancellor, a shrine to the humble beginnings of the NSDAP where Adolf first met the members of the struggling group, the place where Gunther and Klaus had first met Adolf. It was Klaus and Gunther's first stop that evening.

Gunther kept looking around, keeping an eye on the door to see who came and who left and trying to sense the mood of any of his comrades who might pass by. He didn't know what to expect. The rumors of an SA uprising were back, and he thought that must be why Klaus wanted him along. The SA would be more willing to listen to an SA Gruppenführer than someone in an SS uniform. It would show solidarity in the face of any trouble.

Klaus, however, was thinking much differently. His bravado and good nature were forced that night because of his unpleasant assignment—an assignment that he had actually requested. Klaus's attentions to Heydrich's activities had gotten him caught up in a terrible twist of party politics. Ernst Röhm had gotten out of hand and had ended up on the wrong side of Adolf's plans for the party. Adolf was going to keep his word to the army that the Sturmabteilung would be brought into line, and the time had come to correct the situation. Klaus had heard about the events that were about to unfold, and he also knew from the tone of the planning that it would be a severe exercise in discipline. Certain people were referred to as "irredeemable" to the party's true direction.

Klaus knew what that meant; he knew those people wouldn't survive, and then one day that knowledge was borne out when he became privy to a list of names.

Gunther Metzdorf.

He checked it carefully. He even managed to make discreet inquiries to make sure there was no mistake.

He had tried to warn Gunther. He had tried to tell him, but Gunther wouldn't heed his warning, and now some clerk had neatly typed his name on a piece of paper with a dozen other names, and the list had been initialed by Reinhard Heydrich of the SD.

The night went slowly as the two friends strolled about the empty streets, stopping every now and again at a different beer hall and then continuing on their way.

Marienplatz was deserted at 2:00 in the morning. The moon managed to peek though rain clouds for just a moment as Gunther, a bit unsteady from all the beer, looked up at the darkened figures in the clock tower of the Neuen Rathaus. Klaus had been stalling all night, not knowing if he could do what he had committed himself to. He had said that he would take care of Gunther. He thought it would be better that way. Why should he allow his friend to be arrested and tortured? Why should he have to go through all that just to die in the end anyway? The moment seemed perfect. It seemed to last forever, as Klaus drew his pistol and pointed it at the back of Gunther's head.

The gun went off.

Klaus twitched as the pistol jumped in his hand and the flash and echoing report filled the square. Gunther jerked too, but in response to the impact of the nine-millimeter bullet, and he staggered back a step, putting out his hand to Klaus so that Klaus might steady him. He didn't even know that it was Klaus who had shot him. Klaus took Gunther's hand and lowered him gently to the pavement, kneeling beside him.

"I'm sorry . . . ," Klaus choked out as he looked at his friend's bloody face. The bullet had torn away pieces of Gunther's skull above his left eye, allowing his life's blood to run freely down his cheek and onto his brown shirt, down to the red, white, and black armband, before falling in a pool on the cobblestones.

It was the sort of thing that Klaus had thought he could do when it was discussed, and he had gotten permission to take care of Gunther on his own. He thought it would be an act of mercy, humane and painless. Gunther would die instantly, and it would all be over. It was for the best that way. But as he knelt there with the pistol in his hand and Gunther gasping for breath, he wanted to take it all back. It was all wrong. Gunther didn't deserve to die.

"They let me do it so it would be over quickly," Klaus tried to explain to his dying friend.

Unable to speak because of his wounds, Gunther could only stare at Klaus with a look of surprise.

"It's better this way," Klaus whispered as tears rolled down his face. He patted Gunther's hair. "No torture."

Gunther's breathing became uneven as he gasped for air, then arched his back for an instant before falling back against the cool cobblestones of the square.

"God, I've made a mess of it," Klaus said to himself quietly, still holding Gunther and seeing the pool of blood on the cobblestones for the first time. The clouds opened again for an instant and the moon shined down, casting silver reflections and illuminating the white of Gunther's eye, the one that wasn't bathed in his own blood, the one that stared relentlessly at his killer.

Klaus heard someone coming down one of the

side streets, talking softly, but he just sat there, not caring who it might be, not caring if they found him there with the pistol beside him. He could soon make out the voices of a man and a woman coming closer, but just as he expected to see their faces contorted in fear and shock, to hear the woman scream as they came upon him, the voices began to fade. The unknown couple had turned and walked away from the square into an adjacent street, never coming close enough to see Gunther and his murderer lost in the darkness. The moon once again became shrouded in clouds as a hard July rain began to fall, and Klaus began to sob openly.

IT WAS LATE afternoon the next day when the police called. They had been busy. Members of the SA had been arrested all across Germany the night before and throughout the day.

Amalie watched her hand replace the telephone receiver in its cradle, as though it were someone else's. She was numb. She hadn't been concerned by Gunther's absence, since he had been spending so much time away from home, and she hadn't expected any bad news.

Maybe she needed to cry. No, she couldn't. She had to go identify the body. What seemed ironic was that she had finally come to the realization that she had to leave him and now he had . . . left her. How could she tell Jakob?

When Jakob got home from school that day and found Friedrich, Klaus, and Klaus's family there, he knew something was wrong. He stared blankly at his mother when she told him what had happened, that his father had been attacked by a group of men and shot in the ensuing fight, and he just turned and walked out the door. Amalie thought he had just gone out to get some air and was surprised when she realized he wasn't anywhere to be found.

She was still looking out the door when Klaus came up behind her.

"Amalie," Klaus said hesitantly, "I would be honored if you would let me give a eulogy for Gunther."

Amalie tensed up. The last thing she wanted was for this to turn into some kind of honorable Nazi military funeral. Even though she had been told it was a group of Communists who had attacked Gunther and Klaus and killed Gunther, she knew it was the party that had killed him. They had been killing him for years.

"No," Amalie said with more finality than she had intended, and she quickly tried to make her declaration less curt. "I mean, I would rather not have a eulogy. Just a service . . ."

Klaus looked at her for a moment, searching for an argument to persuade her, but decided to let it pass.

The mood was stifling as they all tried to make conversation, and all Amalie could think of was how much she wanted everyone to leave. She almost stopped Klaus as he raised his glass of wine and began rambling on, but instead she just hid in the kitchen.

"It all seemed so easy as a child," he began grandiosely. "You just accepted things . . . Why?" he asked the ceiling in pseudo-Shakespearean soliloquy. "I want God to walk down his golden stairway and explain in simple terms why. The time has come for God to account. I don't mean to sound like I'm calling God on the carpet. It would just be nice if we could talk a bit, man to creator, and he could let me in on some of his inside jokes. There is no greater comedian than God."

Everyone else was getting uncomfortable as Klaus continued, not sure what their role would be. Should they applaud?

Instead, a blossoming silence filled the room until finally Friedrich mercifully suggested that Amalie might like to be alone. Klaus began to insist that this was no time for "the widow" to be left alone, but Gertrude, remembering how it had been when she went through the same thing, agreed that Friedrich was right and Amalie might prefer to be alone for a while. Amalie reappeared from the kitchen and managed a smile for Gertie to acknowledge that she was right, and Gertie gave Amalie a warm hug and a kiss as everyone filed out of the house.

"I'll stay with Friedrich tonight," Gertie said. "I'll see you in the morning."

Klaus sidled up to Gertie as she came out. "Now, what will she do all alone?"

"She'll cry," Getrude answered sadly, a tear of her own running down her face as she quickly moved away and took Friedrich's hand.

Between bouts of crying, Amalie tried to listen to the radio, then tried to read, but she couldn't stop worrying about Jakob. It had been hours since he had left the house. At last she realized where he would be, but when she called Rebecca's mother and asked for Rebecca, Mrs. Geschwind didn't know where her daughter was. Amalie explained what had happened and said that there was probably nothing to worry about, that Jakob and Rebecca were most likely just out somewhere talking.

The rain of the previous night had given way to a beautiful starry sky as Jakob and Rebecca sat in the darkness on an iron bench in a nearby park.

"It feels so strange . . . like I didn't even know him."

"You didn't know your father?"

"I mean . . . as a man."

"What?"

"I can't picture him when he was a boy or when he was in the army or when he was my age."

"What do you think he was like?"

"I don't know. Different . . . different than me."

"Why?"

"He seemed so certain of things. Everything was clear-cut. I don't feel like I know anything."

"Just because he thought he knew something doesn't mean he was right."

"I know, but that's not what I mean. It's not whether he was right or wrong, it's just that he was so sure of himself."

"Are you sure that's so good?"

"Even if he was wrong . . . everyone's wrong at sometime or another. I'm not talking about being right or wrong. I just wish I could be as confident."

Rebecca nodded.

"I don't think he loved me."

The statement was meant to shock Rebecca, and she was supposed to protest, insisting that Gunther had loved his son. Her silence spoke volumes.

"He never said it," Jakob continued. "He was happy when I'd win something, like sports, but it was almost like I was something he owned, and when I did well it was the same as if he had done it himself."

"Are you mad at him?"

Jakob looked at her with surprise. He hadn't expected that question. "No," he finally answered. "Just sad, I guess."

"It seems to me that if I had all that to say to someone and then they went and died before I could say it. . . I'd be mad."

Silence.

"I suppose I'm a little mad."

Rebecca listened patiently and tried to keep him talking because she knew it was important to him. She knew what it was like to be left with all the unanswered questions, since her father had died before she was four years old. Jakob began to realize something important about Becca that night. There are always people who are more than willing to tell you who they think you are, and there are those who commiserate with you in your confusion, and then there are those special few who stay with you as you fumble in the darkness, trying to find your way. Someone who helps you through. She was one of those, willing to listen when you're afraid and talk when you're tired of talking and just be there when you need silence.

When they finally found themselves back at Jakob's house, it was late and Jakob wasn't thinking clearly. He went inside and left the door open, and Rebecca followed, closing the door behind her. Jakob went to his room and lay down to sleep but found himself just staring at the ceiling. He was surprised when Rebecca appeared in the doorway, the moonlight illuminating the soft skin of her face and arms with a gentle glow as she seemed to float toward him. She reached out and took his hand, feeling how cold it was. He pulled her hand to his chest, pressing it to the center of him as burning tears blurred his sight and his mind. She lay down on the bed beside him.

He wasn't even sure what he was crying for. Was he crying for Gunther, the man? For his father? For the things they hadn't said to each other? For the things they had? It wasn't even the questions that hurt. It was the very real, almost physical pain that came from knowing that his father was gone forever. Knowing as a man that it was true and yet hoping as a child that if he just wanted it badly enough, if he railed and ranted, threw a tantrum, that maybe it would change, maybe God would relent.

Rebecca didn't say a word. She only drew closer, resting her head on his chest and draping her arms around him as they lay on the bed in the warmth and silence of the night.

Amalie was shocked when she opened Jakob's door the next morning and saw Jakob and Rebecca lying there intertwined. Her first instinct was to wake them up and create an embarrassing scene, voicing her strong disapproval and sending Rebecca home. That was what her mother would have done. Instead, she found herself watching them, lying there so natural and innocent, fully dressed, as though they had collapsed into sleep. It was like looking at a portrait, but then the unnerving thought came to her that she was staring at her son and his girlfriend in the most intimate of moments. Embarrassed, she quietly closed the door and leaned against the wall just outside the bedroom.

She realized that it wouldn't be long until Jakob left home. He would start at some university next year, if she could still afford it with Gunther gone. Gunther gone . . . her son a man. The world had changed again. *My God!* she thought, *he's only two years younger than Gunther when we married . . . only one year younger than me . . . but he's so young.*

Gertrude came in the front door as Amalie stood in the hallway. She headed straight for the kitchen to start breakfast and asked Amalie if she was feeling better. Amalie just nodded, not knowing what to do about Jakob and Rebecca, but apparently they had been awakened by Gertrude's activity in the kitchen and realized the awkward situation they were in.

Rebecca was embarrassed as she came fumbling out of Jakob's room, trying to straighten her wrinkled clothing and unable to make eye contact with Amalie or Gertrude. Gertrude was shocked when she realized what was going on, and she glanced at Rebecca with a scolding look, then went back to making breakfast without saying a word. Gertrude couldn't approve of such an unseemly thing no matter how much she loved both Jakob and Rebecca.

Amalie was sitting in the living room pretending to read a book when Rebecca stopped in front of her.

"Mrs. Metzdorf . . . I'm sorry, Rebecca stumbled as she tried to explain. "Nothing happened."

Amalie remained expressionless as Rebecca realized what she had said.

"I mean, I'm sorry that we . . ." Rebecca suddenly stopped talking and knelt beside Amalie's chair. "Nothing happened, Frau Metzdorf . . . We just talked. He needed me," she said in a half whisper.

Amalie was caught off guard by this statement. She thought she was in control of this situation, a mother with a right to her righteous indignation at catching her son with a girl in his room. It was one of those strange times when an adult realizes that they are the adult and must react in a certain way, whether they truly believe it or not, and then she remembered that she knew who Rebecca and Jakob were.

Amalie took the day off work, as well as the next week, as she had to decide what she and Jakob and Gertrude would do. Gunther's mother and father arrived that afternoon. Ethan would be coming early the next day, in time for the funeral the following afternoon.

Marie couldn't understand why her son had been killed. No one could tell her who this group of men were and why they had shot her son. "A child should not die before the parents," she kept saying at various times throughout the day.

It was hard for Jakob to sleep that night. He woke from a fitful sleep and was frightened as he looked at the window and saw the outline of a man.

"Father?" he whispered loudly, but the figure didn't move. Jakob lay still for an eternity, waiting to see what the menacing black outline against the hazy grayness of the night beyond would do.

Finally he reached over and turned on the lamp beside his bed. It was only his suit hanging on the curtain rod. His mother must have had his only suit cleaned for him to wear to the funeral the next day and hung it there. Jakob hadn't even noticed it before. Maybe she came in after he had fallen asleep. He turned off the light and tried to get comfortable laying on his side, but finally gave up and turned onto his back, staring at the ceiling. He could feel his heart still racing from the moment of panic and looked down at his chest to see if he could actually see it beating. *So,* he thought to himself, *I am the man in the window that I was afraid of.*

The strangest images danced in and out of his mind. "I didn't even know him. Would his mother go crazy?" She seemed so calm. She hardly even cried. Didn't she care? She had said she wanted to divorce him . . . but of course he hadn't cried much himself, especially when there was anyone around. His face actually hurt sometimes from trying to keep a controlled expression around friends and relatives. The desire to cry burned at the corners of his eyes, but he wouldn't give in. He wasn't a little boy. He was a man, and he would not cry in front of people. It seemed so strange when people came to offer their condolences, staring into his eyes intently as if they were studying his face, expecting to see him literally break apart. He was no longer a boy. He had been his father's son, protected and diminished in his shadow, but their struggle was over. Jakob had won through default, the victory thrust upon him.

The sun was shining when the car came to pick up Amalie, Jakob, and Gertrude. They didn't talk as the car worked its way through the streets of Munich to the church. Amalie thought to herself that it would have seemed more appropriate if the weather had been dark and cold and full of rain, as if the world were mourning.

Oskar had arranged the funeral, which was fine with Amalie. She could have done it if she hadn't had a choice, but she felt relieved when Oskar suggested that his son should be buried with a Lutheran service. She couldn't very well have gone to a synagogue to ask if a rabbi would say kaddish[34] over her husband, who happened to be a group leader in the Brownshirts.

She had never been to a synagogue in Munich. The last time she had attended any service was when she visited her father in Salzburg. Ethan never asked his daughter whether she went to services because he was sure that he already knew the answer.

The service was pious and impersonal, assuring the family and friends that Jesus was coming to soothe their pain and relieve them of their sorrow, that Gunther was now floating up to the clouds where he would be happy, looking down on them all and waiting until they finally joined him when they achieved their final reward.

Things went quickly the next week. Ethan agreed that they should come to Salzburg, and that Jakob would certainly be able to find a good university there. Gertrude began to wonder what would happen to her, but then Friedrich surprised her with the news that he had actually managed, through the good graces of a friendly party member, to lease the apartment that the Haas family had lived in before

---

[34]The Hebrew prayer said for the dead.

the war. It was a strange twist for Gertrude to be planning to return to the apartment on Franz Joseph Strasse where she had been living when she first met Gunther and Amalie. Things had come full circle. She knew she should be happy, now that she had a place of her own and Friedrich was in a position to help her live comfortably, but now she would lose Amalie . . . and Jakob . . . and Fürstenried. She was sixty-six years old. It seemed so hard to start over again.

A few days later, Friedrich was sitting at his desk in his crowded little office, his nose buried in a manila folder, when one of the clerks called out with a note of excitement, "Haas! Obersturmbannführer Heydrich wants you in his office. Now!"

Friedrich's heart leapt to his throat as he rushed down the long hallway to Heydrich's office, stopping at the desk in front of the forbidding, massive red oak door. "Yes?" the young man at the desk said sternly as Friedrich stood at attention, trying to compose himself.

"Obersturmbannführer Heydrich sent for me. Haas, Friedrich Haas."

The secretary quickly glanced over some notes in front of him and agreed that, yes, Friedrich had in fact been sent for, and the young man told him to follow as he knocked on the door and announced Friedrich.

"Come in, Haas," Heydrich said in that unnerving high-pitched voice of his—unnerving because it seemed almost comical, whereas the man himself was anything but humorous.

"Yes, sir," Friedrich said as he stood at attention.

"No need for that," Heydrich said as he leafed through papers in a manila folder and motioned Friedrich to a chair. "Sit down." Friedrich tried to get comfortable as his cold superior officer continued reading, as though Friedrich wasn't there. "Haas," Heydrich finally said, putting the folder down on his desk, "our Führer has told me of a great service that you performed some years ago."

Friedrich knew he was referring to the coverup of Geli's murder, but he said nothing, waiting to see what Heydrich would say next.

"And you have done well to say nothing. You've been very loyal . . ."

Heydrich was trying to read the man sitting in front of him and took Friedrich's silence as a positive sign. Even when Friedrich was being complimented, he didn't lose his head and acknowledge his part in the coverup. Heydrich let the silence lay heavy in the room, watching as Friedrich tried very hard to conceal his nervousness and succeeded fairly well.

"I will only ask one question about the past," Heydrich finally said, staring at Friedrich as though he might bore into his skull with the intensity of his gaze. "Are you the man?"

The question was cryptic, and Friedrich suddenly felt his head swimming. *The man?* he thought to himself. *The man who killed Geli, or the man who covered it up? What was he being asked?* "I'm sorry," Friedrich finally said slowly. "What man?"

Heydrich wasn't put off by the fact that Friedrich didn't understand the question. Obviously Friedrich wasn't as intelligent as he hoped, but intelligence wasn't the greatest virtue in such matters. In reality, of course, Friedrich would have had to have been a mind reader to know Heydrich's meaning.

"Loyalty," Heydrich shot back loudly. "Are you that same man who served so loyally before, and can you be counted on to do so again."

The word loyalty, even in the early days of the SS, was a mystical concept that was nothing less than a direct bond between man and God, and the use of that word was always the impetus for dramatic and heartfelt affirmation between an officer and a soldier.

"Of course," Friedrich said emphatically.

Once again Heydrich paused and considered the man in front of him. "We will need you to go to Berlin," he finally said as he handed Friedrich written orders. "Check with Hans for everything else," he continued, referring to his secretary.

Friedrich remained in the chair to see if there was anything else, but Heydrich seemed annoyed that he had to bother telling Friedrich that that was all and he could go.

Once outside the door, Friedrich realized that every muscle in his body had tensed up as he sat in that chair in Heydrich's office, and he finally relaxed as he walked over to Heydrich's secretary to confirm his travel arrangements.

A week later Friedrich found himself in the office of a nameless SS official receiving final instructions for his assignment.

"And so you will be the Führer's replacement driver."

"Yes, sir."

"I cannot stress how important this mission is. If you have any doubts . . ."

"No, sir," Friedrich said loudly and emphatically, an assertion that saved his life, because the officer had orders to shoot Friedrich on the spot if he had shown any reticence or questioned the mission, since he had already been briefed on the details.

Friedrich Haas had been chosen to replace Hitler's chauffeur because of his war experience as a medic, not just because of his prior service to the Führer.

Later that morning he found himself driving Adolf to the estate of Paul von Hindenburg, where the old man lay sick in bed. Friedrich dutifully followed closely behind Adolf, carrying his large black briefcase as Adolf entered Hindenburg's grand residence.

Hindenburg was eighty-four years old that year, and Adolf had requested an audience to insist that the old man retire and turn the presidency over to him, but Hindenburg was intractable. They talked for a while in polite tones that masked the contempt each man felt for the other. Hindenburg seemed upset with the actions at the end of June when members of the SA were assassinated. The fate of the Sturmabteilung didn't concern Hindenburg, but one of the sideshows of the purge was that Franz von Papen had been placed under house arrest. Hindenburg had a personal fondness for his "Franzchen," who had been one of the string of Chancellors since the presidential elections, and he demanded a promise from Adolf that Papen would be protected. Adolf acceded, but Friedrich could tell that Adolf was growing tired of the conversation. The only person in the room besides Hindenburg, Adolf, and Friedrich was a nurse who sat by the old man's bed, in case he should want anything, and at this moment Adolf decided that he was thirsty and asked if the nurse might go out and get a fresh pitcher of water and clean glasses . . . and ice too, if it wasn't too much trouble. Adolf did his best to be charming as he made the request and followed the nurse to the door, closing it and making sure it latched as she left.

Friedrich instantly realized that this was the time to act, knowing that he only had a moment or two at the most. He had been instructed earlier that it might become necessary for him to administer a syringe full of an hallucinogenic drug, which would eventually bring on paralysis and death.

He opened the briefcase, where the syringe was hidden in a pocket, as Hindenburg rested with his eyes closed. The old man was taken completely by surprise as Friedrich suddenly jumped on him in the bed and began pulling up the sleeve of the his nightshirt to give him the injection before he knew what was happening. Hindenburg struggled and they wrestled about, but Friedrich quickly bested the old man, putting his knee on the Hindenburg's arm to hold it down while he covered his mouth with the bed linens so he could not call out.

During the struggle, Adolf continued to talk for the benefit of anyone who might listen at the door, so that they would think he was still in conference with the Reichspresident.

Hindenburg was already weak from illness at this

point, and even though he was a much bigger man than Friedrich, Friedrich managed to subdue him until the drug took effect.

In the struggle, however, the needle broke off in Hindenburg's arm, and Friedrich looked up at Adolf, not saying a word as Adolf continued talking but pointing at the needle. Adolf couldn't really see what had happened, but it was obvious that something had gone wrong.

There were only a few millimeters of the needle sticking out, and Friedrich had to work hard, pinching the skin around the entry wound to force the needle out enough so that he could get hold of it. He finally managed to work it out and set it on the bedside table, then fell quickly to his knees, looking under the bed for the rest of the syringe. He found it immediately and set it on the table next to the piece of needle. He then noticed that there were spots of blood all over Hindenburg's nightshirt and realized that he would have to change it. He pulled out a handkerchief and quickly wiped up the spots of blood from the puncture wound, then wrapped the broken needle and the rest of the syringe in the handkerchief and set it on the bedside table.

Adolf, who had been pacing and watching the door nervously as he talked, finally turned to Friedrich and asked in a quieter voice, "Are you ready? Are we ready to leave?"

"Not quite. Almost," Friedrich said as he waved Hitler off, indicating that he should go back to his pacing.

Friedrich had noticed that Hindenburg was still bleeding ever so slightly from the needle puncture, which had been aggravated by removing the broken needle. He tried to think what to do and noticed a large Meerschaum pipe in its stand on a small table near the bed. He opened the small drawer in the table and was pleased to find matches and pipe cleaners. He took one of the pipe cleaners and lit a match, burning off the bristles of the pipe cleaner, exposing the twisted wires at its core, and then returned to Hindenburg. The old man lay helpless, muttering on as the drug began to affect his mind after it had all but paralyzed him, allowing only the most rudimentary movement, as the old man might flop an arm across his chest or move his head from side to side. The pipe cleaner was so hot that when he touched it to the small puncture, it sizzled as it came in contact with the skin, cauterizing the wound and assuring it wouldn't bleed anymore.

Friedrich knew this was all taking much too long, and Adolf was becoming more and more nervous. He quickly put the burnt pipe cleaner in the handkerchief package so that he would be sure to remove all evidence of the crime. A nightshirt! He had to find another nightshirt and change the old man, or the spots of blood might give everything away. Adolf couldn't imagine what Friedrich was up to as he quickly rifled through a bureau drawer. Friedrich soon fished out another nightshirt that fortunately was the same as the one Hindenburg was wearing, and he hurried over and expertly stripped the old man in an instant, a talent he had developed during the war when patients had to be cleaned up fast, and wrestled to get the clean nightshirt onto him.

Adolf was amazed as Friedrich flew about the

room one last time, stuffing the nightshirt and the rest of the evidence into the empty briefcase he had brought. "We're ready," he said to Adolf as he quickly smoothed his hair back with his hand.

Without hesitation, Adolf threw open the doors just as the nurse was returning with the water and glasses, causing her to drop the tray, sending the glassware crashing to the floor as he stormed through the waiting room, with Friedrich close behind, shouting angrily, "The old man is gone! He's completely senile! He doesn't even recognize me!"

Hindenburg's secretary immediately called the doctor and rushed into the bedroom as Adolf and Friedrich left the manor.

Once they were in the car and had actually left the grounds of Hindenburg's estate, Adolf finally asked Friedrich how long it would take.

"From what I've been told, he will be dead by tomorrow afternoon."

Friedrich watched Adolf's face in the mirror as he told him, and he was glad to see that the Führer took no pleasure in the news. As a matter of fact, Adolf looked noticeably saddened, as though he wished it didn't have to be the way it was, but then that was just what Friedrich thought he saw in Adolf's face.

FRIEDRICH WAS relieved when the train passed through Dachau. He was almost home after his mission. He had been told he had done a great service for Germany, and that he would be remembered and rewarded, but somehow he couldn't escape the feeling that he should find a way to protect himself. Today they were grateful and appreciative, but what about tomorrow? What would it take for him to become expendable?

"Amalie, I need to meet you somewhere."

"Friedrich? Is that you?" Amalie asked, thinking she recognized the voice on the phone, but wondering why it sounded so . . .

"Yes. Could you meet me at the apartment on Franz Joseph?"

"With your mother?"

"No. Alone."

"When?"

"Tomorrow . . . Wednesday. At two o'clock."

"What's going on?"

"It's nothing, really. I just need to talk to you before you leave."

"All right."

"Who was that?" Gertie asked as she came into the living room.

Amalie was startled and wondered how much Gertie had heard "Oh, that? Uh, that was just . . . David. He wants me to meet him tomorrow to tie up some loose ends."

"You'll still be able to help me move, won't you?" Gertrude asked with annoyance, afraid that Amalie would go back on her promise.

"Oh, of course. This is just for Wednesday. I'll be free all day Thursday. Don't worry, Gertie, I won't let you down."

Amalie found herself getting nervous as she got closer to the apartment, wondering what Friedrich could possibly want to talk to her about. There was no answer when she knocked on the door, but when she tried the knob, she found it was unlocked, so she walked in. Friedrich was sitting in the middle of the front room in the only chair in the apartment, a small wooden folding chair, staring out the window.

"Friedrich?"

Friedrich hadn't heard her come in and jerked his head suddenly toward her.

"I'm sorry," she said. "I didn't mean to startle you."

"I was just thinking. This place . . . all these years."

"I think I'll feel the same way about going back to Salzburg."

"Yes, probably. We get so far away from home sometimes, and then when we return, we don't even recognize it. Home doesn't change . . . we do."

"Friedrich," Amalie said as though she needed to draw him back to the present. "What did you want to talk to me about."

"Things get complicated, Amalie," he said wearily, his speech slightly slurred. "I've seen things . . . done things . . . that I never would have dreamed."

"Are you in trouble, Friedrich? Do you need money?"

"No, it's not that," he said, shaking his head emphatically. It was clear that he had been drinking, and he stopped talking as he tried to pull words together out of a mental fog. He hadn't thought about what he would say when they met, and so he was at a loss. "I need someone to trust," he finally said.

"Trust?" Amalie asked, still not knowing what this could possibly be about.

"Yes . . . Can I trust you Amalie?"

"Of course, Friedrich. We've been friends a long time."

"I know. I hoped you would say that. I've got a package . . . and a couple of letters that I may need some day, but right now it would be best if I had a friend take care of them. Someone who would be out of the country."

"You want me to smuggle something out of the country?"

"It's not like that. It's not something illegal. It's only important to me and a few other people. You wouldn't be stopped by the police or anything. Even if they found it they wouldn't stop you."

"You don't want to tell me what it is?"

"I'd prefer not to."

"Curiosity killed the . . . ," Amalie started to say, but the look on Friedrich's face stopped her. He was very serious.

"Can you do it?"

Amalie thought for a moment. Her instinct was to say yes, but part of her was afraid. "Yes," she finally said, and with that Friedrich picked up a small brown box from the floor beside him and offered it to Amalie. She smiled nervously as she took it.

"When are you leaving?" Friedrich asked.

"Sunday. We'll help your mother move tomorrow and finish up everything at the house on Friday and Saturday."

IT WAS HARD for Amalie to ignore the box when she got home. She had already decided that she would open it once she had some time to herself when they were in Salzburg, but she had to keep it away from Gertrude and Jakob for the next few days.

The next day was just like all moving days, with a bit of confusion, a lot of cleaning and scrubbing, and everyone being tired at the end of the day. Amalie had given Gertrude much of the furniture from the house because she didn't want to ship it to Salzburg and store it until she and Jakob found a home of their own.

It was hard saying good-bye to Munich, saying good-by to Gertie, to David and his father. Rebecca couldn't even try to pretend that it would be all right after Jakob left. They spent every moment together until it was time to board the train, and then she couldn't stop crying even when they stood on the platform waving good-bye and Gertie put her arm around her.

It was a long ride back to Salzburg for Amalie, back to where she had come from such a long time ago, feeling like her life was over.

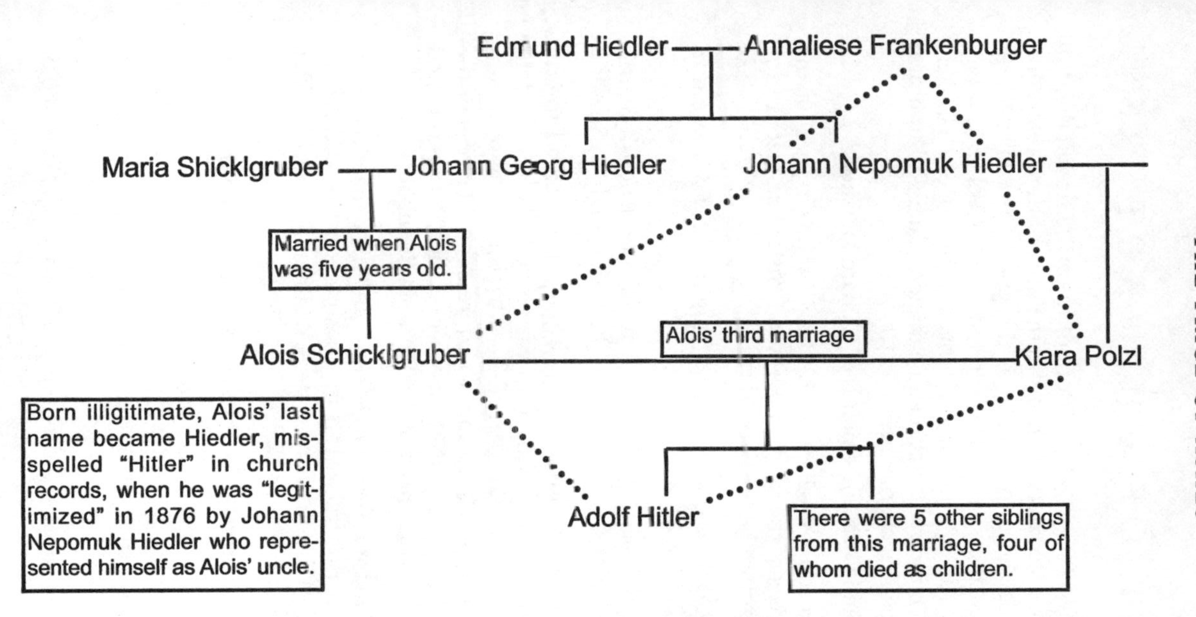

Part of Adolf Hitler's family tree diagrammed by Amalie for Ethan. The dotted lines show the connections that Amalie made from the Johann Nepomuk Hiedler deathbed confession.

LIST OF CHARACTERS

The Jakob's Star Trilogy is a work of historical fiction that follows the Metzdorf family from the time of their relocation from Salzburg to Munich at the end of the First World War on through to the Intefadeh in Israel in the late 1980s. An "F" following a name on the list of characters below indicates a fictional character, while "N" indicates nonfictional characters.

Alfred and Otto *(F)*—Friends of Richard Werthers.

Max Amann *(N)*—Part of the Nazi inner circle from the early days of the party whom Adolf Hitler had met as a soldier during the First World War.

Sister Angelina *(F)*—Nun who taught with Edith Stein in Speyer.

Anna and Lissa *(F)*—Two girls from one of Edith Stein's classes at the Catholic school where she taught in Speyer.

Count Anton Arco-Valley *(N)*—Count who wanted to join the Thule Society, a group very much like the nascent Nazi party, but was denied membership because he was half Jewish. In an attempt to impress the members of the Thule Society and thus gain acceptance, he assassinated Kurt Eisner, the head of the Bavarian Republic.

Prince Max von Baden *(N)*—German Reichschancellor who oversaw the transition of power from the abdicating Kaiser Wilhelm to the new Weimar Republic under President Friedrich Ebert.

Father Berghorst *(F)*—Priest arrested with Edith Stein in Echt.

Otto von Bismarck *(N)*—19th-century German statesman credited with the founding of a unified German state in 1871.

Father Brumgart *(F)*—Retired priest from the Dollersheim parish in Austria.

Emily Dickinson *(N)*—19th-century American poet.

Friedrich Ebert *(N)*—Leader of the German Social Democrat party in 1918 who became the first president of the Weimar Republic, which replaced the monarchical rule of Kaiser Wilhelm II of the Hohenzollerns at the end of World War I.

Kurt Eisner *(N)*—Social Democrat leader of the postwar government of Bavaria that replaced King Ludwig of the Wittlesbach dynasty in that region.

Eli *(F)*—Friend of Istvan Bartalan recruited to help Jakob Stein-Metzdorf on his mission in South America.

Annaliese Frankenburger *(F)*—See Johanna Hiedler.

David Frieder *(F)*—Munich book publisher, head of Frieder and Son Publishing, which his father, Sam, had started years before; Amalie Stein-Metzdorf began working for David as an assistant copyright editor in February 1919.

Sam Frieder *(F)*—Father of David Frieder; founder of Frieder and Son Publishing who retired before the end of the war and made a hobby of following the tumultuous political scene in Germany.

Joseph Goebbels *(N)*—Nazi party's minister of propaganda; was headquarted in Berlin long before the Nazi party received the majority votes under the Weimar elections that brought them to power.

Hermann Göring *(N)*—World War I flying ace who became a confederate of Adolf Hitler in the early days of the Nazi party and eventually head of the German Luftwaffe during the Second World War.

Katrina Grunewald *(F)*—Klaus Grunewald's wife.

Klaus Grunewald *(F)*—Gunther Metzdorf's front-line comrade during the First World War; a conserative, right-wing militarist.

Friedrich Haas *(F)*—Young German befriended by Gunther Metzdorf while the two are looking for work in postwar Munich; Friedrich had been an ambulance driver in the medical corps and so in Gunther's mind qualified as a member of "the brotherhood of front-line soldiers," which later became a qualifying phrase of the emerging Nazi party.

Gertrude Haas *(F)*—Mother of Friedrich Haas and good friend of Amalie Stein-Metzdorf, who became part of the Metzdorf family when she moved in with them after losing her home during the crippling inflation of the early Weimar years.

Manfred Haas *(F)*—Gertrude Haas's late husband; Friedrich Haas's father.

Hans, Peter, and Stefan *(F)*—Friends of Ernst Toller.

Rudolph Hess *(N)*—Deputy führer to Adolph Hitler who flew to England during the war in an attempt to present a plan for peace; he was arrested and eventually became the only surviving defendant of those found guilty during the Nuremburg trials, becoming the sole prisoner in Spandau prison until his death in the late 1980s.

Hiedler family *(N)*—Hitler was a misspelling of the name Hiedler in church records when Alois Hitler was legitimized in 1876.

Johanna Hiedler *(N);* **Johann Georg Hiedler** *(N);* **Johann Polzl** *(N);* **Johann Nepomuk Hiedler** *(N);* **Edmund Hiedler** *(F);* **Annaliese Frankenburger** *(F)*—A mixed cast of fictional and actual ancestors of Adolf Hitler.

Paul von Hindenburg *(N)*—Head of the German High Command during the First World War who became president of the Weimar Republic after the death of Friedrich Ebert in 1925.

Adolf Hitler *(N)*—Leader of the National Socialist German Workers' Party (Nationalsozialistische Deutsche Arbeiterpartei).

Alois Hitler *(N)*—Adolf Hitler's father.

Alois Hitler Jr. *(N)*—Adolf Hitler's half brother.

Klara Hitler née Polzl *(N)*—Adolf Hitler's mother.

William Hitler *(N)*—A nephew of Adolf Hitler.

Eleonore Hoffman née Stein *(F)*—Amalie's sister.

Louis Arthur Hoffman *(F)*—Amalie's brother-in-law; married to her sister Eleonore.

Rachel Hoffman *(F)*—Louis and Eleonore's older daughter

Sophie Hoffman *(F)*—Louis and Eleonore's younger daughter.

Joseph Hubert *(F)*—Longtime friend of David Frieder, Amalie's boss.

Gustav von Kahr **(N)**—A leader of the Bavarian provincial government at the time of Hitler's Beer Hall *Putsch* on November 9, 1923.

Eugen von Knilling *(N)*—A leader of the Bavarian provincial government at the time of Hitler's Beer Hall *Putsch* on November 9, 1923.

Liesl Kraus *(F)*—Reporter with a Munich newspaper whose name Amalie assumes.

Eugen Levin *(N)*—Communist revolutionary sent from Moscow to revitalize the faltering revolution in Munich in 1919.

Karl Liebknecht *(N)*—Contemporary of Rosa Luxemburg; Liebknecht agitated for a Communist uprising in Germany during the war and ended up in jail until the Social Democrats released him and he once again took up the Communist cause.

Otto von Lossow *(N)*—A leader of the Bavarian provincial government at the time of Hitler's Beer Hall *Putsch* on November 9, 1923.

Erich von Ludendorff *(N)*—Quartermaster General of the German High Command during the First World War; orchestrated the surrender of Germany, the abdication of Kaiser Wilhelm, and the succession of the Social Democrat Party as leaders of the new Weimar Republic.

Rosa Luxemburg *(N)*—"Little Rosa," born of Jewish parents in Poland; Communist activist in Germany before, during, and after the First World War; was jailed for her activities during the war, but was released when the Social Democrats took over.

Franziska Matzelsberger *(N)*—First wife of Alois Hitler (Adolf Hitler's father); mother of Angela and Alois Jr.; Angela Hitler married Leo Raubal, and their daughter was Angela "Geli" Raubal, Adolf Hitler's niece, with whom he had an affair.

Otto Maus *(F)*—Middle-aged author of books of the American West; client of Frieder and Son Publishing who lived in Ried, Austria; Amalie, as an agent of Frieder and Son, worked with Otto on some of his books.

Amalie Stein-Metzdorf *(F)*—Born in Salzburg, Austria, in 1895 to Ruth and Ethan Stein; the Steins are reform Jews; Amalie is the wife of Gunther and mother of Jakob, her only child.

Gunther Metzdorf *(F)*—Husband of Amalie and father of Jakob; served in the Austrian infantry on the Russian front in the First World War; moved his family to Munich at the end of the war.

Jakob Stein-Metzdorf *(F)*—Amalie's son; born in 1916.

Maria Metzdorf *(F)*—Gunther Metzdorf's mother.

Oskar Metzdorf *(F)*—Gunther Metzdorf's father.

Benito Mussolini *(N)*—Leader of the Italian Fascist party, which took over the Italian government in 1922. Adolf Hitler, as head of the German Nazi party, sought to emulate Mussolini's early successes.

Czar Nicholas II *(N)*—Czar of Russia at the turn of the century and during the First World War, Nicholas Romanoff was a cousin of Wilhelm Hohenzollern, both men being descended from Queen Victoria of England, who was their grandmother; Nicholas II was deposed during the Bolshevik revolution in 1917, and subsequently he and his family were murdered by members of the Bolshevist faction, although it was rumored that Nicholas's youngest daughter, Anastasia, and his son, Alexeyevich, somehow escaped the slaughter. The rumor is still alive in light of a recent discovery of the burial site of the Romanoff family where the bodies of the two youngest children were not found.

General John "Black Jack" Pershing *(N)*—General in command of the American Expeditionary Force, the American military contingent sent to France during the First World War.

Dr. Rosenau *(F)*—Doctor who operated on Gunther Metzdorf's father, Oskar.

Maria Schicklgruber *(N)*—Alois Hitler's mother; Adolf Hitler's paternal grandmother.

Hans Ritter von Seisser *(N)*—See Gustav von Kahr.

Ethan Stein *(F)*—Amalie's father; owner of a publishing house in Austria.

Ruth Stein *(F)*—Amalie's mother who died of influenza when Amalie was twelve years old.

Berchtwald Stemper *(F)*—Gunther Metzdorf's uncle.

Greta Stemper *(F)*—Gunther Metzdorf's aunt.

Father Strachler *(F)*—Parish priest in Dollersheim before Father Brumgart.

Gregor Strasser *(N)*—Leader of the Sturmabteilung, the military arm of the Nazi party also known as the Brownshirts, in Berlin before the Nazi purge of 1934.

Ernst Toller *(N)*—Munich playwright who led a bloodless takeover of the Bavarian government after the assassination of Kurt Eisner; later, after he was deposed by the Communist leadership of Eugen Levin, he led the revolutionary forces in battle against right-wing "Freikorps" units that tried to take over Munich.

Lorenz Weber *(F)*—Comrade of Gunther Metzdorf killed during the First World War.

Karl Werthers *(F)*—Friend and co-worker of Manfred Haas.

Richard Werthers *(F)*—Boyhood friend of Friedrich Haas whose father worked with Friedrich's father, Manfred; the two hadn't seen each other for years when they meet again in the story; Richard was drafted toward the end of the war and had just finished his training as the war ended and was swept up in the revolutionary fervor of 1918–19.

Horst Wessel *(N)*—Berlin pimp who was also a member of the Nazi party; after he was killed in a fight over a woman by a man who happened to be a member of the Communist party, Josef Goebbels created the myth that Wessel had died fighting for the Nazi party, and a song was soon written celebrating this myth, a song that included such sentiments as "when Jewish blood drips from the knife, then we will all be happy."

Kaiser Wilhelm *(N)*—Last German emperor, ending two hundred years of Hohenzollern rule (apart from their role as rulers of Prussia prior to that period), which began with the unification of Germany by Otto von Bismarck in 1871.

Zeigel *(F)*—Nickname for one of Friedrich Haas's co-workers; German for "brick."